The New JUNIOR CLASSICS

VOLUME FIVE · STORIES THAT NEVER GROW OLD

The New JUNIOR CLASSICS

Edited by MABEL WILLIAMS and MARCIA DALPHIN

With Introduction by WILLIAM ALLAN NEILSON, *Former President of Smith College; Introduction to First Edition by* CHARLES W. ELIOT, *Former President of Harvard University*

DE LUXE EDITION

*With Over One Thousand
Illustrations in Color*

VOLUME
FIVE

STORIES
THAT NEVER
GROW OLD

P. F. COLLIER & SON CORPORATION

CONTENTS

v

THE JUNIOR CLASSICS

(The sources of the stories in this volume will be found listed on page 493.)

ALICE'S ADVENTURES IN WONDERLAND

By LEWIS CARROLL

With Illustrations by SIR JOHN TENNIEL

I: DOWN THE RABBIT HOLE

ALICE was beginning to get very tired of sitting by her sister on the bank, and of having nothing to do: once or twice she had peeped into the book her sister was reading, but it had no pictures or conversations in it, "and what is the use of a book," thought Alice, "without pictures or conversations?"

So she was considering, in her own mind (as well as she could, for the hot day made her feel very sleepy and stupid), whether the pleasure of making a daisy-chain would be worth the trouble of getting up and picking the daisies, when suddenly a White Rabbit with pink eyes ran close by her.

There was nothing so *very* remarkable in that; nor did Alice think it so *very* much out of the way to hear the Rabbit say to itself "Oh dear! Oh, dear! I shall be too late!" (when she thought it over afterward, it occurred to her that she ought to have wondered at this, but

I

at the time it all seemed quite natural); but, when the Rabbit actually *took a watch out of its waistcoat pocket,* and looked at it, and then hurried on, Alice started to her feet, for it flashed across her mind that she had never before seen a rabbit with either a waistcoat pocket, or a watch to take out of it, and, burning with curiosity, she ran across the field after it, and was just in time to see it pop down a large rabbit hole under the hedge.

In another moment down went Alice after it, never once considering how in the world she was to get out again.

The rabbit-hole went straight on like a tunnel for some way, and then dipped suddenly down, so suddenly that Alice had not a moment to think about stopping herself before she found herself falling down what seemed to be a very deep well.

Either the well was very deep, or she fell very slowly, for she had plenty of time as she went down to look about her, and to wonder what was going to happen next. First, she tried to look down and make out what she was coming to, but it was too dark to see anything: then she looked at the sides of the well, and noticed that they were filled with cupboards and book-shelves: here and there she saw maps and pictures hung upon pegs. She took down a jar from one of the shelves as she passed: it was labeled "ORANGE MARMALADE," but to her great disappointment it was empty: she did not like to drop the jar, for fear of killing somebody underneath, so managed to put it into one of the cupboards as she fell past it.

"Well!" thought Alice to herself. "After such a fall as this, I shall think nothing of tumbling downstairs! How brave they'll all think me at home! Why, I wouldn't say anything about it, even if I fell off the top of the house!" (Which was very likely true.)

Down, down, down. Would the fall *never* come to an end? "I wonder how many mile I've fallen by this time?" she said aloud. "I must be getting somewhere near the center of the earth. Let me see: that would be four thousand miles down, I think—" (for, you see, Alice had learned several things of this sort in her lessons in the school room, and though this was not a *very* good opportunity for showing off her knowledge, as there was no one to listen to her, still it was good practice to say it over) "—yes, that's about the right distance— but then I wonder what Latitude or Longitude I've got to?" (Alice had not the slightest idea what Latitude was, or Longitude either, but she thought they were nice grand words to say).

Presently she began again. "I wonder if I shall fall right *through* the earth! How funny it'll seem to come out among the people that walk with their heads downward! The antipathies, I think—" (she was rather glad there *was* no one listening, this time, as it did n't sound at all the right word) "—but I shall have to ask them what the name of the country is, you know. Please, Ma'am, is this New Zea-land? Or Australia?" (and she tried to curtsey as she spoke—fancy, *curtseying* as you're falling through the air! Do you think you could manage it?) "And what an ignorant little girl she'll think me for ask-ing! No, it'll never do to ask: perhaps I shall see it written up some-where."

Down, down, down. There was nothing else to do, so Alice soon began talking again. "Dinah'll miss me very much tonight, I should think!" (Dinah was the cat.) "I hope they'll remember her saucer of milk at tea-time. Dinah, my dear! I wish you were down here with me! There are no mice in the air, I'm afraid, but you might catch a bat, and that's very like a mouse, you know. But do cats eat bats, I wonder?" And here Alice began to get rather sleepy, and went on say-ing to herself, in a dreamy sort of way, "Do cats eat bats? Do cats eat bats?" and sometimes "Do bats eat cats?" for, you see, as she could n't answer either question, it did n't much matter which way she put it.

3

She felt that she was dozing off, and had just began to dream that she was walking hand in hand with Dinah, and was saying to her, very earnestly, "Now, Dinah, tell me the truth: did you ever eat a bat?" when suddenly, thump! thump! down she came upon a heap of sticks and dry leaves, and the fall was over.

Alice was not a bit hurt, and she jumped up onto her feet in a moment: she looked up, but it was all dark overhead: before her was another long passage, and the White Rabbit was still in sight, hurrying down it. There was not a moment to be lost: away went Alice like the wind, and was just in time to hear it say, as it turned a corner, "Oh my ears and whiskers, how late it's getting!" She was close behind it when she turned the corner, but the Rabbit was no longer to be seen: she found herself in a long, low hall, which was lit up by a row of lamps hanging from the roof.

There were doors all round the hall, but they were all locked; and when Alice had been all the way down one side and up the other, trying every door, she walked sadly down the middle, wondering how she was ever to get out again.

Suddenly she came upon a little three-legged table, all made of solid glass: there was nothing on it but a tiny golden key, and Alice's first idea was that this might belong to one of the doors of the hall; but alas! either the locks were too large, or the key was too small, but at any rate it would not open any of them. However, on the second time round, she came upon a low curtain she had not noticed before, and behind it was a little door about fifteen inches high: she tried the little golden key in the lock, and to her great delight it fitted!

Alice opened the door and found that it led into a small passage, not much larger than a rat-hole: she knelt down and looked along the passage into the loveliest garden you ever saw. How she longed to get out of that dark hall, and wander about among those beds of bright flowers and those cool fountains, but she could not even get her head through the doorway; "and even if my head *would* go through," thought poor Alice, "it would be of very little use without my shoulders. Oh, how I wish I could shut up like a telescope! I think I could, if I only knew how to begin." For, you see, so many out-of-the-way things had happened lately, that Alice had begun to think that very few things indeed were really impossible.

There seemed to be no use in waiting by the little door, so she went back
to the table, half hoping she might find
another key on it, or at any rate a book
of rules for shutting people up like tel-
escopes: this time she found a little bottle on it ("which certainly was not here
before," said Alice), and tied round the
neck of the bottle was a paper label,
with the words "DRINK ME" beautifully printed on it in large letters.

It was all very well to say "Drink me," but the wise little Alice was not going to do *that* in a hurry. "No, I'll look first," she said, "and see whether it's marked '*poison*' or not"; for she had read several nice little stories about children who had got burned, and eaten up by wild beasts, and other unpleasant things, all because they *would* not remember the simple rules their friends had taught them: such as, that a red-hot poker will burn you if you hold it too long; and that, if you cut your finger *very* deeply with a knife, it usually bleeds; and she had never forgotten that, if you drink much from a bottle marked "poison," it is almost certain to disagree with you sooner or later.

However, this bottle was *not* marked "poison," so Alice ventured to taste it, and, finding it very nice (it had, in fact, a sort of mixed flavor of cherry-tart, custard, pineapple, roast turkey, toffy, and hot buttered toast), she very soon finished it off.

"What a curious feeling!" said Alice. "I must be shutting up like a telescope!"

And so it was indeed: she was now only ten inches high, and her face brightened up at the thought that she was now the right size for going through the little door into that lovely garden. First, however, she waited for a few minutes to see if she was going to shrink any further: she felt a little nervous about this; "for it might end, you know," said Alice to herself, "in my going out altogether, like a candle. I wonder what I should be like then?" And she tried to fancy what the flame of a candle looks like after the candle is blown out, for she could not remember ever having seen such a thing.

After a while, finding that nothing more happened, she decided on going into the garden at once; but, alas for poor Alice! when she got to the door, she found she had forgotten the little golden key, and when she went back to the table for it, she found she could not possibly reach it: she could see it quite plainly through the glass, and she tried her best to climb up one of the legs of the table, but it was too slippery; and when she had tired herself out with trying, the poor little thing sat down and cried.

"Come, there's no use in crying like that!" said Alice to herself rather sharply. "I advise you to leave off this minute!" She generally gave herself very good advice (though she very seldom followed it), and sometimes she scolded herself so severely as to bring tears into her eyes; and once she remembered trying to box her own ears for having cheated herself in a game of croquet she was playing against herself, for this curious child was very fond of pretending to be two people. "But it's no use now," thought poor Alice, "to pretend to be two people! Why, there's hardly enough of me left to make *one* respectable person!"

Soon her eye fell on a little glass box that was lying under the table: she opened it, and found in it a very small cake, on which the words "EAT ME" were beautifully marked in currants. "Well, I'll eat it," said Alice, "and if it makes me grow larger, I can reach the key; and if it makes me grow smaller, I can creep under the door: so either way I'll get into the garden, and I don't care which happens!"

She ate a little bit, and said anxiously to herself, "Which way? Which way?" holding her hand on the top of her head to feel which way it was growing; and she was quite surprised to find that she remained the same size. To be sure, this is what generally happens when one eats cake; but Alice had got so much into the way of expecting nothing but out-of-the-way things to happen, that it seemed quite dull and stupid for life to go on in the common way.

So she set to work, and very soon finished off the cake.

* * * * *

* * * *

* * * * *

II: THE POOL OF TEARS

"Curiouser and curiouser!" cried Alice (she was so much surprised, that for the moment she quite forgot how to speak good English). "Now I'm opening out like the largest telescope that ever was! Good-bye, feet!" (for when she looked down at her feet, they seemed to be almost out of sight, they were getting so far off). "Oh, my poor little feet, I wonder who will put on your shoes and stockings for you now, dears? I'm sure *I* shan't be able! I shall be a great deal too far off to trouble myself about you: you must manage the best way you can—but I must be kind to them," thought Alice, "or perhaps they won't walk the way I want to go! Let me see. I'll give them a new pair of boots every Christmas."

And she went on planning to herself how she would manage it. "They must go by the carrier," she thought; "and how funny it'll seem, sending presents to one's own feet! And how odd the directions will look!

"Alice's Right Foot, Esq.,
        "Hearthrug,
                "near the Fender,
                        "(with Alice's love).

Oh, dear, what nonsense I'm talking!"

Just at this moment her head struck against the roof of the hall:

in fact she was now rather more than nine feet high, and she at once took up the little golden key and hurried off to the garden door.

Poor Alice! It was as much as she could do, lying down on one side, to look through into the garden with one eye; but to get through was more hopeless than ever: she sat down and began to cry again.

"You ought to be ashamed of yourself," said Alice, "a great girl like you" (she might well say this), "to go on crying in this way!

Stop this moment, I tell you!" But she went on all the same, shedding gallons of tears, until there was a large pool all round her, about four inches deep, and reaching half down the hall.

After a time she heard a little pattering of feet in the distance, and she hastily dried her eyes to see what was coming. It was the White Rabbit returning, splendidly dressed, with a pair of white kid gloves in one hand and a large fan in the other: he came trotting along in a great hurry, muttering to himself, as he came, "Oh! The Duchess, the Duchess! Oh! *Won't* she be savage if I've kept her waiting!" Alice felt so desperate that she was ready to ask help of anyone: so, when the Rabbit came near her, she began, in a low, timid voice, "If you please, Sir—" The Rabbit started violently, dropped the white kid gloves and the fan, and scurried away into the darkness as hard as he could go.

Alice took up the fan and gloves, and, as the hall was very hot, she kept fanning herself all the time she went on talking. "Dear, dear! How queer everything is today! And yesterday things went on just as usual. I wonder if I've been changed in the night? Let me think: *was* I the same when I got up this morning? I almost think I can remember feeling a little different. But if I'm not the same, the next question is 'Who in the world am I? Ah, *that's* the great puzzle!" And she began thinking over all the children she knew that were of the same age as herself, to see if she could have been changed for any of them.

"I'm sure I'm not Ada," she said, "for her hair goes in such long ringlets, and mine doesn't go in ringlets at all; and I'm sure I can't be Mabel, for I know all sorts of things, and she, oh, she knows such a very little! Besides, *she's* she, and *I'm* I, and—oh, dear, how puzzling it all is! I'll try if I know all the things I used to know. Let me see: four times five is twelve, and four times six is thirteen, and four times seven is—oh dear! I shall never get to twenty at that rate! However, the Multiplication-Table does n't signify: let's try Geography. London is the capital of Paris, and Paris is the capital of Rome, and Rome—no, *that's* all wrong, I'm certain! I must have been changed for Mabel! I'll try and say *'How doth the little—','* and she crossed her hands on her lap, as if she were saying lessons, and began to repeat it, but her voice sounded hoarse and strange, and the words did not come the same as they used to do:—

> "How doth the little crocodile
> Improve his shining tail,
> And pour the waters of the Nile
> On every golden scale!

> "How cheerfully he seems to grin,
> How neatly spreads his claws,
> And welcomes little fishes in
> With gently smiling jaws!"

"I'm sure those are not the right words," said poor Alice, and her eyes filled with tears again as she went on, "I must be Mabel after all, and I shall have to go and live in that poky little house, and have next to no toys to play with, and oh, ever so many lessons to learn! No, I've made up my mind about it: if I'm Mabel, I'll stay down here! It'll be no use their putting their heads down and saying, 'Come up again, dear!' I shall only look up and say, 'Who am I, then? Tell me that first, and then, if I like being that person, I'll come up: if not, I'll stay down here till I'm somebody else'—but, oh dear!" cried Alice, with a sudden burst of tears, "I do wish they *would* put their heads down! I am so *very* tired of being all alone here!"

As she said this she looked down at her hands, and was surprised to see that she had put on one of the Rabbit's little white kid gloves while she was talking. "How *can* I have done that?" she thought. "I must be growing small again." She got up and went to the table to measure herself by it, and found that, as nearly as she could guess, she was now about two feet high, and was going on shrinking rapidly: she soon found out that the cause of this was the fan she was holding, and she dropped it hastily, just in time to save herself from shrinking away altogether.

"That *was* a narrow escape!" said Alice, a good deal frightened at the sudden change, but very glad to find herself still in existence. "And now for the garden!" And she ran with all speed back to the little door; but, alas! the little door was shut again, and the little golden key was lying on the glass table as before, "and things are worse than ever," thought the poor child, "for I never was so small as this before, never! And I declare it's too bad, that it is!"

As she said these words her foot slipped, and in another moment, splash! she was up to her chin in salt water. Her first idea was that she had somehow fallen into the sea, "and in that case I can go back by railway," she said to herself. (Alice had been to the seaside once in her life, and had come to the general conclusion that, wherever you go to on the English coast, you find a number of bathing machines in the sea, some children digging in the sand with wooden spades, then a row of lodging houses, and behind them a railway station.) However, she soon made out that she was in the pool of tears which she had wept when she was nine feet high.

"I wish I hadn't cried so much!" said Alice, as she swam about, trying to find her way out. "I shall be punished for it now, I suppose, by being drowned in my own tears! That *will* be a queer thing, to be sure! However, everything is queer today."

Just then she heard something splashing about in the pool a little way off, and she swam nearer to make out what it was: at first she thought it must be a walrus or hippopotamus, but then she remembered how small she was now, and she soon made out that it was only a mouse that had slipped in like herself.

"Would it be of any use, now," thought Alice, "to speak to this mouse? Everything is so out-of-the-way down here, that I should think very likely it can talk: at any rate, there's no harm in trying." So she began: "O Mouse, do you know the way out of this pool? I am very tired of swimming about here O Mouse!" (Alice thought this must be the right way of speaking to a mouse: she had never done such a thing before, but she remembered having seen, in her brother's Latin Grammar, "A mouse—of a mouse—to a mouse—a mouse—O mouse!") The mouse looked at her rather inquisitively, and seemed to her to wink with one of its little eyes, but it said nothing.

"Perhaps it doesn't understand English," thought Alice. "I daresay it's a French mouse, come over with William the Conqueror." (For with all her knowledge of history, Alice had no very clear notion how long ago anything had happened.) So she began again: "Où est ma chatte?" which was the first sentence in her French lesson book. The Mouse gave a sudden leap out of the water, and seemed to quiver all over with fright. "Oh, I beg your pardon!" cried Alice hastily, afraid that she had hurt the poor animal's feelings. "I quite forgot you didn't like cats."

"Not like cats!" cried the Mouse in a shrill, passionate voice. "Would *you* like cats, if you were me?"

"Well, perhaps not," said Alice in a soothing tone: "don't be angry about it. And yet I wish I could show you our cat Dinah. I think you'd take a fancy to cats, if you could only see her. She is such a dear quiet thing," Alice went on, half to herself, as she swam lazily about in the pool, "and she sits purring so nicely by the fire, licking her paws and washing her face—and she is such a nice soft thing to nurse —and she's such a capital one for catching mice—oh, I beg your pardon!" cried Alice again, for this time the Mouse was bristling all over, and she felt certain it must be really offended. "We won't talk about her any more, if you'd rather not."

"We, indeed!" cried the Mouse, who was trembling down to the end of its tail. "As if *I* would talk on such a subject! Our family al-

ways *hated* cats: nasty, low, vulgar things! Don't let me hear the name again!"

"I won't indeed!" said Alice, in a great hurry to change the subject of conversation. "Are you—are you fond—of—of dogs?" The Mouse did not answer, so Alice went on eagerly: "There is such a nice little dog, near our house, I should like to show you! A little bright-eyed terrier, you know, with oh, such long curly brown hair! And it'll fetch things when you throw them, and it'll sit up and beg for its dinner, and all sorts of things—I can't remember half of them—and it belongs to a farmer, you know, and he says it's so useful, it's worth a hundred pounds! He says it kills all the rats, and—oh dear!" cried Alice in a sorrowful tone. "I'm afraid I've offended it again!" For the Mouse was swimming away from her as hard as it could go, and making quite a commotion in the pool as it went.

So she called softly after it, "Mouse dear! Do come back again, and we won't talk about cats, or dogs either, if you don't like them!" When the Mouse heard this, it turned round and swam slowly back to her: its face was quite pale (with passion, Alice thought), and it said, in a low trembling voice, "Let us get to the shore, and then I'll tell you my history, and you'll understand why it is I hate cats and dogs."

It was high time to go, for the pool was getting quite crowded with the birds and animals that had fallen into it: there was a Duck and a Dodo, a Lory and Eaglet, and several other curious creatures. Alice led the way, and the whole party swam to the shore.

III: A CAUCUS-RACE AND

A LONG TALE

They were, indeed, a queer-looking party that assembled on the bank—the birds with draggled feathers, the animals with their fur clinging close to them, and all dripping wet, cross, and uncomfortable.

The first question of course was, how to get dry again: they had a consultation about this, and after a few minutes it seemed quite natural to Alice to find herself talking familiarly with them, as if she had known them all her life. Indeed, she had quite a long argument with the Lory, who at last turned sulky, and would only say "I'm older than you, and must know better." And this Alice would not allow, without knowing how old it was; and, as the Lory positively refused to tell its age, there was no more to be said.

At last the Mouse, who seemed to be a person of some authority among them, called out, "Sit down, all of you, and listen to me! *I'll* soon make you dry enough!" They all sat down at once, in a large ring, with the Mouse in the middle. Alice kept her eyes anxiously fixed on it, for she felt sure she would catch a bad cold if she did not get dry very soon.

"Ahem!" said the Mouse with an important air, "Are you all ready? This is the driest thing I know. Silence all round, if you please! 'William the Conqueror, whose cause was favored by the pope, was soon submitted to by the English, who wanted leaders and had been of late much accustomed to usurpation and conquest. Edwin and Morcar, the earls of Mercia and Northumbria—' "

"Ugh!" said the Lory, with a shiver.

"I beg your pardon!" said the Mouse, frowning, but very politely. "Did you speak?"

"Not I!" said the Lory, hastily.

"I thought you did," said the Mouse. "I proceed. 'Edwin and Morcar, the earls of Mercia and Northumbria, declared for him; and even Stigand, the patriotic archbishop of Canterbury, found it advisable—' "

"Found *what*?" said the Duck.

"Found *it*," the Mouse replied, rather crossly: "of course you know what 'it' means."

"I know what 'it' means well enough, when *I* find a thing," said the Duck; "it's generally a frog, or a worm. The question is, what did the archbishop find!"

The Mouse did not notice this question, but hurriedly went on, " '—found it advisable to go with Edgar Atheling to meet William and offer him the crown. William's conduct at first was moderate. But the insolence of his Normans—' How are you getting on now, my dear?" it continued, turning to Alice as it spoke.

"As wet as ever," said Alice, in a melancholy tone; "it does n't seem to dry me at all."

"In that case," said the Dodo, solemnly, rising to its feet, "I move that the meeting adjourn, for the immediate adoption of more energetic remedies—"

"Speak English!" said the Eaglet. "I don't know the meaning of half those long words, and, what's more, I don't believe you do either!" And the Eaglet bent down its head to hide a smile: some of the other birds tittered audibly.

"What I was going to say," said the Dodo in an offended tone, "was, that the best thing to get us dry would be a Caucus-race."

"What *is* a Caucus-race?" said Alice; not that she much wanted to know, but the Dodo had paused as if it thought that *somebody* ought to speak, and no one else seemed inclined to say anything.

"Why," said the Dodo, "the best way to explain it is to do it." (And, as you might like to try the thing yourself, some winter day, I will tell you how the Dodo managed it.)

First it marked out a race-course, in a sort of circle ("the exact shape does n't matter," it said), and then all the party were placed along the course, here and there. There was no "One, two, three, and away!" but they began running when they liked, and left off when they liked, so that it was not easy to know when the race was over. However, when they had been running half an hour or so, and were quite dry again, the Dodo suddenly called out "The race is over!" and they all crowded round it, panting, and asking, "But who has won?"

This question the Dodo could not answer without a great deal of thought, and it stood for a long time with one finger pressed upon its forehead (the position in which you usually see Shakespeare, in the pictures of him), while the rest waited in silence. At last the Dodo said, "*Everybody* has won, and *all* must have prizes."

"But who is to give the prizes?" quite a chorus of voices asked.

"Why, *she,* of course," said the Dodo, pointing to Alice with one finger; and the whole party at once crowded round her, calling out, in a confused way, "Prizes! Prizes!"

Alice had no idea what to do, and in despair she put her hand in her pocket, and pulled out a box of comfits (luckily the salt water had not got into it), and handed them round as prizes. There was exactly one a-piece, all round.

"But she must have a prize herself, you know," said the Mouse.

"Of course," the Dodo replied very gravely. "What else have you got in your pocket?" it went on, turning to Alice.

"Only a thimble," said Alice sadly.

"Hand it over here," said the Dodo.

Then they all crowded round her once more, while the Dodo solemnly presented the thimble, saying, "We beg your acceptance of this elegant thimble"; and, when it had finished this short speech, they all cheered.

Alice thought the whole thing very absurd, but they all looked so grave that she did not dare to laugh; and, as she could not think of anything to say, she simply bowed, and took the thimble, looking as solemn as she could.

The next thing was to eat the comfits: this caused some noise and confusion, as the large birds complained that they could not taste theirs, and the small ones choked and had to be patted on the back. However, it was over at last, and they sat down again in a ring, and begged the Mouse to tell them something more.

19

"You promised to tell me your history, you know," said Alice, "and why it is you hate—C and D," she added in a whisper, half afraid that it would be offended again.

"Mine is a long and a sad tale!" said the Mouse turning to Alice, and sighing.

"It *is* a long tail, certainly," said Alice, looking down with wonder at the Mouse's tail; "but why do you call it sad?" And she kept on puzzling about it while the Mouse was speaking, so that her idea of the tale was something like this:

```
        "Fury said to
          a mouse, That
            he met in the
              house, 'Let
                 us both go
                  to law: I
                    will prose-
                    cute you.—
                   Come, I'll
                  take no de-
                nial: We
              must have
            the trial;
          For really
        this morn-
      ing I've
     nothing
    to do.'
     Said the
       mouse to
        the cur,
         'Such a
          trial, dear
            Sir, With
             no jury
              or judge,
                would
               be wast-
              ing our
             breath.'
           'I'll be
          judge,
        I'll be
      jury,'
     said
    cun-
    ning
    old
    Fury:
     'I'll
      try
       the
        whole
         cause,
          and
         con-
        demn
      you to
     death.'"
```

"You are not attending!" said the Mouse to Alice, severely. "What are you thinking of?"

"I beg your pardon," said Alice very humbly: "you had got to the fifth bend, I think?"

"I had *not!*" cried the Mouse, sharply and very angrily.

"A knot!" said Alice, always ready to make herself useful, and looking anxiously about her. "Oh, do let me help to undo it!"

"I shall do nothing of the sort," said the Mouse, getting up and walking away. "You insult me by talking such nonsense!"

"I didn't mean it!" pleaded poor Alice. "But you're so easily offended, you know!"

The Mouse only growled in reply.

"Please come back, and finish your story!" Alice called after it. And the others all joined in chorus, "Yes, please do!" But the Mouse only shook its head impatiently, and walked a little quicker.

"What a pity it wouldn't stay!" sighed the Lory, as soon as it was quite out of sight. And an old Crab took the opportunity of saying to her daughter, "Ah, my dear! Let this be a lesson to you never to lose *your* temper!" "Hold your tongue, Ma!" said the young Crab a little snappishly. "You're enough to try the patience of an oyster!"

"I wish I had our Dinah here, I know I do!" said Alice aloud, addressing nobody in particular. *"She'd* soon fetch it back!"

"And who is Dinah, if I might venture to ask the question?" said the Lory.

Alice replied eagerly, for she was always ready to talk about her pet: "Dinah's our cat. And she's such a capital one for catching mice, you can't think! And oh, I wish you could see her after the birds! Why, she'll eat a little bird as soon as look at it!"

This speech caused a remarkable sensation among the party. Some of the birds hurried off at once: one old Magpie began wrapping itself up very carefully, remarking, "I really must be getting home, the night air doesn't suit my throat!" and a Canary called out in a trembling voice, to its children, "Come away, my dears! It's high time you were all in bed!" On various pretexts they all moved off, and Alice was soon left alone.

"I wish I hadn't mentioned Dinah!" she said to herself in a melancholy tone. "Nobody seems to like her, down here, and I'm sure she's the best cat in the world! Oh, my dear Dinah! I wonder if I shall ever see you any more!" And here poor Alice began to cry again, for she felt very lonely and low-spirited. In a little while, however, she again heard a little pattering of footsteps in the distance, and she looked up eagerly, half hoping that the Mouse had changed his mind, and was coming back to finish his story.

IV: THE RABBIT SENDS IN

A LITTLE BILL

It was the White Rabbit, trotting slowly back again, and looking anxiously about as it went, as if it had lost something; and she heard it muttering to itself, "The Duchess! The Duchess! Oh, my dear paws! Oh, my fur and whiskers! She'll get me executed, as sure as ferrets are ferrets! Where *can* I have dropped them, I wonder?" Alice guessed in a moment that it was looking for the fan and the pair of white kid gloves, and she very good-naturedly began hunting about for them, but they were nowhere to be seen—everything seemed to have changed since her swim in the pool; and the great hall, with the glass table and the little door, had vanished completely.

Very soon the Rabbit noticed Alice, as she went hunting about, and called out to her, in an angry tone, "Why, Mary Ann, what *are* you doing out here? Run home this moment, and fetch me a pair of gloves and a fan! Quick, now!" And Alice was so much frightened that she ran off at once in the direction it pointed to, without trying to explain the mistake that it had made.

"He took me for his housemaid," she said to herself as she ran.

"How surprised he'll be when he finds out who I am! But I'd better take him his fan and gloves—that is, if I can find them." As she said this, she came upon a neat little house, on the door of which was a bright brass plate with the name "W. RABBIT" engraved upon it. She went in without knocking, and hurried upstairs, in great fear lest she should meet the real Mary Ann, and be turned out of the house before she had found the fan and gloves.

"How queer it seems," Alice said to herself, "to be going messages for a rabbit! I suppose Dinah'll be sending me on messages next!" And she began fancying the sort of thing that would happen: " 'Miss Alice! Come here directly, and get ready for your walk!' 'Coming in a minute, nurse! But I've got to watch this mouse-hole till Dinah comes back, and see that the mouse does n't get out.' Only I don't think," Alice went on, "that they'd let Dinah stop in the house if it began ordering people about like that!"

By this time she had found her way into a tidy little room with a table in the window, and on it (as she had hoped) a fan and two or three pairs of tiny white kid gloves: she took up the fan and a pair of the gloves, and was just going to leave the room, when her eye fell upon a little bottle that stood near the looking glass. There was no label this time with the words, "DRINK ME," but nevertheless she uncorked it and put it to her lips. "I know *something* interesting is sure to happen," she said to herself, "whenever I eat or drink any-thing: so I'll just see what this bottle does. I do hope it'll make me grow large again, for really I'm quite tired of being such a tiny little thing!"

It did so indeed, and much sooner than she had expected: before she had drunk half the bottle, she found her head pressing against the ceiling, and had to stoop to save her neck from being broken. She hastily put down the bottle, saying to herself "That's quite enough—I hope I shan't grow any more—As it is, I can't get out at the door—I do wish I had n't drunk quite so much!"

Alas! It was too late to wish that! She went on growing, and

growing, and very soon had to kneel down on the floor: in another minute there was not even room for this, and she tried the effect of lying down with one elbow against the door, and the other arm curled round her head. Still she went on growing, and, as a last resource, she put one arm out of the window, and one foot up the chimney, and said to herself, "Now I can do no more, whatever happens. What *will* become of me?"

Luckily for Alice, the little magic bottle had now had its full effect, and she grew no larger: still it was very uncomfortable, and, as there seemed to be no sort of chance of her ever getting out of the room again, no wonder she felt unhappy.

"It was much pleasanter at home," thought poor Alice, "when one wasn't always growing larger and smaller, and being ordered about by mice and rabbits. I almost wish I had n't gone down that rabbit-hole—and yet—and yet—it's curious, you know, this sort of life! I do wonder what *can* have happened to me! When I used to read fairy tales, I fancied that kind of thing never happened, and now here I am in the middle of one! There ought to be a book written about me, that there ought! And when I grow up I'll write one—but I'm grown up now," she added in a sorrowful tone: "at least there's no room to grow up any more *here*."

"But then," thought Alice, "shall I *never* get any older than I am now? That'll be a comfort, one way—never to be an old woman—but then—always to have lessons to learn! Oh, I shouldn't like *that*."

"Oh, you foolish Alice!" she answered herself. "How can you learn lessons in here? Why, there's hardly room for *you*, and no room at all for any lesson-books!"

And so she went on, taking first one side and then the other, and making quite a conversation of it altogether; but after a few minutes she heard a voice outside, and stopped to listen.

"Mary Ann! Mary Ann!" said the voice. "Fetch me my gloves this moment!" Then came a little pattering of feet on the stairs. Alice knew it was the Rabbit coming to look for her, and she trembled till she shook the house, quite forgetting that she was now about a thousand times as large as the Rabbit, and had no reason to be afraid of it.

Presently the Rabbit came up to the door, and tried to open it; but, as the door opened inward, and Alice's elbow was pressed hard against it, that attempt proved a failure. Alice heard it say to itself, "Then I'll go round and get in at the window."

"*That* you won't" thought Alice, and, after waiting till she fancied she heard the Rabbit just under the window, she suddenly spread out her hand, and made a snatch in the air. She did not get hold of anything, but she heard a little shriek and a fall, and a crash of broken glass, from which she concluded that it was just possible it had fallen into a cucumber frame, or something of the sort.

Next came an angry voice—the Rabbit's—"Pat! Pat! Where are you?" And then a voice she had never heard before, "Sure then I'm here! Digging for apples, yer honor!"

"Digging for apples, indeed!" said the Rabbit, angrily. "Here! Come and help me out of *this!*" (Sounds of more broken glass.)

"Now tell me, Pat, what's that in the window?"

"Sure, it's an arm, yer honor!" (He pronounced it "arrum.")

"An arm, you goose! Who ever saw one that size? Why, it fills the whole window!"

"Sure, it does, yer honor: but it's an arm for all that."

"Well, it's got no business there, at any rate: go and take it away!"

There was a long silence after this, and Alice could only hear whispers now and then; such as "Sure, I don't like it, yer honor, at all, at all!" "Do as I tell you, you coward!" and at last she spread out her hand again, and made another snatch in the air. This time there were *two* little shrieks, and more sounds of broken glass. "What a number of cucumber frames there must be!" thought Alice. "I wonder what they'll do next! As for pulling me out of the window, I only wish they *could!* I'm sure *I* don't want to stay in here any longer!"

She waited for some time without hearing anything more: at last came a rumbling of little cart wheels, and the sound of a good many voices all talking together: she made out the words: "Where's the other ladder?—Why, I hadn't to bring but one. Bill's got the other—Bill! Fetch it here, lad!—Here, put 'em up at this corner—No, tie 'em together first—they don't reach half high enough yet—Oh, they'll do well enough. Don't be particular—Here, Bill! Catch hold of this rope—Will the roof bear?—Mind that loose slate—Oh, it's coming down! Heads below!" (a loud crash)—"Now, who did that?—It was Bill, I fancy—Who's to go down the chimney?—Nay, *I* shan't! *You* do it!—*That* I won't, then!—Bill's got to go down—Here, Bill! The master says you've got to go down the chimney!"

"Oh! So Bill's got to come down the chimney, has he?" said Alice to herself. "Why, they seem to put everything upon Bill! I wouldn't be in Bill's place for a good deal: this fireplace is narrow, to be sure; but I *think* I can kick a little!"

She drew her foot as far down the chimney as she could, and waited till she heard a little animal (she couldn't guess of what sort it was) scratching and scrambling about in the chimney close above her: then, saying to herself, "This is Bill," she gave one sharp kick, and waited to see what would happen next.

The first thing she heard was a general chorus of, "There goes Bill!" then the Rabbit's voice alone—"Catch him, you by the hedge!" then silence, and then another confusion of voices—"Hold up his head—Brandy now—Don't choke him—How was it, old fellow? What happened to you? Tell us all about it!"

Last came a little feeble, squeaking voice ("That's Bill," thought Alice), "Well I hardly know—No more, thank ye; I'm better now—but I'm a deal too flustered to tell you—all I know is, something comes at me like a Jack-in-the-box, and up I goes like a sky-rocket!"

"So you did, old fellow!" said the others.

"We must burn the house down!" said the Rabbit's voice. And Alice called out, as loud as she could, "If you do, I'll set Dinah at you!"

There was a dead silence instantly, and Alice thought to herself, "I wonder what they *will* do next! If they had any sense, they'd take the roof off." After a minute or two, they began moving about again, and Alice heard the Rabbit say, "A barrowful will do, to begin with."

"A barrowful of *what?*" thought Alice. But she had not long to doubt, for the next moment a shower of little pebbles came rattling in at the window, and some of them hit her in the face. "I'll put a stop to this," she said to herself, and shouted out, "You'd better not do that again!" which produced another dead silence.

Alice noticed, with some surprise, that the pebbles were all turning into little cakes as they lay on the floor, and a bright idea came into her head. "If I eat one of these cakes," she thought, "it's sure to make *some* change in my size; and, as it can't possibly make me larger, it must make me smaller, I suppose."

So she swallowed one of the cakes, and was delighted to find that she began shrinking directly. As soon as she was small enough to get through the door, she ran out of the house, and found quite a crowd of little animals and birds waiting outside. The poor little Lizard, Bill, was in the middle, being held up by two guinea pigs, who were giving it something out of a bottle. They all made a rush at Alice the moment she appeared; but she ran off as hard as she could, and soon found herself safe in a thick wood.

"The first thing I've got to do," said Alice to herself, as she wandered about in the wood, "is to grow to my right size again; and the second thing is to find my way into that lovely garden. I think that will be the best plan."

It sounded an excellent plan, no doubt, and very neatly and simply arranged: the only difficulty was, that she had not the smallest idea how to set about it; and, while she was peering about anxiously among the trees, a little sharp bark just over her head made her look up in a great hurry.

An enormous puppy was looking down at her with large round eyes, and feebly stretching out one paw, trying to touch her. "Poor little thing!" said Alice, in a coaxing tone, and she tried hard to whistle to it; but she was terribly frightened all the time at the thought that it might be hungry, in which case it would be very likely to eat her up in spite of all her coaxing.

Hardly knowing what she did, she picked up a little bit of stick, and held it out to the puppy: whereupon the puppy jumped into the air off all its feet at once, with a yelp of delight, and rushed at the stick, and made believe to worry it: then Alice dodged behind a great thistle, to keep herself from being run over; and, the moment she appeared on the other side, the puppy made another rush at the stick, and tumbled head over heels in its hurry to get hold of it: then Alice, thinking it was very like having a game of play with a cart horse, and expecting every moment to be trampled under its feet, ran round the thistle again: then the puppy began a series of short charges at the stick, running a very little way forward each time and a long way back, and barking hoarsely all the while, till at last it sat down a good way off, panting, with its tongue hanging out of its mouth, and its great eyes half shut.

This seemed to Alice a good opportunity for making her escape: so she set off at once, and ran till she was quite tired and out of breath, and till the puppy's bark sounded quite faint in the distance.

"And yet what a dear little puppy it was!" said Alice, as she leaned against a buttercup to rest herself, and fanned herself with one of the leaves. "I should have liked teaching it tricks very much, if—if I'd only been the right size to do it! Oh, dear! I'd nearly forgotten

that I've got to grow up again! Let me see—how *is* it to be managed? I suppose I ought to eat or drink something or other; but the great question is, 'What?'"

The great question certainly was "What?" Alice looked all round her at the flowers and the blades of grass, but she could not see anything that looked like the right thing to eat or drink under the circumstances. There was a large mushroom growing near her, about the same height as herself; and, when she had looked under it, and on both sides of it, and behind it, it occurred to her that she might as well look and see what was on the top of it.

She stretched herself up on tiptoe, and peeped over the edge of the mushroom, and her eyes immediately met those of a large blue caterpillar, that was sitting on the top, with his arms folded, quietly smoking a long hookah, and taking not the smallest notice of her or of anything else.

V: ADVICE FROM A CATERPILLAR

The Caterpillar and Alice looked at each other for some time in silence: at last the Caterpillar took the hookah out of its mouth, and addressed her in a languid, sleepy voice.

"Who are *you?*" said the Caterpillar.

This was not an encouraging opening for a conversation. Alice replied, rather shyly, "I—I hardly know, Sir, just at present—at least I know who I *was* when I got up this morning, but I think I must have been changed several times since then."

"What do you mean by that?" said the Caterpillar, sternly. "Explain yourself!"

"I can't explain *myself,* I'm afraid, Sir," said Alice, "because I'm not myself, you see."

"I don't see," said the Caterpillar.

"I'm afraid I can't put it more clearly," Alice replied, very politely, "for I can't understand it myself, to begin with; and being so many different sizes in a day is very confusing."

"It isn't," said the Caterpillar.

"Well, perhaps you haven't found it so yet," said Alice; "but when you have to turn into a chrysalis—you will some day, you know—and then after that into a butterfly, I should think you'll feel it a little queer, won't you?"

"Not a bit," said the Caterpillar.

"Well, perhaps your feelings may be different," said Alice: "all I know is, it would feel very queer to *me*."

"You!" said the Caterpillar contemptuously. "Who are *you*?"

Which brought them back again to the beginning of the conversation. Alice felt a little irritated at the Caterpillar's making such *very* short remarks, and she drew herself up and said, very gravely, "I think you ought to tell me who *you* are, first."

"Why?" said the Caterpillar.

Here was another puzzling question; and, as Alice could not think of any good reason, and the Caterpillar seemed to be in a *very* unpleasant state of mind, she turned away.

"Come back!" the Caterpillar called after her. "I've something important to say!"

This sounded promising, certainly. Alice turned and came back again.

"Keep your temper," said the Caterpillar.

"Is that all?" said Alice, swallowing down her anger as well as she could.

"No," said the Caterpillar.

Alice thought she might as well wait, as she had nothing else to do, and perhaps after all it might tell her something worth hearing. For some minutes it puffed away without speaking; but at last it unfolded its arms, took the hookah out of its mouth again, and said, "So you think you're changed, do you?"

"I'm afraid I am, Sir," said Alice. "I can't remember things as I used — and I don't keep the same size for ten minutes together!"

"Can't remember *what* things?" said the Caterpillar.

"Well, I've tried to say, '*How doth the little busy bee,*' but it all came different!" Alice replied in a very melancholy voice.

"Repeat, '*You are old, Father William,*'" said the Caterpillar.
Alice folded her hands, and began:

"You are old, Father William," the young man said,
 "And your hair has become very white;
And yet you incessantly stand on your head—
 Do you think, at your age, it is right?"

"In my youth," Father William replied to his son,
 "I feared it might injure the brain;
But, now that I'm perfectly sure I have none,
 Why, I do it again and again."

"You are old," said the youth, "as I mentioned before,
 And have grown most uncommonly fat;
Yet you turned a back-somersault in at the door—
 Pray, what is the reason of that?"

"In my youth," said the sage, as he shook his gray locks,
    "I kept all my limbs very supple
By the use of this ointment—one shilling the box—
    Allow me to sell you a couple?"

"You are old," said the youth, "and your jaws are too weak
   For anything tougher than suet;
Yet you finished the goose, with the bones and the beak—
   Pray, how did you manage to do it?"

"In my youth," said his father, "I took to the law,
   And argued each case with my wife;
And the muscular strength, which it gave to my jaw
   Has lasted the rest of my life."

"You are old," said the youth, "one would hardly suppose
   That your eye was as steady as ever;
Yet you balanced an eel on the end of your nose—
   What made you so awfully clever?"

"I have answered three questions, and that is enough,"
   Said his father. "Don't give yourself airs!
Do you think I can listen all day to such stuff?
   Be off, or I'll kick you downstairs!"

"That is not said right," said the Caterpillar.

"Not *quite* right, I'm afraid," said Alice, timidly: "some of the words have got altered."

"It is wrong from beginning to end," said the Caterpillar, decidedly; and there was silence for some minutes.

The Caterpillar was the first to speak.

"What size do you want to be?" it asked.

"Oh, I'm not particular as to size," Alice hastily replied; "only one does n't like changing so often, you know."

"I *don't* know," said the Caterpillar.

Alice said nothing: she had never been so much contradicted in all her life before, and she felt that she was losing her temper.

"Are you content now?" said the Caterpillar.

"Well, I should like to be a *little* larger, Sir, if you would n't mind," said Alice: "three inches is such a wretched height to be."

"It is a very good height indeed!" said the Caterpillar angrily, rearing itself upright as it spoke (it was exactly three inches high).

"But I'm not used to it!" pleaded poor Alice in a piteous tone. And she thought to herself, "I wish the creature would n't be so easily offended!"

"You'll get used to it in time," said the Caterpillar; and it put the hookah into its mouth, and began smoking again.

This time Alice waited patiently until it chose to speak again. In a minute or two the Caterpillar took the hookah out of its mouth, and yawned once or twice, and shook itself. Then it got down off the mushroom, and crawled away into the grass, merely remarking, as it went, "One side will make you grow taller, and the other side will make you grow shorter."

"One side of *what*? The other side of *what*?" thought Alice to herself.

"Of the mushroom," said the Caterpillar, just as if she had asked it aloud; and in another moment it was out of sight.

Alice remained looking thoughtfully at the mushroom for a minute, trying to make out which were the two sides of it; and, as it was perfectly round, she found this a very difficult question. However, at last she stretched her arms round it as far as they would go, and broke off a bit of the edge with each hand.

"And now which is which?" she said to herself, and nibbled a little of the right-hand bit to try the effect. The next moment she felt a violent blow underneath her chin: it had struck her foot!

She was a good deal frightened by this very sudden change, but she felt that there was no time to be lost, as she was shrinking rapidly: so she set to work at once to eat some of the other bit. Her chin was pressed so closely against her foot, that there was hardly room to open her mouth; but she did it at last, and managed to swallow a morsel of the left-hand bit.

*   *   *   *   *   *

   *   *   *   *   *

   *   *   *   *   *   *

"Come, my head's free at last!" said Alice in a tone of delight, which changed into alarm in another moment, when she found that her shoulders were nowhere to be found: all she could see, when she looked down, was an immense length of neck, which seemed to rise like a stalk out a sea of green leaves that lay far below her.

"What *can* all that green stuff be?" said Alice. "And where *have* my shoulders got to? And oh, my poor hands, how is it I can't see you?" She was moving them about, as she spoke, but no result seemed to follow, except a little shaking among the distant green leaves.

As there seemed to be no chance of getting her hands up to her head, she tried to get her head down to *them,* and was delighted to find that her neck would bend about easily in any direction, like a serpent. She had just succeeded in curving it down into a graceful zigzag, and was going to dive in among the leaves, which she found to be nothing but the tops of the trees under which she had been wandering, when a sharp hiss made her draw back in a hurry: a large pigeon had flown into her face, and was beating her violently with its wings.

"Serpent!" screamed the Pigeon.

"I'm *not* a serpent!" said Alice indignantly. "Let me alone!"

"Serpent, I say again!" repeated the Pigeon, but in a more subdued tone, and added, with a kind of sob, "I've tried every way, but nothing seems to suit them!"

"I haven't the least idea what you're talking about," said Alice.

"I've tried the roots of trees, and I've tried banks, and I've tried hedges," the Pigeon went on, without attending to her; "but those serpents! There's no pleasing them!"

Alice was more and more puzzled, but she thought there was no use in saying anything more till the Pigeon had finished.

"As if it wasn't trouble enough hatching the eggs," said the Pigeon; "but I must be on the lookout for serpents, night and day! Why, I haven't had a wink of sleep these three weeks!"

"I'm very sorry you've been annoyed," said Alice, who was beginning to see its meaning.

"And just as I'd taken the highest tree in the wood," continued the Pigeon, raising its voice to a shriek, "and just as I was thinking I should be free of them at last, they must needs come wriggling down from the sky! Ugh, Serpent!"

"But I'm *not* a serpent, I tell you!" said Alice. "I'm a— I'm a—"

"Well! *What* are you?" said the Pigeon. "I can see you're trying to invent something!"

"I—I'm a little girl," said Alice, rather doubtfully, as she remembered the number of changes she had gone through, that day.

"A likely story indeed!" said the Pigeon, in a tone of the deepest contempt. "I've seen a good many little girls in my time, but never *one* with such a neck as that! No, no! You're a serpent; and there's no use denying it. I suppose you'll be telling me next that you never tasted an egg!"

"I *have* tasted eggs, certainly," said Alice, who was a very truthful child; "but little girls eat eggs quite as much as serpents do, you know."

"I don't believe it," said the Pigeon; "but if they do, why, then they're a kind of serpent: that's all I can say."

This was such a new idea to Alice that she was quite silent for a minute or two, which gave the Pigeon the opportunity of adding, "You're looking for eggs, I know *that* well enough; and what does it matter to me whether you're a little girl or a serpent?"

"It matters a good deal to *me*," said Alice, hastily; "but I'm not looking for eggs, as it happens; and, if I was, I should n't want *yours:* I don't like them raw."

"Well, be off, then!" said the Pigeon in a sulky tone, as it settled down again into its nest. Alice crouched down among the trees as well as she could, for her neck kept getting entangled among the branches, and every now and then she had to stop and untwist it. After a while she remembered that she still held the pieces of mushroom in her hands, and she set to work very carefully, nibbling first at one and then at the other, and growing sometimes taller, and sometimes shorter, until she had succeeded in bringing herself down to her usual height.

It was so long since she had been anything near the right size that it felt quite strange at first; but she got used to it in a few minutes, and began talking to herself, as usual, "Come, there's half my plan done now! How puzzling all these changes are! I'm never sure what I'm going to be, from one minute to another! However, I've got back to my right size: the next thing is, to get into that beautiful garden—how *is* that to be done, I wonder?" As she said this, she came suddenly upon an open place, with a little house in it about four feet high. "Whoever lives there," thought Alice, "it'll never do to come upon them *this* size: why, I should frighten them out of their wits!" So she began nibbling at the right-hand bit again, and did not venture to go near the house till she had brought herself down to nine inches high.

VI: PIG AND PEPPER

For a minute or two she stood looking at the house, and wondering what to do next, when suddenly a footman in livery came running out of the wood —(she considered him to be a footman because he was in livery: otherwise, judging by his face only, she would have called him a fish)—and rapped loudly at the door with his knuckles. It was opened by another footman in livery, with a round face, and large eyes like a frog; and both footmen, Alice noticed, had powdered hair that curled all over their heads. She felt very curious to know what it was all about, and crept a little way out of the wood to listen.

The Fish-Footman began by producing from under his arm a great letter, nearly as large as himself, and this he handed over to the other, saying, in a solemn tone, "For the Duchess. An invitation from the Queen to play croquet." The Frog-Footman repeated, in the same solemn tone, only changing the order of the words a little, "From the Queen. An invitation for the Duchess to play croquet."

Then they both bowed low, and their curls got entangled together.

Alice laughed so much at this, that she had to run back into the wood for fear of their hearing her; and when she next peeped out, the Fish-Footman was gone, and the other was sitting on the ground near the door, staring stupidly up into the sky.

Alice went timidly up to the door, and knocked.

"There's no sort of use in knocking," said the Footman, "and that for two reasons. First, because I'm on the same side of the door as you are: secondly, because they're making such a noise inside, no one could possibly hear you." And certainly there *was* a most extraordinary noise going on within—a constant howling and sneezing, and every now and then a great crash, as if a dish or kettle had been broken to pieces.

"Please, then," said Alice, "how am I to get in?"

"There might be some sense in your knocking," the Footman went on, without attending to her, "if we had the door between us. For instance, if you were *inside,* you might knock and I could let you out, you know." He was looking up into the sky all the time he was speaking, and this Alice thought decidedly uncivil. "But perhaps he can't help it," she said to herself; "his eyes are so *very* nearly at the top of his head. But at any rate he might answer questions—How am I to get in?" she repeated, aloud.

"I shall sit here," the Footman remarked, "till tomorrow—"

At this moment the door of the house opened, and a large plate came skimming out, straight at the Footman's head: it just grazed his nose, and broke to pieces against one of the trees behind him.

"—or next day, maybe," the Footman continued in the same tone, exactly as if nothing had happened.

"How am I to get in?" asked Alice again, in a louder tone.

"*Are* you to get in at all?" said the Footman. "That's the first question, you know."

It was, no doubt: only Alice did not like to be told so. "It's really dreadful," she muttered to herself, "the way all the creatures argue. It's enough to drive one crazy!"

The Footman seemed to think this a good opportunity for repeat-

ing his remark, with variations. "I shall sit here," he said, "on and off, for days and days."

"But what am *I* to do?" said Alice.

"Anything you like," said the Footman, and began whistling.

"Oh, there's no use in talking to him," said Alice desperately: "he's perfectly idiotic!" And she opened the door and went in.

The door led right into a large kitchen, which was full of smoke from one end to the other: the Duchess was sitting on a three-legged stool in the middle, nursing a baby: the cook was leaning over the fire, stirring a large caldron which seemed to be full of soup.

"There's certainly too much pepper in that soup!" Alice said to herself, as well as she could for sneezing.

There was certainly too much of it in the *air*. Even the Duchess sneezed occasionally; and as for the baby, it was sneezing and howling alternately without a moment's pause. The only two creatures in the kitchen, that did *not* sneeze, were the cook, and a large cat, which was lying on the hearth and grinning from ear to ear.

"Please would you tell me," said Alice, a little timidly, for she was not quite sure whether it was good manners for her to speak first, "why your cat grins like that?"

"It's a Cheshire-Cat," said the Duchess, "and that's why. Pig!"

She said the last word with such sudden violence that Alice quite jumped; but she saw in another moment that it was addressed to the baby, and not to her, so she took courage, and went on again:

"I didn't know that Cheshire-Cats always grinned; in fact, I didn't know that cats *could* grin."

"They all can," said the Duchess; "and most of 'em do."

"I don't know of any that do," Alice said, very politely, feeling quite pleased to have got into a conversation.

"You don't know much," said the Duchess; "and that's a fact."

Alice did not at all like the tone of this remark, and thought it would be as well to introduce some other subject of conversation. While she was trying to fix on one, the cook took the caldron of soup off the fire, and at once set to work throwing everything within her reach at the Duchess and the baby—the fire-irons came first; then followed a shower of saucepans, plates, and dishes. The Duchess took no notice of them even when they hit her; and the baby was howling

so much already, that it was quite impossible to say whether the blows hurt it or not.

"Oh, *please* mind what you're doing!" cried Alice, jumping up and down in an agony of terror. "Oh, there goes his *precious* nose!" as an unusually large saucepan flew close by it, and very nearly carried it off.

"If everybody minded their own business," the Duchess said, in a hoarse growl, "the world would go round a deal faster than it does."

"Which would *not* be an advantage," said Alice, who felt very glad to get an opportunity of showing off a little of her knowledge.

47

"Just think what work it would make with the day and night! You see the earth takes twenty-four hours to turn round on its axis—"

"Talking of axes," said the Duchess, "chop off her head!"

Alice glanced rather anxiously at the cook, to see if she meant to take the hint; but the cook was busily stirring the soup, and seemed not to be listening, so she went on again: "Twenty-four hours, I *think;* or is it twelve? I—"

"Oh, don't bother *me!*" said the Duchess. "I never could abide figures!" And with that she began nursing her child again, singing a sort of lullaby to it as she did so, and giving it a violent shake at the end of every line:—

> "Speak roughly to your little boy,
>   And beat him when he sneezes:
> He only does it to annoy,
>   Because he knows it teases."

CHORUS

(in which the cook and the baby joined):

> "Wow! wow! wow!"

While the Duchess sang the second verse of the song, she kept tossing the baby violently up and down, and the poor little thing howled so, that Alice could hardly hear the words:

> "I speak severely to my boy,
>   I beat him when he sneezes;
> For he can thoroughly enjoy
>   The pepper when he pleases!"

CHORUS

> "Wow! wow! wow!"

"Here! You may nurse it a bit, if you like!" the Duchess said to Alice, flinging the baby at her as she spoke. "I must go and get ready to play croquet with the Queen," and she hurried out of the room. The cook threw a frying-pan after her as she went, but it just missed her.

Alice caught the baby with some difficulty, as it was a queer-shaped little creature, and held out its arms and legs in all directions, "just like a starfish," thought Alice. The poor little thing was snorting like a steam-engine when she caught it, and kept doubling itself up and straightening itself out again, so that altogether, for the first minute or two, it was as much as she could do to hold it.

As soon as she had made out the proper way of nursing it (which was to twist it up into a sort of knot, and then keep tight hold of its right ear and left foot, so as to prevent its undoing itself), she carried it out into the open air. "If I don't take this child away with me," thought Alice, "they're sure to kill it in a day or two. Would n't it be murder to leave it behind?" She said the last words out loud, and the little thing grunted in reply (it had left off sneezing by this time). "Don't grunt," said Alice; "that's not at all a proper way of expressing yourself."

The baby grunted again, and Alice looked very anxiously into its face to see what was the matter with it. There could be no doubt that it had a *very* turn-up nose, much more like a snout than a real nose: also its eyes were getting extremely small for a baby: altogether Alice did not like the look of the thing at all. "But perhaps it was only sobbing," she thought, and looked into its eyes again, to see if there were any tears.

No, there were no tears. "If you're going to turn into a pig, my dear," said Alice, seriously, "I'll have nothing more to do with you. Mind now!" The poor little thing sobbed again (or grunted, it was

impossible to say which), and they went on for some while in silence.

Alice was just beginning to think to herself, "Now, what am I to do with this creature, when I get it home?" when it grunted again, so violently, that she looked down into its face in some alarm. This time there could be *no* mistake about it: it was neither more nor less than a pig, and she felt that it would be quite absurd for her to carry it any further.

So she set the little creature down, and felt quite relieved to see it trot away quietly into the wood. "If it had grown up," she said to herself, "it would have made a dreadfully ugly child: but it makes rather a handsome pig, I think." And she began thinking over other children she knew, who might do very well as pigs, and was just saying to herself, "if one only knew the right way to change them—" when she was a little startled by seeing the Cheshire-Cat sitting on a bough of a tree a few yards off.

The Cat only grinned when it saw Alice. It looked good-natured, she thought: still it had *very* long claws and a great many teeth, so she felt that it ought to be treated with respect.

"Cheshire-Puss," she began, rather timidly, as she did not at all know whether it would like the name: however, it only grinned a little wider. "Come, it's pleased so far," thought Alice, and she went on. "Would you tell me, please, which way I ought to go from here?"

"That depends a good deal on where you want to get to," said the Cat.

"I don't much care where—" said Alice.

"Then it does n't matter which way you go," said the Cat.

"—so long as I get *somewhere*," Alice added as an explanation.

"Oh, you're sure to do that," said the Cat, "if you only walk long enough."

Alice felt that this could not be denied, so she tried another question. "What sort of people live about here?"

"In *that* direction," the Cat said, waving its right paw round, "lives a Hatter: and in *that* direction," waving the other paw, "lives a March Hare. Visit either you like: they're both mad."

"But I don't want to go among mad people," Alice remarked.

"Oh, you can't help that," said the Cat: "we're all mad here. I'm mad. You're mad."

"How do you know I'm mad?" said Alice.

"You must be," said the Cat, "or you would n't have come here."

Alice did n't think that proved it at all: however, she went on: "And how do you know that you're mad?"

"To begin with," said the Cat, "a dog's not mad. You grant that?"

"I suppose so," said Alice.

"Well, then," the Cat went on, "you see a dog growls when it's angry, and wags its tail when it's pleased. Now *I* growl when I'm pleased, and wag my tail when I'm angry. Therefore I'm mad."

"*I* call it purring, not growling," said Alice.

"Call it what you like," said the Cat. "Do you play croquet with the Queen today?"

"I should like it very much," said Alice, "but I haven't been invited yet."

"You'll see me there," said the Cat, and vanished.

Alice was not much surprised at this, she was getting so well used to queer things happening. While she was still looking at the place where it had been, it suddenly appeared again.

"By the by, what became of the baby?" said the Cat. "I'd nearly forgotten to ask."

"It turned into a pig," Alice answered very quietly, just as if the Cat had come back in a natural way.

"I thought it would," said the Cat, and vanished again.

Alice waited a little, half expecting to see it again, but it did not appear, and after a minute or two she walked on in the direction in which the March Hare was said to live. "I've seen hatters before," she said to herself: "the March Hare will be much the most inter-esting, and perhaps, as this is May, it won't be raving mad—at least not so mad as it was in March." As she said this, she looked up, and there was the Cat again sitting on a branch of a tree.

"Did you say 'pig,' or 'fig'?" said the Cat.

"I said 'pig,' " replied Alice, "and I wish you would n't keep appearing and vanishing so suddenly: you make one quite giddy!"

"All right," said the Cat; and this time it vanished quite slowly, beginning with the end of the tail, and ending with the grin, which remained some time after the rest of it had gone.

"Well! I've often seen a cat without a grin," thought Alice, "but a grin without a cat! It's the most curious thing I ever saw in all my life!"

She had not gone much farther before she came in sight of the house of the March Hare: she thought it must be the right house, because the chimneys were shaped like ears and the roof was thatched with fur. It was so large a house, that she did not like to go nearer till she had nibbled some more of the left-hand bit of mushroom, and raised herself to about two feet high: even then she walked up toward it rather timidly, saying to herself, "Suppose it should be raving mad after all! I almost wish I'd gone to see the Hatter instead!"

VII: A MAD TEA-PARTY

There was a table set out under a tree in front of the house, and the March Hare and the Hatter were having tea at it: a Dormouse was sitting between them, fast asleep, and the other two were using it as a cushion, resting their elbows on it, and talking over its head. "Very uncomfortable for the Dormouse," thought Alice; "only as it's asleep, I suppose it does n't mind."

The table was a large one, but the three were all crowded together at one corner of it. "No room! No room!" they cried out when they saw Alice coming. "There's *plenty* of room!" said Alice indignantly, and she sat down in a large arm-chair at one end of the table.

"Have some wine," the March Hare said in an encouraging tone.

Alice looked all round the table, but there was nothing on it but tea. "I don't see any wine," she remarked.

"There isn't any," said the March Hare.

"Then it was n't very civil of you to offer it," said Alice, angrily.

"It was n't very civil of you to sit down without being invited," said the March Hare.

"I did n't know it was *your* table," said Alice: "it's laid for a great many more than three."

"Your hair wants cutting," said the Hatter. He had been looking at Alice for some time with great curiosity, and this was his first speech.

"You should learn not to make personal remarks," Alice said with some severity: "it's very rude."

The Hatter opened his eyes very wide on hearing this: but all he *said* was: "Why is a raven like a writing-desk?"

"Come, we shall have some fun now!" thought Alice. "I'm glad they've begun asking riddles—I believe I can guess that," she added, aloud.

"Do you mean that you think you can find out the answer to it?" said the March Hare.

"Exactly so," said Alice.

"Then you should say what you mean," the March Hare went on.

"I do," Alice hastily replied; "at least—at least I mean what I say—that's the same thing, you know."

"Not the same thing a bit!" said the Hatter. "Why, you might just as well say that 'I see what I eat' is the same thing as 'I eat what I see'!"

"You might just as well say," added the March Hare, "that 'I like what I get' is the same thing as 'I get what I like'!"

"You might just as well say," added the Dormouse, which seemed to be talking in its sleep, "that 'I breathe when I sleep' is the same thing as 'I sleep when I breathe'!"

"It *is* the same thing with you," said the Hatter, and here the conversation dropped, and the party sat silent for a minute, while Alice thought over all she could remember about ravens and writing-desks, which wasn't much.

The Hatter was the first to break the silence. "What day of the month is it?" he said turning to Alice: he had taken his watch out of his pocket, and was looking at it uneasily, shaking it every now and then, and holding it to his ear.

Alice considered a little, and then said, "The fourth."

"Two days wrong!" sighed the Hatter. "I told you butter wouldn't suit the works," he added, looking angrily at the March Hare.

"It was the *best* butter," the March Hare meekly replied.

"Yes, but some crumbs must have got in as well," the Hatter grumbled: "you shouldn't have put it in with the bread-knife."

The March Hare took the watch and looked at it gloomily: then he dipped it into his cup of tea, and looked at it again: but he could think of nothing better to say than his first remark, "It was the *best* butter, you know."

Alice had been looking over his shoulder with some curiosity. "What a funny watch!" she remarked. "It tells the day of the month, and doesn't tell what o'clock it is!"

"Why should it?" muttered the Hatter. "Does *your* watch tell you what year it is?"

"Of course not," Alice replied very readily: "but that's because it stays the same year for such a long time together."

"Which is just the case with *mine*," said the Hatter.

Alice felt dreadfully puzzled. The Hatter's remark seemed to her have no sort of meaning in it, and yet it was certainly English. "I don't quite understand you," she said, as politely as she could.

"The Dormouse is asleep again," said the Hatter, and he poured a little hot tea upon its nose.

The Dormouse shook its head impatiently, and said, without opening its eyes, "Of course, of course: just what I was going to re-mark myself."

"Have you guessed the riddle yet?" the Hatter said, turning to Alice again.

"No, I give it up," Alice replied. "What's the answer?"

"I haven't the slightest idea," said the Hatter.

"Nor I," said the March Hare.

Alice sighed wearily. "I think you might do something better with the time," she said, "than wasting it in asking riddles that have no answers."

"If you knew Time as well as I do," said the Hatter, "you wouldn't talk about wasting *it*. It's *him*."

"I don't know what you mean," said Alice.

"Of course you don't!" the Hatter said, tossing his head contemptuously. "I dare say you never even spoke to Time!"

"Perhaps not," Alice cautiously replied; "but I know I have to beat time when I learn music."

"Ah! That accounts for it," said the Hatter. "He won't stand beating. Now, if you only kept on good terms with him, he'd do almost anything you like with the clock. For instance, suppose it were nine o'clock in the morning, just time to begin lessons: you'd only have to whisper a hint to Time, and round goes the clock in a twinkling! Half-past one, time for dinner!"

("I only wish it was," the March Hare said to itself in a whisper.)

"That would be grand, certainly," said Alice thoughtfully: "but then—I should n't be hungry for it, you know."

"Not at first, perhaps," said the Hatter: "but you could keep it to half-past one as long as you liked."

"Is that the way *you* manage?" Alice asked.

The Hatter shook his head mournfully. "Not I!" he replied. "We quarreled last March—just before *he* went mad, you know—" pointing with his teaspoon at the March Hare) "—it was at the great concert given by the Queen of Hearts, and I had to sing:

'Twinkle, twinkle, little bat!
How I wonder what you're at!'

You know the song, perhaps?"

"I've heard something like it," said Alice.

"It goes on, you know," the Hatter continued, "in this way:—

'Up above the world you fly,
Like a tea-tray in the sky.
Twinkle, twinkle—'"

Here the Dormouse shook itself, and began singing in its sleep, *"Twinkle, twinkle, twinkle, twinkle—"* and went on so long that they had to pinch it to make it stop.

"Well, I'd hardly finished the first verse," said the Hatter, "when the Queen bawled out 'He's murdering the time! Off with his head!'"

"How dreadfully savage!" exclaimed Alice.

"And ever since that," the Hatter went on in a mournful tone, "he won't do a thing I ask! It's always six o'clock now."

A bright idea came into Alice's head. "Is that the reason so many tea-things are put out here?" she asked.

"Yes, that's it," said the Hatter with a sigh: "it's always tea-time, and we've no time to wash the things between whiles."

"Then you keep moving round, I suppose?" said Alice.

"Exactly so," said the Hatter: "as the things get used up."

"But what happens when you come to the beginning again?" Alice ventured to ask.

"Suppose we change the subject," the March Hare interrupted, yawning. "I'm getting tired of this. I vote the young lady tells us a story."

"I'm afraid I don't know one," said Alice, rather alarmed at the proposal.

"Then the Dormouse shall!" they both cried. "Wake up, Dormouse!" And they pinched it on both sides at once.

The Dormouse slowly opened its eyes. "I was n't asleep," it said in a hoarse, feeble voice, "I heard every word you fellows were saying."

"Tell us a story!" said the March Hare.

"Yes, please do!" pleaded Alice.

"And be quick about it," added the Hatter, "or you'll be asleep again before it's done."

"Once upon a time there were three little sisters," the Dormouse began in a great hurry; "and their names were Elsie, Lacie, and Tillie; and they lived at the bottom of a well—"

"What did they live on?" said Alice, who always took a great interest in questions of eating and drinking.

"They lived on treacle," said the Dormouse, after thinking a minute or two.

"They could n't have done that, you know," Alice gently remarked. "They'd have been ill."

"So they were," said the Dormouse; "*very* ill."

Alice tried a little to fancy to herself what such an extraordinary way of living would be like, but it puzzled her too much: so she went on:

"But why did they live at the bottom of a well?"

"Take some more tea," the March Hare said to Alice, very earnestly.

"I've had nothing yet," Alice replied in an offended tone: "so I can't take more."

"You mean you can't take *less*," said the Hatter: "it's very easy to take *more* than nothing."

"Nobody asked *your* opinion," said Alice.

"Who's making personal remarks now?" the Hatter asked triumphantly.

Alice did not quite know what to say to this: so she helped herself to some tea and bread-and-butter, and then turned to the Dormouse, and repeated her quesion. "Why did they live at the bottom of a well?"

The Dormouse again took a minute or two to think about it, and then said, "It was a treacle-well."

"There's no such thing!" Alice was beginning very angrily, but the Hatter and the March Hare went, "Sh! Sh!" and the Dormouse sulkily remarked, "If you can't be civil, you'd better finish the story for yourself."

"No, please go on!" Alice said very humbly. "I won't interrupt you again. I dare say there may be *one*."

"One, indeed!" said the Dormouse indignantly. However, he consented to go on. "And so these three little sisters—they were learning to draw, you know—"

"What did they draw?" said Alice, quite forgetting her promise.

"Treacle," said the Dormouse, without considering at all, this time.

"I want a clean cup," interrupted the Hatter: "let's all move one place on."

He moved on as he spoke, and the Dormouse followed him: the March Hare moved into the Dormouse's place, and Alice rather unwillingly took the place of the March Hare. The Hatter was the only one who got any advantage from the change; and Alice was a good deal worse off than before, as the March Hare had just upset the milk-jug into his plate.

Alice did not wish to offend the Dormouse again, so she began very cautiously: "But I don't understand. Where did they draw the treacle from?"

"You can draw water out of a water-well," said the Hatter; "so I should think you could draw treacle out of a treacle-well—eh, stupid?"

"But they were *in* the well," Alice said to the Dormouse, not choosing to notice this last remark.

"Of course they were," said the Dormouse: "well in."

This answer so confused poor Alice, that she let the Dormouse go on for some time without interrupting it.

"They were learning to draw," the Dormouse went on, yawning and rubbing its eyes, for it was getting very sleepy; "and they drew all manner of things—everything that begins with an M—"

"Why with an M?" said Alice.

"Why not?" said the March Hare.

Alice was silent.

The Dormouse had closed its eyes by this time, and was going off into a doze; but, on being pinched by the Hatter, it woke up again with a little shriek, and went on: "—that begins with an M, such as mouse-traps, and the moon, and memory, and muchness—you know you say things are 'much of a muchness'—did you ever see such a thing as a drawing of a muchness?"

"Really, now you ask me," said Alice, very much confused, "I don't think—"

"Then you should n't talk," said the Hatter.

This piece of rudeness was more than Alice could bear: she got up in great disgust, and walked off: the Dormouse fell asleep instantly, and neither of the others took the least notice of her going, though she looked back once or twice, half hoping that they would call after her: the last time she saw them, they were trying to put the Dormouse into the teapot.

"At any rate I'll never go *there* again!" said Alice, as she picked her way through the wood. "It's the stupidest tea-party I ever was at in all my life!"

Just as she said this, she noticed that one of the trees had a door leading right into it. "That's very curious!" she thought. "But everything's curious today. I think I may as well go in at once." And in she went.

Once more she found herself in the long hall, and close to the little glass table. "Now, I'll manage better this time," she said to herself, and began by taking the little golden key, and unlocking the door that led into the garden. Then she set to work nibbling at the mushroom (she had kept a piece of it in her pocket) till she was about a foot high: then she walked down the little passage: and *then*—she found herself at last in the beautiful garden, among the bright flower beds and the cool fountains.

VIII: THE QUEEN'S

CROQUET GROUND

A large rose tree stood near the entrance of the garden: the roses growing on it were white, but there were three gardeners at it, busily painting them red. Alice thought this a very curious thing, and she went nearer to watch them, and, just as she came up to them, she heard one of them say "Look out, now, Five! Don't go splashing paint over me like that!"

"I could n't help it," said Five, in a sulky tone. "Seven jogged my elbow."

On which Seven looked up and said, "That's right, Five! Always lay the blame on others!"

"*You'd* better not talk!" said Five. "I heard the Queen say only yesterday you deserved to be beheaded."

"What for?" said the one who had spoken first.

"That's none of *your* business, Two!" said Seven.

"Yes, it *is* his business!" said Five. "And I'll tell him—it was for bringing the cook tulip-roots instead of onions."

Seven flung down his brush, and had just begun, "Well, of all the unjust things—" when his eye chanced to fall upon Alice, as she stood watching them, and he checked himself suddenly: the others looked round also, and all of them bowed low.

"Would you tell me, please," said Alice, a little timidly, "why you are painting those roses?"

Five and Seven said nothing, but looked at Two. Two began, in a low voice, "Why, the fact is, you see, Miss, this here ought to have been a *red* rose tree, and we put a white one in by mistake; and, if the Queen was to find it out, we should all have our heads cut off, you know. So you see, Miss, we're doing our best, afore she comes, to—" At this moment, Five, who had been anxiously looking across the garden, called out, "The Queen! The Queen!" and the three gardeners instantly threw themselves flat upon their faces. There was a sound of many footsteps, and Alice looked round, eager to see the Queen.

First came ten soldiers carrying clubs: these were all shaped like the three gardeners, oblong and flat, with their hands and feet at the corners: next the ten courtiers: these were ornamented all over with diamonds, and walked two and two, as the soldiers did. After these came the royal children: there were ten of them, and the little dears came jumping merrily along, hand in hand, in couples: they were all ornamented with hearts. Next came the guests, mostly Kings and Queens, and among them Alice recognized the White Rabbit: it was talking in a hurried nervous manner, smiling at everything that was said, and went by without noticing her. Then followed the Knave of Hearts, carrying the King's crown on a crimson velvet cushion; and, last of all this grand procession, came THE KING AND THE QUEEN OF HEARTS.

Alice was rather doubtful whether she ought not to lie down on her face like the three gardeners, but she could not remember ever having heard of such a rule at processions; "and besides, what would be the use of a procession," thought she, "if people had all to lie down on their faces, so that they couldn't see it?" So she stood where she was, and waited.

When the procession came opposite to Alice, they all stopped and

looked at her, and the Queen said, severely, "Who is this?" She said it to the Knave of Hearts, who only bowed and smiled in reply.

"Idiot!" said the Queen, tossing her head impatiently: and, turning to Alice, she went on: "What's your name, child?"

"My name is Alice, so please your Majesty," said Alice very politely; but she added, to herself, "Why, they're only a pack of cards after all. I needn't be afraid of them!"

"And who are *these*?" said the Queen, pointing to the three gardeners who were lying round the rose tree; for, you see, as they were lying on their faces, and the pattern on their backs was the same as the rest of the pack, she could not tell whether they were gardeners, or soldiers, or courtiers, or three of her own children.

"How should *I* know!" said Alice, surprised at her own courage. "It's no business of mine."

The Queen turned crimson with fury, and, after glaring at her for a moment like a wild beast, began screaming, "Off with her head! Off with—"

"Nonsense!" said Alice, very loudly and decidedly, and the Queen was silent.

The King laid his hand upon her arm, and timidly said, "Consider, my dear: she is only a child!"

The Queen turned angrily away from him, and said to the Knave, "Turn them over!"

The Knave did so, very carefully, with one foot.

"Get up!" said the Queen in a shrill, loud voice, and the three gardeners instantly jumped up, and began bowing to the King, the Queen, the royal children, and everybody else.

"Leave off that!" screamed the Queen. "You make me giddy." And then, turning to the rose tree, she went on, "What *have* you been doing here?"

"May it please your Majesty," said Two, in a very humble tone, going down on one knee as he spoke, "we were trying—"

"*I* see!" said the Queen, who had meanwhile been examining the roses. "Off with their heads!" and the procession moved on, three of the soldiers remaining behind to execute the unfortunate gardeners, who ran to Alice for protection.

"You shan't be beheaded!" said Alice, and she put them into a large flower pot that stood near. The three soldiers wandered about for a minute or two, looking for them, and then quietly marched off after the others.

"Are their heads off?" shouted the Queen.

"Their heads are gone, if it please your Majesty!" the soldiers shouted in reply.

"That's right!" shouted the Queen. "Can you play croquet?"

The soldiers were silent, and looked at Alice, as the question was evidently meant for her.

"Yes!" shouted Alice.

"Come on, then!" roared the Queen, and Alice joined the procession, wondering very much what would happen next.

"It's—it's a very fine day!" said a timid voice at her side. She was walking by the White Rabbit, who was peeping anxiously into her face.

"Very," said Alice. "Where's the Duchess?"

"Hush! Hush!" said the Rabbit in a low hurried tone. He looked anxiously over his shoulder as he spoke, and then raised himself upon tiptoe, put his mouth close to her ear, and whispered, "She's under sentence of execution."

"What for?" said Alice.

"Did you say, 'What a pity!'?" the Rabbit asked.

"No, I did n't," said Alice. "I don't think it's at all a pity. I said, 'What for?'"

"She boxed the Queen's ears—" the Rabbit began. Alice gave a little scream of laughter. "Oh, hush!" the Rabbit whispered in a frightened tone. "The Queen will hear you! You see she came rather late, and the Queen said—"

"Get to your places!" shouted the Queen in a voice of thunder, and people began running about in all directions, tumbling up against each other: however, they got settled down in a minute or two, and the game began.

Alice thought she had never seen such a curious croquet ground in her life: it was all ridges and furrows: the croquet balls were live hedgehogs, and the mallets live flamingoes, and the soldiers had to double themselves up and stand on their hands and feet, to make the arches.

The chief difficulty Alice found at first was in managing her flamingo: she succeeded in getting its body tucked away comfortably enough under her arm, with its legs hanging down, but generally, just as she had got its neck nicely straightened out, and was going to give the hedgehog a blow with its head, it *would* twist itself round and look up in her face, with such a puzzled expression that she could not help bursting out laughing; and, when she had got its head down, and was going to begin again, it was very provoking to find that the hedgehog had unrolled itself, and was in the act of crawling away: besides all this, there was generally a ridge or a furrow in the way wherever she wanted to send the hedgehog to, and, as the doubled-up soldiers were always getting up and walking off to other parts of the ground, Alice soon came to the conclusion that it was a very difficult game indeed.

The players all played at once, without waiting for turns, quarreling all the while, and fighting for the hedgehogs; and in a very short time the Queen was in a furious passion, and went stamping about and shouting, "Off with his head!" or "Off with her head!" about once in a minute.

Alice began to feel very uneasy: to be sure she had not as yet had any dispute with the Queen, but she knew that it might happen any minute, "and then," thought she, "what would become of me? They're dreadfully fond of beheading people here: the great wonder is that there's any one left alive!"

She was looking about for some way of escape, and wondering whether she could get away without being seen when she noticed a curious appearance in the air: it puzzled her very much at first, but after watching it a minute or two she made it out to be a grin, and she said to herself, "It's the Cheshire-Cat: now I shall have somebody to talk to."

"How are you getting on?" said the Cat, as soon as there was mouth enough for it to speak with.

Alice waited till the eyes appeared, and then nodded. "It's no use speaking to it," she thought, "till its ears have come, or at least one of them." In another minute the whole head appeared, and then Alice put down her flamingo, and began an account of the game, feeling very glad she had some one to listen to her. The Cat seemed to think that there was enough of it now in sight, and no more of it appeared.

"I don't think they play at all fairly," Alice began, in rather a complaining tone, "and they all quarrel so dreadfully one can't hear one's self speak—and they don't seem to have any rules in particular: at least, if there are, nobody attends to them—and you've no idea how confusing it is all the things being alive: for instance, there's the arch I've got to go through next walking about at the other end of the ground—and I should have croqueted the Queen's hedgehog just now, only it ran away when it saw mine coming!"

"How do you like the Queen?" said the Cat in a low voice.

"Not at all," said Alice: "she's so extremely—" Just then she noticed that the Queen was close behind her, listening: so she went on "—likely to win, that it's hardly worth while finishing the game."

The Queen smiled and passed on.

"Who *are* you talking to?" said the King, coming up to Alice, and looking at the Cat's head with great curiosity.

"It's a friend of mine—a Cheshire-Cat," said Alice: "allow me to introduce it."

"I don't like the look of it at all," said the King: "however, it may kiss my hand, if it likes."

"I'd rather not," the Cat remarked.

"Don't be impertinent," said the King, "and don't look at me like that!" He got behind Alice as he spoke.

"A cat may look at a king," said Alice. "I've read that in some book, but I don't remember where."

"Well, it must be removed," said the King very decidedly; and he called to the Queen, who was passing at the moment, "My dear! I wish you would have this cat removed!"

The Queen had only one way of settling all difficulties, great or small. "Off with his head!" she said without even looking round.

"I'll fetch the executioner myself," said the King eagerly, and he hurried off.

Alice thought she might as well go back and see how the game was going on, as she heard the Queen's voice in the distance, screaming with passion. She had already heard her sentence three of the players to be executed for having missed their turns, and she did not like the look of things at all, as the game was in such confusion that she never knew whether it was her turn or not. So she went off in search of her hedgehog.

The hedgehog was engaged in a fight with another hedgehog, which seemed to Alice an excellent opportunity for croqueting one of them with the other: the only difficulty was, that her flamingo was gone across to the other side of the garden, where Alice could see it trying in a helpless sort of way to fly up into a tree.

By the time she had caught the flamingo and brought it back, the fight was over, and both the hedgehogs were out of sight: "but it does n't matter much," thought Alice, "as all the arches are gone from this side of the ground." So she tucked it away under her arm, that it might not escape again, and went back to have a little more conversation with her friend.

When she got back to the Cheshire-Cat, she was surprised to find quite a large crowd collected round it: there was a dispute going on between the executioner, the King, and the Queen, who were all talking at once, while all the rest were quite silent, and looked very uncomfortable.

The moment Alice appeared, she was appealed to by all three to settle the question, and they repeated their arguments to her, though, as they all spoke at once, she found it very hard to make out exactly what they said.

The executioner's argument was, that you couldn't cut off a head unless there was a body to cut it off from: that he had never had to do such a thing before, and he wasn't going to begin at *his* time of life.

The King's argument was that anything that had a head could be beheaded, and that you weren't to talk nonsense.

The Queen's argument was that, if something wasn't done about it in less than no time, she'd have everybody executed, all round. (It was this last remark that had made the whole party look so grave and anxious.)

Alice could think of nothing else to say but "It belongs to the Duchess: you'd better ask *her* about it."

"She's in prison," the Queen said to the executioner: "fetch her here." And the executioner went off like an arrow.

The Cat's head began fading away the moment he was gone, and, by the time he had come back with the Duchess, it had entirely disappeared: so the King and the executioner ran wildly up and down, looking for it, while the rest of the party went back to the game.

IX: THE MOCK TURTLE'S STORY

"You can't think how glad I am to see you, again, you dear old thing!" said the Duchess, as she tucked her arm affectionately into Alice's, and they walked off together.

Alice was very glad to find her in such a pleasant temper, and thought to herself that perhaps it was only the pepper that had made her so savage when they met in the kitchen.

"When *I'm* a Duchess," she said to herself (not in a very hopeful tone, though), "I won't have any pepper in my kitchen *at all*. Soup does very well without— Maybe it's always pepper that makes people hot-tempered," she went on, very much pleased at having found out a new kind of rule, "and vinegar that makes them sour—and camomile that makes them bitter—and—and barley-sugar and such things that make children sweet-tempered. I only wish people knew *that* then they wouldn't be so stingy about it, you know—"

She had quite forgotten the Duchess by this time, and was a little startled when she heard her voice close to her ear. "You're thinking about something, my dear, and that makes you forget to talk. I can't tell you just now what the moral of that is, but I shall remember it in a bit."

"Perhaps it hasn't one," Alice ventured to remark.

"Tut, tut, child!" said the Duchess. "Everything's got a moral, if only you can find it." And she squeezed herself up closer to Alice's side as she spoke.

Alice did not much like her keeping so close to her: first, because the Duchess was *very* ugly; and secondly, because she was exactly the right height to rest her chin on Alice's shoulder, and it was an uncomfortably sharp chin. However, she did not like to be rude: so she bore it as well as she could.

"The game's going on rather better now," she said, by way of keeping up the conversation a little.

" 'Tis so," said the Duchess: "and the moral of that is—'Oh, 'tis love, 'tis love, that makes the world go round!' "

"Somebody said," Alice whispered, "that it's done by everybody minding their own business!"

"Ah, well! It means much the same thing," said the Duchess, digging her sharp little chin into Alice's shoulder as she added, "and the moral of *that* is—'Take care of the sense, and the sounds will take care of themselves.' "

"How fond she is of finding morals in things!" Alice thought to herself.

"I dare say you're wondering why I don't put my arm round your waist," the Duchess said, after a pause: "the reason is, that I'm doubtful about the temper of your flamingo. Shall I try the experiment?"

"He might bite," Alice cautiously replied, not feeling at all anxious to have the experiment tried.

"Very true," said the Duchess: "flamingoes and mustard both bite. And the moral of that is—'Birds of a feather flock together.' "

"Only mustard isn't a bird," Alice remarked.

"Right, as usual," said the Duchess: "what a clear way you have of putting things!"

"It's a mineral, I *think*," said Alice.

"Of course it is," said the Duchess, who seemed ready to agree to everything that Alice said: "there's a large mustard mine near here. And the moral of that is—'The more there is of mine, the less there is of yours.'"

"Oh, I know!" exclaimed Alice, who had not attended to this last remark. "It's a vegetable. It does n't look like one, but it is."

"I quite agree with you," said the Duchess; "and the moral of that is—'Be what you would seem to be'—or, if you'd like it put more simply—'Never imagine yourself not to be otherwise than what it might appear to others that what you were or might have been was not otherwise than what you had been would have appeared to them to be otherwise.'"

"I think I should understand that better," Alice said very politely, "if I had it written down: but I can't quite follow it as you say it."

"That's nothing to what I could say if I chose," the Duchess replied, in a pleased tone.

"Pray don't trouble yourself to say it any longer than that," said Alice.

"Oh, don't talk about trouble!" said the Duchess. "I make you a present of everything I've said as yet."

"A cheap sort of present," thought Alice. "I'm glad people don't give birthday presents like that!" But she did not venture to say it out loud.

"Thinking again?" the Duchess asked, with another dig of her sharp little chin.

"I've a right to think," said Alice sharply, for she was beginning to feel a little worried.

"Just about as much right," said the Duchess, "as pigs have to fly; and the m—"

But here, to Alice's great surprise, the Duchess's voice died away, even in the middle of her favorite word "moral," and the arm that was linked into hers began to tremble. Alice looked up, and there stood the Queen in front of them, with her arms folded, frowning like a thunderstorm.

"A fine day, your Majesty!" the Duchess began in a low, weak voice.

"Now, I give you fair warning," shouted the Queen, stamping on the ground as she spoke; "either you or your head must be off, and that in about half no time! Take your choice!"

The Duchess took her choice, and was gone in a moment.

"Let's go on with the game," the Queen said to Alice; and Alice was too much frightened to say a word, but slowly followed her back to the croquet ground.

The other guests had taken advantage of the Queen's absence, and were resting in the shade: however, the moment they saw her they hurried back to the game, the Queen merely remarking that a moment's delay would cost them their lives.

All the time they were playing the Queen never left off quarreling with the other players and shouting, "Off with his head!" or "Off with her head!" Those whom she sentenced were taken into custody by the soldiers, who of course had to leave off being arches to do this, so that, by the end of half an hour or so, there were no arches left, and all the players, except the King, the Queen, and Alice, were in custody and under sentence of execution.

Then the Queen left off, quite out of breath, and said to Alice: "Have you seen the Mock Turtle yet?"

"No," said Alice. "I don't even know what a Mock Turtle is."

"It's the thing Mock Turtle soup is made from," said the Queen.

"I never saw one, or heard of one," said Alice.

77

"Come on, then," said the Queen, "and he shall tell you his history."

As they walked off together, Alice heard the King say in a low voice, to the company generally, "You are all pardoned." "Come, *that's* a good thing!" she said to herself, for she had felt quite unhappy at the number of executions the Queen had ordered.

They very soon came upon a Gryphon, lying fast asleep in the sun.

(If you don't know what a Gryphon is, look at the picture.) "Up, lazy thing!" said the Queen, "and take this young lady to see the Mock Turtle, and to hear his history. I must go back and see after some executions I have ordered"; and she walked off leaving Alice alone with the Gryphon. Alice did not quite like the look of the creature, but on the whole she thought it would be quite as safe to stay with it as to go after that savage Queen: so she waited.

The Gryphon sat up and rubbed its eyes: then it watched the Queen till she was out of sight: then it chuckled.

"What fun!" said the Gryphon, half to itself, half to Alice.

"What *is* the fun?" said Alice.

"Why, *she*," said the Gryphon. "It's all her fancy, that: they never executes nobody, you know. Come on!"

"Everybody says 'Come on!' here," thought Alice, as she went slowly after it: "I never was so ordered about before, in all my life, never!"

They had not gone far before they saw the Mock Turtle in the distance, sitting sad and lonely on a little ledge of rock, and, as they came nearer, Alice could hear him sighing as if his heart would break. She pitied him deeply. "What is his sorrow?" she asked the Gryphon. And the Gryphon answered, very nearly in the same words as before, "It's all his fancy, that: he has n't got no sorrow, you know. Come on!"

So they went up to the Mock Turtle, who looked at them with large eyes full of tears, but said nothing.

"This here young lady," said the Gryphon, "she wants to know your history, she do."

"I'll tell it her," said the Mock Turtle in a deep, hollow tone. "Sit down, both of you, and don't speak a word till I've finished."

So they sat down, and nobody spoke for some minutes. Alice thought to herself "I don't see how he can *ever* finish, if he does n't begin." But she waited patiently.

"Once," said the Mock Turtle at last, with a deep sigh. "I was a real Turtle."

These words were followed by a very long silence, broken only by an occasional exclamation of "Hjckrrh!" from the Gryphon, and the constant heavy sobbing of the Mock Turtle. Alice was very nearly getting up and saying, "Thank you, Sir, for your interesting story," but she could not help thinking there *must* be more to come, so she sat still and said nothing.

"When we were little," the Mock Turtle went on at last, more calmly, though still sobbing a little now and then, "we went to school in the sea. The master was an old Turtle—we use to call him Tortoise—"

"Why did you call him Tortoise, if he was n't one?" Alice asked.

"We called him Tortoise because he taught us," said the Mock Turtle angrily. "Really you are very dull!"

"You ought to be ashamed of yourself for asking such a simple question," added the Gryphon; and then they both sat silent and looked at poor Alice, who felt ready to sink into the earth. At last the Gryphon said to the Mock Turtle, "Drive on, old fellow! Don't be all day about it!" and he went on in these words:

"Yes, we went to school in the sea, though you may n't believe it—"

"I never said I did n't!" interrupted Alice.

"You did," said the Mock Turtle.

"Hold your tongue!" added the Gryphon, before Alice could speak again. The Mock Turtle went on:

"We had the best of educations—in fact, we went to school every day—"

"*I've* been to a day-school, too," said Alice. "You need n't be so proud as all that."

"With extras?" asked the Mock Turtle, a little anxiously.

"Yes," said Alice; "we learned French and music."

"And washing?" said the Mock Turtle.

"Certainly not!" said Alice indignantly.

"Ah! Then yours was n't a really good school," said the Mock Turtle in a tone of great relief. "Now, at *ours,* they had, at the end of the bill, 'French, music, *and washing*—extra.' "

"You could n't have wanted it much," said Alice; "living at the bottom of the sea."

"I could n't afford to learn it," said the Mock Turtle with a sigh. "I only took the regular course."

"What was that?" inquired Alice.

"Reeling and Writhing, of course, to begin with," the Mock Turtle replied: "and then the different branches of Arithmetic—Ambition, Distraction, Uglification, and Derision."

"I never heard of 'Uglification,'" Alice ventured to say. "What is it?"

The Gryphon lifted up both its paws in surprise. "Never heard of uglifying!" it exclaimed. "You know what to beautify is, I suppose?"

"Yes," said Alice doubtfully: "it means—to—make—anything—prettier."

"Well, then," the Gryphon went on, "if you don't know what to uglify is, you *are* a simpleton."

Alice did not feel encouraged to ask any more questions about it: so she turned to the Mock Turtle, and said, "What else had you to learn?"

"Well, there was Mystery," the Mock Turtle replied, counting off the subjects on his flappers—"Mystery, ancient and modern, with Seaography: then Drawling—the Drawling-master was an old conger-eel, that used to come once a week: *he* taught us Drawling, Stretching, and Fainting in Coils."

"What was *that* like?" said Alice.

"Well, I can't show it you, myself," the Mock Turtle said: "I'm too stiff. And the Gryphon never learned it."

"Hadn't time," said the Gryphon: "I went to the Classical master though. He was an old crab, *he* was."

"I never went to him," the Mock Turtle said with a sigh. "He taught Laughing and Grief, they used to say."

"So he did, so he did," said the Gryphon, sighing in his turn, and both creatures hid their faces in their paws.

"And how many hours a day did you do lessons?" said Alice, in a hurry to change the subject.

"Ten hours the first day," said the Mock Turtle: "nine the next, and so on."

"What a curious plan!" exclaimed Alice.

"That's the reason they're called lessons," the Gryphon remarked: "because they lessen from day to day."

This was quite a new idea to Alice, and she thought it over a little before she made her next remark. "Then the eleventh day must have been a holiday?"

"Of course it was," said the Mock Turtle.

"And how did you manage on the twelfth?" Alice went on eagerly.

"That's enough about lessons," the Gryphon interrupted in a very decided tone. "Tell her something about the games now."

X: THE LOBSTER-QUADRILLE

The Mock Turtle sighed deeply, and drew the back of one flapper across his eyes. He looked at Alice and tried to speak, but, for a minute or two, sobs choked his voice. "Same as if he had a bone in his throat," said the Gryphon; and it set to work shaking him and punching him in the back. At last the Mock Turtle recovered his voice, and, with tears running down his cheeks, he went on again:

"You may not have lived much under the sea—" ("I haven't," said Alice)—"and perhaps you were never even introduced to a lobster—" (Alice began to say, "I once tasted—" but checked herself hastily, and said, "No, never") "—so you can have no idea what a delightful thing a Lobster-Quadrille is!"

"No, indeed," said Alice. "What sort of a dance is it?"

"Why," said the Gryphon, "you first form into a line along the seashore—"

"Two lines!" cried the Mock Turtle. "Seals, turtles, salmon, and so on: then, when you've cleared all the jelly-fish out of the way—"

"*That* generally takes some time," interrupted the Gryphon.

"—you advance twice—"

"Each with a lobster as a partner!" cried the Gryphon.

"Of course," the Mock Turtle said: "advance twice, set to partners—"

"—change lobsters, and retire in same order," continued the Gryphon.

"Then you know," the Mock Turtle went on, "you throw the—"

"The lobsters!" shouted the Gryphon, with a bound into the air.

"—as far out to sea as you can—"

"Swim after them!" screamed the Gryphon.

"Turn a somersault in the sea!" cried the Mock Turtle, capering wildly about.

"Change lobsters again!" yelled the Gryphon at the top of its voice.

"Back to land again, and—that's all the first figure," said the Mock Turtle, suddenly dropping his voice; and the two creatures, who had been jumping about like mad things all this time, sat down again very sadly and quietly, and looked at Alice.

"It must be a very pretty dance," said Alice timidly.

"Would you like to see a little of it?" said the Mock Turtle.

"Very much indeed," said Alice.

"Come, let's try the first figure!" said the Mock Turtle to the Gryphon. "We can do it without lobsters, you know. Which shall sing?"

"Oh, *you* sing," said the Gryphon. "I've forgotten the words."

So they began solemnly dancing round and round Alice, every now and then treading on her toes when they passed too close, and waving their fore-paws to mark the time, while the Mock Turtle sang this, very slowly and sadly:

"Will you walk a little faster?" said a whiting to a snail,
"There's a porpoise close behind us, and he's treading on my tail."
See how eagerly the lobsters and the turtles all advance!
They are waiting on the shingle—will you come and join the dance?
    Will you, won't you, will you, won't you, will you join the dance?
    Will you, won't you, will you, won't you, won't you join the dance?

"You can really have no notion how delightful it will be
When they take us up and throw us, with the lobsters, out to sea!"
But the snail replied, "Too far, too far!" and gave a look askance—
Said he thanked the whiting kindly, but he would not join the dance.
    Would not, could not, would not, could not, would not join the dance.
    Would not, could not, would not, could not, could not join the dance.

"What matters it how far we go?" his scaly friend replied.
"There is another shore, you know, upon the other side.
The further off from England the nearer is to France—
Then turn not pale, beloved snail, but come and join the dance.
    Will you, won't you, will you, won't you, will you join the dance;
    Will you, won't you, will you, won't you, won't you join the dance?"

"Thank you, it's a very interesting dance to watch," said Alice, feeling very glad that it was over at last: "and I do so like that curious song about the whiting!"

"Oh, as to the whiting," said the Mock Turtle, "they—you've seen them, of course?"

"Yes," said Alice, "I've often seen them at dinn—" she checked herself hastily.

"I don't know where Dinn may be," said the Mock Turtle; "but, if you've seen them so often, of course you know what they're like?"

"I believe so," Alice replied thoughtfully. "They have their tails in their mouths—and they're all over crumbs."

"You're wrong about the crumbs," said the Mock Turtle: "crumbs would all wash off in the sea. But they *have* their tails in their mouths; and the reason is—" here the Mock Turtle yawned and shut his eyes. "Tell her about the reason and all that," he said to the Gryphon.

"The reason is," said the Gryphon, "that they *would* go with the lobsters to the dance. So they got thrown out to sea. So they had to fall a long way. So they got their tails fast in their mouths. So they couldn't get them out again. That's all."

"Thank you," said Alice, "it's very interesting. I never knew so much about a whiting before."

"I can tell you more than that, if you like," said the Gryphon. "Do you know why it's called a whiting?"

"I never thought about it," said Alice. "Why?"

"It does the boots and shoes," the Gryphon replied very solemnly.

Alice was thoroughly puzzled. "Does the boots and shoes!" she repeated in a wondering tone.

"Why, what are *your* shoes done with?" said the Gryphon. "I mean, what makes them so shiny?"

Alice looked down at them, and considered a little before she gave her answer. "They're done with blacking, I believe."

"Boots and shoes under the sea," the Gryphon went on in a deep voice, "are done with whiting. Now you know."

"And what are they made of?" Alice asked in a tone of great curiosity.

"Soles and eels, of course," the Gryphon replied, rather impatiently: "any shrimp could have told you that."

"If I'd been the whiting," said Alice, whose thoughts were still running on the song, "I'd have said to the porpoise, 'Keep back, please! We don't want *you* with us!'"

"They were obliged to have him with them," the Mock Turtle said. "No wise fish would go anywhere without a porpoise."

"Wouldn't it really?" said Alice, in a tone of great surprise.

"Of course not," said the Mock Turtle. "Why, if a fish came to *me,* and told me he was going a journey, I should say, 'With what porpoise?'"

"Don't you mean 'purpose'?" said Alice.

"I mean what I say," the Mock Turtle replied, in an offended tone. And the Gryphon added, "Come let's hear some of *your* adventures."

"I could tell you my adventures—beginning from this morning," said Alice a little timidly; "but it's no use going back to yesterday, because I was a different person then."

"Explain all that," said the Mock Turtle.

"No, no! The adventures first," said the Gryphon in an impatient tone: "explanations take such a dreadful time."

So Alice began telling them her adventures from the time when she first saw the White Rabbit. She was a little nervous about it, just at first, the two creatures got so close to her, one on each side, and opened their eyes and mouths so *very* wide; but she gained courage as she went on. Her listeners were perfectly quiet till she got to the part about her repeating, *"You are old, Father William,"* to the Caterpillar, and the words all coming different, and then the Mock Turtle drew a long breath, and said, "That's very curious!"

"It's all about as curious as it can be," said the Gryphon.

"It all came different!" the Mock Turtle repeated thoughtfully. "I should like to hear her try and repeat something now. Tell her to begin." He looked at the Gryphon as if he thought it had some kind of authority over Alice.

"Stand up and repeat, *' 'Tis the voice of the sluggard,' "* said the Gryphon.

"How the creatures order one about, and make one repeat lessons!" thought Alice. "I might just as well be at school at once." However, she got up, and began to repeat it, but her head was so full of the Lobster-Quadrille, that she hardly knew what she was saying; and the words came very queer indeed:

" 'Tis the voice of the Lobster: I heard him declare
 'You have baked me too brown, I must sugar my hair.'

As a duck with its eyelids, so he with his nose
Trims his belt and his buttons, and turns out his toes.
When the sands are all dry, he is gay as a lark,
And will talk in contemptuous tones of the shark:
But, when the tide rises and sharks are around,
His voice has a timid and tremulous sound."

"That's different from what *I* used to say when I was a child," said the Gryphon.

"Well, *I* never heard it before," said the Mock Turtle, "but it sounds uncommon nonsense."

Alice said nothing: she had sat down with her face in her hands, wondering if anything would *ever* happen in a natural way again.

"I should like to have it explained," said the Mock Turtle.

"She can't explain it," said the Gryphon hastily. "Go on with the next verse."

"But about his toes?" the Mock Turtle persisted. "How *could* he turn them out with his nose, you know?"

"It's the first position in dancing," Alice said; but she was dreadfully puzzled by the whole thing, and longed to change the subject.

"Go on with the next verse," the Gryphon repeated: "it begins, '*I passed by his garden.*'"

Alice did not dare to disobey, though she felt sure it would all come wrong, and she went on in a trembling voice:—

89

"I passed by his garden, and marked, with one eye,
    How the Owl and the Panther were sharing a pie:
The Panther took pie-crust, and gravy, and meat,
    While the Owl had the dish as its share of the treat.
When the pie was all finished, the Owl, as a boon,
    Was kindly permitted to pocket the spoon:
While the Panther received knife and fork with a growl,
    And concluded the banquet by—"

"What *is* the use of repeating all that stuff?" the Mock Turtle interrupted, "if you don't explain it as you go on? It's by far the most confusing thing *I* ever heard!"

"Yes, I think you'd better leave off," said the Gryphon, and Alice was only too glad to do so.

"Shall we try another figure of the Lobster-Quadrille?" the Gryphon went on. "Or would you like the Mock Turtle to sing you another song?"

"Oh, a song, please, if the Mock Turtle would be so kind," Alice replied, so eagerly that the Gryphon said, in a rather offended tone, "H'm! No accounting for tastes! Sing her '*Turtle Soup,*' will you, old fellow?"

The Mock Turtle sighed deeply, and began, in a voice choked with sobs, to sing this:—

"Beautiful Soup, so rich and green,
    Waiting in a hot tureen!
Who for such dainties would not stoop?
Soup of the evening, beautiful Soup!
Soup of the evening, beautiful Soup!
        Beau—ootiful Soo—oop!
        Beau—ootiful Soo—oop!
    Soo—oop of the e—e—evening,
        Beautiful, beautiful Soup!

90

"Beautiful Soup! Who cares for fish,
　Game, or any other dish?
　Who would not give all else for two p
　ennyworth only of beautiful Soup?
　Pennyworth only of beautiful Soup?
　　Beau—ootiful Soo—oop!
　　Beau—ootiful Soo—oop!
　Soo—oop of the e—e—evening,
　　Beautiful, beauti—FUL SOUP!"

"Chorus again!" cried the Gryphon, and the Mock Turtle had just began to repeat it, when a cry of "The trial's beginning!" was heard in the distance.

"Come on!" cried the Gryphon, and, taking Alice by the hand, it hurried off without waiting for the end of the song.

"What trial is it?" Alice panted as she ran; but the Gryphon only answered, "Come on!" and ran the faster, while more and more faintly came, carried on the breeze that followed them, the melancholy words:—

"Soo—oop of the e—e—evening,
　Beautiful, beautiful Soup!"

XI: WHO STOLE THE TARTS?

The King and Queen of Hearts were seated on their throne when they arrived, with a great crowd assembled about them—all sorts of little birds and beasts, as well as the whole pack of cards: the Knave was standing before them, in chains, with a soldier on each side to guard him, and near the King was the White Rabbit, with a trumpet in one hand, and a scroll of parchment in the other. In the very middle of the court was a table with a large dish of tarts upon it: they looked so good, that it made Alice quite hungry to look at them —"I wish they'd get the trial done," she thought, "and hand round the refreshments!" But there seemed to be no chance of this; so she began looking at everything about her to pass away the time.

Alice had never been in a court of justice before, but she had read about them in books, and she was quite pleased to find that she knew the name of nearly everything there. "That's the judge," she said to herself, "because of his great wig."

The judge, by the way, was the King; and, as he wore his crown over the wig (look at page 93 if you want to see how he did it), he did not look at all comfortable, and it was certainly not becoming.

"And that's the jury-box," thought Alice; "and those twelve creatures" (she was obliged to say "creatures," you see, because some

of them were animals, and some were birds), "I suppose they are the jurors." She said this last word two or three times over to herself, being rather proud of it: for she thought, and rightly too, that very few little girls of her age knew the meaning of it at all. However, "jury-men" would have done just as well.

The twelve jurors were all writing very busily on slates.

"What are they doing?" Alice whispered to the Gryphon. "They can't have anything to put down yet, before the trial's begun."

"They're putting down their names," the Gryphon whispered in reply, "for fear they should forget them before the end of the trial."

"Stupid things!" Alice began in a loud indignant voice; but she stopped herself hastily, for the White Rabbit cried out, "Silence in the court!" and the King put on his spectacles and looked anxiously round, to make out who was talking.

Alice could see, as well as if she were looking over their shoulders, that all the jurors were writing down "Stupid things!" on their slates, and she could even make out that one of them didn't know how to spell "stupid," and that he had to ask his neighbor to tell him. "A nice muddle their slates'll be in, before the trial's over!" thought Alice.

One of the jurors had a pencil that squeaked. This, of course, Alice could *not* stand, and she went round the court and got behind him, and very soon found an opportunity of taking it away. She did it so quickly that the poor little juror (it was Bill, the Lizard) could not make out at all what had become of it; so, after hunting all about for it, he was obliged to write with one finger for the rest of the day; and this was of very little use as it left no mark on the slate.

"Herald, read the accusation!" said the King.

On this the White Rabbit blew three blasts on the trumpet, and then unrolled the parchment-scroll, and read as follows:—

"The Queen of Hearts, she made some tarts,
  All on a summer day:
The Knave of Hearts, he stole those tarts
  And took them quite away!"

"Consider your verdict," the King said to the jury.

"Not yet, not yet!" the Rabbit hastily interrupted. "There's a great deal to come before that!"

"Call the first witness," said the King; and the White Rabbit blew three blasts on the trumpet, and called out:

"First witness!"

The first witness was the Hatter. He came in with a teacup in one hand and a piece of bread-and-butter in the other. "I beg pardon, your Majesty," he began, "for bringing these in; but I hadn't quite finished my tea when I was sent for."

"You ought to have finished," said the King. "When did you begin?"

The Hatter looked at the March Hare, who had followed him into the court, arm-in-arm with the Dormouse. "Fourteenth of March, I *think* it was," he said.

"Fifteenth," said the March Hare.

"Sixteenth," said the Dormouse.

"Write that down," the King said to the jury; and the jury eagerly wrote down all three dates on their slates, and then added them up, and reduced the answer to shillings and pence.

"Take off your hat," the King said to the Hatter.

"It isn't mine," said the Hatter.

"*Stolen!*" the King exclaimed, turning to the jury, who instantly made a memorandum of the fact.

"I keep them to sell," the Hatter added as an explanation. "I've none of my own. I'm a hatter."

Here the Queen put on her spectacles, and began staring hard at the Hatter, who turned pale and fidgeted.

"Give your evidence," said the King; "and don't be nervous, or I'll have you executed on the spot."

This did not seem to encourage the witness at all: he kept shifting from one foot to the other, looking uneasily at the Queen, and in his confusion he bit a large piece out of his teacup instead of the bread-and-butter.

Just at this moment Alice felt a very curious sensation, which puzzled her a good deal until she made out what it was: she was beginning to grow larger again, and she thought at first she would get up and leave the court; but on second thought she decided to remain where she was as long as there was room for her.

"I wish you wouldn't squeeze so," said the Dormouse, who was sitting next to her. "I can hardly breathe."

"I can't help it," said Alice very meekly: "I'm growing."

"You've no right to grow *here*," said the Dormouse.

"Don't talk nonsense," said Alice more boldly: "you know you're growing too."

"Yes, but *I* grow at a reasonable pace," said the Dormouse: "not in that ridiculous fashion." And he got up very sulkily and crossed over to the other side of the court.

All this time the Queen had never left off staring at the Hatter, and, just as the Dormouse crossed the court, she said, to one of the officers of the court, "Bring me the list of the singers in the last concert!" on which the wretched Hatter trembled so that he shook off both his shoes.

"Give your evidence," the King repeated angrily, "or I'll have you executed, whether you're nervous or not."

"I'm a poor man, your Majesty," the Hatter began, in a trembling voice, "and I had n't begun my tea—not above a week or so—and what with the bread-and-butter getting so thin—and the twinkling of the tea—"

"The twinkling of *what?*" said the King.

"It *began* with the tea," the Hatter replied.

"Of course twinkling *begins* with a T!" said the King sharply. "Do you take me for a dunce? Go on!"

"I'm a poor man," the Hatter went on, "and most things twinkled after that—only the March Hare said—"

"I did n't!" the March Hare interrupted in a great hurry.

"You did!" said the Hatter.

"I deny it!" said the March Hare.

"He denies it," said the King: "leave out that part."

"Well, at any rate, the Dormouse said—" the Hatter went on, looking anxiously round to see if he would deny it too; but the Dormouse denied nothing, being fast asleep.

"After that," continued the Hatter, "I cut some more bread and butter—"

"But what did the Dormouse say?" one of the jury asked.

"That I can't remember," said the Hatter.

"You *must* remember," remarked the King, "or I'll have you executed."

The miserable Hatter dropped his teacup and bread-and-butter, and went down on one knee. "I'm a poor man, your Majesty," he began.

"You're a *very* poor *speaker,*" said the King.

Here one of the guinea-pigs cheered, and was immediately suppressed by the officers of the court. (As that is rather a hard word, I will just explain to you how it was done. They had a large canvas bag, which tied up at the mouth with strings: into this they slipped the guinea-pig, head first, and then sat upon it.)

"I'm glad I've seen that done," thought Alice. "I've so often read in the newspapers, at the end of trials, 'There was some attempt at applause, which was immediately suppressed by the officers of the court,' and I never understood what it meant till now."

"If that's all you know about it, you may stand down," continued the King.

"I can't go no lower," said the Hatter: "I'm on the floor, as it is."

"Then you may *sit* down," the King replied.

Here the other guinea-pig cheered, and was suppressed.

"Come, that finishes the guinea-pigs!" thought Alice. "Now we shall go on better."

"I'd rather finish my tea," said the Hatter, with an anxious look at the Queen, who was reading the list of singers.

"You may go," said the King, and the Hatter hurriedly left the court, without even waiting to put his shoes on.

"—and just take his head off outside," the Queen added to one of the officers; but the Hatter was out of sight before the officer could get to the door.

"Call the next witness!" said the King. The next witness was the Duchess's cook. She carried the pepper-box in her hand, and Alice guessed who it was, even before she got into the court, by the way the people near the door began sneezing all at once.

"Give your evidence," said the King.

"Shan't," said the cook.

The King looked anxiously at the White Rabbit, who said, in a low voice, "Your Majesty must cross-examine *this* witness."

"Well, if I must, I must," the King said with a melancholy air, and, after folding his arms and frowning at the cook till his eyes were nearly out of sight, he said, in a deep voice, "What are tarts made of?"

"Pepper, mostly," said the cook.

"Treacle," said a sleepy voice behind her.

"Collar that Dormouse!" the Queen shrieked out. "Behead that Dormouse! Turn that Dormouse out of court! Suppress him! Pinch him! Off with his whiskers!"

For some minutes the whole court was in confusion, getting the Dormouse turned out, and, by the time they had settled down again, the cook had disappeared.

"Never mind!" said the King, with an air of great relief. "Call the next witness." And, he added, in an undertone to the Queen, "Really, my dear, *you* must cross-examine the next witness. It quite makes my forehead ache!"

Alice watched the White Rabbit as he fumbled over the list, feeling very curious to see what the next witness would be like, "—for they haven't got much evidence *yet*," she said to herself. Imagine her surprise, when the White Rabbit read out, at the top of his shrill little voice, the name "Alice!"

XII: ALICE'S EVIDENCE

"Here!" cried Alice, quite forgetting in the flurry of the moment how large she had grown in the last few minutes, and she jumped up in such a hurry that she tipped over the jury-box with the edge of her skirt, upsetting all the jurymen on to the heads of the crowd below, and there they lay sprawling about, reminding her very much of a globe of gold-fish she had accidentally upset the week before.

"Oh, I *beg* your pardon!" she exclaimed in a tone of great dismay, and began picking them up again as quickly as she could, for the accident of the gold-fish kept running in her head, and she had a vague sort of idea that they must be collected at once and put back into the jury-box, or they would die.

"The trial cannot proceed," said the King, in a very grave voice, "until all the jurymen are back in their proper places—*all*," he repeated with great emphasis, looking hard at Alice as he said so.

Alice looked at the jury-box, and saw that, in her haste, she had put the Lizard in head downward, and the poor little thing was waving its tail about in a melancholy way, being quite unable to move. She soon got it out again, and put it right; "not that it signifies much," she said to herself; "I should think it would be *quite* as much use in the trial one way up as the other."

As soon as the jury had a little recovered from the shock of being upset, and their slates and pencils had been found and handed back to them, they set to work very diligently to write out a history of the accident, all except the Lizard, who seemed too much overcome to do anything but sit with its mouth open, gazing up into the roof of the court.

"What do you know about this business?" the King said to Alice.

"Nothing," said Alice.

"Nothing *whatever?*" persisted the King.

"Nothing whatever," said Alice.

"That's very important," the King said, turning to the jury. They were just beginning to write this down on their slates, when the White Rabbit interrupted: "*Un*important, your Majesty means, of course," he said, in a very respectful tone, but frowning and making faces at him as he spoke.

"*Un*important, of course, I meant," the King hastily said, and went on to himself in an undertone, "important—unimportant—un-important—important—" as if he were trying which word sounded best.

Some of the jury wrote it down "important," and some "unim-portant." Alice could see this, as she was near enough to look over their slates; "but it doesn't matter a bit," she thought to herself.

At this moment the King, who had been for some time busily writing in his note-book, called out, "Silence!" and read out from his book, "Rule Forty-two. *All persons more than a mile high to leave the court.*"

Everybody looked at Alice.

"*I'm* not a mile high," said Alice.

"You are," said the King.

"Nearly two miles high," added the Queen.

"Well, I shan't go, at any rate," said Alice: "besides, that's not a regular rule: you invented it just now."

"It's the oldest rule in the book," said the King.

"Then it ought to be Number One," said Alice.

The King turned pale, and shut his note-book hastily. "Consider your verdict," he said to the jury, in a low trembling voice.

"There's more evidence to come yet, please your Majesty," said the White Rabbit, jumping up in a great hurry: "this paper has just been picked up."

"What's in it?" said the Queen.

"I haven't opened it yet," said the White Rabbit; "but it seems to be a letter, written by the prisoner to—to somebody."

"It must have been that," said the King, "unless it was written to nobody, which isn't usual, you know."

"Who is it directed to?" said one of the jurymen.

"It isn't directed at all," said the White Rabbit: "in fact, there's nothing written on the *outside*." He folded the paper as he spoke, and added, "It isn't a letter, after all, it's a set of verses."

"Are they in the prisoner's handwriting?" asked another of the jurymen.

"No, they're not," said the White Rabbit, "and that's the queerest thing about it." (The jury all looked puzzled.)

"He must have imitated somebody else's hand," said the King. (The jury all brightened up again.)

"Please your Majesty," said the Knave, "I didn't write it and they can't prove that I did: there's no name signed at the end."

"If you didn't sign it," said the King, "that only makes the matter worse. You *must* have meant some mischief, or else you'd have signed your name like an honest man."

There was a general clapping of hands at this: it was the first really clever thing the King had said that day.

"That *proves* his guilt, of course," said the Queen: "so, off with—"

"It doesn't prove anything of the sort!" said Alice. "Why, you don't even know what they're about!"

"Read them," said the King.

The White Rabbit put on his spectacles. "Where shall I begin, please your Majesty?" he asked.

"Begin at the beginning," the King said very gravely, "and go on till you come to the end: then stop."

There was dead silence in the court, while the White Rabbit read out these verses:

"They told me you had been to her,
And mentioned me to **him**:
She gave me a good character,
But said I could not swim.

He sent them word I had not gone
(We know it to be true):
If she should push the matter on,
What would become of you?

I gave her one, they gave him **two**,
You gave us three or more;
They all returned from him to you,
Though they were mine before.

If I or she should chance to be
Involved in this affair,
He trusts to you to set them free,
Exactly as we were.

My notion was that you had been
  (Before she had this fit)
An obstacle that came between
  Him, and ourselves, and it.

Don't let him know she liked them best,
  For this must ever be
A secret, kept from all the rest,
  Between yourself and me."

"That's the most important piece of evidence we've heard yet," said the King, rubbing his hands; "so now let the jury—"

"If any one of them can explain it," said Alice (she had grown so large in the last few minutes that she wasn't a bit afraid of interrupting him), "I'll give him sixpence. *I* don't believe there's an atom of meaning in it."

The jury all wrote down, on their slates, *"She* doesn't believe there's an atom of meaning in it," but none of them attempted to explain the paper.

"If there's no meaning in it," said the King, "that saves a world of trouble, you know, as we needn't try to find any. And yet I don't know," he went on, spreading out the verses on his knee, and looking at them with one eye; "I seem to see some meaning in them, after all. '—*said I could not swim—*' you can't swim, can you?" he added, turning to the Knave.

The Knave shook his head sadly.

"Do I look like it?" he said. (Which he certainly did *not,* being made entirely of cardboard.)

"All right, so far," said the King; and he went on muttering over the verses to himself: " '*We know it to be true*'—that's the jury of course—'*If she should push the matter on*'—that must be the Queen—'*What would become of you?*'—What, indeed!—'*I gave her one, they gave him two*'—why, that must be what he did with the tarts, you know—"

"But it goes on '*they all returned from him to you,*' " said Alice.

"Why, there they are!" said the King triumphantly, pointing to the tarts on the table. "Nothing can be clearer than *that*. Then again —'*before she had this fit*'—you never had *fits*, my dear, I think?" he said to the Queen.

"Never!" said the Queen, furiously, throwing an inkstand at the Lizard as she spoke. (The unfortunate little Bill had left off writing on his slate with one finger, as he found it made no mark; but he now hastily began again, using the ink, that was trickling down his face, as long as it lasted.)

"Then the words don't *fit* you," said the King, looking round the court with a smile. There was a dead silence.

"It's a pun!" the King added in an angry tone, and everybody laughed. "Let the jury consider their verdict," the King said, for about the twentieth time that day.

"No, no!" said the Queen. "Sentence first—verdict afterwards."

"Stuff and nonsense!" said Alice loudly. "The idea of having the sentence first!"

"Hold your tongue!" said the Queen, turning purple.

"I won't!" said Alice.

"Off with her head!" the Queen shouted at the top of her voice. Nobody moved.

"Who cares for *you?*" said Alice (she had grown to her full size by this time). "You're nothing put a pack of cards!"

At this the whole pack rose up into the air, and came flying down upon her; she gave a little scream, half of fright and half of anger, and tried to beat them off, and found herself lying on the bank, with her head in the lap of her sister, who was gently brushing away some dead leaves that had fluttered down from the trees upon her face.

"Wake up, Alice dear!" said her sister. "Why, what a long sleep you've had!"

"Oh, I've had such a curious dream!" said Alice. And she told her sister, as well as she could remember them, all these strange adventures of hers that you have just been reading about; and, when she had finished, her sister kissed her, and said, "It *was* a curious dream, dear, certainly; but now run in to your tea; it's getting late." So Alice got up and ran off, thinking while she ran, as well she might, what a wonderful dream it had been.

THE KING OF THE GOLDEN RIVER

By *JOHN RUSKIN*

Illustrations by
RICHARD DOYLE

I

IN a secluded and mountainous part of Stiria there was, in old time, a valley of the most surprising and luxuriant fertility. It was surrounded, on all sides, by steep and rocky mountains, rising into peaks, which were always covered with snow, and from which a number of torrents descended in constant cataracts. One of these fell westward, over the face of a crag so high, that, when the sun had set to everything else, and all below was darkness, his beams still shone full upon this waterfall, so that it looked like a shower of gold. It was, therefore, called by the people of the neighborhood the Golden River. It was strange that none of these streams fell into the valley itself. They all descended on the other side of the mountains, and wound away through broad plains and by populous cities. But the clouds were drawn so constantly to the snowy hills, and rested so softly in the circular hollow, that in time of drought and heat, when all the country round was burnt up, there was still rain in the little valley; and its crops were so heavy, and its hay so high, and its apples so red, and its grapes so blue, and its wine so rich, and its honey so sweet, that it was a marvel to everyone who beheld it, and was commonly called the Treasure Valley.

The whole of this little valley belonged to three brothers, called Schwartz, Hans, and Gluck. Schwartz and Hans, the two elder brothers, were very ugly men, with overhanging eyebrows and small dull eyes, which were always half shut, so that you couldn't see into *them,* and always fancied they saw very far into *you.* They lived by farming the Treasure Valley, and very good farmers they were. They killed everything that did not pay for its eating. They shot the blackbirds, because they pecked the fruit; and killed the hedge-hogs, lest they should suck the cows; they poisoned the crickets for eating the crumbs in the kitchen; and smothered the cicadas, which used to sing all summer in the lime trees. They worked their servants without any wages, till they would not work any more, and then quarreled with them, and turned them out of doors without paying them. It would have been very odd, if with such a farm, and such a system of farming, they hadn't got very rich; and very rich they *did* get. They generally contrived to keep their corn by them till it was very dear, and then sell it for twice its value; they had heaps of gold lying about on their floors, yet it was never known that they had given so much as a penny or a crust in charity; they never went to Mass; grumbled perpetually at paying tithes; and were, in a word, of so cruel and grinding a temper, as to receive from all those with whom they had any dealings, the nickname of the "Black Brothers."

The youngest brother, Gluck, was as completely opposed, in both appearance and character, to his seniors as could possibly be imagined or desired. He was not above twelve years old, fair, blue-eyed, and kind in temper to every living thing. He did not, of course, agree particularly well with his brothers, or rather, they did not agree with *him*. He was usually appointed to the honorable office of turnspit, when there was anything to roast, which was not often; for, to do the brothers justice, they were hardly less sparing upon themselves than upon other people. At other times he used to clean the shoes, floors, and sometimes the plates, occasionally getting what was left on them, by way of encouragement, and a wholesome quantity of dry blows, by way of education.

Things went on in this manner for a long time. At last came a very wet summer, and everything went wrong in the country around. The hay had hardly been got in, when the haystacks were floated bodily down to the sea by an inundation; the vines were cut to pieces with the hail; the corn was all killed by a black blight; only in the Treasure Valley, as usual, all was safe. As it had rain when there was rain nowhere else, so it had sun when there was sun nowhere else. Everybody came to buy corn at the farm, and went away pouring maledictions on the Black Brothers. They asked what they liked, and got it, except from the poor people, who could only beg, and several of whom were starved at their very door, without the slightest regard or notice.

It was drawing toward winter, and very cold weather, when one day the two elder brothers had gone out, with their usual warning to little Gluck, who was left to mind the roast, that he was to let nobody in, and give nothing out. Gluck sat down quite close to the fire, for it was raining very hard, and the kitchen walls were by no means dry or comfortable looking. He turned and turned, and the roast got nice and brown. "What a pity," thought Gluck, "my brothers never ask anybody to dinner. I'm sure, when they've got such a nice piece of mutton as this, and nobody else has got so much as a piece of dry bread, it would do their hearts good to have somebody to eat it with them."

Just as he spoke, there came a double knock at the house door, yet heavy and dull, as though the knocker had been tied up—more like a puff than a knock.

"It must be the wind," said Gluck; "nobody else would venture to knock double knocks at our door."

No; it was n't the wind: there it came again very hard, and what was particularly astounding, the knocker seemed to be in a hurry, and not to be in the least afraid of the consequences. Gluck went to the window, opened it, and put his head out to see who it was.

It was the most extraordinary-looking little gentleman he had ever seen in his life. He had a very large nose, slightly brass-colored; his cheeks were very round, and very red, and might have warranted a supposition that he had been blowing a refractory fire for the last eight-and-forty hours; his eyes twinkled merrily through long silky eyelashes, his mustaches curled twice round like a corkscrew on each side of his mouth, and his hair, of a curious mixed pepper-and-salt color, descended far over his shoulders. He was about four feet six in height, and wore a conical pointed cap of nearly the same alti-tude, decorated with a black feather some three feet long. His doublet was prolonged behind into something resembling a violent exaggera-tion of what is now termed a "swallow tail," but was much obscured by the swelling folds of an enormous black, glossy-looking cloak, which must have been very much too long in calm weather, as the wind, whistling round the old house, carried it clear out from the wearer's shoulders to about four times his own length.

Gluck was so perfectly paralyzed by the singular appearance of his visitor, that he remained fixed without uttering a word, until the old gentleman, having performed another, and a more energetic concerto on the knocker, turned round to look after his fly-away cloak. In so doing he caught sight of Gluck's little yellow head jammed in the window, with its mouth and eyes very wide open indeed.

"Hullo!" said the little gentleman, "that's not the way to answer the door: I'm wet, let me in."

To do the little gentleman justice, he *was* wet. His feather hung down between his legs like a beaten puppy's tail, dripping like an umbrella; and from the ends of his mustaches the water was running into his waistcoat pockets, and out again like a mill stream.

"I beg pardon, sir," said Gluck, "I'm very sorry, but I really can't."

"Can't what!" said the old gentleman.

"I can't let you in, sir—I can't, indeed; my brothers would beat me to death, sir, if I thought of such a thing. What do you want, sir?"

"Want?" said the old gentleman, petulantly. "I want fire, and shelter; and there's your great fire there blazing, crackling, and dancing on the walls, with nobody to feel it. Let me in, I say; I only want to warm myself."

Gluck had had his head, by this time, so long out of the window, that he began to feel it was really unpleasantly cold, and when he turned, and saw the beautiful fire rustling and roaring, and throwing long bright tongues up the chimney, as if it were licking its chops at the savory smell of the leg of mutton, his heart melted within him that it should be burning away for nothing. "He does look *very* wet," said little Gluck; "I'll just let him in for a quarter of an hour." Round he went to the door, and opened it; and as the little gentleman walked in, there came a gust of wind through the house that made the old chimneys totter.

Gluck put his head out to see who it was.

"That's a good boy," said the little gentleman. "Never mind your brothers. I'll talk to them."

"Pray, sir, don't do any such thing," said Gluck. "I can't let you stay till they come; they'd be the death of me."

"Dear me," said the old gentleman. "I'm very sorry to hear that. How long may I stay?"

"Only till the mutton's done, sir," replied Gluck, "and it's very brown."

Then the old gentleman walked into the kitchen, and sat himself down on the hob, with the top of his cap accommodated up the chimney, for it was a great deal too high for the roof.

"You'll soon dry there, sir," said Gluck, and sat down again to turn the mutton. But the old gentleman did not *dry* there, but went on drip, drip, dripping among the cinders, and the fire fizzed, and sputtered, and began to look very black, and uncomfortable: never was such a cloak; every fold in it ran like a gutter.

"I beg pardon, sir," said Gluck at length, after watching the water spreading in long quicksilver-like streams over the floor for a quarter of an hour; "mayn't I take your cloak?"

"No, thank you," said the old gentleman.

"Your cap, sir?"

"I am all right, thank you," said the old gentleman rather gruffly.

"But—sir—I'm very sorry," said Gluck, hesitatingly; "but—really, sir—you're—putting the fire out."

"It'll take longer to do the mutton, then," replied his visitor dryly.

Gluck was very much puzzled by the behavior of his guest; it was such a strange mixture of coolness and humility.

He turned away at the string meditatively for another five minutes.

"That mutton looks very nice," said the old gentleman at length. "Can't you give me a little bit?"

"Impossible, sir," said Gluck.

"I'm very hungry," continued the old gentleman: "I've had nothing to eat yesterday, nor today. They surely could n't miss a bit from the knuckle!"

He spoke in so very melancholy a tone, that it quite melted Gluck's heart. "They promised me one slice today, sir," said he; "I can give you that, but not a bit more."

"That's a good boy," said the old gentleman again.

Then Gluck warmed a plate, and sharpened a knife. "I don't care if I do get beaten for it," thought he. Just as he had cut a large slice out of the mutton, there came a tremendous rap at the door. The old gentleman jumped off the hob, as if it had suddenly become inconveniently warm. Gluck fitted the slice into the mutton again, with desperate efforts at exactitude, and ran to open the door.

"What did you keep us waiting in the rain for?" said Schwartz, as he walked in, throwing his umbrella in Gluck's face. "Ay! what for, indeed, you little vagabond?" said Hans, administering an educational box on the ear, as he followed his brother into the kitchen.

"Bless my soul!" said Schwartz when he opened the door.

"Amen," said the little gentleman, who had taken his cap off, and was standing in the middle of the kitchen, bowing with the utmost possible velocity.

"Who's that?" said Schwartz, catching up a rolling-pin, and turning to Gluck with a fierce frown.

"I don't know, indeed, brother," said Gluck in great terror.

"How did he get in?" roared Schwartz.

"My dear brother," said Gluck, deprecatingly, "he was so *very* wet!"

The rolling-pin was descending on Gluck's head; but, at the instant, the old gentleman interposed his conical cap, on which it crashed with a shock that shook the water out of it all over the room. What was very odd, the rolling-pin no sooner touched the cap, than it flew out of Schwartz's hand, spinning like a straw in a high wind, and fell into the corner at the further end of the room.

"Who are you, sir?" demanded Schwartz, turning upon him.

"What's your business?" snarled Hans.

"I'm a poor old man, sir," the little gentleman began very modestly, "and I saw your fire through the window, and begged shelter for a quarter of an hour."

"Have the goodness to walk out again, then," said Schwartz. "We've quite enough water in our kitchen, without making it a drying house."

"Amen," said the little gentleman.

"It is a cold day to turn an old man out in, sir; look at my gray hairs." They hung down to his shoulders, as I told you before.

"Ay!" said Hans, "there are enough of them to keep you warm. Walk!"

"I'm very, very hungry, sir; couldn't you spare me a bit of bread before I go?"

"Bread, indeed!" said Schwartz; "do you suppose we've nothing to do with our bread, but to give it to such red-nosed fellows as you?"

"Why don't you sell your feather?" said Hans, sneeringly. "Out with you."

"A little bit," said the old gentleman.

"Be off!" said Schwartz.

"Pray, gentlemen——"

"Off and be hanged!" cried Hans, seizing him by the collar. But he had no sooner touched the old gentleman's collar, than away he went after the rolling-pin, spinning round and round, till he fell into the corner on top of it. Then Schwartz was very angry, and ran at the old gentleman to turn him out; but he also had hardly touched him, when away he went after Hans and the rolling-pin, and hit his head against the wall as he tumbled into the corner.

And so there they lay, all three.

Then the old gentleman spun himself round with velocity in the opposite direction; continued to spin until his long cloak was all wound neatly about him; clapped his cap on his head, very much on one side (for it could not stand upright without going through the ceiling), gave an additional twist to his corkscrew mustaches, and replied with perfect coolness: "Gentlemen, I wish you a very good morning. At twelve o'clock tonight I'll call again; after such a refusal of hospitality as I have just experienced, you will not be surprised if that visit is the last I ever pay you."

"If ever I catch you here again," muttered Schwartz, coming, half frightened, out of the corner—but, before he could finish his sentence, the old gentleman had shut the house door behind him with a great bang: and there drove past the window, at the same instant, a wreath of ragged cloud, that whirled and rolled away down the valley in all manner of shapes; turning over and over in the air; and melting away at last in a gush of rain.

"A very pretty business, indeed, Mr. Gluck!" said Schwartz. "Dish the mutton, sir. If ever I catch you at such a trick again—bless me, why, the mutton's been cut!"

"You promised me one slice, brother, you know," said Gluck.

"Oh, and you were cutting it hot, I suppose, and going to catch all the gravy. It'll be long before I promise you such a thing again. Leave the room, sir; and have the kindness to wait in the coal-cellar till I call you."

Gluck left the room melancholy enough. The brothers ate as much mutton as they could, locked the rest in the cupboard, and proceeded to get very drunk after dinner.

Such a night as it was! Howling wind, and rushing rain, without intermission. The brothers had just sense enough left to put up all the shutters, and double bar the door, before they went to bed. They usually slept in the same room. As the clock struck twelve, they were both awakened by a tremendous crash. Their door burst open with a violence that shook the house from top to bottom.

"What's that?" cried Schwartz, starting up in his bed.

"Only I," said the little gentleman.

The two brothers sat up on their bolster, and stared into the darkness. The room was full of water, and by a misty moonbeam, which found its way through a hole in the shutter, they could see in the midst of it an enormous foam globe, spinning round, and bobbing up and down like a cork, on which, as on a most luxurious cushion, reclined the little old gentleman, cap and all. There was plenty of room for it now, for the roof was off.

"Sorry to incommode you," said their visitor, ironically. "I'm afraid your beds are dampish; perhaps you had better go to your brother's room: I've left the ceiling on there."

They required no second admonition, but rushed into Gluck's room, wet through, and in an agony of terror.

"You'll find my card on the kitchen table," the old gentleman called after them. "Remember, the *last* visit."

"Pray Heaven it may!" said Schwartz, shuddering. And the foam globe disappeared.

Dawn came at last, and the two brothers looked out of Gluck's little window in the morning. The Treasure Valley was one mass of ruin and desolation. The inundation had swept away trees, crops, and cattle, and left in their stead a waste of red sand and gray mud. The two brothers crept shivering and horror-struck into the kitchen. The water had gutted the whole first floor; corn, money, almost every movable thing had been swept away, and there was left only a small white card on the kitchen table. On it, in large, breezy, long-legged letters, were engraved the words:——

SOUTH-WEST WIND, ESQUIRE

II

South-West Wind, Esquire, was as good as his word. After the momentous visit above related, he entered the Treasure Valley no more; and, what was worse, he had so much influence with his relations, the West Winds in general, and used it so effectually, that they all adopted a similar line of conduct. So no rain fell in the valley from one year's end to another. Though everything remained green and flourishing in the plains below, the inheritance of the three brothers was a desert. What had once been the richest soil in the kingdom, became a shifting heap of red sand; and the brothers, unable longer to contend with the adverse skies, abandoned their valueless patrimony in despair, to seek some means of gaining a livelihood among the cities and people of the plains.

All their money was gone, and they had nothing left but some curious old-fashioned pieces of gold plate, the last remnants of their ill-gotten wealth.

"Suppose we turn goldsmiths?" said Schwartz to Hans, as they entered the large city. "It is a good knave's trade; we can put a great deal of copper into the gold, without anyone's finding it out."

The thought was agreed to be a very good one; they hired a furnace, and turned goldsmiths. But two slight circumstances affected their trade: the first, that people did not approve of the coppered gold; the second, that the two elder brothers, whenever they had sold anything, used to leave little Gluck to mind the furnace, and go and drink out the money in the ale-house next door. So they melted all their gold, without making money enough to buy more, and were at last reduced to one large drinking mug, which an uncle of his had given to little Gluck, and which he was very fond of, and would not have parted with for the world; though he never drank anything out of it but milk and water. The mug was a very odd mug to look at. The handle was formed of two wreaths of flowing golden hair, so finely spun that it looked more like silk than metal, and these wreaths descended into, and mixed with, a beard and whiskers of the same exquisite workmanship, which surrounded and decorated a very fierce little face, of the reddest gold imaginable, right in the front of the mug, with a pair of eyes in it which seemed to command its whole circumference. It was impossible to drink out of the mug, without being subjected to an intense gaze out of the side of these eyes; and Schwartz positively averred, that once, after emptying it, full of Rhenish, seventeen times, he had seen them wink! When it came to the mug's turn to be made into spoons, it half broke poor little Gluck's heart; but the brothers only laughed at him, tossed the mug into the melting-pot, and staggered out to the ale-house: leaving him, as usual, to pour the gold into bars, when it was all ready.

When they were gone, Gluck took a farewell look at his old friend in the melting-pot. The flowing hair was all gone; nothing remained but the red nose, and the sparkling eyes, which looked more malicious than ever. "And no wonder," thought Gluck, "after being treated in that way." He sauntered disconsolately to the window, and sat himself down to catch the fresh evening air, and escape the hot breath of the furnace. Now this window commanded a direct view of the range of mountains, which, as I told you before, overhung the Treasure Valley, and more especially of the peak from which fell the Golden River. It was just at the close of the day, and, when Gluck sat down at the window, he saw the rocks of the mountain tops, all crimson and purple with the sunset; and there were bright tongues of fiery cloud burning and quivering about them; and the river, brighter than all, fell, in a waving column of pure gold, from precipice to precipice, with the double arch of a broad purple rainbow stretched across it, flushing and fading alternately in the wreaths of spray.

"Ah!" said Gluck aloud, after he had looked at it for a while, "if that river were really all gold, what a nice thing it would be."

"No, it wouldn't, Gluck," said a clear, metallic voice, close at his ear.

"Bless me, what's that?" exclaimed Gluck, jumping up. There was nobody there. He looked round the room, and under the table, and a great many times behind him, but there was certainly nobody there, and he sat down again at the window.

This time he didn't speak, but he couldn't help thinking again that it would be very convenient if the river were really all gold.

"Not at all, my boy," said the same voice, louder than before.

"Bless me!" said Gluck again, "what *is* that?" He looked again into all the corners and cupboards, and then began turning round and round as fast as he could in the middle of the room, thinking there was somebody behind him, when the same voice struck again on his ear. It was singing now, very merrily, "Lala-lira-la"; no words, only a soft running effervescent melody, something like that of a kettle on the boil. Gluck looked out of the window. No, it was certainly in the house. Upstairs, and downstairs. No, it was certainly in that very room, coming in quicker time and clearer notes every moment. "Lala-lira-la." All at once it struck Gluck that it sounded louder near the furnace. He ran to the opening and looked in; yes, he saw right, it seemed to be coming, not only out of the furnace, but out of the pot. He uncovered it, and ran back in a great fright, for the pot was certainly singing! He stood in the farthest corner of the room, with his hands up and his mouth open, for a minute or two, when the singing stopped, and the voice became clear and pronunciative.

"Hullo!" said the voice.

Gluck made no answer.

"Hullo! Gluck, my boy," said the pot again.

Gluck summoned all his energies, walked straight up to the crucible, drew it out of the furnace, and looked in. The gold was all melted, and its surface as smooth and polished as a river; but instead of reflecting little Gluck's head, as he looked in, he saw meeting his glance from beneath the gold, the red nose and sharp eyes of his old friend of the mug, a thousand times redder and sharper than ever he had seen them in his life.

"Come, Gluck, my boy," said the voice out of the pot again, "I'm all right; pour me out."

But Gluck was too much astonished to do anything of the kind.

"Pour me out, I say," said the voice, rather gruffly. Still Gluck couldn't move.

"*Will* you pour me out?" said the voice, passionately. "I'm too hot."

By a violent effort, Gluck recovered the use of his limbs, took hold of the crucible and sloped it, so as to pour out the gold. But, instead of a liquid stream, there came out, first a pair of pretty little yellow legs, then some coat tails, then a pair of arms stuck a-kimbo, and finally the well-known head of his friend the mug; all which articles, uniting as they rolled out, stood up energetically on the floor, in the shape of a little golden dwarf, about a foot and a half high.

"That's right!" said the dwarf, stretching out first his legs, and then his arms, and then shaking his head up and down, and as far round as it would go, for five minutes without stopping, apparently with the view of ascertaining if he were quite correctly put together, while Gluck stood contemplating him in speechless amazement. He was dressed in a slashed doublet of spun gold, so fine in its texture, that the prismatic colors gleamed over it as if on a surface of mother of pearl; and, over this brilliant doublet, his hair and beard fell full half way to the ground in waving curls, so exquisitely delicate, that Gluck could hardly tell where they ended; they seemed to melt into air. The features of the face, however, were by no means finished with the same delicacy; they were rather coarse, slightly inclining to coppery in complexion, and indicative, in expression, of a very pertinacious and intractable disposition in their small proprietor. When the dwarf had finished his self-examination, he turned his small sharp eyes full on Gluck, and stared at him deliberately for a minute or two. "No, it wouldn't, Gluck, my boy," said the little man.

This was certainly rather an abrupt and unconnected mode of commencing conversation. It might indeed be supposed to refer to the course of Gluck's thoughts, which had first produced the dwarf's

Gluck stood contemplating him in speechless amazement.

observations out of the pot; but whatever it referred to, Gluck had no inclination to dispute the dictum.

"Wouldn't it, sir?" said Gluck, very mildly and submissively indeed.

"No," said the dwarf, conclusively, "no, it wouldn't." And with that the dwarf pulled his cap hard over his brows, and took two turns, of three feet long, up and down the room, lifting his legs up very high, and setting them down very hard. This pause gave time for Gluck to collect his thoughts a little, and, seeing no great reason to view his diminutive visitor with dread, and feeling his curiosity overcome his amazement, he ventured on a question of peculiar delicacy.

"Pray, sir," said Gluck, rather hesitatingly, "were you my mug?"

On which the little man turned sharp round, walked straight up to Gluck, and drew himself up to his full height. "I," said the little man, "am the King of the Golden River." Whereupon he turned about again, and took two more turns, some six feet long, in order to allow time for the consternation which this announcement produced in his auditor to evaporate.

After which, he again walked up to Gluck and stood still, as if expecting some comment on his communication.

Gluck determined to say something at all events. "I hope your Majesty is very well," said Gluck.

"Listen!" said the little man, deigning no reply to this polite inquiry. "I am the King of what you mortals call the Golden River. The shape you saw me in, was owing to the malice of a stronger king, from whose enchantments you have this instant freed me. What I have seen of you, and your conduct to your wicked brothers, renders me willing to serve you; therefore, attend to what I tell you. Whoever shall climb to the top of that mountain from which you see the Golden River issue, and shall cast into the stream at its source, three drops of holy water, for him, and for him only, the river shall turn to gold. But no one failing in his first, can succeed in a second attempt; and if any one shall cast unholy water into the river, it will overwhelm him, and he will become a black stone." So saying, the King of the Golden River turned away and deliberately walked into the center of the hottest flame of the furnace.

His figure became red, white, transparent, dazzling—a blaze of intense light—rose, trembled, and disappeared. The King of the Golden River had evaporated.

"Oh!" cried poor Gluck, running to look up the chimney after him; "Oh, dear, dear, dear me! My mug! my mug! my mug!"

III

The King of the Golden River had hardly made the extraordinary exit related in the last chapter, before Hans and Schwartz came roaring into the house, very savagely drunk. The discovery of the total loss of their last piece of plate had the effect of sobering them just enough to enable them to stand over Gluck, beating him very steadily for a quarter of an hour; at the expiration of which period they dropped into a couple of chairs, and requested to know what he had got to say for himself. Gluck told them his story, of which, of course, they did not believe a word. They beat him again, till their arms were tired, and staggered to bed. In the morning, however, the steadiness with which he adhered to his story obtained him some degree of credence; the immediate consequence of which was, that the two brothers, after wrangling a long time on the knotty question, which of them should try his fortune first, drew their swords and began fighting. The noise of the fray alarmed the neighbors, who, finding they could not pacify the combatants, sent for the constable.

Hans, on hearing this, contrived to escape, and hid himself; but Schwartz was taken before the magistrate, fined for breaking the peace, and, having drunk out his last penny the evening before, was thrown into prison till he should pay.

When Hans heard this, he was much delighted, and determined

to set out immediately for the Golden River. How to get the holy water, was the question. He went to the priest, but the priest could not give any holy water to so abandoned a character. So Hans went to vespers in the evening for the first time in his life, and, under pretense of crossing himself, stole a cupful, and returned home in triumph.

Next morning he got up before the sun rose, put the holy water into a strong flask, and two bottles of wine and some meat in a basket, slung them over his back, took his alpine staff in his hand, and set off for the mountains.

On his way out of the town he had to pass the prison, and as he looked in at the windows, whom should he see but Schwartz himself peeping out of the bars, and looking very disconsolate.

"Good morning, brother," said Hans; "have you any message for the King of the Golden River?"

Schwartz gnashed his teeth with rage, and shook the bars with all his strength; but Hans only laughed at him, and advising him to make himself comfortable till he came back again, shouldered his basket, shook the bottle of holy water in Schwartz's face till it frothed again, and marched off in the highest spirits in the world.

It was, indeed, a morning that might have made any one happy, even with no Golden River to seek for. Level lines of dewy mist lay stretched along the valley, out of which rose the massy mountains—their lower cliffs in pale gray shadow, hardly distinguishable from the floating vapor, but gradually ascending till they caught the sunlight, which ran in sharp touches of ruddy color, along the angular crags, and pierced, in long level rays, through their fringes of spear-like pine. Far above, shot up red splintered masses of castellated rock, jagged and shivered into myriads of fantastic forms, with here and there a streak of sunlit snow, traced down their chasms like a line of forked lightning; and, far beyond, and far above all these, fainter than the morning clouds, but purer and changeless, slept, in the blue sky, the utmost peaks of the eternal snow.

The Golden River, which sprang from one of the lower and snowless elevations, was now nearly in shadow; all but the uppermost jets of spray, which rose like slow smoke above the undulating line of the cataract, and floated away in feeble wreaths upon the morning wind.

On this object, and on this alone, Hans's eyes and thoughts were fixed; forgetting the distance he had to traverse, he set off at an imprudent rate of walking, which greatly exhausted him before he had scaled the first range of the green and low hills. He was, moreover, surprised, on surmounting them, to find that a large glacier, of whose existence, notwithstanding his previous knowledge of the mountains, he had been absolutely ignorant, lay between him and the source of the Golden River. He entered on it with the boldness of a practised mountaineer; yet he thought he had never traversed so strange or so dangerous a glacier in his life. The ice was excessively slippery, and out of all its chasms came wild sounds of gushing water; not monotonous or low, but changeful and loud, rising occasionally into drifting passages of wild melody, then breaking off into short melancholy tones, or sudden shrieks, resembling those of human voices in distress or pain. The ice was broken into thousands of confused shapes, but none, Hans thought, like the ordinary forms of splintered ice. There seemed a curious *expression* about all their outlines—a perpetual resemblance to living features, distorted and scornful. Myriads of deceitful shadows, and lurid lights, played and floated about and through the pale blue pinnacles, dazzling and confusing the sight of the traveler; while his ears grew dull and his head giddy with the constant gush and roar of the concealed waters. These painful circumstances increased upon him as he advanced; the ice crashed and yawned into fresh chasms at his feet, tottering spires nodded around him, and fell thundering across his path; and though he had repeatedly faced these dangers on the most terrific glaciers, and in the wildest weather, it was with a new and oppressive feeling of panic terror that he leaped the last chasm, and flung himself, exhausted and shuddering, on the firm turf of the mountain.

He had been compelled to abandon his basket of food, which became a perilous incumbrance on the glacier, and had now no means of refreshing himself but by breaking off and eating some of the pieces of ice. This, however, relieved his thirst; an hour's repose recruited his hardy frame, and with the indomitable spirit of avarice, he resumed his laborious journey.

His way now lay straight up a ridge of bare red rocks, without a blade of grass to ease the foot, or a projecting angle to afford an inch of shade from the south sun. It was past noon, and the rays beat intensely upon the steep path, while the whole atmosphere was motionless, and penetrated with heat. Intense thirst was soon added to the bodily fatigue with which Hans was now afflicted; glance after glance he cast on the flask of water which hung at his belt. "Three drops are enough," at last thought he; "I may, at least, cool my lips with it."

He opened the flask, and was raising it to his lips, when his eye fell on an object lying on the rock beside him; he thought it moved. It was a small dog, apparently in the last agony of death from thirst. Its tongue was out, its jaws dry, its limbs extended lifelessly, and a swarm of black ants were crawling about its lips and throat. Its eye moved to the bottle which Hans held in his hand. He raised it, drank, spurned the animal with his foot, and passed on. And he did not know how it was, but he thought that a strange shadow had suddenly come across the blue sky.

The path became steeper and more rugged every moment; and the high hill air, instead of refreshing him, seemed to throw his blood into a fever. The noise of the hill cataracts sounded like mockery in his ears; they were all distant, and his thirst increased every moment. Another hour passed, and he again looked down to the flask at his side; it was half empty; but there was much more than three drops in it. He stopped to open it, and again, as he did so, something moved in the path above him.

It was a fair child, stretched nearly lifeless on the rock, its breast heaving with thirst, its eyes closed, and its lips parched and burning. Hans eyed it deliberately, drank, and passed on. And a dark gray cloud came over the sun, and long, snake-like shadows crept up along the mountain-sides. Hans struggled on. The sun was sinking, but its descent seemed to bring no coolness; the leaden weight of the dead air pressed upon his brow and heart, but the goal was near. He saw the cataract of the Golden River springing from the hillside, scarcely five hundred feet above him. He paused for a moment to breathe, and sprang on to complete his task.

At this instant a faint cry fell on his ear. He turned and saw a gray-haired old man extended on the rocks. His eyes were sunk, his features deadly pale, and gathered into an expression of despair. "Water!" he stretched his arms to Hans, and cried feebly. "Water! I am dying."

"I have none," replied Hans; "thou hast had thy share of life." He strode over the prostrate body, and darted on. And a flash of blue lightning rose out of the East, shaped like a sword; it shook thrice over the whole heaven, and left it dark with one heavy impenetrable shade. The sun was setting; it plunged toward the horizon like a red-hot ball.

The roar of the Golden River rose on Hans's ear. He stood at the brink of the chasm through which it ran. Its waves were filled with the red glory of the sunset; they shook their crests like tongues of fire, and flashes of bloody light gleamed along their foam. Their sound came mightier and mightier on his senses; his brain grew giddy with the prolonged thunder. Shuddering he drew the flask from his girdle, and hurled it into the center of the torrent. As he did so, an icy chill shot through his limbs; he staggered, shrieked, and fell. The waters closed over his cry. And the moaning of the river rose wildly into the night, as it gushed over THE BLACK STONE.

IV

Poor little Gluck waited very anxiously alone in the house, for Hans's return. Finding he did not come back, he was terribly frightened, and went and told Schwartz in the prison, all that had happened. Then Schwartz was very much pleased, and said that Hans must certainly have been turned into a black stone, and he should have all the gold to himself. But Gluck was very sorry, and cried all night. When he got up in the morning, there was no bread in the house, nor any money; so Gluck went and hired himself to another goldsmith, and he worked so hard, and so neatly, and so long every day, that he soon got money enough together to pay his brother's fine; and he went, and gave it all to Schwartz, and Schwartz got out of prison. Then Schwartz was quite pleased, and said he should have some of the gold of the river. But Gluck only begged he would go and see what had become of Hans.

Now when Schwartz had heard that Hans had stolen the holy

water, he thought to himself that such a proceeding might not be considered altogether correct by the King of the Golden River, and determined to manage matters better. So he took some more of Gluck's money, and went to a bad man, who gave him some holy water very readily for it. Then Schwartz was sure it was all quite right. So Schwartz got up early in the morning before the sun rose, and took some bread and wine, in a basket, and put his holy water in a flask, and set off for the mountains. Like his brother he was much surprised at the sight of the glacier, and had great difficulty in crossing it, even after leaving his basket behind him. The day was cloudless, but not bright: there was a heavy purple haze hanging over the sky, and the hills looked lowering and gloomy. And as Schwartz climbed the steep rock path, the thirst came upon him, as it had upon his brother, until he lifted his flask to his lips to drink. Then he saw the fair child lying near him on the rocks, and it cried to him, and moaned for water.

"Water, indeed," said Schwartz; "I haven't half enough for myself," and passed on. And as he went he thought the sunbeams grew more dim, and he saw a low bank of black cloud rising out of the West; and, when he had climbed for another hour, the thirst overcame him again, and he would have drunk. Then he saw the old man lying before him on the path, and heard him cry out for water. "Water, indeed," said Schwartz, "I haven't half enough for myself," and on he went.

Then again the light seemed to fade from before his eyes, and he looked up, and, behold, a mist, of the color of blood, had come over the sun; and the bank of black cloud had risen very high, and its edges were tossing and tumbling like the waves of the angry sea. And they cast long shadows, which flickered over Schwartz's path.

Then Schwartz climbed for another hour, and again his thirst returned; and as he lifted his flask to his lips, he thought he saw his brother Hans lying exhausted on the path before him, and, as he gazed, the figure stretched its arms to him, and cried for water. "Ha, ha," laughed Schwartz, "are you there? Remember the prison bars, my boy. Water, indeed! Do you suppose I carried it all the way up here for *you?*" And he strode over the figure; yet, as he passed, he thought he saw a strange expression of mockery about its lips. And, when he had gone a few yards farther, he looked back; but the figure was not there.

And a sudden horror came over Schwartz, he knew not why; but the thirst for gold prevailed over his fear, and he rushed on. And the bank of black cloud rose to the zenith, and out of it came bursts of spiry lightning, and waves of darkness seemed to heave and float between their flashes, over the whole heavens. And the sky where the sun was setting was all level, and like a lake of blood; and a strong wind came out of that sky, tearing its crimson clouds into fragments, and scattering them far into the darkness. And when Schwartz stood by the brink of the Golden River, its wares were black, like thunder clouds, but their foam was like fire; and the roar of the waters below, and the thunder above met, as he cast the flask into the stream.

And, as he did so, the lightning glared in his eyes, and the earth gave way beneath him, and the waters closed over his cry. And the moaning of the river rose wildly into the night, as it gushed over the TWO BLACK STONES.

V

When Gluck found that Schwartz did not come back, he was very sorry, and did not know what to do. He had no money, and was obliged to go and hire himself again to the goldsmith, who worked him very hard, and gave him very little money. So, after a month or two Gluck grew tired, and made up his mind to go and try his fortune with the Golden River. "The little king looked very kind," thought he. "I don't think he will turn me into a black stone." So he went to the priest, and the priest gave him some holy water as soon as he asked for it. Then Gluck took some bread in his basket, and the bottle of water, and set off very early for the mountains.

If the glacier had occasioned a great deal of fatigue to his brothers, it was twenty times worse for him, who was neither so strong nor so practised on the mountains. He had several very bad falls, lost his basket and bread, and was very much frightened at the strange noises under the ice. He lay a long time to rest on the grass, after he had got over, and began to climb the hill just in the hottest part of the day. When he had climbed for an hour, he got dreadfully thirsty, and was going to drink like his brothers, when he saw an old man coming down the path above him, looking very feeble, and leaning on a staff. "My son," said the old man, "I am faint with thirst; give me some of that water." Then Gluck looked at him, and when he saw that he was pale and weary, he gave him the water. "Only pray don't drink it all," said Gluck. But the old man drank a great deal, and gave him back the bottle two-thirds empty. Then he bade him good speed, and Gluck went on again merrily. And the path became easier to his feet, and two or three blades of grass appeared upon it, and some grasshoppers began singing on the bank beside it; and Gluck thought he had never heard such merry singing.

Then he went on for another hour, and the thirst increased on him so that he thought he should be forced to drink. But, as he raised the flask, he saw a little child lying panting by the road-side, and it cried out piteously for water. Then Gluck struggled with himself, and determined to bear the thirst a little longer; and he put the bottle to the child's lips, and it drank it all but a few drops.

Then it smiled on him, and got up, and ran down the hill; and Gluck looked after it, till it became as small as a little star, and then turned and began climbing again. And then there were all kinds of sweet flowers growing on the rocks, bright green moss, with pale pink starry flowers, and soft belled gentians, more blue than the sky at its deepest, and pure white transparent lilies. And crimson and purple butterflies darted hither and thither, and the sky sent down such pure light that Gluck had never felt so happy in his life.

Then it smiled on him, and got up, and ran down the hill.

Yet, when he had climbed for another hour, his thirst became intolerable again; and, when he looked at his bottle, he saw that there were only five or six drops left in it, and he could not venture to drink. And, as he was hanging the flask to his belt again, he saw a little dog lying on the rocks, gasping for breath—just as Hans had seen it on the day of his ascent. And Gluck stopped and looked at it, and then at the Golden River, not five hundred yards above him; and he thought of the dwarf's words, "that no one could succeed, except in his first attempt"; and he tried to pass the dog, but it whined piteously, and Gluck stopped again. "Poor beastie," said Gluck, "it'll be dead when I come down again if I don't help it." Then he looked closer and closer at it, and its eye turned on him so mournfully, that he could not stand it. "Confound the king and his gold, too," said Gluck; and he opened the flask, and poured all the water into the dog's mouth.

The dog sprang up and stood on its hind legs. Its tail disappeared, its ears became long, longer, silky, golden; its nose became very red, its eyes became very twinkling; in three seconds the dog was gone, and before Gluck stood his old acquaintance, the King of the Golden River.

"Thank you," said the monarch; "but don't be frightened, it's all right"; for Gluck showed manifest symptoms of consternation at this unlooked-for reply to his last observation. "Why did n't you come before," continued the dwarf, "instead of sending me those rascally brothers of yours, for me to have the trouble of turning into stones? Very hard stones they make, too."

"Oh, dear me!" said Gluck, "have you really been so cruel?"

"Cruel!" said the dwarf, "they poured unholy water into my stream: do you suppose I'm going to allow that?"

"Why," said Gluck, "I am sure, sir—your Majesty, I mean—they got the water out of the church font."

"Very probably," replied the dwarf; "but," and his countenance grew stern as he spoke, "the water which has been refused to the cry of the weary and dying, is unholy, though it had been blessed by every saint in heaven; and the water which is found in the vessel of mercy is holy, though it had been defiled with corpses."

So saying the dwarf stooped and plucked a lily that grew at his feet. On its white leaves there hung three drops of clear dew. And the dwarf shook them into the flask which Gluck held in his hand. "Cast these into the river," he said, "and descend on the other side of the mountains into the Treasure Valley. And so good speed."

As he spoke the figure of the dwarf became indistinct. The playing colors of his robe formed themselves into a prismatic mist of dewy light: he stood for an instant veiled with them as with the belt of a broad rainbow. The colors grew faint, the mist rose into the air; the monarch had evaporated.

And Gluck climbed to the brink of the Golden River, and its waves were as clear as crystal, and as brilliant as the sun. And, when he cast the three drops of dew into the stream, there opened where they fell, a small circular whirlpool, into which the waters descended with a musical noise.

Gluck stood watching it for some time, very much disappointed, because not only the river was not turned into gold, but its waters seemed much diminished in quantity. Yet he obeyed his friend the dwarf, and descended the other side of the mountains toward the Treasure Valley; and, as he went, he thought he heard the noise of water working its way under the ground. And, when he came in sight of the Treasure Valley, behold, a river, like the Golden River, was springing from a new cleft of the rocks above it, and was flowing in innumerable streams among the dry heaps of red sand.

And as Gluck gazed, fresh grass sprang beside the new streams, and creeping plants grew, and climbed among the moistening soil. Young flowers opened suddenly along the river sides, as stars leap out when twilight is deepening, and thickets of myrtle, and tendrils of vine, cast lengthening shadows over the valley as they grew. And thus the Treasure Valley became a garden again, and the inheritance, which had been lost by cruelty, was regained by love.

And Gluck went and dwelt in the valley, and the poor were never driven from his door: so that his barns became full of corn, and his house of treasure. And, for him, the river had, according to the dwarf's promise, become a River of Gold.

And, to this day, the inhabitants of the valley point out the place where the three drops of holy dew were cast into the stream, and trace the course of the Golden River under the ground, until it emerges in the Treasure Valley. And at the top of the cataract of the Golden River, are still to be seen TWO BLACK STONES, round which the waters howl mournfully every day at sunset; and these stones are still called by the people of the valley THE BLACK BROTHERS.

JACKANAPES

By *JULIANA HORATIA EWING*

With *Illustrations by*
RANDOLPH CALDECOTT

If I might buffet for may love, or
bound my horse for her favors, I could
lay on like a butcher, and sit like a
Jackanapes, never off.
—*King Henry V*, Act V, Scene 2.

I: THE BLACK CAPTAIN GOES TO WAR

TWO Donkeys and the Geese lived on the Green, and all other residents of any social standing lived in houses round it. The houses had no names. Everybody's address was "The Green," but the Postman and the people of the place knew where each family lived. As to the rest of the world, what has one to do with the rest of the world when he is safe at home on his own Goose Green? Moreover, if a stranger did come on any lawful business, he might ask his way at the shop.

Most of the inhabitants were long-lived, early deaths (like that of the little Miss Jessamine) being exceptional; and most of the old people were proud of their age, especially the sexton, who would be ninety-nine come Martinmas, and whose father remembered a man who had carried arrows, as a boy, for the battle of Flodden Field.

The Gray Goose and the big Miss Jessamine were the only elderly persons who kept their ages secret. Indeed, Miss Jessamine never mentioned any one's age, or recalled the exact year in which anything had happened. She said that she had been taught that it was bad manners to do so "in a mixed assembly."

The Gray Goose also avoided dates; but this was partly because her brain, though intelligent, was not mathematical, and computation was beyond her. She never got farther than "last Michaelmas," "the Michaelmas before that," and "the Michaelmas before the Michaelmas before that." After this her head, which was small, became confused, and she said, "Ga, ga!" and changed the subject.

But she remembered the little Miss Jessamine, the Miss Jessamine with the "conspicuous" hair. Her aunt, the big Miss Jessamine, said it was her only fault. The hair was clean, was abundant, was glossy; but do what you would with it, it never looked quite like other people's. And at church, after Saturday night's wash, it shone like the best brass fender after a spring cleaning. In short, it was conspicuous, which does not become a young woman, especially in church.

Those were worrying times altogether, and the Green was used for strange purposes. A political meeting was held on it with the village Cobbler in the chair, and a speaker who came by stage-coach from the town, where they had wrecked the bakers' shops, and discussed the price of bread. He came a second time by stage; but the people had heard something about him in the meanwhile, and they did not keep him on the Green. They took him to the pond and tried to make him swim, which he could not do, and the whole affair was very disturbing to all quiet and peaceable fowls. After which another man came, and preached sermons on the Green, and a great many people went to hear him; for those were "trying times," and folk ran hither and thither for comfort. And then what did they do but drill the ploughboys on the Green, to get them ready to fight the French, and teach them the goose-step! However, that came to an end at last; for Bony was sent to St. Helena, and the ploughboys were sent back to the plough.

Everybody lived in fear of Bony in those days, especially the naughty children, who were kept in order during the day by threats of "Bony shall have you," and who had nightmares about him in the dark. They thought he was an Ogre in a cocked hat. The Gray Goose thought he was a Fox, and that all the men of England were going out in red coats to hunt him. It was no use to argue the point; for she had a very small head, and when one idea got into it there was no room for another.

Besides, the Gray Goose never saw Bony, nor did the children, which rather spoilt the terror of him, so that the Black Captain became more effective as a Bogy with hardened offenders. The Gray Goose remembered *his* coming to the place perfectly. What he came for she did not pretend to know. It was all part and parcel of the war and bad times. He was called the Black Captain, partly because of himself and partly because of his wonderful black mare. Strange stories were afloat of how far and how fast that mare could go when her master's hand was on her mane and he whispered in her ear. Indeed, some people thought we might reckon ourselves very lucky if we were not out of the frying-pan into the fire, and had not got a certain well-known Gentleman of the Road to protect us against the French. But that, of course, made him none the less useful to the Johnsons' Nurse when the little Miss Johnsons were naughty.

"You leave off crying this minnit, Miss Jane, or I'll give you right away to that horrid wicked officer. Jemima! just look out o' the windy, if you please, and see if the Black Cap'n's a-coming with his horse to carry away Miss Jane."

And there, sure enough, the Black Captain strode by, with his sword clattering as if it did not know whose head to cut off first. But he did not call for Miss Jane that time. He went on to the Green, where he came so suddenly upon the eldest Master Johnson, sitting in a puddle on purpose, in his new nankeen skeleton suit, that the young gentleman thought judgment had overtaken him at last, and abandoned himself to the howlings of despair. His howls were redoubled when he was clutched from behind and swung over the Black Captain's shoulder; but in five minutes his tears were stanched, and he was playing with the officer's accouterments. All of which the Gray Goose saw with her own eyes, and heard afterwards that that bad boy had been whining to go back to the Black Captain ever since, which showed how hardened he was, and that nobody but Bonaparte himself could be expected to do him any good.

But those were "trying times." It was bad enough when the pickle of a large and respectable family cried for the Black Captain; when it came to the little Miss Jessamine crying for him, one felt that the sooner the French landed and had done with it, the better.

The big Miss Jessamine's objection to him was that he was a soldier; and this prejudice was shared by all the Green. "A soldier," as the speaker from the town had observed, "is a blood-thirsty, unsettled sort of a rascal, that the peaceable, home-loving, bread-winning citizen can never conscientiously look on as a brother till he has beaten his sword into a ploughshare and his spear into a pruning-hook."

On the other hand, there was some truth in what the Postman (an old soldier) said in reply—that the sword has to cut a way for us out of many a scrape into which our bread-winners get us when they drive their ploughshares into fallows that don't belong to them. Indeed, whilst our most peaceful citizens were prosperous chiefly by means of cotton, of sugar, and of the rise and fall of the money-market (not to speak of such salable matters as opium, firearms, and "black ivory"), disturbances were apt to arise in India, Africa, and other outlandish parts, where the fathers of our domestic race were making fortunes for their families. And for that matter, even on the Green, we did not wish the military to leave us in the lurch, so long as there was any fear that the French were coming.

To let the Black Captain have little Miss Jessamine, however, was another matter. Her aunt would not hear of it; and then, to crown all, it appeared that the Captain's father did not think the young lady good enough for his son. Never was any affair more clearly brought to a conclusion.

But those were "trying times"; and one moonlight night, when the Gray Goose was sound asleep upon one leg, the Green was rudely shaken under her by the thud of a horse's feet. "Ga, ga!" said she, putting down the other leg and running away.

By the time she returned to her place not a thing was to be seen or heard. The horse had passed like a shot. But next day there was hurrying and skurrying and cackling at a very early hour, all about the white house with the black beams, where Miss Jessamine lived. And when the sun was so low and the shadows so long on the grass that the Gray Goose felt ready to run away at the sight of her own neck, little Miss Jane Johnson and her "particular friend" Clarinda sat under the big oak tree on the Green, and Jane pinched Clarinda's little finger till she found that she could keep a secret, and then she told her in confidence that she had heard from Nurse and Jemima that Miss Jessamine's niece had been a very naughty girl, and that that horrid wicked officer had come for her on his black horse and carried her right away.

"Will she never come back?" asked Clarinda.

"Oh, no!" said Jane, decidedly. "Bony never brings people back."

"Not never no more?" sobbed Clarinda, for she was weak-minded, and could not bear to think that Bony never, never let naughty people go home again.

Next day Jane had heard more.

"He has taken her to a Green."

"A Goose Green?" asked Clarinda.

"No. A Gretna Green. Don't ask so many questions, child," said Jane, who, having no more to tell, gave herself airs.

Jane was wrong on one point. Miss Jessamine's niece did come back, and she and her husband were forgiven. The Gray Goose remembered it well; it was Michaelmas-tide, the Michaelmas before the Michaelmas before the Michaelmas—but, ga ga! What does the date matter? It was autumn, harvest-time, and everybody was so busy prophesying and praying about the crops, that the young couple wandered through the lanes, and got blackberries for Miss Jessamine's celebrated crab and blackberry jam, and made guys of themselves with bryony-wreaths, and not a soul troubled his head about them, except the children and the Postman. The children dogged the Black Captain's footsteps (his bubble reputation as an Ogre having burst), clamoring for a ride on the black mare. And the Postman would go somewhat out of his postal way to catch the Captain's dark eye, and show that he had not forgotten how to salute an officer.

But they were "trying times." One afternoon the black mare was stepping gently up and down the grass, with her head at her master's shoulder, and as many children crowded on to her silky back as if she had been an elephant in a menagerie; and the next afternoon she

carried him away, sword and *sabre-tache* clattering war music at her side, and the old Postman waiting for them, rigid with salutation, at the four cross-roads.

War and bad times! It was a hard winter; and the big Miss Jessamine and the little Miss Jessamine (but she was Mrs. Black-Cap-

145

tain now) lived very economically, that they might help their poorer neighbors. They neither entertained nor went into company; but the young lady always went up the village as far as the *George and Dragon,* for air and exercise, when the London Mail [Coach] came in.

One day (it was a day in the following June) it came in earlier than usual, and the young lady was not there to meet it.

But a crowd soon gathered round the *George and Dragon,* gaping to see the Mail Coach dressed with flowers and oak-leaves, and the guard wearing a laurel wreath over and above his royal livery. The ribbons that decked the horses were stained and flecked with the warmth and foam of the pace at which they had come, for they had pressed on with the news of Victory.

Miss Jessamine was sitting with her niece under the oak tree on the Green, when the Postman put a newspaper silently into her hand. Her niece turned quickly—

"Is there news?"

"Don't agitate yourself, my dear," said her aunt. "I will read it aloud, and then we can enjoy it together: a far more comfortable method, my love, than when you go up to the village, and come home out of breath, having snatched half the news as you run."

"I am all attention, dear aunt," said the little lady, clasping her hands tightly on her lap.

Then Miss Jessamine read aloud—she was proud of her reading—and the old soldier stood at attention behind her, with such a blending of pride and pity on his face as it was strange to see:—

> "DOWNING STREET,
> "*June* 22, 1815, 1 A. M."

"That's one in the morning," gasped the Postman; "beg your pardon, mum."

But though he apologized, he could not refrain from echoing here and there a weighty word: "Glorious victory"—"Two hundred pieces of artillery"—"Immense quantity of ammunition"—and so forth.

"The loss of the British Army upon this occasion has unfortunately been most severe. It had not been possible to make out a return of the killed and wounded when Major Percy left headquarters. The names of the officers killed and wounded, as far as they can be collected, are annexed.

"I have the honor—"

"The list, aunt! Read the list!"

"My love—my darling—let us go in and—"

"No. Now! now!"

To one thing the supremely afflicted are entitled in their sorrow —to be obeyed; and yet it is the last kindness that people commonly will do them. But Miss Jessamine did. Steadying her voice as best she might, she read on; and the old soldier stood bareheaded to hear that first Roll of the Dead at Waterloo, which began with the Duke of Brunswick and ended with Ensign Brown. Five-and-thirty British Captains fell asleep that day on the Bed of Honor, and the Black Captain slept among them.

· · ·

There are killed and wounded by war, of whom no returns reach Downing Street.

Three days later, the Captain's wife had joined him, and Miss Jessamine was kneeling by the cradle of their orphan son, a purple-red morsel of humanity, with conspicuously golden hair.

"Will he live, Doctor?"

"Live? God bless my soul, ma'am! Look at him! The young Jackanapes!"

II: TWO YELLOW THINGS

The Gray Goose remembered quite well the year that Jackanapes began to walk, for it was the year that the speckled hen for the first time in all her motherly life got out of patience when she was sitting. She had been rather proud of the eggs—they were unusually large—but she never felt quite comfortable on them; and whether it was because she used to get cramp and go off the nest, or because the season was bad, or what, she never could tell; but every egg was addled but one, and the one that did hatch gave her more trouble than any chick she had ever reared.

It was a fine, downy, bright yellow little thing, but it had a monstrous big nose and feet, and such an ungainly walk as she knew no other instance of in her well-bred and high-stepping family. And as to behavior, it was not that it was either quarrelsome or moping, but simply unlike the rest. When the other chicks hopped and cheeped on the Green about their mother's feet, this solitary yellow brat went waddling off on its own responsibility, and do or cluck what the speckled hen would, it went to play in the pond.

It was off one day as usual, and the hen was fussing and fuming after it, when the Postman, going to deliver a letter at Miss Jessamine's door, was nearly knocked over by the good lady herself, who, bursting out of the house with her cap just off and her bonnet just not on, fell into his arms, crying—

"Baby! Baby! Jackanapes! Jackanapes!"

If the Postman loved anything on earth, he loved the Captain's yellow-haired child; so, propping Miss Jessamine against her own door-post, he followed the direction of her trembling fingers and made for the Green.

Jackanapes had had the start of the Postman by nearly ten minutes. The world—the round green world with an oak tree on it—was just becoming very interesting to him. He had tried, vigorously but

ineffectually, to mount a passing pig, the last time he was taken out walking; but then he was encumbered with a nurse. Now he was his own master, and might, by courage and energy, become the master of that delightful downy, dumpy, yellow thing that was bobbing along over the green grass in front of him. Forward! Charge! He aimed well, and grabbed it, but only to feel the delicious downiness and dumpiness slipping through his fingers as he fell upon his face. "Quawk!" said the yellow thing, and wabbled off sideways. It was this oblique movement that enabled Jackanapes to come up with it, for it was bound for the pond, and therefore obliged to come back into line. He failed again from top-heaviness, and his prey escaped sideways as before, and, as before, lost ground in getting back to the direct road to the pond.

And at the pond the Postman found them both—one yellow thing rocking safely on the ripples that lie beyond duck-weed, and the other washing his draggled frock with tears because he, too, had tried to sit upon the pond and it wouldn't hold him.

III: THE FAIR AND THE RED-HAIRED PONY

Young Mrs. Johnson, who was a mother of many, hardly knew which to pity more—Miss Jessamine for having her little ways and her antimacassars rumpled by a young Jackanapes, or the boy himself for being brought up by an old maid.

Oddly enough, she would probably have pitied neither, had Jackanapes been a girl. (One is so apt to think that what works smoothest, works to the highest ends, having no patience for the results of friction.) That father in God who bade the young men to be pure and the maidens brave, greatly disturbed a member of his congregation, who thought that the great preacher had made a slip of the tongue.

"That the girls should have purity, and the boys courage, is what you would say, good father?"

"Nature has done that," was the reply; "I meant what I said."

In good sooth, a young maid is all the better for learning some robuster virtues than maidenliness and not to move the antimacassars; and the robuster virtues require some fresh air and freedom. As, on the other hand, Jackanapes (who had a boy's full share of the little beast and the young monkey in his natural composition) was none the worse, at his tender years, for learning some maidenliness—so far as maidenliness means decency, pity, unselfishness, and pretty behavior.

And it is due to him to say that he was an obedient boy, and a boy whose word could be depended on, long before his grandfather the General came to live at the Green.

He was obedient; that is, he did what his great-aunt told him. But—oh, dear! oh, dear!—the pranks he played, which it had never entered into her head to forbid!

It was when he had just been put into skeletons (frocks never suited him) that he became very friendly with Master Tony Johnson, a younger brother of the young gentleman who sat in the puddle on purpose. Tony was not enterprising, and Jackanapes led him by the nose. One summer's evening they were out late, and Miss Jessamine was becoming anxious, when Jackanapes presented himself with a ghastly face all besmirched with tears. He was unusually subdued.

"I'm afraid," he sobbed—"if you please, I'm very much afraid that Tony Johnson's dying in the churchyard."

Miss Jessamine was just beginning to be distracted, when she smelt Jackanapes. "You naughty, naughty boys! Do you mean to tell me that you've been smoking?"

"Not pipes," urged Jackanapes; "upon my honor, aunty, not pipes. Only cigars like Mr. Johnson's! and only made of brown paper with a very, very little tobacco from the shop inside them."

Whereupon Miss Jessamine sent a servant to the churchyard, who found Tony Johnson lying on a tombstone, very sick, and having ceased to entertain any hopes of his own recovery.

If it could be possible that any "unpleasantness" could arise between two such amiable neighbors as Miss Jessamine and Mrs. Johnson, and if the still more incredible paradox can be that ladies may differ over a point on which they are agreed, that point was the admitted fact that Tony Johnson was "delicate"; and the difference lay chiefly in this: Mrs. Johnson said that Tony was delicate—meaning that he was more finely strung, more sensitive, a properer subject for pampering and petting than Jackanapes, and that, consequently, Jackanapes was to blame for leading Tony into scrapes which resulted in his being chilled, frightened, or (most frequently) sick. But when Miss Jessamine said that Tony Johnson was delicate, she meant that he was more puling, less manly, and less healthily brought up than Jackanapes, who, when they got into mischief together, was certainly not to blame because his friend could not get wet, sit a kicking donkey, ride in the giddy-go-round, bear the noise of a cracker, or smoke brown paper with impunity, as he could.

Not that there was ever the slightest quarrel between the ladies. It never even came near it, except the day after Tony had been so very sick with riding Bucephalus in the giddy-go-round. Mrs. Johnson had explained to Miss Jessamine that the reason Tony was so easily upset was the unusual sensitiveness (as a doctor had explained it to her) of the nervous centers in her family—"Fiddlestick!" So Mrs. Johnson understood Miss Jessamine to say; but it appeared that she only said "Treaclestick?" which is quite another thing, and of which Tony was undoubtedly fond.

It was at the Fair that Tony was made ill by riding on Bucephalus. Once a year the Goose Green became the scene of a carnival. First of all, carts and caravans were rumbling up all along, day and night. Jackanapes could hear them as he lay in bed, and could hardly sleep for speculating what booths and whirligigs he should find fairly established when he and his dog Spitfire went out after breakfast. As a matter of fact, he seldom had to wait so long for news of the Fair. The Postman knew the window out of which Jackanapes' yellow head would come, and was ready with his report.

"Royal Theayter, Master Jackanapes, in the old place, but be careful o' them seats, sir; they're rickettier than ever. Two sweets and a ginger beer under the oak tree, and the Flying Boats is just a-coming along the road."

No doubt it was partly because he had already suffered severely in the Flying Boats that Tony collapsed so quickly in the giddy-go-round. He only mounted Bucephalus (who was spotted, and had no tail) because Jackanapes urged him, and held out the ingenious hope that the round-and-round feeling would very likely cure the up-and-down sensation. It did not however, and Tony tumbled off during the first revolution.

Jackanapes was not absolutely free from qualms; but having once mounted the Black Prince, he stuck to him as a horseman should. During the first round he waved his hat, and observed with some concern that the Black Prince had lost an ear since last Fair; at the second, he looked a little pale, but sat upright, though somewhat unnecessarily rigid; at the third round he shut his eyes. During the fourth his hat fell off, and he clasped his horse's neck. By the fifth he had laid his yellow head against the Black Prince's mane, and so clung anyhow till the hobby-horses stopped, when the proprietor assisted him to alight, and he sat down rather suddenly and said he had enjoyed it very much.

The Gray Goose always ran away at the first approach of the caravans, and never came back to the Green till there was nothing left of the Fair but footmarks and oyster-shells. Running away was her pet principle; the only system, she maintained, by which you can live long and easily and lose nothing. If you run away when you see danger, you can come back when all is safe. Run quickly, return slowly, hold your head high, and gabble as loud as you can, and you'll preserve the respect of the Goose Green to a peaceful old age. Why should you struggle and get hurt, if you can lower your head and swerve, and not lose a feather? Why in the world should anyone spoil the pleasure of life, or risk his skin, if he can help it?

" 'What's the use?'
Said the Goose."

Before answering which one might have to consider what world, which life, and whether his skin were a goose-skin; but the Gray Goose's head would never have held all that.

Grass soon grows over footprints, and the village children took the oyster-shells to trim their gardens with; but the year after Tony rode Bucephalus there lingered another relic of Fair-time in which Jackanapes was deeply interested. "The Green" proper was originally only part of a straggling common, which in its turn merged into some wilder waste land where gypsies sometimes squatted if the authorities would allow them, especially after the annual Fair. And it was after the Fair that Jackanapes, out rambling by himself, was knocked over by the Gypsy's son riding the Gypsy's red-haired pony at breakneck pace across the common.

Jackanapes got up and shook himself, none the worse except for being heels over head in love with the red-haired pony. What a rate he went at! How he spurned the ground with his nimble feet! How his red coat shone in the sunshine! And what bright eyes peeped out of his dark forelock as it was blown by the wind!

The Gypsy boy had had a fright, and he was willing enough to reward Jackanapes for not having been hurt, by consenting to let him have a ride.

"Do you mean to kill the little fine gentleman, and swing us all on the gibbet, you rascal?" screamed the Gypsy mother, who came up just as Jackanapes and the pony set off.

"He would get on," replied her son. "It'll not kill him. He'll fall on his yellow head, and it's as tough as a cocoanut."

But Jackanapes did not fall. He stuck to the red-haired pony as he had stuck to the hobby-horse; but, oh, how different the delight of this wild gallop with flesh and blood! Just as his legs were beginning to feel as if he did not feel them, the Gypsy boy cried, "Lollo!"

Round went the pony so unceremoniously that with as little ceremony Jackanapes clung to his neck; and he did not properly recover
himself before Lollo stopped with a jerk at the place where they had
started.

"Is his name Lollo?" asked Jackanapes, his hand lingering in the
wiry mane.

"Yes."

"What does Lollo mean?"

"Red."

"Is Lollo your pony?"

"No. My father's." And the Gypsy boy led Lollo away.

At the first opportunity Jackanapes stole away again to the common. This time he saw the Gypsy father, smoking a dirty pipe.

"Lollo is your pony, isn't he?" said Jackanapes.

"Yes."

"He's a very nice one."

"He's a racer."

"You don't want to sell him, do you?"

"Fifteen pounds," said the Gypsy father; and Jackanapes sighed
and went home again. That very afternoon he and Tony rode the
two donkeys; and Tony managed to get thrown, and even Jackanapes' donkey kicked. But it was jolting, clumsy work after
the elastic swiftness and the dainty mischief of the red-haired
pony.

A few days later, Miss Jessamine spoke very seriously to Jackanapes. She was a good deal agitated as she told him that his grandfather the General was coming to the Green, and that he must be
on his very best behavior during the visit. If it had been feasible to
leave off calling him Jackanapes and to get used to his baptismal
name of Theodore before the day after tomorrow (when the General

was due), it would have been satisfactory. But Miss Jessamine feared it would be impossible in practice, and she had scruples about it on principle. It would not seem quite truthful, although she had always most fully intended that he should be called Theodore when he had outgrown the ridiculous appropriateness of his nickname. The fact was that he had not outgrown it, but he must take care to remember who was meant when his grandfather said Theodore.

Indeed, for that matter he must take care all along.

"You are apt to be giddy, Jackanapes," said Miss Jessamine.

"Yes, aunt," said Jackanapes, thinking of the hobby-horses.

"You are a good boy, Jackanapes. Thank God, I can tell your grandfather that. An obedient boy, an honorable boy, and a kind-hearted boy. But you are—in short, you *are* a Boy, Jackanapes. And I hope," added Miss Jessamine, desperate with the results of experience, "that the General knows that Boys will be Boys."

What mischief could be foreseen, Jackanapes promised to guard against. He was to keep his clothes and his hands clean, to look over his catechism, not to put sticky things in his pockets, to keep that hair of his smooth ("It's the wind that blows it, aunty," said Jackanapes—"I'll send by the coach for some bear's-grease," said Miss Jessamine, tying a knot in her pocket-handkerchief), not to burst in at the parlor door, not to talk at the top of his voice, not to crumple his Sunday frill, and to sit quite quiet during the sermon, to be sure to say "sir" to the General, to be careful about rubbing his shoes on the door-mat, and to bring his lesson-books to his aunt at once that she might iron down the dogs'-ears. The General arrived; and for the first day all went well, except that Jackanapes' hair was as wild as usual, for the hair-dresser had no bear's-grease left. He began to feel more at ease with his grandfather, and disposed to talk confidentially with him, as he did with the Postman. All that the General felt, it would take too long to tell; but the result was the same. He was disposed to talk confidentially with Jackanapes.

"Mons'ous pretty place this," he said, looking out of the lattice

on to the Green, where the grass was vivid with sunset and the shadows were long and peaceful.

"You should see it in Fair-week, sir," said Jackanapes, shaking his yellow mop, and leaning back in his one of the two Chippendale arm-chairs in which they sat.

"A fine time that, eh?" said the General, with a twinkle in his left eye (the other was glass).

Jackanapes shook his hair once more. "I enjoyed this last one the best of all," he said. "I'd so much money."

"By George, it's not a common complaint in these bad times. How much had ye?"

"I'd two shillings. A new shilling aunty gave me, and elevenpence I had saved up, and a penny from the Postman—*sir!*" added Jackanapes with a jerk, having forgotten it.

"And how did ye spend it—*sir?*" inquired the General.

Jackanapes spread his ten fingers on the arms of his chair, and shut his eyes that he might count the more conscientiously.

"Watch-stand for aunty, threepence. Trumpet for myself, twopence; that's fivepence. Gingernuts for Tony, twopence, and a mug with a Grenadier on for the Postman, fourpence; that's elevenpence. Shooting-gallery, a penny; that's a shilling. Giddy-go-round, a penny; that's one and a penny. Treating Tony, one and twopence. Flying Boats (Tony paid for himself), a penny, one and threepence. Shooting-gallery again, one and fourpence; Fat Woman, a penny, one and fivepence. Giddy-go-round again, one and sixpence. Shooting-gallery, one and sevenpence. Treating Tony, and then he would n't shoot, so I did, one and eightpence. Living Skeleton, a penny—no, Tony treated me, the Living Skeleton does n't count. Skittles, a penny, one and ninepence. Mermaid (but when we got inside she was dead), a penny, one and tenpence. Theater, a penny (Priscilla Partington, or the Green Lane Murder. A beautiful young lady, sir, with pink cheeks and a real pistol); that's one and elevenpence. Ginger beer, a penny (I *was* so thirsty!) two shillings. And then the Shooting-gallery man gave me a turn for nothing, because, he said, I was a real gentleman, and spent my money like a man."

"So you do, sir, so you do!" cried the General. "Egad, sir, you spent it like a prince. And now I suppose you've not got a penny in your pocket?"

"Yes, I have," said Jackanapes. "Two pennies. They are saving up." And Jackanapes jingled them with his hand.

"You don't want money except at Fair-times, I suppose?" said the General.

Jackanapes shook his mop.

"If I could have as much as I want, I should know what to buy," said he.

"And how much do you want, if you could get it?"

"Wait a minute, sir, till I think what twopence from fifteen pounds leaves. Two from nothing you can't, but borrow twelve. Two from twelve, ten, and carry one. Please remember ten, sir, when I ask you. One from nothing you can't, borrow twenty. One from twenty, nineteen, and carry one. One from fifteen, fourteen. Fourteen pounds nineteen and—what did I tell you to remember?"

"Ten," said the General.

"Fourteen pounds nineteen shillings and tenpence, then, is what I want," said Jackanapes.

"God bless my soul! what for?"

"To buy Lollo with. Lollo means red, sir. The Gypsy's red-haired pony, sir. Oh, he *is* beautiful! You should see his coat in the sunshine! You should see his mane! You should see his tail! Such little feet, sir, and they go like lightning! Such a dear face, too, and eyes like a mouse! But he's a racer, and the Gypsy wants fifteen pounds for him."

"If he's a racer you couldn't ride him. Could you?"

"No—o, sir, but I can stick to him. I did the other day."

"The dooce you did! Well, I'm fond of riding myself; and if the beast is as good as you say, he might suit me."

"You're too tall for Lollo, I think," said Jackanapes, measuring his grandfather with his eye.

"I can double up my legs, I suppose. We'll have a look at him tomorrow."

"Don't you weigh a good deal?" asked Jackanapes.

"Chiefly waistcoats," said the General, slapping the breast of his military frock-coat. "We'll have the little racer on the Green the first thing in the morning. Glad you mentioned it, grandson; glad you mentioned it."

The General was as good as his word. Next morning the Gypsy and Lollo, Miss Jessamine, Jackanapes and his grandfather and his dog Spitfire, were all gathered at one end of the Green in a group, which so aroused the innocent curiosity of Mrs. Johnson, as she saw it from one of her upper windows, that she and the children took their early promenade rather earlier than usual. The General talked to the Gypsy, and Jackanapes fondled Lollo's mane, and did not know whether he should be more glad or miserable if his grandfather bought him.

"Jackanapes!"

"Yes, sir!"

"I've bought Lollo, but I believe you were right. He hardly stands high enough for me. If you can ride him to the other end of the Green, I'll give him to you."

How Jackanapes tumbled on to Lollo's back he never knew. He had just gathered up the reins when the Gypsy father took him by the arm.

"If you want to make Lollo go fast, my little gentleman—"

"*I* can make him go!" said Jackanapes; and drawing from his pocket the trumpet he had bought in the Fair, he blew a blast both loud and shrill.

Away went Lollo, and away went Jackanapes' hat. His golden hair flew out, an aureole from which his cheeks shone red and distended with trumpeting. Away went Spitfire, mad with the rapture of the race and the wind in his silky ears. Away went the geese, the cocks, the hens, and the whole family of Johnson. Lucy clung to her mamma, Jane saved Emily by the gathers of her gown, and Tony saved himself by a somersault.

The Gray Goose was just returning when Jackanapes and Lollo rode back, Spitfire panting behind.

"Good, my little gentleman, good!" said the Gypsy. "You were born to the saddle. You've the flat thigh, the strong knee, the wiry back, and the light caressing hand; all you want is to learn the whisper. Come here!"

"What was that dirty fellow talking about, grandson?" asked the General.

"I can't tell you, sir. It's a secret."

They were sitting in the window again, in the two Chippendale arm-chairs, the General devouring every line of his grandson's face, with strange spasms crossing his own.

"You must love your aunt very much, Jackanapes?"

"I do, sir," said Jackanapes, warmly.

"And whom do you love next best to your aunt?"

The ties of blood were pressing very strongly on the General him-self, and perhaps he thought of Lollo. But love is not bought in a day, even with fourteen pounds nineteen shillings and tenpence. Jack-anapes answered quite readily, "The Postman."

"Why the Postman?"

"He knew my father," said Jackanapes, "and he tells me about him and about his black mare. My father was a soldier, a brave soldier. He died at Waterloo. When I grow up I want to be a soldier, too."

"So you shall, my boy; so you shall."

"Thank you, grandfather. Aunty does n't want me to be a soldier, for fear of being killed."

"Bless my life! Would she have you get into a feather-bed and stay there? Why, you might be killed by a thunderbolt if you were a butter-merchant!"

"So I might. I shall tell her so. What a funny fellow you are, sir! I say, do you think my father knew the Gypsy's secret? The Postman says he used to whisper to his black mare."

"Your father was taught to ride, as a child, by one of those horse-men of the East who swoop and dart and wheel about a plain like swallows in autumn. Grandson! love me a little, too. I can tell you more about your father than the Postman can."

"I do love you," said Jackanapes. "Before you came I was fright-ened. I'd no notion you were so nice."

"Love me always, boy, whatever I do or leave undone. And—God help me!—whatever you do or leave undone, I'll love you. There shall never be a cloud between us for a day; no, sir, not for an hour. We're imperfect enough, all of us—we need n't be so bitter; and life is uncertain enough at its safest—we need n't waste its opportunities.

God bless my soul! Here sit I, after a dozen battles and some of the worst climates in the world, and by yonder lych gate lies your mother, who didn't move five miles, I suppose, from your aunt's apron-strings—dead in her teens; my golden-haired daughter, whom I never saw!" Jackanapes was terribly troubled.

"Don't cry, Grandfather," he pleaded, his own blue eyes round with tears. "I will love you very much, and I will try to be very good. But I should like to be a soldier."

"You shall, my boy; you shall. You've more claims for a commission than you know of. Cavalry, I suppose, eh; the young Jackanapes? Well, well; if you live to be an honor to your country, this old heart shall grow young again with pride for you; and if you die in the service of your country—egad, sir, it can but break for ye!"

And beating the region which he said was all waistcoats, as if they stifled him, the old man got up and strode out on to the Green.

IV: A RIDE FOR LIFE

Twenty and odd years later the Gray Goose was still alive, and in full possession of her faculties, such as they were. She lived slowly and carefully, and she lived long. So did Miss Jessamine; but the General was dead.

He had lived on the Green for many years, during which he and the Postman saluted each other with a punctiliousness that it almost drilled one to witness. He would have completely spoiled Jackanapes if Miss Jessamine's conscience would have let him; otherwise he somewhat dragooned his neighbors, and was as positive about parish matters as a ratepayer about the army. A stormy-tempered, tender-hearted soldier, irritable with the suffering of wounds of which he never spoke, whom all the village followed to his grave with tears.

The General's death was a great shock to Miss Jessamine, and her nephew stayed with her for some little time after the funeral. Then he was obliged to join his regiment, which was ordered abroad.

One effect of the conquest which the General had gained over the affections of the village was a considerable abatement of the popular prejudice against "the military." Indeed, the village was now somewhat importantly represented in the army. There was the General himself, and the Postman, and the Black Captain's tablet in the church, and Jackanapes, and Tony Johnson, and a Trumpeter.

Tony Johnson had no more natural taste for fighting than for riding, but he was as devoted as ever to Jackanapes. And that was how it came about that Mr. Johnson bought him a commission in the same cavalry regiment that the General's grandson (whose commission had been given him by the Iron Duke) was in; and that he was quite content to be the butt of the mess where Jackanapes was the hero; and that when Jackanapes wrote home to Miss Jessamine, Tony wrote with the same purpose to his mother—namely, to demand her congratulations that they were on active service at last, and were ordered to the front. And he added a postscript, to the effect that she could have no idea how popular Jackanapes was, nor how splendidly he rode the wonderful red charger which he had named after his old friend Lollo.

·   ·   ·

"Sound Retire!"

A Boy Trumpeter, grave with the weight of responsibilities and accouterments beyond his years, and stained so that his own mother would not have known him, with the sweat and dust of battle, did as he was bid; and then, pushing his trumpet pettishly aside, adjusted

his weary legs for the hundredth time to the horse which was a world too big for him, and muttering, "'Tain't a pretty tune," tried to see something of this his first engagement before it came to an end.

Being literally in the thick of it, he could hardly have seen less or known less of what happened in that particular skirmish if he had been at home in England. For many good reasons—including dust and smoke, and that what attention he dared distract from his commanding officer was pretty well absorbed by keeping his hard-mouthed troop-horse in hand, under pain of execration by his neighbors, in the *mêlée*. By and by, when the newspapers came out, if he could get a look at one before it was thumbed to bits, he would learn that the enemy had appeared from ambush in overwhelming numbers, and that orders had been given to fall back, which was done slowly and in good order, the men fighting as they retired.

Born and bred on the Goose Green, the youngest of Mr. Johnson's gardener's numerous offspring, the boy had given his family "no peace" till they let him "go for a soldier" with Master Tony and Master Jackanapes. They consented at last, with more tears than they shed when an older son was sent to jail for poaching; and the boy was perfectly happy in his life, and full of *esprit de corps*. It was this which had been wounded by having to sound retreat for "the young gentlemen's regiment," the first time he served with it before the enemy; and he was also harassed by having completely lost sight of Master Tony. There had been some hard fighting before the backward movement began, and he had caught sight of him once, but not since. On the other hand, all the pulses of his village pride had been stirred by one or two visions of Master Jackanapes whirling about on his wonderful horse. He had been easy to distinguish, since an eccentric blow had bared his head without hurting it; for his close golden mop of hair gleamed in the hot sunshine as brightly as the steel of the sword flashing round it.

Of the missiles that fell pretty thickly, the Boy Trumpeter did not take much notice. First, one can't attend to everything, and his hands were full; secondly, one gets used to anything; thirdly, experience soon teaches one, in spite of proverbs, how very few bullets find their billet. Far more unnerving is the mere suspicion of fear or even of anxiety in the human mass around you. The Boy was beginning to wonder if there were any dark reason for the increasing pressure, and whether they would be allowed to move back more quickly, when the smoke in front lifted for a moment, and he could see the plain, and the enemy's line some two hundreds yards away. And across the plain between them, he saw Master Jackanapes galloping alone at the top of Lollo's speed, their faces to the enemy, his golden head at Lollo's ear.

But at this moment noise and smoke seemed to burst out on every side; the officer shouted to him to sound Retire! and between trumpeting and bumping about on his horse, he saw and heard no more of the incidents of his first battle.

Tony Johnson was always unlucky with horses, from the days of the giddy-go-round onward. On this day—of all days in the year—his own horse was on the sick list, and he had to ride an inferior, ill-conditioned beast, and fell off that, at the very moment when it was a matter of life or death to be able to ride away. The horse fell on him, but struggled up again, and Tony managed to keep hold of it. It was in trying to remount that he discovered, by helplessness and anguish, that one of his legs was crushed and broken, and that no feat of which he was master would get him into the saddle. Not able even to stand alone, awkwardly, agonizingly, unable to mount his restive horse, his life was yet so strong within him! And on one side of him rolled the dust and smoke-cloud of his advancing foes, and on the other, that which covered his retreating friends.

He turned one piteous gaze after them, with a bitter twinge, not of reproach, but of loneliness; and then, dragging himself up by the side of his horse, he turned the other way and drew out his pistol, and waited for the end. Whether he waited seconds or minutes he never knew, before some one gripped him by the arm.

"*Jackanapes! God bless you!* It's my left leg. If you *could* get me on—"

It was like Tony's luck that his pistol went off at his horse's tail, and made it plunge; but Jackanapes threw him across the saddle.

"Hold on anyhow, and stick your spur in. I'll lead him. Keep your head down; they're firing high."

And Jackanapes laid his head down—to Lollo's ear.

It was when they were fairly off, that a sudden upspringing of the enemy in all directions had made it necessary to change the gradual retirement of our force into as rapid a retreat as possible. And

when Jackanapes became aware of this, and felt the lagging and swerving of Tony's horse, he began to wish he had thrown his friend across his own saddle and left their lives to Lollo.

When Tony became aware of it, several things came into his head: 1. That the dangers of their ride for life were now more than doubled; 2. That if Jackanapes and Lollo were not burdened with him they would undoubtedly escape; 3. That Jackanapes' life was infinitely valuable, and his—Tony's—was not; 4. That this, if he could seize it, was the supremest of all the moments in which he had tried to assume the virtues which Jackanapes had by nature; and that if he could be courageous and unselfish now—

He caught at his own reins and spoke very loud—

"Jackanapes! It won't do. You and Lollo must go on. Tell the fellows I gave you back to them with all my heart. Jackanapes, if you love me, leave me!"

There was a daffodil light over the evening sky in front of them, and it shone strangely on Jackanapes' hair and face. He turned with an odd look in his eyes that a vainer man than Tony Johnson might have taken for brotherly pride. Then he shook his mop, and laughed at him.

"*Leave you?* To save my skin? No, Tony, not to save my soul!"

V: SO HE PASSED OVER TO THE OTHER SIDE

Coming out of a hospital tent, at headquarters, the surgeon cannoned against, and rebounded from, another officer—a sallow man, not young, with a face worn more by ungentle experiences than by age, with weary eyes that kept their own counsel, iron-gray hair, and a mustache that was as if a raven had laid its wing cross his lips and sealed them.

"Well?"

"Beg pardon, Major. Didn't see you. Oh, compound fracture and bruises. But it's all right; he'll pull through."

"Thank God."

It was probably an involuntary expression; for prayer and praise were not much in the Major's line, as a jerk of the surgeon's head would have betrayed to an observer. He was a bright little man, with his feelings showing all over him, but with gallantry and contempt of death enough for both sides of his profession; who took a cool head, a white handkerchief, and a case of instruments, where other men went hot-blooded with weapons, and who was the biggest gossip, male or female, of the regiment. Not even the Major's taciturnity daunted him.

"Didn't think he'd as much pluck about him as he has. He'll do all right if he doesn't fret himself into a fever about poor Jackanapes."

"Whom are you talking about?" asked the Major, hoarsely.

"Young Johnson. He—"

"What about Jackanapes?"

"Don't you know? Sad business. Rode back for Johnson, and brought him in; but, monstrous ill luck, hit as they rode. Left lung—"

"Will he recover?"

"No. Sad business. What a frame—what limbs—what health—and what good looks! Finest young fellow—"

"Where is he?"

"In his own tent," said the surgeon, sadly.

The Major wheeled and left him.

•   •   •

171

"Can I do anything else for you?"

"Nothing, thank you. Except— Major! I wish I could get you to appreciate Johnson."

"This is not an easy moment, Jackanapes."

"Let me tell you, sir—*he* never will—that if he could have driven me from him, he would be lying yonder at this moment, and I should be safe and sound."

The Major laid his hand over his mouth, as if to keep back a wish he would have been ashamed to utter.

"I've known old Tony from a child. He's a fool on impulse, a good man and a gentleman in principle. And he acts on principle, which it's not every— Some water, please! Thank you, sir. It's very hot, and yet one's feet get uncommonly cold. Oh, thank you, thank you. He's no fire-eater, but he has a trained conscience and a tender heart, and he'll do his duty when a braver and more selfish man might fail you. But he wants encouragement; and when I'm gone—"

"He shall have encouragement. You have my word for it. Can I do nothing else?"

"Yes, Major. A favor."

"Thank you, Jackanapes."

"Be Lollo's master, and love him as well as you can. He's used to it."

"Wouldn't you rather Johnson had him?"

The blue eyes twinkled in spite of mortal pain.

"Tony *rides* on principle, Major. His legs are bolsters, and will be to the end of the chapter. I couldn't insult dear Lollo; but if you don't care—"

"While I live—which will be longer than I desire or deserve— Lollo shall want nothing but—you. I have too little tenderness for—

My dear boy, you're faint. Can you spare me for a moment?"

"No, stay— Major!"

"What? What?"

"My head drifts so—if you wouldn't mind."

"Yes! Yes!"

"Say a prayer by me. Out loud, please; I am getting deaf."

"My dearest Jackanapes—my dear boy—"

"One of the Church Prayers—Parade Service, you know—"

"I see. But the fact is—God forgive me, Jackanapes!—I'm a very different sort of fellow to some of you youngsters. Look here, let me fetch—"

But Jackanapes' hand was in his, and it would not let go.

There was a brief and bitter silence.

"'Pon my soul, I can only remember the little one at the end."

"Please," whispered Jackanapes.

Pressed by the conviction that what little he could do it was his duty to do, the Major, kneeling, bared his head, and spoke loudly, clearly, and very reverently—

"The grace of our Lord Jesus Christ—"

Jackanapes moved his left hand to his right one, which still held the Major's—

"The love of God—"

And with that—Jackanapes died.

VI: FAITHFUL LOLLO

Jackanapes' death was sad news for the Goose Green, a sorrow just qualified by honorable pride in his gallantry and devotion. Only the Cobbler dissented; but that was his way. He said he saw nothing in it but foolhardiness and vainglory. They might both have been killed, as easy as not; and then where would ye have been? A man's life was a man's life, and one life was as good as another. No one would catch him throwing his away. And, for that matter, Mrs. Johnson could spare a child a great deal better than Miss Jessamine.

But the parson preached Jackanapes' funeral sermon on the text, "Whosoever will save his life shall lose it, and whosoever will lose his life for my sake shall find it"; and all the village went and wept to hear him.

Nor did Miss Jessamine see her loss from the Cobbler's point of view. On the contrary, Mrs. Johnson said she never to her dying day should forget how, when she went to condole with her, the old lady came forward, with gentlewomanly self-control, and kissed her, and thanked God that her dear nephew's effort had been blessed with success, and that this sad war had made no gap in her friend's large and happy home-circle.

"But she's a noble, unselfish woman," sobbed Mrs. Johnson, "and she taught Jackanapes to be the same; and that's how it is that my

Tony has been spared to me. And it must be sheer goodness in Miss Jessamine, for what can she know of a mother's feeling? And I'm sure most people seem to think that if you've a large family you don't know one from another any more than they do, and that a lot of children are like a lot of store apples—if one's taken it won't be missed."

Lollo—the first Lollo, the Gypsy's Lollo—very aged, draws Miss

Jessamine's bath-chair slowly up and down the Goose Green in the sunshine.

The Ex-postman walks beside him, which Lollo tolerates to the level of his shoulder. If the Postman advances any nearer to his head, Lollo quickens his pace; and were the Postman to persist in the injudicious attempt, there is, as Miss Jessamine says, no knowing what might happen.

In the opinion of the Goose Green, Miss Jessamine has borne her troubles "wonderfully." Indeed, today, some of the less delicate and less intimate of those who see everything from the upper windows say (well, behind her back) that "the old lady seems quite lively with her military beaux again."

The meaning of this is, that Captain Johnson is leaning over one side of her chair, while by the other bends a brother officer who is staying with him, and who has manifested an extraordinary interest in Lollo. He bends lower and lower, and Miss Jessamine calls to the Postman to request Lollo to be kind enough to stop, while she is fumbling for something which always hangs by her side, and has got entangled with her spectacles.

It is a twopenny trumpet, bought years ago in the village fair; and over it she and Captain Johnson tell, as best they can, between them, the story of Jackanapes' ride across the Goose Green; and how he won Lollo—the Gypsy's Lollo—the racer Lollo—dear Lollo—faithful Lollo—Lollo the never vanquished—Lollo the tender servant of his mistress. And Lollo's ears twitch at every mention of his name.

Their hearer does not speak, but he never moves his eyes from the trumpet; and when the tale is told, he lifts Miss Jessamine's hand and presses his heavy black mustache in silence to her trembling fingers.

The sun, setting gently to his rest, embroiders the somber foliage of the oak-tree with threads of gold. The Gray Goose is sensible of an atmosphere of repose, and puts up one leg for the night. The grass glows with a more vivid green, and, in answer to a ringing call from Tony, his sisters fluttering over the daisies in pale-hued muslins, come out of their ever-open door, like pretty pigeons from a dovecote.

And if the good gossips' eyes do not deceive them, all the Miss Johnsons and both the officers go wandering off into the lanes, where bryony wreaths still twine about the brambles.

●　　●　　●

A sorrowful story, and ending badly?

Nay, Jackanapes, for the End is not yet.

A life wasted that might have been useful?

Men who have died for men, in all ages, forgive the thought!

There is a heritage of heroic example and noble obligation, not reckoned in the Wealth of Nations, but essential to a nation's life; the contempt of which, in any people, may, not slowly, mean even its commercial fall. Very sweet are the uses of prosperity, the harvests of peace and progress, the fostering sunshine of health and happiness, and length of days in the land.

But there be things—oh, sons of what has deserved the name of Great Britain, forget it now!—"the good of" which and "the use of" which are beyond all calculation of wordly goods and earthly uses: things such as Love, and Honor, and the Soul of Man, which cannot be bought with a price, and which do not die with death. And they who would fain live happily ever after should not leave these things out of the lessons of their lives.

A MIDSUMMER NIGHT'S
DREAM *of WILLIAM SHAKESPEARE*

Retold by CHARLES
AND MARY LAMB

Illustrations by W. HEATH ROBINSON

THERE was a law in the city of Athens which gave to its citizens the power of compelling their daughters to marry whomsoever they pleased; for upon a daughter's refusing to marry the man her father had chosen to be her husband, the father was empowered by this law to cause her to be put to death; but as fathers do not often desire the death of their own daughters, even though they do happen to prove a little refractory, this law was seldom or never put in execution, though perhaps the young ladies of that city were not unfrequently threatened by their parents with the terrors of it.

There was one instance, however, of an old man, whose name was Egeus, who actually did come before Theseus (at that time the reigning Duke of Athens), to complain that his daughter Hermia, whom he had commanded to marry Demetrius, a young man of a noble Athenian family, refused to obey him, because she loved another young Athenian, named Lysander. Egeus demanded justice of Theseus, and desired that this cruel law might be put in force against his daughter.

Hermia pleaded in excuse for her disobedience, that Demetrius had formerly professed love for her dear friend Helena, and that Helena loved Demetrius to distraction: but this honorable reason which Hermia gave for not obeying her father's command moved not the stern Egeus.

Theseus, though a great and merciful prince, had no power to alter the laws of his country; therefore he could only give Hermia four days to consider of it; and at the end of that time, if she still refused to marry Demetrius, she was to be put to death.

When Hermia was dismissed from the presence of the Duke, she went to her lover Lysander, and told him the peril she was in, and that she must either give him up and marry Demetrius, or lose her life in four days.

Lysander was in great affliction at hearing these evil tidings; but recollecting that he had an aunt who lived at some distance from Athens, and that at the place where she lived the cruel law could not be put in force against Hermia (this law not extending beyond the boundaries of the city), he proposed to Hermia that she should steal out of her father's house that night, and go with him to his aunt's house, where he would marry her.

"I will meet you," said Lysander, "in the wood a few miles without the city; in that delightful wood, where we have so often walked with Helena in the pleasant month of May."

To this proposal Hermia joyfully agreed; and she told no one of her intended flight but her friend Helena. Helena (as maidens will do foolish things for love) very ungenerously resolved to go and tell this to Demetrius, though she could hope no benefit from betraying her friend's secret, but the poor pleasure of following her faithless lover to the wood; for she well knew that Demetrius would go thither in pursuit of Hermia.

The wood, in which Lysander and Hermia proposed to meet, was the favorite haunt of those little beings known by the name of *Fairies*.

Oberon the King, and Titania the Queen, of the Fairies, and all their tiny train of followers, in this wood held their midnight revels.

Between this little King and Queen of sprites there happened, at this time, a sad disagreement; they never met by moonlight in the shady walks of this pleasant wood, but they were quarreling, till all their fairy elves would creep into acorn-cups and hide themselves for fear.

The cause of this unhappy derangement was Titania's refusing to give Oberon a little changeling boy, whose mother had been Titania's friend; and upon her death the fairy Queen stole the child from its nurse, and brought him up in the woods.

The night on which the lovers were to meet in this wood, as Titania was walking with some of her maids of honor, she met Oberon attended by his train of fairy courtiers.

"Ill met by moonlight, proud Titania," said the fairy King.

The Queen replied. "What, jealous Oberon, is it you? Fairies, skip hence; I have forsworn his company."

"Tarry, rash fairy," said Oberon; "am not I thy lord? Why does Titania cross her Oberon? Give me your little changeling boy to be my page."

"Set your heart at rest," answered the Queen; "your whole fairy kingdom buys not the boy of me." She then left her lord in great anger.

"Well, go your way," said Oberon: "before the morning dawns I will torment you for this injury."

Oberon then sent for Puck, his chief favorite and privy counselor.

Puck (or as he was sometimes called, Robin Goodfellow) was a shrewd and knavish sprite, that used to play comical pranks in the neighboring villages; sometimes getting into the butter-churn, and while he was dancing his fantastic shape in the churn, in vain the dairymaid would labor to change her cream into butter: nor had the village swains any better success; whenever Puck chose to play his freaks in the brewing copper, the ale was sure to be spoiled. When a few good neighbors were met to drink some comfortable ale together, Puck would jump into the bowl of ale in the likeness of a roasted crab (an apple), and when some old goody was going to drink, he would bob against her lips, and spill the ale over her withered chin; and presently after, when the same old dame was gravely seating herself to tell her neighbors a sad and melancholy story, Puck would slip her three-legged stool from under her, and down toppled the poor old woman, and then the old gossips would hold their sides

and laugh at her, and swear they never wasted a merrier hour.

"Come hither, Puck," said Oberon to this little merry wanderer of the night; "fetch me the flower which maids call *Love in Idleness;* the juice of that little purple flower laid on the eyelids of those who sleep, will make them, when they awake, dote on the first thing they see. Some of the juice of that flower I will drop on the eyelids of my Titania when she is asleep; and the first thing she looks upon when she opens her eyes she will fall in love with, even though it be a lion or a bear, a meddling monkey, or a busy ape; and before I will take this charm from off her sight, which I can do with another charm I know of, I will make her give me that boy to be my page."

Puck, who loved mischief to his heart, was highly diverted with this intended frolic of his master, and ran to seek the flower; and while Oberon was waiting the return of Puck, he observed Demetrius and Helena enter the wood: he overheard Demetrius reproaching Helena for following him, and after many unkind words on his part, and gentle expostulations from Helena, reminding him of his former love and professions of true faith to her, he left her (as he said) to the mercy of the wild beasts, and she ran after him as swiftly as she could.

The fairy King, who was always friendly to true lovers, felt great compassion for Helena; and perhaps, as Lysander said they used to walk by moonlight in this pleasant wood, Oberon might have seen Helena in those happy times when she was beloved by Demetrius. However that might be, when Puck returned with the little purple flower, Oberon said to his favorite, "Take a part of this flower: there has been a sweet Athenian lady here, who is in love with a disdainful youth; if you find him sleeping, drop some of the love-juice in his eyes, but contrive to do it when she is near him, that the first thing he sees when he awakes may be this despised lady. You will know the man by the Athenian garments which he wears."

Puck promised to manage this matter very dexterously; and then

Oberon went, unperceived by Titania, to her bower, where she was preparing to go to rest. Her fairy bower was a bank, where grew wild thyme, cowslips, and sweet violets, under a canopy of woodbine, musk-roses, and eglantine. There Titania always slept some part of the night; her coverlet the enameled skin of a snake, which, though a small mantle, was wide enough to wrap a fairy in.

He found Titania giving orders to her fairies, how they were to employ themselves while she slept. "Some of you," said Her Majesty, "must kill cankers in the musk-rose buds, and some wage war with the bats for their leathern wings, to make my small elves coats; and some of you keep watch that the clamorous owl, that nightly hoots, come not near me: but first sing me to sleep." Then they began to sing this song:

> "You spotted snakes with double tongue,
>   Thorny hedgehogs, be not seen;
> Newts and blind-worms do no wrong,
>   Come not near our Fairy Queen.
>
> "Philomel, with melody,
>   Sing in our sweet lullaby,
> Lulla, lulla, lullaby; lulla, lulla, lullaby;
>   Never harm,
>   Nor spell, nor charm,
>   Come our lovely lady nigh;
> So good night, with lullaby."

When the fairies had sung their Queen asleep with this pretty lullaby, they left her to perform the important services she had enjoined them. Oberon then softly drew near his Titania, and dropped some of the love-juice on her eyelids, saying,

> "What thou seest when thou dost wake,
> Do it for thy true-love take."

But to return to Hermia, who made her escape out of her father's house that night, to avoid the death she was doomed to for refusing to marry Demetrius. When she entered the wood, she found her dear Lysander waiting for her, to conduct her to his aunt's house; but before they had passed half through the wood, Hermia was so much fatigued, that Lysander, who was very careful of this dear lady, who had proved her affection for him even by hazarding her life for his sake, persuaded her to rest till morning on a bank of soft moss, and lying down himself on the ground at some little distance, they soon fell fast asleep. Here they were found by Puck, who, seeing a handsome young man asleep, and perceiving that his clothes were made in the Athenian fashion, and that a pretty lady was sleeping near him, concluded that this must be the Athenian maid and her disdainful lover whom Oberon had sent him to seek; and he naturally enough conjectured that, as they were alone together, she must be the first thing he would see when he awoke; so, without more ado, he proceeded to pour some of the juice of the little purple flower into his eyes. But it so fell out, that Helena came that way, and, instead of Hermia, was the first object Lysander beheld when he opened his eyes; and, strange to relate, so powerful was the love-charm, all his love for Hermia vanished away, and Lysander fell in love with Helena.

Had he first seen Hermia when he awoke, the blunder Puck com-

"What thou seest when thou dost wake,
Do it for thy true-love take."

185

mitted would have been of no consequence, for he could not love that faithful lady too well; but for poor Lysander to be forced by a fairy love-charm to forget his own true Hermia, and to run after another lady, and leave Hermia asleep quite alone in a wood at midnight, was a sad chance, indeed.

Thus this misfortune happened. Helena, as has been before related, endeavored to keep pace with Demetrius when he ran away so rudely from her; but she could not continue the unequal race long, men being always better runners in a long race than ladies. Helena soon lost sight of Demetrius; and, as she was wandering about, dejected and forlorn, she arrived at the place where Lysander was sleeping. "Ah!" said she, "thus is Lysander lying on the ground: is he dead or asleep?" Then gently touching him, she said, "Good sir, if you are alive, awake." Upon this Lysander opened his eyes, and (the love-charm beginning to work) immediately addressed her in terms of extravagant love and admiration; telling her she as much excelled Hermia in beauty as a dove does a raven, and that he would run through fire for her sweet sake; and many more such lover-like speeches. Helena knowing Lysander was her friend Hermia's lover, and that he was solemnly engaged to marry her, was in the utmost rage when she heard herself addressed in this manner; for she thought (as well she might) that Lysander was making a jest of her. "Oh!" said she, "why was I born to be mocked and scorned by everyone? Is it not enough, is it not enough, young man, that I can never get a sweet look or a kind word from Demetrius; but you, sir, must pretend in this disdainful manner to court me? I thought, Lysander, you were a lord of more true gentleness." Saying these words in great anger, she ran away; and Lysander followed her, quite forgetful of his own Hermia, who was still asleep.

When Hermia awoke, she was in a sad fright at finding herself alone. She wandered about the wood, not knowing what was become of Lysander, or which way to go to seek for him. In the meantime Demetrius, not being able to find Hermia and his rival Lysander, and fatigued with his fruitless search, was observed by Oberon fast asleep. Oberon had learnt, by some questions he had asked of Puck, that he had applied the love-charm to the wrong person's eyes; and now having found the person first intended, he touched the eyelids of the sleeping Demetrius with the love-juice, and he instantly awoke; and the first thing he saw being Helena, he, as Lysander had done before, began to address love-speeches to her; and just at that moment Lysander, followed by Hermia (for through Puck's unlucky mistake it was now become Hermia's turn to run after her lover), made his appearance; and then Lysander and Demetrius, both speaking together, made love to Helena, they being each one under the influence of the same potent charm.

The astonished Helena thought that Demetrius, Lysander, and her once dear friend Hermia, were all in a plot together to make a jest of her.

Hermia was as much surprised as Helena; she knew not why Lysander and Demetrius, who both before loved her, were now become the lovers of Helena; and to Hermia the matter seemed to be no jest.

The ladies, who before had always been the dearest of friends, now fell to high words together.

"Unkind Hermia," said Helena, "it is you have set Lysander on, to vex me with mock praises; and your other lover Demetrius, who used almost to spurn me with his foot, have you not bid him call me goddess, nymph, rare, precious, and celestial? He would not speak thus to me, whom he hates, if you did not set him on to make a jest of me. Unkind Hermia, to join with men in scorning your poor friend. Have you forgot our school-day friendship? How often, Hermia, have we two, sitting on one cushion, both singing one song, with our needles working the same flower, both on the same sampler wrought; growing up together in fashion of a double cherry, scarcely seeming parted? Hermia, it is not friendly in you, it is not maidenly, to join with men in scorning your poor friend."

"I am amazed at your passionate words," said Hermia: "I scorn you not; it seems you scorn me." "Aye, do," returned Helena, "persevere, counterfeit serious looks, and make mouths at me when I turn my back; then wink at each other, and hold the sweet jest up. If you had any pity, grace, or manners, you would not use me thus."

While Helena and Hermia were speaking these angry words to each other, Demetrius and Lysander left them, to fight together in the wood for the love of Helena.

When they found the gentlemen had left them, they departed, and once more wandered weary in the wood in search of their lovers.

As soon as they were gone, the fairy King, who with little Puck had been listening to their quarrels, said to him, "This is your negligence, Puck; or did you do this willfully?"

"Believe me, King of Shadows," answered Puck, "it was a mistake; did not you tell me I should know the man by his Athenian garments? However, I am not sorry that has happened, for I think their jangling makes excellent sport."

"You heard," said Oberon, "that Demetrius and Lysander are gone to seek a convenient place to fight in. I command you to overhang the night with a thick fog, and lead these quarrelsome lovers so astray in the dark, that they shall not be able to find each other. Counterfeit each of their voices to the other, and with bitter taunts provoke them to follow you, while they think it is their rival's tongue they hear. See you do this, till they are so weary they can go no further; and when you find they are asleep, drop the juice of this flower into Lysander's eyes, and when he awakes he will forget his new love for Helena, and return to his old passion for Hermia; and then the two fair ladies may each one be happy with the man she loves, and they will think all that has passed a vexatious dream. About this quickly, Puck; and I will go and see what sweet love my Titania has found."

Titania was still sleeping, and Oberon seeing a clown[1] near her, who had lost his way in the wood, and was likewise asleep: "This fellow," said he, "shall be my Titania's true love"; and clapping an ass's head over the clown's, it seemed to fit him as well as if it had grown upon his shoulders. Though Oberon fixed it on very gently, it awakened him and, rising, unconscious of what Oberon had done, he went towards the bower where the fairy Queen slept.

"Ah! what angel is that I see?" said Titania, opening her eyes, and the juice of the little purple flower beginning to take effect: "Are you as wise as you are beautiful?"

"Why, mistress," said the foolish clown, "if I have wit enough to find the way out of this wood, I have enough to serve my turn."

"Out of the wood do not desire to go," said the enamored Queen. "I am a spirit of no common rate. I love you. Go with me, and I will give you fairies to attend upon you."

She then called four of her fairies: their names were Pease-Blossom, Cobweb, Moth, and Mustard-Seed.

"Attend," said the Queen, "upon this sweet gentleman; hop in his

---

[1] This clown was one Nick Bottom, a weaver, who, with other workmen, was in the wood to rehearse an "interlude" they were to act before the Duke and Duchess of Athens. The play, called "The most lamentable comedy, and most cruel death of Pyramus and Thisby," is very amusingly presented in the last act of *A Midsummer Night's Dream,* Bottom taking the part of Pyramus. [In the play by Shakespeare, it is Puck who actually puts the ass's head upon the shoulders of Bottom, making his fellow-workers flee from him in terror. The mischievous Puck then leads him to the sleeping fairy Queen.]

walks, and gambol in his sight; feed him with grapes and apricots, and steal for him the honey-bags from the bees. Come, sit with me," said she to the clown, "and let me play with your amiable hairy

"Come, sit with me," said Titania.

cheeks, my beautiful ass, and kiss your fair large ears, my gentle joy!"

"Where is Pease-Blossom?" said the ass-headed clown, not much regarding the fairy Queen's courtship, but very proud of his new attendants.

190

"Here, sir," said little Pease-Blossom.

"Scratch my head," said the clown. "Where is Cobweb?"

"Here, sir," said Cobweb.

"Good Mr. Cobweb," said the foolish clown, "kill me the red bumble-bee on the top of that thistle yonder; and, good Mr. Cobweb, bring me the honey-bag. Do not fret yourself too much in the action, Mr. Cobweb, and take care the honey-bag break not; I should be sorry to have you overflown with a honey-bag. Where is Mustard-Seed?"

"Here, sir," said Mustard-Seed; "what is your will?"

"Nothing," said the clown, "good Mr. Mustard-Seed, but to help Mr. Pease-Blossom to scratch; I must go to a barber's, Mr. Mustard-Seed, for methinks I am marvelous hairy about the face."

"My sweet love," said the Queen, "what will you have to eat? I have a venturous fairy shall seek the squirrel's hoard, and fetch you some new nuts."

"I had rather have a handful of dried pease," said the clown, who with his ass's head had got an ass's appetite. "But, I pray, let none of your people disturb me, for I have a mind to sleep."

"Sleep, then," said the Queen, "and I will wind you in my arms. Oh, how I love you! How I dote upon you!"

When the fairy King saw the clown sleeping in the arms of his Queen, he advanced within her sight, and reproached her with having lavished her favors upon an ass. This she could not deny, as the clown was then sleeping within her arms, with his ass's head crowned by her with flowers.

When Oberon had teased her for some time, he again demanded the changeling boy; which she, ashamed of being discovered by her lord with her new favorite, did not dare to refuse him.

Oberon, having thus obtained the little boy he had so long wished for to be his page, took pity on the disgraceful situation into which, by his merry contrivance, he had brought his Titania, and threw some of the juice of the other flower into her eyes; and the fairy Queen immediately recovered her senses, and wondered at her late dotage, saying how she now loathed the sight of the strange monster.

Oberon likewise took the ass's head from off the clown and left him to finish his nap with his own fool's head upon his shoulders.

Oberon and his Titania being now perfectly reconciled, he related to her the history of the lovers, and their midnight quarrels; and she agreed to go with him, and see the end of their adventures.

The fairy King and Queen found the lovers and their fair ladies, at no great distance from each other, sleeping on a grass-plot; for Puck, to make amends for his former mistake, had contrived with the utmost diligence to bring them all to the same spot, unknown to each other; and he had carefully removed the charm from off the eyes of Lysander with the antidote the fairy King gave to him.

Hermia first awoke, and finding her lost Lysander asleep so near her, was looking at him and wondering at his strange inconstancy. Lysander, presently opening his eyes, and seeing his dear Hermia, recovered his reason which the fairy charm had before clouded, and with his reason, his love for Hermia; and they began to talk over the adventures of the night, doubting if these things had really happened, or if they had both been dreaming the same bewildering dream.

Helena and Demetrius were by this time awake; and a sweet sleep having quieted Helena's disturbed and angry spirits, she listened with delight to the professions of love which Demetrius still made to her, and which, to her surprise as well as pleasure, she began to perceive were sincere.

These fair night-wandering ladies, now no longer rivals, became once more true friends; all the unkind words which had passed were forgiven, and they calmly consulted together what was best to be done in their present situation. It was soon agreed that, as Demetrius had given up his pretensions to Hermia, he should endeavor to prevail upon her father to revoke the cruel sentence of death which had been passed against her. Demetrius was preparing to return to Athens for this friendly purpose, when they were surprised with the sight of Egeus, Hermia's father, who came to the wood in pursuit of his runaway daughter.

When Egeus understood that Demetrius would not now marry his daughter, he no longer opposed her marriage with Lysander, but gave his consent that they should be wedded on the fourth day from that time, being the same day on which Hermia had been condemned to lose her life; and on that same day Helena joyfully agreed to marry her beloved and now faithful Demetrius.

The fairy King and Queen, who were invisible spectators of this reconciliation, and now saw the happy ending of the lovers' history brought about through the good offices of Oberon, received so much pleasure, that these kind spirits resolved to celebrate the approaching nuptials with sports and revels throughout their fairy kingdom.

And now, if any are offended with this story of fairies and their pranks, as judging it incredible and strange, they have only to think that they have been asleep and dreaming, and that all these adventures were visions which they saw in their sleep: and I hope none of my readers will be so unreasonable as to be offended with a pretty, harmless, Midsummer Night's Dream.

THE GOLD BUG

By *EDGAR ALLAN POE*

Illustrations by WARREN CHAPPELL

What ho! what ho! this fellow is dancing mad!
He hath been bitten by the Tarantula.
—*"All in the Wrong"*

MANY years ago, I contracted an intimacy with a Mr. William Legrand. He was of an ancient Huguenot family, and had once been wealthy; but a series of misfortunes had reduced him to want. To avoid the mortification consequent upon his disasters, he left New Orleans, the city of his forefathers, and took up his residence at Sullivan's Island, near Charleston, South Carolina.

This island is a very singular one. It consists of little else than the sea sand, and is about three miles long. Its breadth at no point exceeds a quarter of a mile. It is separated from the mainland by a scarcely perceptible creek, oozing its way through a wilderness of reeds and slime, a favorite resort of the marsh-hen. The vegetation, as might be supposed, is scant, or at least dwarfish. No trees of any magnitude are to be seen. Near the western extremity, where Fort Moultrie stands, and where are some miserable frame buildings, tenanted, during summer, by the fugitives from Charleston dust and fever, may be found, indeed, the bristly palmetto; but the whole island, with the exception of this western point, and a line of hard, white beach on the seacoast, is covered with a dense undergrowth of the sweet myrtle, so much prized by the horticulturists of England. The shrub here often attains the height of fifteen or twenty feet, and forms an almost impenetrable copice, burthening the air with its fragrance.

In the inmost recesses of this copice, not far from the eastern or more remote end of the island, Legrand had built himself a small hut, which he occupied when I first, by mere accident, made his acquaintance. This soon ripened into friendship—for there was much in the recluse to excite interest and esteem. I found him well educated, with unusual powers of mind, but infected with misanthropy, and subject to perverse moods of alternate enthusiasm and melancholy. He had with him many books, but rarely employed them. His chief amusements were gunning and fishing, or sauntering along the beach and through the myrtles, in quest of shells or entomological specimens—his collection of the latter might have been envied by a Swammerdamm. In these excursions he was usually accompanied by an old negro, called Jupiter, who had been manumitted before the reverses of the family, but who could be induced, neither by threats nor by promises, to abandon what he considered his right of attendance upon the footsteps of his young "Massa Will." It is not improbable that the relatives of Legrand, conceiving him to be somewhat unsettled in intellect, had contrived to instil this obstinacy into Jupiter, with a view to the supervision and guardianship of the wanderer.

The winters in the latitude of Sullivan's Island are seldom very severe, and in the fall of the year it is a rare event indeed when a fire is considered necessary. About the middle of October, 18—, there occurred, however, a day of remarkable chilliness. Just before sunset I scrambled my way through the evergreens to the hut of my friend, whom I had not visited for several weeks—my residence being, at that time, in Charleston, a distance of nine miles from the Island, while the facilities of passage and re-passage were very far behind those of the present day. Upon reaching the hut I rapped, as was my custom, and getting no reply, sought for the key where I knew it was secreted, unlocked the door and went in. A fine fire was blazing upon the hearth. It was a novelty, and by no means an ungrateful one. I threw off an overcoat, took an arm chair by the crackling logs, and awaited patiently the arrival of my hosts.

Soon after dark they arrived, and gave me a most cordial welcome. Jupiter, grinning from ear to ear, bustled about to prepare some marsh-hens for supper. Legrand was in one of his fits—how else shall I term them?—of enthusiasm. He had found an unknown bivalve, forming a new genus, and, more than this, he had hunted down and secured, with Jupiter's assistance, a *scarabaeus* which he believed to be totally new, but in respect to which he wished to have my opinion on the morrow.

"And why not tonight?" I asked, rubbing my hands over the blaze, and wishing the whole tribe of *scarabaei* at the devil.

"Ah, if I had only known you were here!" said Legrand, "but it's so long since I saw you; and how could I foresee that you would pay me a visit this very night of all others? As I was coming home I met Lieutenant G——, from the fort, and, very foolishly, I lent him the bug; so it will be impossible for you to see it until morning. Stay here tonight, and I will send Jup down for it at sunrise. It is the love-liest thing in creation!"

"What?—sunrise?"

"Nonsense! no!—the bug. It is of a brilliant gold color—about the size of a large hickory-nut—with two jet black spots near one extrem-ity of the back, and another, somewhat longer, at the other. The *antennae* are—"

"Dey aint *no* tin in him, Massa Will, I keep a tellin' on you," here interrupted Jupiter; "de bug is a goole-bug, solid, ebery bit of him, inside and all, sep him wing—never feel half so hebby a bug in my life."

"Well, suppose it is, Jup," replied Legrand, somewhat more earn-estly, it seemed to me, than the case de-manded, "is that any reason for your let-ting the birds burn? The color"—here he turned to me—"is really almost enough to warrant Jupiter's idea. You never saw a more brilliant metallic luster than the scales emit—but of this you cannot judge till tomorrow. In the meantime I can give you some idea of the shape." Saying this, he seated himself at a small table, on which were a pen and ink, but no paper. He looked for some in a drawer, but found none.

Legrand.

"Never mind," said he at length, "this will answer"; and he drew from his waistcoat pocket a scrap of what I took to be very dirty foolscap, and made upon it a rough drawing with the pen. While he did this, I retained my seat by the fire, for I was still chilly. When the design was complete, he handed it to me without rising. As I

197

received it, a loud growl was heard, succeeded by a scratching at the door. Jupiter opened it, and a large Newfoundland, belonging to Legrand, rushed in, leaped upon my shoulders, and loaded me with caresses; for I had shown him much attention during previous visits. When his gambols were over, I looked at the paper, and, to speak the truth, found myself not a little puzzled at what my friend had depicted.

"Well!" I said, after contemplating it for some minutes, "this *is* a strange *scarabaeus,* I must confess: new to me: never saw anything like it before—unless it was a skull, or a death's-head—which it more nearly resembles than anything else that has come under *my* observation."

"A death's-head!" echoed Legrand—"Oh—yes—well, it has something of that appearance upon paper, no doubt. The two upper black spots look like eyes, eh? and the longer one at the bottom like a mouth—and then the shape of the whole is oval."

"Perhaps so," said I; "but, Legrand, I fear you are no artist. I must wait until I see the beetle itself, if I am to form any idea of its personal appearance."

"Well, I don't know," said he, a little nettled. "I draw tolerably—*should* do it at least—have had good masters, and flatter myself that I am not quite a blockhead."

"But, my dear fellow, you are joking, then," said I, "this is a very passable *skull*—indeed, I may say that it is a very *excellent* skull, according to the vulgar notions about such specimens of physiology—and your *scarabaeus* must be the queerest *scarabaeus* in the world if it resembles it. Why, we may get up a very thrilling bit of superstition upon this hint. I presume you will call the bug *Scarabaeus caput hominis,* or something of that kind—there are many similar titles in the Natural Histories. But where are the *antennae* you spoke of?"

"The *antennae!*" said Legrand, who seemed to be getting unaccountably warm upon the subject; "I am sure you must see the *antennae*. I made them as distinct as they are in the original insect, and I presume that is sufficient."

"Well, well," I said, "perhaps you have—still I don't see them"; and I handed him the paper without additional remark, not wishing to ruffle his temper; but I was much surprised at the turn affairs had taken; his ill humor puzzled me—and, as for the drawing of the beetle, there were positively *no antennae* visible, and the whole *did* bear a very close resemblance to the ordinary cuts of a death's-head.

He received the paper very peevishly, and was about to crumple it, apparently to throw it in the fire, when a casual glance at the design seemed suddenly to rivet his attention. In an instant his face grew violently red—in another as excessively pale. For some minutes he continued to scrutinize the drawing minutely where he sat. At length he arose, took a candle from the table, and proceeded to seat himself upon a sea-chest in the farthest corner of the room. Here again he made an anxious examination of the paper; turning it in all directions. He said nothing, however, and his conduct greatly astonished me; yet I thought it prudent not to exacerbate the growing moodiness of his temper by any comment. Presently he took from his coat pocket a wallet, placed the paper carefully in it, and deposited both in a writing desk, which he locked. He now grew more composed in his demeanor; but his original air of enthusiasm had quite disappeared. Yet he seemed not so much sulky as abstracted. As the evening wore away he become more and more absorbed in reverie, from which no sallies of mine could arouse him. It had been my intention to pass the night at the hut, as I had frequently done before, but, seeing my host in this mood, I deemed it proper to take leave. He did not press me to remain, but, as I departed, he shook my hand with even more than his usual cordiality.

It was about a month after this (and during the interval I had seen nothing of Legrand) when I received a visit, at Charleston, from his man, Jupiter. I had never seen the good old negro look so dispirited, and I feared that some serious disaster had befallen my friend.

Jupiter.

"Well, Jup," said I, "what is the matter now?—how is your master?"

"Why, to speak de troof, massa, him not so berry well as mought be."

"Not well! I am truly sorry to hear it. What does he complain of?"

"Dar! dat's it — him nebber 'plain of notin'—but him berry sick for all dat."

"Very sick, Jupiter! — why didn't you say so at once? Is he confined to bed?"

"No, dat he ain't!—he ain't 'find'd nowhar—dat's just whar de shoe pinch—my mind is got to be berry hebby bout poor Massa Will."

"Jupiter, I should like to understand what it is you are talking about. You say your master is sick. Hasn't he told you what ails him?"

"Why, massa, 'taint worf while for me to git mad bout de matter —Massa Will say noffin at all aint de matter wid him—but den what make him go about looking dis here way, wid he head down and he soldiers up, and as white as a gose? And den he keep a syphon all de time—"

"Keeps a what, Jupiter?"

"Keeps a syphon wid de figgurs on de slate—de queerest figgurs I ebber did see. Ise gittin' to be skeered, I tell you. Hab for to keep mighty tight eye pon him 'noovers. Todder day he gib me slip 'fore de sun up and was gone de whole ob de blessed day. I had a big stick ready cut for to gib him d——d good beating when he did come—but Ise sich a fool dat I hadn't de heart arter all—he look so berry poorly."

"Eh?—what?—ah yes!—upon the whole I think you had better not be too severe with the poor fellow—don't flog him, Jupiter—he can't very well stand it—but can you form no idea of what has occasioned this illness, or rather this change of conduct? Has anything unpleasant happened since I saw you?"

"No massa, dey aint bin noffin onpleasant *since* den—'twas '*fore* den I'm feared—'twas de berry day you was dare."

"How? what do you mean?"

"Why, massa, I mean de bug—dare now."

"The what?"

"De bug—I'm berry sartain dat Massa Will bin bit somewhere bout de head by dat goole-bug."

"And what cause have you, Jupiter, for such a supposition?"

"Claws enuff, massa, and mouff, too. I neber did see such a d——d bug—he kick and he bite ebery ting what cum near him. Massa Will cotch him fuss, but had for to let him go 'gin mighty quick, I tell you —den was de time he must ha' got de bite. I didn't like de look ob de bug mouff, myself, nohow, so I wouldn't take hold ob him wid my finger, but I cotch him wid a piece ob paper I found. I rap him up in de paper and stuff piece ob it in he mouff—dat was de way."

"And you think, then, that your master was really bitten by the beetle, and that the bite made him sick?"

"I don't tink noffin about it—I nose it. What make him dream 'bout de goole so much, if 'taint cause he bit by de goole bug? Ise heard 'bout dem goole bugs 'fore dis."

"But how do you know he dreams about gold?"

"How I know? why cause he talk about it in he sleep—dat's how I nose."

"Well, Jup, perhaps you are right; but to what fortunate circumstance am I to attribute the honor of a visit from you today?"

"What de matter, massa?"

"Did you bring any message from Mr. Legrand?"

"No, massa, I bring dis here 'pissel"; and here Jupiter handed me a note which ran thus:

"My Dear——

"Why have I not seen you for so long a time? I hope you have not been so foolish as to take offense, at any little *brusquerie* of mine; but no, that is improbable.

"Since I saw you I have had great cause for anxiety. I have something to tell you, yet scarcely know how to tell it, or whether I should tell it at all.

"I have not been quite well for some days past, and poor old Jup annoys me, almost beyond endurance, by his well-meant attentions. Would you believe it?—he had prepared a huge stick, the other day, with which to chastise me for giving him the slip, and spending the day, *solus,* among the hills on the mainland. I verily believe that my ill looks alone saved me a flogging.

"I have made no addition to my cabinet since we met.

"If you can, in any way, make it convenient, come over with Jupiter. *Do* come. I wish to see you *tonight,* upon business of importance. I assure you that it is of the *highest* importance.

"Ever yours,

"William Legrand."

There was something in the tone of this note which gave me great uneasiness. Its whole style differed materially from that of Legrand. What could he be dreaming of? What new crotchet possessed his excitable brain? What "business of the highest importance" could *he* possibly have to transact? Jupiter's account of him boded no good. I dreaded lest the continued pressure of misfortune had, at length, fairly unsettled the reason of my friend. Without a moment's hesitation, therefore, I prepared to accompany the negro.

Upon reaching the wharf, I noticed a scythe and three spades, all apparently new, lying in the bottom of the boat in which we were to embark.

"What is the meaning of all this, Jup?" I inquired.

"Him syfe, massa, and spade."

"Very true; but what are they doing here?"

"Him de syfe and de spade what Massa Will sis 'pon my buying for him in de town, and de debbil's own lot of money I had to gib for em."

"But what, in the name of all that is mysterious, is your 'Massa Will' going to do with scythes and spades?"

"Dat's more dan *I* know, and debbil take me if I don't b'lieve 'tis more dan he know, too. But it's all cum ob de bug."

Finding that no satisfaction was to be obtained of Jupiter, whose whole intellect seemed to be absorbed by "de bug," I now stepped into the boat and made sail. With a fair and strong breeze we soon ran into the little cove to the northward of Fort Moultrie, and a walk of some two miles brought us to the hut. It was about three in the afternoon when we arrived. Legrand had been awaiting us in eager expectation. He grasped my hand with a nervous *empressement* which alarmed me and strengthened the suspicions already entertained. His countenance was pale even to ghastliness, and his deep-set eyes glared with unnatural luster. After some inquiries respecting his health, I asked him, not knowing what better to say, if he had yet obtained the *scarabaeus* from Lieutenant G——.

"Oh, yes," he replied, coloring violently, "I got it from him the next morning. Nothing should tempt me to part with that *scarabaeus*. Do you know that Jupiter is quite right about it?"

"In what way?" I asked, with a sad foreboding at heart.

"In supposing it to be a bug of *real gold*." He said this with an air of profound seriousness, and I felt inexpressibly shocked.

"This bug is to make my fortune," he continued, with a triumphant smile, "to reinstate me in my family possessions. Is it any wonder, then, that I prize it? Since Fortune has thought fit to bestow it upon me, I have only to use it properly and I shall arrive at the gold of which it is the index. Jupiter, bring me that *scarabaeus!*"

"What! de bug, massa! I'd rubber not go fer trubble dat bug— you mus' git him for your own self." Hereupon Legrand arose, with a grave and stately air, and brought me the beetle from a glass case in which it was enclosed. It was a beautiful *scarabaeus,* and, at that time, unknown to naturalists—of course a great prize in a scientific point of view. There were two round black spots near one extremity of the back, and a long one near the other. The scales were exceedingly hard and glossy, with all the appearance of burnished gold. The weight of the insect was very remarkable, and, taking all things into consideration, I could hardly blame Jupiter for his opinion respecting it; but what to make of Legrand's agreement with that opinion, I could not, for the life of me, tell.

"I sent for you," said he, in a grandiloquent tone, when I had completed my examination of the beetle, "I sent for you, that I might have your counsel and assistance in furthering the views of Fate and of the bug—"

"My dear Legrand," I cried, interrupting him, "you are certainly unwell, and had better use some little precautions. You shall go to bed, and I will remain with you a few days, until you get over this. You are feverish and—"

"Feel my pulse," said he.

I felt it, and, to say the truth, found not the slightest indication of fever.

"But you may be ill and yet have no fever. Allow me this once to prescribe for you. In the first place, go to bed. In the next—"

"You are mistaken," he interposed, "I am as well as I can expect to be under the excitement which I suffer. If you really wish me well, you will relieve this excitement."

"And how is this to be done?"

"Very easily. Jupiter and myself are going upon an expedition into the hills, upon the mainland, and, in this expedition, we shall need the aid of some person in whom we can confide. You are the only one we can trust. Whether we succeed or fail, the excitement which you now perceive in me will be equally allayed."

"I am anxious to oblige you in any way," I replied; "but do you mean to say that this infernal beetle has any connection with your expedition into the hills?"

"It has."

"Then, Legrand, I can become a party to no such absurd proceeding."

"I am sorry—very sorry—for we shall have to try it by ourselves."

"Try it by yourselves! The man is surely mad!—but stay! how long do you propose to be absent?"

"Probably all night. We shall start immediately, and be back, at all events, by sunrise."

"And will you promise me, upon your honor, that when this

freak of yours is over, and the bug business (good God!) settled to
your satisfaction, you will then return home and follow my advice
implicitly, as that of your physician?"

*Legrand contented himself with the scarabaeus, twirling
it to and fro as he went.*

"Yes; I promise; and now let us be off, for we have no time to
lose."

With a heavy heart I accompanied my friend. We started about
four o'clock—Legrand, Jupiter, the dog, and myself. Jupiter had with
him the scythe and spades—the whole of which he insisted upon carrying—more through fear, it seemed to me, of trusting either of the
implements within reach of his master, than from any excess of industry or complaisance. His demeanor was dogged in the extreme,

and "dat d——d bug" were the sole words which escaped his lips during the journey. For my own part, I had charge of a couple of dark lanterns, while Legrand contented himself with the *scarabaeus,* which he carried attached to the end of a bit of whipcord; twirling it to and fro, with the air of a conjurer, as he went. When I observed this last, plain evidence of my friend's aberration of mind, I could scarcely refrain from tears. I thought it best, however, to humor his fancy, at least for the present, or until I could adopt some more energetic measures with a chance of success. In the meantime I endeavored, but all in vain, to sound him in regard to the object of the expedition. Having succeeded in inducing me to accompany him, he seemed unwilling to hold conversation upon any topic of minor importance, and to all my questions vouchsafed no other reply than "we shall see!"

We crossed the creek at the head of the island by means of a skiff, and, ascending the high grounds on the shore of the mainland, proceeded in a northwesterly direction, through a tract of the country excessively wild and desolate, where no trace of a human footstep was to be seen. Legrand led the way with decision; pausing only for an instant, here and there, to consult what appeared to be certain landmarks of his own contrivance upon a former occasion.

In this manner we journeyed for about two hours, and the sun was just setting when we entered a region infinitely more dreary than any yet seen. It was a species of tableland, near the summit of an almost inaccessible hill, densely wooded from base to pinnacle, and interspersed with huge crags that appeared to lie loosely upon the soil, and in many cases were prevented from precipitating themselves into the valleys below, merely by the support of the trees against which they reclined. Deep ravines, in various directions, gave an air of still sterner solemnity to the scene.

The natural platform to which we had clambered was thickly

overgrown with brambles, through which we soon discovered that it would have been impossible to force our way but for the scythe; and Jupiter, by direction of his master, proceeded to clear for us a path to the foot of an enormously tall tulip-tree, which stood, with some eight or ten oaks, upon the level, and far surpassed them all, and all other trees which I had then ever seen, in the beauty of its foliage and form, in the wide spread of its branches, and in the general majesty of its appearance. When we reached this tree, Legrand turned to Jupiter, and asked him if he thought he could climb it. The old man seemed a little staggered by the question, and for some moments made no reply. At length he approached the huge trunk, walked slowly around it, and examined it with minute attention. When he had completed his scrutiny, he merely said,

"Yes, massa, Jup climb any tree he ebber see in he life."

"Then up with you as soon as possible, for it will soon be too dark to see what we are about."

"How far mus go up, massa?" inquired Jupiter.

"Get up the main trunk first, and then I will tell you which way to go—and here—stop! take this beetle with you."

"De bug, Massa Will!—de goole-bug!" cried the negro, drawing back in dismay—"what for mus' tote de bug way up de tree?—d——n if I do!"

"If you are afraid, Jup, a great big negro like you, to take hold of a harmless little dead beetle, why you can carry it up by this string—but, if you do not take it up with you in some way, I shall be under the necessity of breaking your head with this shovel."

"What de matter now, massa?" said Jup, evidently shamed into compliance; "always want for to raise fuss wid ole nigger. Was only funnin anyhow. *Me* feered de bug!—what I keer for de bug?" Here he took cautiously hold of the extreme end of the string, and, maintaining the insect as far from his person as circumstances would permit, prepared to ascend the tree.

In youth, the tulip-tree, or *Liriodendron tulipifera,* the most magnificent of American foresters, has a trunk peculiarly smooth, and often rises to a great height without lateral branches; but, in its riper age, the bark becomes gnarled and uneven, while many short limbs make their appearance on the stem. Thus the difficulty of ascension, in the present case, lay more in semblance than in reality. Embracing the huge cylinder, as closely as possible, with his arms and knees, seizing with his hands some projections, and resting his naked toes upon others, Jupiter, after one or two narrow escapes from falling, at length wriggled himself into the first great fork, and seemed to consider the whole business as virtually accomplished. The *risk* of the achievement was, in fact, now over, although the climber was some sixty or seventy feet from the ground.

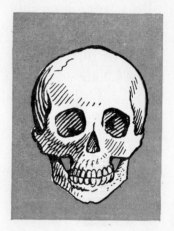

"Which way mus' go now, Massa Will?" he asked.

"Keep up the largest branch—the one on this side," said Legrand. The negro obeyed him promptly, and apparently with but little trouble; ascending higher and higher, until no glimpse of his squat figure could be obtained through the dense foliage which enveloped it. Presently his voice was heard in a sort of halloo.

"How much fudder is got for go?"

"How high up are you?" asked Legrand.

"Ebber so fur," replied the negro; "can see de sky fru de top ob de tree."

"Never mind the sky, but attend to what I say. Look down the trunk and count the limbs below you on this side. How many limbs have you passed?"

"One, two, tree, four, fibe—I done pass fibe big limb, massa, 'pon dis side."

"Then go one limb higher."

In a few minutes the voice was heard again, announcing that the seventh limb was attained.

"Now, Jup," cried Legrand, evidently much excited, "I want you to work your way out upon that limb as far as you can. If you see anything strange, let me know."

By this time what little doubt I might have entertained of my poor friend's insanity, was put finally at rest. I had no alternative but to conclude him stricken with lunacy, and I became seriously anxious about getting him home.

While I was pondering upon what was best to be done, Jupiter's voice was again heard.

"Mos feerd for to ventur 'pon dis limb berry far—'tis dead limb putty much all de way."

"Did you say it was a *dead* limb, Jupiter?" cried Legrand in a quavering voice.

"Yes, massa, him dead as de door-nail—done up for sartain—done departed dis here life."

"What in the name of heaven shall I do?" asked Legrand, seemingly in the greatest distress.

"Do!" said I, glad of an opportunity to interpose a word, "Why, come home and go to bed. Come now!—that's a fine fellow. It's getting late, and besides, you remember your promise."

"Jupiter," cried he, without heeding me in the least, "do you hear me?"

"Yes, Massa Will, hear you ebber so plain."

"Try the wood with your knife, and see if it is *very* rotten."

"Him rotten, massa, sure nuff," replied the negro in a few moments, "but not so berry rotten as mought be. Mought ventur out leetle way 'pon de limb by myself, dat's true."

"By yourself!—what do you mean?"

"Why, I mean de bug. 'Tis *berry* hebby bug. Spose I drop him down fuss, and den de limb won't break wid just de weight ob one nigger."

"You infernal scoundrel!" cried Legrand, apparently much relieved, "what do you mean by telling me such nonsense as that? As sure as you let that beetle fall I'll break your neck. Look here, Jupiter! do you hear me?"

"Yes, massa, need n't hollo at poor nigger dat style."

"Well! now listen!—if you will venture out on the limb as far as you think safe, and not let go the beetle, I'll make you a present of a silver dollar as soon as you get down."

"I'm gwine, Massa Will—deed I is," replied the negro very promptly—"mos' out to the eend now."

"*Out to the end!*" here fairly screamed Legrand. "Do you say you are out to the end of that limb?"

"Soon be to de eend, massa—o-o-o-o-oh! Lor-gol-a-marcy! what *is* dis here 'pon de tree?"

"Well!" cried Legrand, highly delighted. "What is it?"

"Why 'tain't noffin but a skull—somebody bin lef' him head up de tree, and de crows gone gobble ebery bit ob de meat off."

"A skull, you say!—very well!—how is it fastened to the limb?—what holds it on?"

"Sure nuff, massa; mus' look. Why dis berry curous sarcumstance, 'pon my word—dar's a great big nail in de skull, what fastens ob it on to de tree."

"Well, now, Jupiter, do exactly as I tell you—do you hear?"

"Yes, massa."

"Pay attention, then!—find the left eye of the skull."

"Mighty easy ting for to put de bug fru de hole."

"Hum! hoo! dat's good! why dar ain't no eye lef' at all."

"Curse your stupidity! do you know your right hand from your left?"

"Yes, I nose dat—nose all about dat—'tis my lef' hand what I chops de wood wid."

"To be sure! you are left-handed; and your left eye is on the same side as your left hand. Now, I suppose, you can find the left eye of the skull, or the place where the left eye has been. Have you found it?"

Here was a long pause. At length the negro asked,

"Is de lef' eye of de skull 'pon de same side as de lef' hand of de skull, too?—cause de skull ain't got not a bit ob a hand at all—nebber mind! I got de lef' eye now—here de lef' eye! what mus do wid it?"

"Let the beetle drop through it, as far as the string will reach—but be careful and not let go your hold of the string."

"All dat done, Massa Will; mighty easy ting for to put de bug fru de hole—look out for him dar below!"

During this colloquy no portion of Jupiter's person could be seen; but the beetle, which he had suffered to descend, was now visible at the end of the string, and glistened, like a globe of burnished gold, in the last rays of the setting sun, some of which still faintly illumined the eminence upon which we stood. The *scarabaeus* hung quite clear of any branches, and, if allowed to fall, would have fallen at our feet. Legrand immediately took the scythe, and cleared with it a circular space, three or four yards in diameter, just beneath the insect, and, having accomplished this, ordered Jupiter to let go the string and come down from the tree.

Driving a peg, with great nicety, into the ground, at the precise spot where the beetle fell, my friend now produced from his pocket a tape-measure. Fastening one end of this at that point of the trunk of the tree which was nearest the peg, he unrolled it till it reached the peg, and thence farther unrolled it, in the direction already established by the two points of the tree and the peg, for the distance of fifty feet—Jupiter clearing away the brambles with the scythe. At the spot thus attained a second peg was driven, and about this, as a center, a rude circle, about four feet in diameter, described. Taking now a spade himself, and giving one to Jupiter and one to me, Legrand begged us to set about digging as quickly as possible.

To speak the truth, I had no especial relish for such amusement at any time, and, at that particular moment, would most willingly have declined it; for the night was coming on, and I felt much fatigued with the exercise already taken; but I saw no mode of escape, and was fearful of disturbing my poor friend's equanimity by a refusal. Could I have depended, indeed, upon Jupiter's aid, I would have had no hesitation in attempting to get the lunatic home by force; but I was too well assured of the old negro's disposition, to hope that he would assist me, under any circumstances, in a personal contest with his master. I made no doubt that the latter had been infected with some of the innumerable Southern superstitions about money buried, and that his phantasy had received confirmation by the finding of the *scarabaeus,* or, perhaps, by Jupiter's obstinacy in maintaining it to be "a bug of real gold." A mind disposed to lunacy would readily be led away by such suggestions—especially if chiming in with favorite preconceived ideas—and then I called to mind the poor fellow's speech about the beetle's being "the index of his fortune." Upon the whole, I was sadly vexed and puzzled, but, at length, I concluded to make a virtue of necessity—to dig with a good will, and thus the sooner to convince the visionary, by ocular demonstration, of the fallacy of the opinions he entertained.

The lanterns having been lit, we all fell to work with a zeal worthy a more rational cause; and, as the glare fell upon our persons and implements, I could not help thinking how picturesque a group we composed, and how strange and suspicious our labors must have appeared to any interloper who, by chance, might have stumbled upon our whereabouts.

We dug very steadily for two hours. Little was said; and our chief embarrassment lay in the yelpings of the dog, who took exceeding interest in our proceedings. He, at length, became so obstreperous that we grew fearful of his giving the alarm to some stragglers in the vicinity—or, rather, this was the apprehension of Legrand—for myself,

I should have rejoiced at any interruption which might have enabled me to get the wanderer home. The noise was, at length, very effectually silenced by Jupiter, who, getting out of the hole with a dogged air of deliberation, tied the brute's mouth up with one of his suspenders, and then returned, with a grave chuckle, to his task.

When the time mentioned had expired, we had reached a depth of five feet, and yet no signs of any treasure became manifest. A general pause ensued, and I began to hope that the farce was at an end. Legrand, however, although evidently much disconcerted, wiped his brow thoughtfully and recommenced. We had excavated the entire circle of four feet diameter, and now we slightly enlarged the limit, and went to the farther depth of two feet. Still nothing appeared. The gold-seeker, whom I sincerely pitied, at length clambered from the pit, with the bitterest disappointment imprinted upon every feature, and proceeded, slowly and reluctantly, to put on his coat, which he had thrown off at the beginning of his labor. In the meantime I made no remark. Jupiter, at a signal from his master, began to gather up his tools. This done, and the dog having been unmuzzled, we turned in profound silence towards home.

We had taken perhaps a dozen steps in this direction, when, with a loud oath, Legrand strode up to Jupiter and seized him by the collar. The astonished negro opened his eyes and mouth to the fullest extent, let fall the spades, and fell upon his knees.

"You scoundrel," said Legrand, hissing out the syllables from between his clenched teeth—"you infernal black villain!—speak, I tell you—answer me this instant, without prevarication!—which—which is your left eye?"

"Oh, my golly, Massa Will! ain't dis here my lef' eye for sartain?" roared the terrified Jupiter, placing his hand upon his *right* organ of

vision, and holding it there with a desperate pertinacity, as if in immediate dread of his master's attempt at a gouge.

"I thought so!—I knew it!—hurrah!" vociferated Legrand, letting
the negro go, and executing a series of curvets and caracols, much to
the astonishment of his valet, who, arising from his knees, looked,
mutely, from his master to myself, and then from myself to his master.

"Come! we must go back," said the latter, "the game's not up
yet"; and he again led the way to the tulip-tree.

"Jupiter," said he, when we reached its foot, "come here! was the
skull nailed to the limb with the face outward, or with the face to
the limb?"

"De face was out, massa, so dat de crows could get at de eyes good,
widout any trouble."

"Well, then, was it this eye or that through which you let the beetle fall?"—here Legrand touched each of Jupiter's eyes.

" 'Twas dis eye, massa—de lef' eye—jis as you tell me," and here
it was his right eye that the negro indicated.

"That will do—we must try it again."

Here my friend, about whose madness I now saw, or fancied that I
saw, certain indications of method, removed the peg which marked
the spot where the beetle fell, to a spot about three inches to the westward of its former position. Taking, now the tape-measure from the
nearest point of the trunk to the peg, as before, and continuing the
extension in a straight line to the distance of fifty feet, a spot was
indicated, removed, by several yards, from the point at which we had
been digging.

Around the new position a circle, somewhat larger than in the former instance, was now described, and we again set to work with the
spades. I was dreadfully weary, but, scarcely understanding what had
occasioned the change in my thoughts, I felt no longer any great

aversion from the labor imposed. I had become most unaccountably interested—nay, even excited. Perhaps there was something, amid all the extravagant demeanor of Legrand—some air of forethought, or of deliberation, which impressed me. I dug eagerly, and now and then caught myself actually looking, with something that very much resembled expectation, for the fancied treasure, the vision of which had demented my unfortunate companion. At a period when such vagaries of thought most fully possessed me, and when we had been at work perhaps an hour and a half, we were again interrupted by the violent howlings of the dog. His uneasiness, in the first instance, had been, evidently, but the result of playfulness or caprice, but he now assumed a bitter and serious tone. Upon Jupiter's again attempting to muzzle him, he made furious resistance, and leaping into the hole, tore up the mould frantically with

Set to work with the spades.

his claws. In a few seconds he had uncovered a mass of human bones, forming two complete skeletons, intermingled with several buttons of metal, and what appeared to be the dust of decayed woolen. One or two strokes of a spade upturned the blade of a large Spanish knife, and, as we dug farther, three or four loose pieces of gold and silver coin came to light.

At sight of these the joy of Jupiter could scarcely be restrained, but the countenance of his master wore an air of extreme disappointment. He urged us, however, to continue our exertions, and the words were hardly uttered when I stumbled and fell forward, having caught the toe of my boot in a large ring of iron that lay half buried in the loose earth.

We now worked in earnest, and never did I pass ten minutes of more intense excitement. During this interval we had fairly unearthed an oblong chest of wood, which, from its perfect preservation, and wonderful hardness, had plainly been subjected to some mineralizing process—perhaps that of the bichloride of mercury. This box was three feet and a half long, three feet broad, and two and a half feet deep. It was firmly secured by bands of wrought iron, riveted, and forming a kind of trellis-work over the whole. On each side of the chest, near the top, were three rings of iron—six in all—by means of which a firm hold could be obtained by six persons. Our utmost united endeavors served only to disturb the coffer very slightly in its bed. We at once saw the impossibility of removing so great a weight. Luckily, the sole fastenings of the lid consisted of two sliding bolts. These we drew back—trembling and panting with anxiety. In an instant, a treasure of incalculable value lay gleaming before us. As the rays of the lanterns fell within the pit, there flashed upwards, from a confused heap of gold and of jewels, a glow and a glare that absolutely dazzled our eyes.

I shall not pretend to describe the feelings with which I gazed. Amazement was, of course, predominant. Legrand appeared exhausted with excitement, and spoke very few words. Jupiter's countenance wore, for some minutes, as deadly a pallor as it is possible, in the nature of things, for any negro's visage to assume. He seemed stupefied—thunderstricken. Presently he fell upon his knees in the pit, and, burying his naked arms up to the elbows in gold, let them there remain, as if enjoying the luxury of a bath. At length, with a deep sigh, he exclaimed, as if in a soliloquy,

"And dis all cum ob de goole-bug! de putty goole-bug! de poor little goole-bug, what I bossed in dat sabage kind ob style! Ain't you shamed ob yourself, nigger?—answer me dat!"

It became necessary, at last, that I should arouse both master and valet to the expediency of removing the treasure. It was growing late, and it behooved us to make exertion, that we might get everything housed before daylight. It was difficult to say what should be done; and much time was spent in deliberation—so confused were the ideas of all. We, finally, lightened the box by removing two thirds of its contents, when we were enabled, with some trouble, to raise it from the hole. The articles taken out were deposited among the brambles, and the dog left to guard them, with strict orders from Jupiter neither, upon any pretense, to stir from the spot, nor to open his mouth until our return. We then hurriedly made for home with the chest; reaching the hut in safety, but after excessive toil, at one o'clock in the morning. Worn out as we were, it was not in human nature to do more just then. We rested until two, and had supper; starting for the hills immediately afterwards, armed with three stout sacks, which, by good luck, were upon the premises. A little before four we arrived at the pit, divided the remainder of the booty, as equally as might be, among us, and, leaving the holes unfilled, again set out for the hut, at which, for the second time, we deposited our golden burthens, just as the first streaks of the dawn gleamed from over the tree-tops in the East.

We were now thoroughly broken down; but the intense excitement of the time denied us repose. After an unquiet slumber of some three or four hours' duration, we arose, as if by pre-concert, to make examination of our treasure.

The chest had been full to the brim, and we spent the whole day, and the greater part of the next night, in a scrutiny of its contents. There had been nothing like order or arrangement. Everything had been heaped in promiscuously. Having assorted all with care, we found ourselves possessed of even vaster wealth than we had at first supposed. In coin there was rather more than four hundred and fifty thousand dollars—estimating the value of the pieces, as accurately as we could, by the tables of the period. There was not a particle of silver. All was gold of antique date and of great variety—French, Spanish, and German money, with a few English guineas, and some counters, of which we had never seen specimens before. There were several very large and heavy coins, so worn that we could make nothing of their inscriptions. There was no American money. The value of the jewels we found more difficulty in estimating. There were diamonds—some of them exceedingly large and fine—a hundred and ten in all, and not one of them small; eighteen rubies of remarkable brilliancy—three hundred and ten emeralds, all very beautiful; and twenty-one sapphires, with an opal. These stones had all been broken from their settings and thrown loose in the chest. The settings themselves, which we picked out from among the other gold, appeared to have been beaten up with hammers, as if to prevent identification. Besides all this, there was a vast quantity of solid gold ornaments—nearly two hundred massive finger and ear rings—rich chains—thirty of these, if I remember—eighty-three very large and heavy crucifixes—five gold censers of great value—a prodigious golden punch-bowl, ornamented with richly chased vine-leaves and Bacchanalian figures; with two sword-handles exquisitely embossed, and many other smaller articles which I cannot recollect. The weight of these valuables exceeded three hundred and fifty pounds avoirdupois; and in this estimate I have not included one hundred and ninety-seven superb gold watches; three of the number being worth each five hundred dollars, if one. Many of them were very old, and as time keepers valueless; the works having suffered, more or less, from corrosion—but all were richly jeweled and in cases of great worth. We estimated the entire contents of the chest, that night, at a million and a half of dollars; and, upon the subsequent disposal of the trinkets and jewels (a few being retained for our own use), it was found that we had greatly undervalued the treasure.

When, at length, we had concluded our examination, and the intense excitement of the time had, in some measure, subsided, Legrand, who saw that I was dying with impatience for a solution of this most extraordinary riddle, entered into a full detail of all the circumstances connected with it.

"You remember," said he, "the night when I handed you the rough sketch I had made of the *scarabaeus*. You recollect also, that I became quite vexed at you for insisting that my drawing resembled a death's-head. When you first made this assertion I thought you were jesting; but afterwards I called to mind the peculiar spots on the back of the insect, and admitted to myself that your remark had some little foundation in fact. Still, the sneer at my graphic powers irritated me —for I am considered a good artist—and, therefore, when you handed me the scrap of parchment, I was about to crumple it up and throw it angrily into the fire."

"The scrap of paper, you mean," said I.

"No; it had much of the appearance of paper, and at first I supposed it to be such, but when I came to draw upon it, I discovered it, at once, to be a piece of very thin parchment. It was quite dirty, you remember. Well, as I was in the very act of crumpling it up, my glance fell upon the sketch at which you had been looking, and you may imagine my astonishment when I perceived, in fact, the figure of a death's-head just where, it seemed to me, I had made the drawing of the beetle. For a moment I was too much amazed to think with accuracy. I knew that my design was very different in detail from this —although there was a certain similarity in general outline. Presently I took a candle, and seating myself at the other end of the room, proceeded to scrutinize the parchment more closely. Upon turning it over, I saw my own sketch upon the reverse, just as I had made it. My first idea, now, was mere surprise at the really remarkable similarity of outline—at the singular coincidence involved in the fact, that unknown to me, there should have been a skull upon the other side of the parchment, immediately beneath my figure of the *scarabaeus,* and that this skull, not only in outline, but in size, should so closely resemble my drawing. I say the singularity of this coincidence absolutely stupefied me for a time. This is the usual effect of such coincidences. The mind struggles to establish a connection—a sequence of cause and effect—and, being unable to do so, suffers a species of temporary paralysis. But, when I recovered from this stupor, there dawned upon me gradually a conviction which startled me even far more than the coincidence. I began distinctly, positively, to remember that there had been *no* drawing on the parchment when I made my sketch of the *scarabaeus*. I became perfectly certain of this; for I recollected turning up first one side and then the other, in search of the cleanest spot. Had the skull been then there, of course I could not have failed to notice it. Here was indeed a mystery which I felt it impossible to explain; but, even at that early moment, there seemed to glimmer, faintly, within the most remote and secret chamber of my intellect, a glowworm-like conception of that truth which last night's adventure brought to so magnificent a demonstration. I arose at once, and putting the parchment securely away, dismissed all farther reflection until I should be alone.

"When you had gone, and when Jupiter was fast asleep, I betook myself to a more methodical investigation of the affair. In the first place I considered the manner in which the parchment had come into my possession. The spot where we discovered the *scarabaeus* was on the coast of the mainland, about a mile eastward of the island, and but a short distance above high water mark. Upon my taking hold of it, it gave me a sharp bite, which caused me to let it drop. Jupiter, with his accustomed caution, before seizing the insect, which had flown towards him, looked about him for a leaf, or something of that nature, by which to take hold of it. It was at this moment that his eyes, and mine also, fell upon the scrap of parchment, which I then supposed to be paper. It was lying half buried in the sand, a corner sticking up. Near the spot where we found it, I observed the remnants of what appeared to have been a ship's long boat. The wreck seemed to have been there for a very great while; for the resemblance to boat timbers could scarcely be traced.

"Well, Jupiter picked up the parchment, wrapped the beetle in it, and gave it to me. Soon afterwards we turned to go home, and on the way met Lieutenant G——. I showed him the insect, and he begged me to let him take it to the fort. On my consenting, he thrust it forthwith into his waistcoat pocket, without the parchment in which it had been wrapped, and which I had continued to hold in my hand during its inspection. Perhaps he dreaded my changing my mind, and thought it best to make sure of the prize at once—you know how enthusiastic he is on all subjects connected with Natural History. At the same time, without being conscious of it, I must have deposited the parchment in my own pocket.

"You remember that when I went to the table, for the purpose of making a sketch of the beetle, I found no paper where it was usually kept. I looked in the drawer, and found none there. I searched my pockets, hoping to find an old letter—and then my hand fell upon the parchment. I thus detail the precise mode in which it came into my possession; for the circumstances impressed me with peculiar force.

"No doubt you will think me fanciful—but I had already established a kind of *connection*. I had put together two links of a great chain. There was a boat lying on a sea-coast, and not far from the boat was a parchment—*not a paper*—with a skull depicted on it. You will, of course, ask 'where is the connection?' I reply that the skull, or death's-head, is the well-known emblem of the pirate. The flag of the death's-head is hoisted in all engagements.

"I have said that the scrap was parchment, and not paper. Parchment is durable—almost imperishable. Matters of little moment are rarely consigned to parchment; since, for the mere ordinary purposes of drawing or writing, it is not nearly so well adapted as paper. This reflection suggested some meaning—some relevancy—in the death's-head. I did not fail to observe, also, the *form* of the parchment. Although one of its corners had been, by some accident, destroyed, it could be seen that the original form was oblong. It was just such a slip, indeed, as might have been chosen for a memorandum—for a record of something to be long remembered and carefully preserved."

"But," I interposed, "you say that the skull was *not* upon the parchment when you made the drawing of the beetle. How then do you trace any connection between the boat and the skull—since this latter, according to your own admission, must have been designed (God only knows how or by whom) at some period subsequent to your sketching the *scarabaeus*?"

"Ah, hereupon turns the whole mystery; although the secret, at this point, I had comparatively little difficulty in solving. My steps were sure, and could afford but a single result. I reasoned, for example, thus: When I drew the *scarabaeus,* there was no skull apparent on the parchment. When I had completed the drawing, I gave it to you, and observed you narrowly until you returned it. *You,* therefore, did not design the skull, and no one else was present to do it. Then it was not done by human agency. And nevertheless it was done.

"At this stage of my reflections I endeavored to remember, and *did* remember, with entire distinctness, every incident which occurred about the period in question. The weather was chilly (oh, rare and happy accident!) and a fire was blazing on the hearth. I was heated with exercise and sat near the table. You, however, had drawn a chair close to the chimney. Just as I placed the parchment in your hand, and as you were in the act of inspecting it, Wolf, the Newfoundland, entered, and leaped upon your shoulders. With your left hand you caressed him and kept him off, while your right, holding the parchment, was permitted to fall listlessly between your knees, and in close proximity to the fire. At one moment I thought the blaze had caught it, and was about to caution you, but, before I could speak, you had withdrawn it, and were engaged in its examination. When I considered all these particulars, I doubted not for a moment that *heat* had been the agent in bringing to light, on the parchment, the skull which I saw designed on it. You are well aware that chemical preparations exist, and have existed time out of mind, by means of which it is possible to write on either paper or vellum, so that the characters shall become visible only when subjected to the action of fire. Zaffre, digested in *aqua regia,* and diluted with four times its weight of water, is sometimes employed; a green tint results. The regulus of cobalt, dissolved in spirit of nitre, gives a red. These colors disappear at longer or shorter intervals after the material written on cools, but again become apparent upon the re-application of heat.

"I now scrutinized the death's-head with care. Its outer edges—the edges of the drawing nearest the edge of the vellum—were far more *distinct* than the others. It was clear that the action of the caloric had been imperfect or unequal. I immediately kindled a fire, and subjected every portion of the parchment to a glowing heat. At first, the only effect was the strengthening of the faint lines in the skull; but, on persevering in the experiment, there became visible, at the corner of the slip, diagonally opposite to the spot in which the death's-head was delineated, the figure of what I at first supposed to be a goat. A closer scrutiny, however, satisfied me that it was intended for a kid."

"Ha! ha!" said I, "to be sure I have no right to laugh at you—a million and a half of money is too serious a matter for mirth—but you are not about to establish a third link in your chain—you will not find any especial connection between your pirates and a goat—pirates, you know, have nothing to do with goats; they appertain to the farming interest."

"But I have just said that the figure was *not* that of a goat."

"Well, a kid then—pretty much the same thing."

"Pretty much, but not altogether," said Legrand. "You may have heard of one *Captain* Kidd. I at once looked on the figure of the animal as a kind of punning or hieroglyphical signature. I say signature; because its position on the vellum suggested this idea. The death's-head at the corner diagonally opposite, had, in the same manner, the air of a stamp, or seal. But I was sorely put out by the absence of all else—of the body to my imagined instrument—of the text for my context."

"I presume you expected to find a letter between the stamp and the signature."

"Something of that kind. The fact is, I felt irresistibly impressed with a presentiment of some vast good fortune impending. I can scarcely say why. Perhaps, after all, it was rather a desire than an actual belief—but do you know that Jupiter's silly words, about the bug being of solid gold, had a remarkable effect on my fancy? And then the series of accidents and coincidences—these were so *very* extraordinary. Do you observe how mere an accident it was that these events should have occurred on the *sole* day of all the year in which it has been, or may be, sufficiently cool for fire, and that without the fire, or without the intervention of the dog at the precise moment in which he appeared, I should never have become aware of the death's-head, and so never the possessor of the treasure?"

"But proceed—I am all impatience."

"Well; you have heard, of course, the many stories current—the thousand vague rumors afloat about money buried, somewhere on the Atlantic coast, by Kidd and his associates. These rumors must have had some foundation in fact. And that the rumors have existed so long and so continuously could have resulted, it appeared to me, only from the circumstance of the buried treasure still *remaining* entombed. Had Kidd concealed his plunder for a time, and afterwards reclaimed it, the rumors would scarcely have reached us in their present unvarying form. You will observe that the stories told are all about money-seekers, not about money-finders. Had the pirate recovered his money, there the affair would have dropped. It seemed to me that some accident—say the loss of a memorandum indicating its locality—had deprived him of the means of recovering it, and that this accident had become known to his followers, who otherwise might never have heard that treasure had been concealed at all, and who, busying themselves in vain, because unguided attempts to regain it, had given first birth, and then universal currency, to the reports which are now so common. Have you ever heard of any important treasure being unearthed along the coast?"

"Never."

"But that Kidd's accumulations were immense, is well known. I took it for granted, therefore, that the earth still held them; and you will scarcely be surprised when I tell you that I felt a hope, nearly amounting to certainty, that the parchment so strangely found, involved a lost record of the place of deposit."

"But how did you proceed?"

The pirate.

"I held the vellum again to the fire, after increasing the heat; but nothing appeared. I now thought it possible that the coating of dirt might have something to do with the failure; so I carefully rinsed the parchment by pouring warm water over it, and, having done this, I placed it in a tin pan, with the skull downwards, and put the pan upon a furnace of lighted charcoal. In a few minutes, the pan having become thoroughly heated, I removed the slip, and, to my inexpressible joy, found it spotted, in several places, with what appeared to be figures arranged in lines. Again I placed it in the pan, and suffered it to remain another minute. On taking it off, the whole was just as you see it now."

Here Legrand, having re-heated the parchment, submitted it to my inspection. The following characters were rudely traced, in a red tint, between the death's-head and the goat:

53‡‡†305))6*;4826)4‡.)4‡);806*;48†8¶60))
85;(;]8*);:‡*8†83(88)5*†;46(;88*96*?;8)*‡(;485);
5*†2:*‡(;4956*2(5*-4)8¶8*;4069285);)6†8)
4‡‡;1(‡9;48081;8:8‡1;48†85;4)485†528806*81(
‡9;48;(88;4(‡?34;48)4‡;161;:188;‡?;

"But," said I, returning him the slip, "I am as much in the dark as ever. Were all the jewels of Golconda awaiting me on my solution of this enigma, I am quite sure that I should be unable to earn them."

"And yet," said Legrand, "the solution is by no means so difficult as you might be led to imagine from the first hasty inspection of the characters. These characters, as any one might readily guess, form a cipher—that is to say, they convey a meaning; but then, from what is known of Kidd, I could not suppose him capable of constructing any of the more abstruse cryptographs. I made up my mind, at once, that this was of a simple species, such, however, as would appear, to the crude intellect of the sailor, absolutely insoluble without the key."

"And you really solved it?"

"Readily; I have solved others of an abstruseness ten thousand times greater. Circumstances, and a certain bias of mind, have led me to take interest in such riddles, and it may well be doubted whether human ingenuity can construct an enigma of the kind which human ingenuity may not, by proper application, resolve. In fact, having once established connected and legible characters, I scarcely gave a thought to the mere difficulty of developing their import.

"In the present case—indeed in all cases of secret writing—the first question regards the *language* of the cipher; for the principles of solution, so far, especially, as the more simple ciphers are concerned, depend upon, and are varied by, the genius of the particular idiom. In general, there is no alternative but experiment (directed by probabilities) of every tongue known to him who attempts the solution, until the true one be attained. But, with the cipher now before us, all difficulty is removed by the signature. The pun on the word 'Kidd' is appreciable in no other language than the English. But for this consideration I should have begun my attempts with the Spanish and French, as the tongues in which a secret of this kind would most naturally have been written by a pirate of the Spanish main. As it was, I assumed the cryptograph to be English.

"You observe there are no divisions between the words. Had there been divisions, the task would have been comparatively easy. In such case I should have commenced with a collation and analysis of the shorter words, and, had a word of a single letter occurred, as is most likely (*a* or *I,* for example,) I should have considered the solution as assured. But, there being no division, my first step was to ascertain the predominant letters, as well as the least frequent. Counting all, I constructed a table, thus:

Of the character 8 there are 33.

; there are 26.

4 there are 19.

‡) there are 16.

* there are 13.

5 there are 12.

6 there are 11.

† 1 there are 8.

0 there are 6.

9 2 there are 5.

: 3 there are 4.

? there are 3.

¶ there are 2.

] - . there are 1.

"Now, in English, the letter which most frequently occurs is *e*. Afterwards, the succession runs thus: *a o i d h n r s t u y c f g l m w b k p q x z. E,* however, predominates so remarkably that an individual sentence of any length is rarely seen, in which it is not the prevailing character.

"Here, then, we have, in the very beginning, the ground-work for something more than a mere guess. The general use which may be made of the table is obvious—but, in this particular cipher, we shall only very partially require its aid. As our predominant character is 8, we will commence by assuming it as the *e* of the natural alphabet. To verify the supposition, let us observe if the 8 be seen often in couples—for *e* is doubled with great frequency in English—in such words, for example, as 'meet,' 'fleet,' 'speed,' 'seen,' 'been,' 'agree,' &c. In the present instance we see it doubled no less than five times, although the cryptograph is brief.

"Let us assume 8, then, as *e*. Now, of all *words* in the language, 'the' is most usual; let us see, therefore, whether there are not repetitions of any three characters, in the same order of collocation, the last of them being 8. If we discover repetitions of such letters, so arranged, they will most probably represent the word 'the.' On inspection, we find no less than seven such arrangements, the characters being ;48. We may, therefore, assume that the semicolon represents *t,* that 4 represents *h,* and that 8 represents *e*—the last being now well confirmed. Thus a great step has been taken.

"But, having established a single word, we are enabled to establish a vastly important point; that is to say, several commencements and terminations of other words. Let us refer, for example, to the last instance but one, in which the combination ;48 occurs—not far from the end of the cipher. We know that the semicolon immediately ensuing is the commencement of a word, and, of the six characters succeeding this 'the,' we are cognizant of no less than five. Let us set these characters down, thus, by the letters we know them to represent, leaving a space for the unknown—

t eeth.

"Here we are enabled, at once, to discard the '*th,*' as forming no portion of the word commencing with the first *t;* since, by experiment of the entire alphabet for a letter adapted to the vacancy we perceive that no word can be formed of which this *th* can be a part. We are thus narrowed into

t ee,

and, going through the alphabet, if necessary, as before, we arrive at the word 'tree' as the sole possible reading. We thus gain another letter, *r,* represented by (, with the words 'the tree' in juxtaposition.

"Looking beyond these words, for a short distance, we again see the combination ;48, and employ it by way of *termination* to what immediately precedes. We have thus this arrangement:

the tree;4(‡?34 the,

or, substituting the natural letters, where known, it reads thus:

the tree thr‡?3h the.

"Now, if, in place of the unknown characters, we leave blank spaces, or substitute dots, we read thus:

the tree thr...h the,

when the word 'through' makes itself evident at once. But this discovery gives us three new letters, *o, u* and *g,* represented by ‡ ? and 3.

"Looking now, narrowly, through the cipher for combinations of known characters, we find, not very far from the beginning, this arrangement,

83(88, or egree,

which, plainly, is the conclusion of the word 'degree,' and gives us another letter, *d,* represented by †.

"Four letters beyond the word 'degree,' we perceive the combination

;46(;88*

"Translating the known characters, and representing the unknown by dots, as before, we read thus:

th.rtee.

232

an arrangement immediately suggestive of the word 'thirteen,' and again furnishing us with two new characters, *i* and *n,* represented by 6 and *.

"Referring, now, to the beginning of the cryptograph, we find the combination,

53‡‡†.

"Translating, as before, we obtain

.good,

which assures us that the first letter is *A,* and that the first two words are 'A good.'

"To avoid confusion, it is now time that we arrange our key, as far as discovered, in a tabular form. It will stand thus:

5 represents a
† represents d
8 represents e
3 represents g
4 represents h
6 represents i
* represents in
‡ represents o
(represents r
; represents t

"We have, therefore, no less than ten of the most important letters represented, and it will be unnecessary to proceed with the details of the solution. I have said enough to convince you that ciphers of this nature are readily soluble, and to give you some insight into the *rationale* of their development. But be assured that the specimen before us appertains to the very simplest species of cryptograph. It now only remains to give you the full translation of the characters upon the parchment, as unriddled. Here it is:

"'*A good glass in the bishop's hostel in the devil's seat twenty-one degrees and thirteen minutes northeast and by north main branch seventh limb east side shoot from the left eye of the death's head a bee line from the tree through the shot fifty feet out.'*"

"But," said I, "the enigma seems still in as bad a condition as ever. How is it possible to extort a meaning from all this jargon about 'devil's seats,' 'death's-head,' and 'bishop's hotels'?"

"I confess," replied Legrand, "that the matter still wears a serious aspect, when regarded with a casual glance. My first endeavor was to divide the sentence into the natural division intended by the cryptographist."

"You mean, to punctuate it?"

"Something of that kind."

"But how was it possible to effect this?"

"I reflected that it had been a *point* with the writer to run his words together without division, so as to increase the difficulty of solution. Now, a not over-acute man, in pursuing such an object, would be nearly certain to overdo the matter. When, in the course of his composition, he arrived at a break in his subject which would naturally require a pause, or a point, he would be exceedingly apt to run his characters, at this place, more than usually close together. If you will observe the MS., in the present instance, you will easily detect five such cases of unusual crowding. Acting on this hint, I made the division thus:

"'*A good glass in the Bishop's hostel in the Devil's seat—twenty-one degrees and thirteen minutes—northeast and by north—main branch seventh limb east side—shoot from the left eye of the death's-head—a bee-line from the tree through the shot fifty feet out.'*"

"Even this division," said I, "leaves me still in the dark."

"It left me also in the dark," replied Legrand, "for a few days;

during which I made diligent inquiry, in the neighborhood of Sullivan's Island, for any building which went by the name of the
'Bishop's Hotel'; for, of course, I dropped the obsolete word 'hostel.'
Gaining no information on the subject, I was on the point of extending my sphere of search, and proceeding in a more systematic manner, when, one morning, it entered my head, quite suddenly, that
this 'bishop's hostel' might have some reference to an old family,
of the name of Bessop, which, time out of mind, had held possession
of an ancient manor-house, about four miles to the northward of
the Island. I accordingly went over to the plantation, and reinstituted
my inquiries among the older negroes of the place. At length one of
the most aged of the women said that she had heard of such a place
as *Bessop's Castle,* and thought that she could guide me to it, but
that it was not a castle, nor a tavern, but a high rock.

"I offered to pay her well for her trouble, and, after some demur,
she consented to accompany me to the spot. We found it without
much difficulty, when, dismissing her, I proceeded to examine the
place. The 'castle' consisted of an irregular assemblage of cliffs and
rocks—one of the latter being quite remarkable for its height as
well as for its insulated and artificial appearance. I clambered to
its apex, and then felt much at a loss as to what should be next
done.

"While I was busied in reflection, my eyes fell upon a narrow
ledge in the eastern face of the rock, perhaps a yard below the summit
on which I stood. This ledge projected about eighteen inches, and
was not more than a foot wide, while a niche in the cliff just above
it gave it a rude resemblance to one of the hollow-backed chairs used
by our ancestors. I made no doubt that here was the 'devil's seat'
alluded to in the MS., and now I seemed to grasp the full secret of
the riddle.

I let myself down on the ledge, and proceeded to use the glass.

"The 'good glass,' I knew, could have reference to nothing but a telescope; for the word 'glass' is rarely employed in any other sense by seamen. Now here, I at once saw, was a telescope to be used, and a definite point of view, *admitting no variation,* from which to use it. Nor did I hesitate to believe that the phrases, 'twenty-one degrees and thirteen minutes,' and 'northeast and by north,' were intended

236

as directions for the leveling of the glass. Greatly excited by these discoveries, I hurried home, procured a telescope, and returned to the rock.

"I let myself down to the ledge, and found that it was impossible to retain a seat on it unless in one particular position. This fact confirmed my preconceived idea. I proceeded to use the glass. Of course, the 'twenty-one degrees and thirteen minutes' could allude to nothing but elevation above the visible horizon, since the horizontal direction was clearly indicated by the words, 'northeast and by north.' This latter direction I at once established by means of a pocket-compass; then, pointing the glass as nearly at an angle of twenty-one degrees of elevation as I could do it by guess, I moved it cautiously up or down, until my attention was arrested by a circular rift or opening in the foliage of a large tree that overtopped its fellows in the distance. In the center of this rift I perceived a white spot, but could not, at first, distinguish what it was. Adjusting the focus of the telescope, I again looked, and now made it out to be a human skull.

"On this discovery I was so sanguine as to consider the enigma solved; for the phrase 'main branch, seventh limb, east side,' could refer only to the position of the skull on the tree, while 'shoot from the left eye of the death's-head' admitted, also, of but one interpretation, in regard to a search for buried treasure. I perceived that the design was to drop a bullet from the left eye of the skull, and that a bee-line, or, in other words, a straight line, drawn from the nearest point of the trunk through 'the shot' (or the spot where the bullet fell) and thence extended to a distance of fifty feet, would indicate a definite point—and beneath this point I thought it at least *possible* that a deposit of value lay concealed."

"All this," I said, "is exceedingly clear, and, although ingenious, still simple and explicit. When you left the Bishop's Hotel, what then?"

"Why, having carefully taken the bearings of the tree, I turned homewards. The instant that I left 'the devil's seat,' however, the circular rift vanished; nor could I get a glimpse of it afterwards, turn as I would. What seems to me the chief ingenuity in this whole business, is the fact (for repeated experiment has convinced me it *is* a fact) that the circular opening in question is visible from no other attainable point of view than that afforded by the narrow ledge on the face of the rock.

"In this expedition to the 'Bishop's Hotel' I had been attended by Jupiter, who had, no doubt, observed, for some weeks past, the abstraction of my demeanor, and took especial care not to leave me alone. But, on the next day, getting up very early, I contrived to give him the slip, and went into the hills in search of the tree. After much toil I found it. When I came home at night my valet proposed to give me a flogging. With the rest of the adventure I believe you are as well acquainted as myself."

"I suppose," said I, "you missed the spot, in the first attempt at digging, through Jupiter's stupidity in letting the bug fall through the right instead of through the left eye of the skull."

"Precisely. This mistake made a difference of about two inches and a half in the 'shot'—that is to say, in the position of the peg nearest the tree; and had the treasure been *beneath* the 'shot,' the error would have been of little moment; but 'the shot,' together with the nearest point of the tree, were merely two points for the establishment of a line of direction; of course the error, however trivial in the beginning, increased as we proceeded with the line, and by the time we had gone fifty feet, threw us quite off the scent. But for my deep-seated convictions that treasure was here somewhere actually buried, we might have had all our labor in vain."

"I presume the fancy of *the skull*—of letting fall a bullet through the skull's eye—was suggested to Kidd by the piratical flag. No doubt he felt a kind of poetical consistency in recovering his money through this ominous insignium."

"Perhaps so; still I cannot help thinking that common sense had quite as much to do with the matter as poetical consistency. To be visible from the devil's seat, it was necessary that the object, if small, should be *white;* and there is nothing like your human skull for retaining and even increasing its whiteness under exposure to all vicissitudes of weather."

"But your grandiloquence, and your conduct in swinging the beetle—how excessively odd! I was sure you were mad. And why did you insist on letting fall the bug, instead of a bullet, from the skull?"

"Why, to be frank, I felt somewhat annoyed by your evident suspicions touching my sanity, and so resolved to punish you quietly, in my own way, by a little bit of sober mystification. For this reason I swung the beetle, and for this reason I let it fall from the tree. An observation of yours about its great weight suggested the latter idea."

"Yes, I perceive; and now there is only one point which puzzles me. What are we to make of the skeletons found in the hole?"

"That is a question I am no more able to answer than yourself. There seems, however, only one plausible way of accounting for them —and yet it is dreadful to believe in such atrocity as my suggestion would imply. It is clear that Kidd—if Kidd indeed secreted this treasure, which I doubt not—it is clear that he must have had assistance in the labor. But, the worst of this labor concluded, he may have thought it expedient to remove all participants in his secret. Perhaps a couple of blows with a mattock were sufficient, while his coadjutors were busy in the pit; perhaps it required a dozen—who shall tell?"

TALES FROM THE TRAVELS OF BARON MUNCHAUSEN

By *RUDOLPH ERICH RASPE*

Illustrations by GUSTAVE DORÉ

I

The Baron gives an account of his first travels—The astonishing effects of a storm—Arrives at Ceylon; combats and conquers two extraordinary opponents — Returns to Holland.

SOME years before my beard announced approaching manhood, or, in other words, when I was neither man nor boy, but between both, I expressed in repeated conversations a strong desire of seeing the world, from which I was discouraged by my parents, though my father had been no inconsiderable traveler himself, and will appear before I have reached the end of my singular and, I may add, interesting adventures. A cousin, by my mother's side, took a liking to me, often said I was a fine forward youth, and was much inclined to gratify my curiosity. His eloquence had more effect than mine, for my father consented to my accompanying him in a voyage to the island of Ceylon, where his uncle had resided as governor many years.

We sailed from Amsterdam with dispatches from their High Mightinesses the States of Holland. The only circumstance which happened on our voyage worth relating was the wonderful effects of a storm, which had torn up by the roots a great number of trees of enormous bulk and height, in an island where we lay at anchor to take in wood and water. Some of these trees weighed many tons, yet they were carried by the wind so amazingly high, that they appeared like the feathers of small birds floating in the air, for they were at least five miles above the earth. However, as soon as the storm subsided, they all fell perpendicularly into their respective places, and took root again, except the largest, which happened, when it was blown into the air, to have a man and his wife, a very honest old couple, upon its branches gathering cucumbers (in this part of the globe that useful vegetable grows upon trees). The weight of this couple, as the tree descended, overbalanced the trunk, and brought it down in a horizontal position. It fell upon the chief man of the island, and killed him on the spot; he had quitted his house in the storm, under an apprehension of its falling upon him, and was returning through his own garden, when this fortunate accident happened. The word fortunate, here, requires some explanation. The chief was a man of a very avaricious and oppressive disposition, and though he had no family, the natives of the island were half-starved by his oppressive and infamous impositions.

The very goods which he had thus taken from them were spoiling in his stores, while the poor wretches from whom they were plundered were pining in poverty. Though the destruction of this tyrant was accidental, the people chose the cucumber-gatherers for their governors, as a mark of gratitude for destroying, though accidentally, their late tyrant.

After we had repaired the damages we had sustained in this remarkable storm, and taken leave of the new governor and his lady, we sailed with a fair wind for the object of our voyage.

In about six weeks we arrived at Ceylon, where we were received with great marks of friendship and true politeness. The following singular adventures may not prove unentertaining.

After we had resided at Ceylon about a fortnight, I accompanied one of the governor's brothers upon a shooting party. He was a strong, athletic man, and being used to that climate (for he had resided there some years), he bore the violent heat of the sun much better than I could; in our excursion he had made a considerable progress through a thick wood when I was only at the entrance.

Near the banks of a large piece of water, which had engaged my attention, I thought I heard a rustling noise behind; on turning about, I was almost petrified (as who would not be?) at the sight of a lion, which was evidently approaching with the intention of satisfying his appetite with my poor carcass, and that without asking my consent. What was to be done in this horrible dilemma? I had not even a moment for reflection; my piece was charged only with swan-shot, and I had no other about me; however, though I could have no idea of killing such an animal with that weak kind of ammunition, yet I had some hopes of frightening him by the report, and perhaps of wounding him also. I immediately let fly, without waiting till he was within reach, and the report did but enrage him, for he now quickened his pace, and seemed to approach me full speed: I attempted to escape, but that only added (if an addition could be made) to my distress; for the moment I turned about, I found a large crocodile, with his mouth extended almost ready to receive me. On my right hand was the piece of water before mentioned, and on my left a deep precipice, said to have, as I have since learned, a receptacle at the bottom for venomous creatures; in short, I gave myself up for lost, for the lion was now upon his hind legs, just in the act of seizing me; I fell involuntarily to the ground with fear, and, as it afterwards appeared, he sprang over me. I lay some time in a situation which no language can describe, expecting to feel his teeth or talons in some part of me every moment. After waiting in this prostrate situation a few seconds, I heard a violent but unusual noise, different from any sound that had ever before assailed my ears; nor is it at all to be wondered at, when I inform you from whence it proceeded. After listening for some time, I ventured to raise my head and look around, when, to my unspeakable joy, I perceived the lion had, by the eagerness with which he sprung at me, jumped forward, as I fell, into the crocodile's mouth! which, as before observed, was wide open; the head of the one stuck in the throat of the other; and they were struggling to extricate themselves! I fortunately recollected my *couteau de chasse,* which was by my side; with this instrument I severed the lion's head at one blow, and the body fell at my feet! I then with the butt-end of my fowling piece, rammed the head further into the throat of the crocodile, and destroyed him by suffocation, for he could neither gorge nor eject it.

Soon after I had thus gained a complete victory over my two powerful adversaries, my companion arrived in search of me; for finding I did not follow him into the wood, he returned, apprehending I had lost my way, or met with some accident.

After mutual congratulations, we measured the crocodile, which was just forty feet in length.

As soon as we had related this extraordinary adventure to the governor, he sent a wagon and servants, who brought home the two carcasses. The lion's skin was properly preserved, with its hair on, after which it was made into tobacco-pouches, and presented by me, upon our return to Holland, to the burgomasters, who, in return, requested my acceptance of a thousand ducats.

The skin of the crocodile was stuffed in the usual manner, and makes a capital article in their public museum at Amsterdam, where the exhibitor relates the whole story to each spectator, with such additions as he thinks proper. Some of his variations are rather extrava-

The lion had jumped forward, as I fell, into
the crocodile's mouth.

gant; one of them is, that the lion jumped quite through the crocodile, and was making his escape at the back door, when, as soon as
his head appeared, Monsieur the Great Baron (as he is pleased to call
me) cut it off, and three feet of the crocodile's tail with it; nay, so
little attention has this fellow to the truth, that he sometimes adds, as
soon as the crocodile missed his tail, he turned about, snatched the
couteau de chasse out of Monsieur's hand, and swallowed it with such
eagerness that it pierced his heart and killed him immediately!

The little regard which this impudent knave has to veracity makes
me sometimes apprehensive that my *real facts* may fall under suspicion, by being found in company with his confounded inventions.

II

*In which the Baron proves himself a good shot—He loses his horse and
finds a wolf—Makes him draw his sledge—Promises to entertain his company with a relation of such facts as are well deserving their notice.*

I set off from Rome on a journey to Russia, in the midst of winter,
from a just notion that frost and snow must of course mend the roads,
which every traveler had described as uncommonly bad through the
northern parts of Germany, Poland, Courland, and Livonia. I went
on horseback, as the most convenient manner of traveling; I was but
lightly clothed, and of this I felt the inconvenience the more I advanced northeast. What must not a poor old man have suffered in
that severe weather and climate, whom I saw on a bleak common in
Poland, lying on the road, helpless, shivering, and hardly having
wherewithal to cover his nakedness? I pitied the poor soul: though
I felt the severity of the air myself, I threw my mantle over him, and

immediately I heard a voice from the heavens, blessing me for that piece of charity, saying,

"You will be rewarded, my son, for this in time."

I went on: night and darkness overtook me. No village was to be seen. The country was covered with snow, and I was unacquainted with the road.

Tired, I alighted, and fastened my horse to something like a pointed stump of a tree, which appeared above the snow; for the sake of safety I placed my pistols under my arm, and lay down on the snow, where I slept so soundly that I did not open my eyes till full daylight. It is not easy to conceive my astonishment to find myself in the midst of a village, lying in a churchyard; nor was my horse to be seen, but I heard him soon after neigh somewhere above me. On looking upward I beheld him hanging by his bridle to the weather-cock of the steeple. Matters were now very plain to me: the village had been covered with snow overnight; a sudden change of weather had taken place; I had sunk down to the churchyard whilst asleep, gently, and in the same proportion as the snow had melted away; and what in the dark I had taken to be a stump of a little tree appearing above the snow, to which I had tied my horse, proved to have been the cross or weathercock of the steeple!

Without long consideration I took one of my pistols, shot the bridle in two, brought down the horse, and proceeded on my journey. [Here the Baron seems to have forgotten his feelings: he should certainly have ordered his horse a feed of corn, after fasting so long.]

He carried me well—advancing into the interior parts of Russia. I found traveling on horseback rather unfashionable in winter. Therefore, I submitted, as I always do, to the custom of the country, took a single horse sledge, and drove briskly toward St. Petersburg. I do not exactly recollect whether it was in Eastland or Jugemanland, but I remember that in the midst of a dreary forest I spied a terrible wolf making after me with all the speed of a ravenous winter hunger. He soon overtook me. There was no possibility of escape. Mechanically I laid myself down flat in the sledge, and let my horse run for our safety. What I wished, but hardly hoped or expected, happened immediately after. The wolf did not mind me in the least, but took a leap over me, and falling furiously on the horse, began instantly to tear and devour the hind-part of the poor animal, which ran the faster for his pain and terror. Thus unnoticed and safe myself, I lifted my head slyly up, and with horror I beheld that the wolf had eaten his way into the horse's body; it was not long before he had fairly forced himself into it, when I took my advantage, and fell upon him with the butt-end of my whip. This unexpected attack in his rear frightened him so much, that he leaped forward with all his might: the horse's carcass dropped on the ground, but in his place the wolf was in the harness, and I on my part whipping him continually: we both arrived in full career safe at St. Petersburg, contrary to our respective expectations, and very much to the astonishment of the spectators.

I shall not tire you, gentlemen, with the politics, arts, sciences, and history of this magnificent metropolis of Russia, nor trouble you with the various intrigues and pleasant adventures I had in the politer circles of that country, where the lady of the house always receives the visitor with a dram and a salute. I shall confine myself rather to the greater and nobler objects of your attention, horses and dogs, my favorites in the brute creation; also to foxes, wolves, and bears, with which, and game in general, Russia abounds more than any other part of the world; and to such sports, manly exercises, and feats of gallantry and activity, as show the gentleman better than musty Greek or Latin, or all the perfume, finery, and capers of French wits or *petits-maîtres*.

III

An encounter between the Baron's nose and a door-post, with its wonderful effect —Fifty brace of ducks and other fowl destroyed by one shot—Flogs a fox out of his skin—Leads an old sow home in a new way, and vanquishes a wild boar.

For several months (as it was some time before I could obtain a commission in the army) I was perfectly at liberty to sport away my time and money in the most gentleman-like manner. You may easily imagine that I spent much of both out of town with such gallant fellows as knew how to make the most of an open forest country. The very recollection of those amusements gives me fresh spirits, and creates a warm wish for a repetition of them.

One morning I saw, through the windows of my bedroom, that a large pond not far off was covered with wild ducks. In an instant I took my gun from the corner, ran downstairs and out of the house in such a hurry that I imprudently struck my face against the door-post. Fire flew out of my eyes, but it did not prevent my intention; I soon came within shot, when, leveling my piece, I observed to my sorrow that even the flint had sprung from the cock by the violence of the shock I had just received. There was no time to be lost. I presently remembered the effect it had on my eyes, therefore opened the pan, leveled my piece against the wild fowls, and my fist against one of my eyes. [The Baron's eyes have retained fire ever since, and appear particularly illuminated when he relates this anecdote.] A hearty blow drew sparks again; the shot went off, and I killed fifty brace of ducks, twenty widgeons, and three couple of teals.

Presence of mind is the soul of manly exercises. If soldiers and sailors owe to it many of their lucky escapes, hunters and sportsmen are not less beholden to it for many of their successes. In a noble forest in Russia I met a fine black fox, whose valuable skin it would have been a pity to tear by ball or shot. Reynard stood close to a tree. In a twinkling I took out my ball and placed a good spike nail in its room, fired, and hit him so cleverly that I nailed his brush fast to the tree. I now went up to him, took out my hanger, gave him a cross cut over the face, laid hold of my whip, and fairly flogged him out of his fine skin.

Chance and good luck often correct our mistakes; of this I had a singular instance soon after, when, in the depths of a forest, I saw a wild pig and sow running close behind each other. My ball had missed them, yet the foremost pig only ran away, and the sow stood motionless, as fixed to the ground. On examining into the matter, I found the latter one to be an old sow, blind with age, which had taken hold of her pig's tail, in order to be led along by filial duty. My ball, having passed between the two, had cut his leading-string, which the old sow continued to hold in her mouth; and as her former guide did not draw her on any longer, she had stopped of course; I therefore laid hold of the remaining end of the pig's tail, and led the old beast without any further trouble on my part, and without any reluctance or apprehension on the part of the helpless old animal.

Terrible as these wild sows are, yet more fierce and dangerous are the boars, one of which I had once the misfortune to meet in the forest, unprepared for attack or defense. I retired behind an oak tree just when the furious animal leveled a side-blow at me, with such force that his tusks pierced through the tree, by which means he could neither repeat the blow nor retire. Ho, ho! thought I, I shall soon have you now! And immediately I laid hold of a stone, wherewith I hammered and bent his tusks in such a manner that he could not retreat by any means, and must wait my return from the next village, whither I went for ropes and a cart, to secure him properly, and to carry him off safe and alive, in which I perfectly succeeded.

IV

Recollections on Saint Hubert's stag—Shoots a stag with cherry-stones; the wonderful effects of it—Kills a bear by extraordinary dexterity; his danger pathetically described—Attacked by a wolf, which he turns inside out—Is assailed by a mad dog, from which he escapes—The Baron's cloak seized with madness, by which his whole wardrobe is thrown into confusion.

I dare say you have heard of the hunter and sportsman's protector, St. Hubert, and of the noble stag which appeared to him in the forest, with the holy cross between his antlers. I have paid my homage to that saint every year in good fellowship, and seen this stag a thousand times either painted in churches, or embroidered in the stars of his knights; so that, upon the honor and conscience of a good sportsman, I hardly know whether there may not have been formerly, or whether there are not such crossed stags even at this present day. But let me rather tell what I have seen myself.

Having one day spent all my shot, I found myself unexpectedly in the presence of a stately stag, looking at me as unconcernedly as if he had known of my empty pouches. I charged immediately with powder, and upon it a good handful of cherry-stones, for I had sucked the fruit as far as the hurry would permit. Thus I let fly at him, and hit him just in the middle of the forehead between his antlers; it stunned him—he staggered—yet he made off. A year or two after, being with a party in the same forest, I beheld a noble stag with a fine full-grown cherry tree above ten feet high between his antlers. I immediately recollected my former adventure, looked upon him as my property, and brought him to the ground by one shot, which at once gave me the haunch and cherry-sauce, for the tree was covered with the richest fruit, the like I had never tasted before.

Who knows but some passionate, holy sportsman, or sporting abbot or bishop, may have shot, planted, and fixed the cross between the antlers of St. Hubert's stag, in a manner similar to this? They always have been, and still are, famous for plantations of crosses and antlers; and in a case of distress or dilemma, which too often happens to keen sportsmen, one is apt to grasp at anything for safety, and to try any expedient rather than miss the favorable opportunity. I have many times found myself in that trying situation.

What do you say to this, for example? Daylight and powder were spent one day in a Polish forest. When I was going home a terrible

A noble stag with a full-grown cherry tree between his antlers.

bear made up to me in great speed, with open mouth, ready to fall upon me; all my pockets were searched in an instant for powder and ball, but in vain; I found nothing but two spare flints: one I flung with all my might into the monster's open jaws, down his throat. It gave him pain and made him turn about, so that I could level the second at his back-door, which, indeed, I did with wonderful success; for it flew in, met the first flint in the stomach, struck fire, and blew up the bear with a terrible explosion. Though I came safe off that time, yet I should not wish to try it again, or venture against bears with no other ammunition.

There is a kind of fatality in it. The fiercest and most dangerous animals generally come upon me when defenseless, as if they had a notion or an instinctive intimation of it. Thus a frightful wolf rushed upon me so suddenly, and so close, that I could do nothing but follow mechanical instinct, and thrust my fist into his open mouth. For safety's sake I pushed on and on, till my arm was fairly in up to the shoulder. How should I disengage myself? I was not much pleased with my awkward situation—with a wolf face to face; our ogling was not of the most pleasant kind. If I withdrew my arm, then the animal would fly the more furiously upon me; that I saw in his flaming eyes. In short, I laid hold of his tail, turned him inside out like a glove, and flung him to the ground, where I left him.

The same expedient would not have answered against a mad dog, which soon after came running against me in a narrow street at St. Petersburg. Run who can, I thought; and to do this the better, I threw off my fur cloak, and was safe within doors in an instant. I sent my servant for the cloak, and he put it in the wardrobe with my other clothes. The day after I was amazed and frightened by Jack's bawling, "For God's sake, sir, your fur cloak is mad!" I hastened up to him, and found almost all my clothes tossed about and torn to pieces.

The fellow was perfectly right in his apprehensions about the fur cloak's madness. I saw him myself just then falling upon a fine full-dress suit, which he shook and tossed in an unmerciful manner.

V

The effects of great activity and presence of mind—A favorite hound described—Presented with a famous horse by Count Przobossky, with which he performs many extraordinary feats.

All these narrow and lucky escapes, gentlemen, were chances turned to advantage by presence of mind and vigorous exertions, which, taken together, as everybody knows, make the fortunate sportsman, sailor, and soldier; but he would be a very blamable and imprudent sportsman, admiral, or general, who would always depend upon chance and his stars, without troubling himself about those arts which are their particular pursuits, and without providing the very best implements which insure success. I was not blamable either way; for I have always been as remarkable for the excellency of my horses, dogs, guns, and swords, as for the proper manner of using and managing them, so that upon the whole I may hope to be remembered in the forest, upon the turf, and in the field. I shall not enter here into any detail of my stables, kennel, or armory; but a favorite bitch of mine I cannot help mentioning to you; she was a greyhound, and I never had or saw a better. She grew old in my service, and was not remarkable for her size, but rather for her uncommon swiftness. I always coursed with her. Had you seen her you must have admired her, and would not have wondered at my predilection, and at my coursing her so much. She ran so fast, so much, and so long in my service, that she actually ran off her legs; so that, in the latter part of her life, I was under the necessity of working and using her only as a terrier, in which quality she still served me many years.

I remember this, my wonderful bitch, with the same pleasure and tenderness as a superb Lithuanian horse, which no money could have bought. He became mine by an accident, which gave me an opportunity of showing my horsemanship to a great advantage. I was at Count Przobossky's noble country-seat in Lithuania, and remained with the ladies at tea in the drawing room, while the gentlemen were down in the yard to see a young horse of blood which had just arrived. We suddenly heard a noise of distress; I hastened downstairs, and found the horse so unruly that nobody durst approach or mount him. The most resolute horsemen stood dismayed and aghast; despondency was expressed in every countenance, when, in one leap, I was on his back, took him by surprise, and worked him quite into gentleness and obedience, with the best display of horsemanship I was master of. Fully to show this to the ladies, and save them unneccessary trouble, I forced him to leap in at one of the open windows of the tea-room, walked around several times, pace, trot, and gallop, and at last made him mount the tea-table, there to repeat his lessons in a pretty style of miniature which was exceedingly pleasing to the ladies, for he performed them amazingly well, and did not break either cup or saucer. It placed me so high in their opinion, and so well in that of the noble lord, that, with his usual politeness, he begged I would accept of this young horse, and ride him full career to conquest and honor in the campaign against the Turks, which was soon to be opened, under the command of Count Munich.

I could not indeed have received a more agreeable present, nor a more ominous one at the opening of that campaign, in which I made my apprenticeship as a soldier. A horse so gentle, so spirited, and so fierce—at once a lamb and a Bucephalus—put me always in mind of the soldier's and the gentleman's duty! of young Alexander, and of the astonishing things he performed in the field.

We took the field, among several other reasons, it seems, with an intention to retrieve the character of the Russian arms, which had been blemished a little by Czar Peter's last campaign on the Pruth; and this we fully accomplished by several very fatiguing and glorious campaigns under the command of that great general I mentioned.

Modesty forbids individuals to arrogate to themselves great successes or victories, the glory of which is generally engrossed by the commander—nay, which is rather awkward, by kings and queens who never smelled gunpowder but at the field-days and reviews of their troops; never saw a field of battle, or an enemy in battle array.

Nor do I claim any particular share of glory in the great engagements with the enemy. We all did our duty, which, in the patriot's, soldier's and gentleman's language, is a very comprehensive word, of great honor, meaning, and import, and of which the generality of idle quidnuncs and coffee-house politicians can hardly form any but a very mean and contemptible idea. However, having had the command of a body of hussars, I went upon several expeditions, with discretionary powers; and the success I then met with is, I think, fairly and only to be placed to my account, and to that of the brave fellows whom I led on to conquest and to victory.

We had very hot work once in the van of the army, when we

drove the Turks into Oczakow. My spirited Lithuanian had almost brought me into a scrape: I had an advanced fore-post, and saw the enemy coming against me in a cloud of dust, which left me rather uncertain about their actual numbers and real intentions: to wrap myself up in a similar cloud was common prudence, but would not have much advanced my knowledge, or answered the end for which I had been sent out; therefore I let my flankers on both wings spread to the right and left, and make what dust they could, and I myself led on straight upon the enemy, to have a nearer sight of them; in this I was gratified, for they stood and fought, till, for fear of my flankers, they began to move off rather disorderly. This was the moment to fall upon them with spirit; we broke them entirely—made a terrible havoc, and drove them not only back to a walled town in their rear, but through it, contrary to our most sanguine expectation.

The swiftness of my Lithuanian enabled me to be foremost in the pursuit; and seeing the enemy fairly flying through the opposite gate, I thought it would be prudent to stop in the market-place, to order the men to rendezvous. I stopped, gentlemen; but judge of my astonishment when in this market-place I saw not one of my hussars about me! Are they scouring the other streets? or what is become of them? They could not be far off, and must, at all events, soon join me. In that expectation I walked my panting Lithuanian to a spring in this market-place and let him drink. He drank uncommonly, with an eagerness not to be satisfied, but natural enough; for when I looked around for my men, what should I see, gentlemen! the hind part of the poor creature—croup and legs—was missing, as if he had been cut in two, and the water ran out as it came in, without refreshing or doing him any good! How it could have happened was quite a mystery to me, till I returned with him to the town gate. There I saw that when I rushed in pell-mell with the flying enemy, they had

The hind part of the poor creature was missing,
as if it had been cut in two.

dropped the portcullis (a heavy falling door, with sharp spikes at the bottom, let down suddenly to prevent the entrance of an enemy into a fortified town) unperceived by me, which had totally cut off his hind part, that still lay quivering on the outside of the gate. It would have been an irreparable loss, had not our farrier contrived to bring both parts together while hot. He sewed them up with sprigs and young shoots of laurels that were at hand; the wound healed, and, what could not have happened but to so glorious a horse, the sprigs took root in his body, grew up and formed a bower over me; so that afterwards I could go upon many other expeditions in the shade of my own and my horse's laurels.

VI

The Baron is made a prisoner of war, and sold for a slave—Keeps the Sultan's bees, which are attacked by two bears—Loses one of his bees; a silver hatchet, which he throws at the bears, rebounds and flies up to the moon; brings it back by an ingenious invention; falls to the earth on his return, and helps himself out of a pit— Extricates himself from a carriage which meets his in a narrow road, in a manner never before attempted nor practiced, since—The wonderful effects of the frost upon his servant's French horn.

Success was not always with me. I had the misfortune to be over-powered by numbers, to be made prisoner of war; and, what is worse, but always usual among the Turks, to be sold for a slave. [The Baron was afterwards in great favor with the Grand Seignior, as will appear hereafter.] In that state of humiliation my daily task was not very hard and laborious, but rather singular and irksome. It was to drive the Sultan's bees every morning to their pasture-grounds, to attend them all day long, and against night to drive them back to their hives.

One evening I missed a bee, and soon observed that two bears had fallen upon her to tear her to pieces for the honey she carried. I had nothing like an offensive weapon in my hands but the silver hatchet, which is the badge of the Sultan's gardeners and farmers. I threw it at the robbers, with an intention to frighten them away, and set the poor bee at liberty; but by an unlucky turn of my arm, it flew upward, and continued rising till it reached the moon. How should I recover it? how fetch it down again? I recollected that Turkey-beans grow very quick, and run up to an astonishing height. I planted one immediately; it grew, and actually fastened itself to one of the moon's horns. I had no more to do now but to climb up by it into the moon, where I safely arrived, and had a troublesome piece of business before I could find my silver hatchet, in a place where everything has the brightness of silver; at last, however, I found it in a heap of chaff and chopped straw.

I was now for returning: but, alas! the heat of the sun had dried up my bean; it was totally useless for my descent; so I fell to work and twisted me a rope of that chopped straw, as long and as well as I could make it. This I fastened to one of the moon's horns, and slid down to the end of it. Here I held myself fast with the left hand, and with the hatchet in my right, I cut the long, now useless, end of the upper part, which, when tied to the lower end, brought me a good deal lower. This repeated splicing and tying of the rope did not improve its quality, or bring me down to the Sultan's farm. I was four or five miles from the earth at least when it broke; I fell to the ground with such amazing violence that I found myself stunned, and in a hole nine fathoms deep at least, made by the weight of my body falling from so great a height. I recovered, but knew not how to get out again; however, I dug slopes or steps with my finger-nails [the Baron's nails then were of forty years' growth], and easily accomplished it.

Peace was soon after concluded with the Turks, and gaining my liberty, I left St. Petersburg at the time of that singular revolution, when the emperor in his cradle, his mother, the Duke of Brunswick, her father, Field Marshal Munich, and many others were sent to Siberia. The winter was then so uncommonly severe all over Europe, that ever since the sun seems to be frost-bitten. At my return to this place, I felt on the road greater inconveniences than those I had experienced on my setting out.

I traveled post, and finding myself in a narrow lane, bid the postilion give a signal with his horn, that other travelers might not meet us in the narrow passage. He blew with all his might; but his efforts were in vain, he could not make the horn sound, which was unaccountable and rather unfortunate, for soon after we found ourselves in the presence of another coach coming the other way. There was no proceeding; however, I got out of my carriage, and being pretty strong, placed it, wheels and all, upon my head. I then jumped over a hedge about nine feet high (which considering the weight of the coach, was rather difficult) into a field, and came out again by another jump into the road beyond the other carriage. I then went back for the horses, and placing one upon my head, and the other under my left arm, by the same means brought them to my coach, put to, and proceeded to an inn at the end of our stage. I should have told you that the horse under my arm was very spirited, and not above four

I went back for the horses, and carried them to my coach.

years old. In making my second spring over the hedge he expressed great dislike to that violent kind of motion by kicking and snorting; however, I confined his hind legs by putting them into my coat pocket. After we arrived at the inn, my postilion and I refreshed ourselves: he hung his horn on a peg near the kitchen fire; I sat on the other side.

Suddenly we heard a *tereng! tereng! teng! teng!* We looked around, and now found the reason why the postilion had not been able to sound his horn; his tunes were frozen up in the horn, and came out now, by thawing, plain enough, and much to the credit of the driver; so that the honest fellow entertained us for some time with a variety of tunes, without putting his mouth to the horn—The King of Prussia's March—Over the Hill and Over the Dale—with many other favorite tunes; at length the thawing entertainment concluded, as I shall this short account of my Russian travels.

GULLIVER'S VOYAGE TO LILLIPUT

By JONATHAN SWIFT: Edited by PADRAIC COLUM

With Illustrations by WILLY POGANY

I: *The Author gives some account of himself and family, his first induce-ments to travel—He is shipwrecked and swims for his life, gets safe on shore in the country of* Lilliput, *is made a prisoner and carried up country.*

MY father had a small estate in Nottinghamshire; I was the third of five sons. He sent me to Emanuel College in Cambridge, at fourteen years old, where I resided three years, and applied myself close to my studies; but the charge of maintaining me (although I had a very scanty allowance) being too great for a narrow fortune, I was bound apprentice to Mr. James Bates, an eminent surgeon in London, with whom I continued four years; and my father now and then sending me small sums of money, I laid them out in learning navigation, and other parts of the mathematics, useful to those who intend to travel, as I always believed it would be some time or other my fortune to do. When I left Mr. Bates, I went down to my father; where, by the assistance of him and my uncle John, and some other relations, I got forty pounds, and a promise of thirty pounds a year to maintain me at Leyden: there I studied physic two years and seven months, knowing it would be useful in long voyages.

Soon after my return from Leyden, I was recommended by my good master, Mr. Bates, to be surgeon to the *Swallow,* Captain Abraham Pannell, commander; with whom I continued three years and a half, making a voyage or two into the Levant, and some other parts. When I came back I resolved to settle in London, to which Mr. Bates, my master, encouraged me, and by him I was recommended to several patients. I took part of a small house in the Old Jury; and being advised to alter my condition, I married Mrs. Mary Burton, second daughter to Mr. Edmund Burton, hosier, in Newgate-street, with whom I received four hundred pounds for a portion.

But, my good master Bates dying in two years after, and I having few friends, my business began to fail; for my conscience would not suffer me to imitate the bad practice of too many among my brethren. Having therefore consulted with my wife, and some of my acquaintance, I determined to go again to sea. I was surgeon successively in two ships, and made several voyages, for six years, to the East and West Indies, by which I got some addition to my fortune. My hours of leisure I spent in reading the best authors, ancient and modern, being always provided with a good number of books; and when I was ashore, in observing the manners and dispositions of the people, as well as learning their language, wherein I had a great facility by the strength of my memory.

The last of these voyages not proving very fortunate, I grew weary of the sea, and intended to stay at home with my wife and family. I removed from the Old Jury to Fetter-Lane, and from thence to Wapping, hoping to get business among the sailors; but it would not turn to account. After three years' expectation that things would mend, I accepted an advantageous offer from Captain William Prichard, master of the *Antelope,* who was making a voyage to the South Sea. We set sail from Bristol, May 4, 1699, and our voyage at first was very prosperous.

It would not be proper, for some reasons, to trouble the reader with the particulars of our adventures in those seas: let it suffice to inform him, that in our passage from thence to the East Indies, we were driven by a violent storm to the northwest of Van Diemen's Land. By an observation, we found ourselves in the latitude of 30 degrees 2 minutes south. Twelve of our crew were dead by immoderate labor, and ill food, the rest were in a very weak condition. On the fifth of November, which was the beginning of summer in those parts, the weather being very hazy, the seamen spied a rock, within half a cable's length of the ship; but the wind was so strong, that we were driven directly upon it, and immediately split. Six of the crew, of whom I was one, having let down the boat into the sea, made a shift to get clear of the ship, and the rock. We rowed, by my computation, about three leagues, till we were able to work no longer, being already spent with labor while we were in the ship. We therefore trusted ourselves to the mercy of the waves, and in about half an hour the boat was overset by a sudden flurry from the north. What became of my companions in the boat, as well as of those who escaped on the rock, or were left in the vessel, I cannot tell; but conclude they were all lost. For my own part, I swam as fortune directed me, and was pushed forward by wind and tide. I often let my legs drop, and could feel no bottom: but when I was almost gone, and able to struggle no longer, I found myself within my depth; and by this time the storm was much abated. The declivity was so small, that I walked near a mile before I got to the shore, which I conjectured was about eight o'clock in the evening. I then advanced forward near half a mile, but could not discover any sign of houses or inhabitants; at least I was in so weak a condition, that I did not observe them. I was extremely tired, and with that, and the heat of the weather, and about half a pint of brandy that I drank as I left the ship, I found myself much inclined to sleep. I lay down on the grass, which was very short and soft, where I slept sounder than ever I remember to have done in my life, and, as I reckoned, about nine hours; for when I awaked, it was just daylight. I attempted to arise, but was not able to stir: for as I happened to lie on my back, I found my arms and legs were strongly fastened on each side of the ground; and my hair, which was long and thick, tied down in the same manner. I likewise felt several slender ligatures across my body, from my arm-pits to my thighs. I could only look upward, the sun began to grow hot, and the light offended my eyes. I heard a confused noise about me, but in the posture I lay, could see nothing except the sky. In a little time I felt something alive moving on my left leg, which advancing gently forward over my breast, came almost up to my chin; when bending my eyes downward as much as I could, I perceived it to be a human creature not six inches high,[1] with a bow and arrow in his hands, and a quiver at his back. In the meantime, I felt at least forty more of the same kind (as I conjectured) following the first. I was in the utmost astonishment, and roared so loud, that they all ran back in a fright; and some of them, as I was afterwards told, were hurt with the falls they got by leaping from my sides upon the ground. However, they soon returned, and one of them, who ventured so far as to get a full sight of my face, lifting up his hands and eyes by way of admiration,

[1] The people of Lilliput measure in inches about what a man measures in feet; a person of six inches would be tall among them. Everything in the country is of a size proportional to the inhabitants: horses, wagons, temples, trees, animals are in inches what ours would be in feet.

cried out in a shrill, but distinct voice, *Hekinah degul:* the others repeated the same words several times, but then I knew not what they
meant: I lay all this while, as the reader may believe, in great uneasiness: at length, struggling to get loose, I had the fortune to break the
strings, and wrench out the pegs that fastened my left arm to the
ground; for, by lifting it up to my face, I discovered the methods
they had taken to bind me, and at the same time with a violent pull,
which gave me excessive pain, I a little loosened the strings that tied
down my hair on the left side, so that I was just able to turn my head
about two inches. But the creatures ran off a second time, before I
could seize them; whereupon there was a great shout in a very shrill
accent, and after it ceased, I heard one of them cry aloud *Tolgo
phonac;* when in an instant I felt about a hundred arrows discharged
on my left hand, which pricked me like so many needles; and besides,
they shot another flight into the air, as we do bombs in Europe,
whereof many, I suppose, fell on my body (though I felt them not),
and some on my face, which I immediately covered with my left
hand. When this shower of arrows was over, I fell a-groaning with
grief and pain, and then striving again to get loose, they discharged
another volley larger than the first, and some of them attempted with
spears to stick me in the sides; but, by good luck, I had on a buff
jerkin, which they could not pierce. I thought it the most prudent
method to lie still, and my design was to continue so till night, when,
my left hand being already loose, I could easily free myself; and as
for the inhabitants, I had reason to believe I might be a match for
the greatest armies they could bring against me, if they were all of the
same size with him that I saw. But fortune disposed otherwise of me.
When the people observed I was quiet, they discharged no more
arrows; but, by the noise I heard, I knew their numbers increased;
and about four yards from me, over against my right ear, I heard a

knocking for above an hour, like that of people at work; when turning my head that way, as well as the pegs and strings would permit me, I saw a stage erected, about a foot and a half from the ground, capable of holding four of the inhabitants, with two or three ladders to mount it: from whence one of them, who seemed to be a person of quality, made me a long speech, whereof I understood not one syllable. But I should have mentioned, that before the principal person began his oration, he cried out three times, *Langro dehul sans* (these words and the former were afterwards repeated and explained to me). Whereupon immediately about fifty of the inhabitants came and cut the strings that fastened the left side of my head, which gave me the liberty of turning it to the right, and of observing the person and gesture of him that was to speak. He appeared to be of middle age, and taller than any of the other three who attended him, whereof one was a page that held up his train, and seemed to be somewhat longer than my middle finger; the other two stood one on each side to support him. He acted every part of an orator, and I could observe many periods of threatenings, and others of promises, pity, and kindness. I answered in a few words, but in the most submissive manner, lifting up my left hand, and both my eyes to the sun, as calling him for a witness; and being almost famished with hunger, having not eaten a morsel for some hours before I left the ship, I found the demands of nature so strong upon me, that I could not forbear showing my impatience (perhaps against the strict rules of decency) by putting my finger frequently on my mouth, to signify that I wanted food. The *Hurgo* (for so they call a great lord, as I afterwards learned) understood me very well. He descended from the stage, and commanded that several ladders should be applied to my sides, on which above a hundred of the inhabitants mounted and walked toward my mouth, laden with baskets full of meat, which had been provided and sent thither by the King's orders, upon the first intelligence he received of me. I observed there was the flesh of several animals, but could not distinguish them by the taste. There were shoulders, legs, and loins, shaped like those of mutton, and very well dressed, but smaller than the wings of a lark. I ate them by two or three at a mouthful, and took three loaves at a time, about the bigness of musket bullets. They supplied me as fast as they could, showing a thousand marks of wonder and astonishment at my bulk and appetite. I then made another sign that I wanted drink. They found by my eating, that a small quantity would not suffice me; and being a most ingenious people, they slung up with great dexterity one of their largest hogsheads, then rolled it towards my hand, and beat out the top; I drank it off at a draught, which I might well do, for it did not hold half a pint,[1] and tasted like a small wine of Burgundy, but much more delicious. They brought me a second hogshead, which I drank in the same manner, and made signs for more, but they had none to give me. When I had performed these wonders, they shouted for joy, and danced upon my breast, repeating several times as they did at first, *Hekinah degul.* They made me a sign that I should throw down the two hogsheads, but first warning the people below to stand out of the way, crying aloud, *Borach mivola,* and when they saw the vessels in the air, there was an universal shout of *Hekinah degul.* I confess I was often tempted, while they were passing backwards and forwards on my body, to seize forty or fifty of the first that came in my reach, and dash them against the ground. But the remembrance of what I had felt, which probably might not be the worst they could do, and the promise of honor I made them, for so I interpreted my submissive behavior, soon drove out these imaginations. Besides, I now

[1] Our measure would be 1,728 times as great as that of the Lilliputians; half a pint would thus be equivalent to 108 Lilliputian gallons.

considered myself as bound by the laws of hospitality to a people who had treated me with so much expense and magnificence. However, in my thoughts, I could not sufficiently wonder at the intrepidity of these diminutive mortals, who durst venture to mount and walk upon my body, while one of my hands was at liberty, without trembling at the very sight of so prodigious a creature as I must appear to them. After some time, when they observed that I made no more demands for meat, there appeared before me a person of high rank from his Imperial Majesty. His Excellency, having mounted on the small of my right leg, advanced forwards up to my face, with about a dozen of his retinue. And producing his credentials under the Signet Royal, which he applied close to my eyes, spoke about ten minutes, without any signs of anger, but with a kind of determinate resolution; often pointing forwards, which as I afterwards found, was towards the capital city, about half a mile distant, whither it was agreed by his Majesty in council that I must be conveyed. I answered in few words, but to no purpose, and made a sign with my hand that was loose, putting it to the other (but over his Excellency's head for fear of hurting him or his train) and then to my own head and body, to signify that I desired my liberty. It appeared that he understood me well enough, for he shook his head by way of disapprobation, and held his hand in a posture to show that I must be carried as a prisoner. However, he made other signs to let me understand that I should have meat and drink enough, and very good treatment. Whereupon I once more thought of attempting to break my bonds; but again, when I felt the smart of their arrows, upon my face and hands, which were all in blisters, and many of the darts still sticking in them, and observing likewise that the number of my enemies increased, I gave tokens to let them know that they might do with me what they pleased. Upon this, the *Hurgo* and his train withdrew, with much civility and cheerful countenances.

Soon after I heard a general shout, with frequent repetitions of the words, *Peplom selan,* and I felt great numbers of people on my left side relaxing the cords to such a degree, that I was able to turn upon my right side. But before this, they had daubed my face and both my hands with a sort of ointment very pleasant to the smell, which in a few minutes removed all the smart of their arrows. These circumstances, added to the refreshment I had received by their victuals and drink, which were very nourishing, disposed me to sleep. I slept about eight hours, as I was afterwards assured; and it was no wonder, for the physicians, by the Emperor's order, had mingled a sleepy potion in the hogshead of wine.

It seems that upon the first moment I was discovered sleeping on the ground after my landing, the Emperor had early notice of it by an express; and determined in council that I should be tied in the manner I have related (which was done in the night while I slept), that plenty of meat and drink should be sent to me, and a machine prepared to carry me to the capital city.

This resolution perhaps may appear very bold and dangerous, and I am confident would not be imitated by any prince in Europe on the like occasion; however, in my opinion, it was extremely prudent, as well as generous: for supposing these people had endeavored to kill me with their spears and arrows while I was asleep, I should certainly have awaked with the first sense of smart, which might so far have roused my rage and strength, as to have enabled me to break the strings wherewith I was tied; after which, as they were not able to make resistance, so they could expect no mercy.

These people are most excellent mathematicians, and arrived to a great perfection in mechanics, by the countenance and encouragement of the Emperor, who is a renowned patron of learning. This prince hath several machines fixed on wheels, for the carriage of trees and

Fifteen hundred of the Emperor's horses

were used to draw me to the metropolis.

275

other great weights. He often builds his largest men of war, whereof some are nine foot long, in the woods, where the timber grows, and has them carried on these engines three or four hundred yards to the sea. Five hundred carpenters and engineers were immediately set at work to prepare the greatest engine they had. It was a frame of wood raised three inches from the ground, about seven foot long and four wide, moving upon twenty-two wheels. The shout I heard was upon the arrival of this engine, which it seems set out in four hours after my landing. It was brought parallel to me as I lay. But the principal difficulty was to raise and place me in this vehicle. Eighty poles, each of one foot high, were erected for this purpose, and very strong cords of the bigness of packthread were fastened by hooks to many bandages, which the workmen had girt round my neck, my hands, my body, and my legs. Nine hundred of the strongest men were employed to draw up these cords by many pulleys fastened on the poles, and thus, in less than three hours, I was raised and slung into the engine, and there tied fast. All this I was told, for, while the whole operation was performing, I lay in a profound sleep, by the force of that soporiferous medicine infused into my liquor. Fifteen hundred of the Emperor's largest horses, each about four inches and a half high, were employed to draw me towards the metropolis, which, as I said, was half a mile distant.

About four hours after we began our journey, I awaked by a very ridiculous accident; for the carriage being stopped a while to adjust something that was out of order, two or three of the young natives had the curiosity to see how I looked when I was asleep; they climbed up into the engine, and advancing very softly to my face, one of them, an officer in the guards, put the sharp end of his half-pike a good way up into my left nostril, which tickled my nose like a straw, and made me sneeze violently: whereupon they stole off unperceived, and it was three weeks before I knew the cause of my awaking so suddenly. We made a long march the remaining part of that day, and rested at night with five hundred guards on each side of me, half with torches, and half with bows and arrows, ready to shoot me if I should offer to stir. The next morning at sunrise we continued our march and arrived within two hundred yards of the city gates about noon. The Emperor, and all his court, came out to meet us; but his great officers would by no means suffer his Majesty to endanger his person by mounting on my body.

At the place where the carriage stopped, there stood an ancient temple, esteemed to be the largest in the whole kingdom; which having been polluted some years before by an unnatural murder, was, according to the zeal of those people, looked upon as profane, and therefore had been applied to common uses, and all the ornaments and furniture carried away. In this edifice it was determined I should lodge. The great gate fronting to the north was about four foot high, and almost two foot wide, through which I could easily creep. On each side of the gate was a small window not above six inches from the ground: into that on the left side, the King's smiths conveyed fourscore and eleven chains, like those that hang to a lady's watch in Europe and almost as large, which were locked to my left leg with six and thirty padlocks. Over against this temple, on t'other side of the great highway, at twenty foot distance, there was a turret at least five foot high. Here the Emperor ascended, with many principal lords of his court, to have an opportunity of viewing me, as I was told, for I could not see them. It was reckoned that above a hundred thousand inhabitants came out of the town upon the same errand; and, in spite of my guards, I believe there could not be fewer than ten thousand at several times, who mounted my body by the help of ladders. But a proclamation was soon issued to forbid it upon pain of death. When the workmen found it was impossible for me to break loose, they cut all the strings that bound me; whereupon I rose up, with as melancholy a disposition as ever I had in my life. But the noise and astonishment of the people at seeing me rise and walk, are not to be expressed. The chains that held my left leg were about two yards long, and gave me not only the liberty of walking backwards and forwards in a semi-circle; but, being fixed within four inches of the gate, allowed me to creep in, and lie at my full length in the temple.

II: *The Emperor of* Lilliput, *attended by several of the nobility, comes to see the Author in his confinement—The Emperor's person and habit described—Learned men appointed to teach the Author their language—He gains favor by his mild disposition—His pockets are searched, and his sword and pistols taken from him.*

When I found myself on my feet, I looked about me, and must confess I never beheld a more entertaining prospect. The country round appeared like a continued garden, and the enclosed fields, which were generally forty foot square, resembled so many beds of flowers. These fields were intermingled with woods of half a stang,[1] and the tallest trees, as I could judge, appeared to be seven foot high. I viewed the town on my left hand, which looked like the painted scene of a city in a theater.

The Emperor was already descended from the tower, and advancing on horseback toward me, which had like to have cost him dear; for the beast, though very well trained, yet wholly unused to such a sight, which appeared as if a mountain moved before him, reared up on his hinder feet: but that prince, who is an excellent horseman, kept

[1] A stang is a pole or perch; sixteen feet and a half.

his seat, till his attendants ran in, and held the bridle, while his Majesty had time to dismount. When he alighted, he surveyed me round with great admiration, but kept beyond the length of my chain. He ordered his cooks and butlers, who were already prepared, to give me victuals and drink, which they pushed forward in a sort of vehicles upon wheels, till I could reach them. I took these vehicles, and soon emptied them all; twenty of them were filled with meat, and ten with liquor; each of the former afforded me two or three good mouthfuls, and I emptied the liquor of ten vessels, which was contained in earthen vials, into one vehicle, drinking it off at a draught; and so I did with the rest. The Empress, and young Princes of the blood of both sexes, attended by many ladies, sat at some distance in their chairs; but upon the accident that happened to the Emperor's horse, they alighted, and came near his person, which I am now going to describe.

He is taller by almost the breadth of my nail, than any of his court; which alone is enough to strike an awe into the beholders. His features are strong and masculine, with an Austrian lip and arched nose, his complexion olive, his countenance erect, his body and limbs well proportioned, all his motions graceful, and his deportment majestic. He was then past his prime, being twenty-eight years and three quarters old, of which he had reigned about seven, in great felicity, and generally victorious. For the better convenience of beholding him, I lay on my side, so that my face was parallel to his, and he stood but three yards off: however, I have had him since many times in my hand, and therefore cannot be deceived in the description. His dress was very plain and simple, and the fashion of it between the Asiatic and the European: but he had on his head a light helmet of gold, adorned with jewels, and a plume on the crest. He held his sword drawn in his hand, to defend himself, if I should happen to break loose; it was almost three inches long, the hilt and scabbard were gold enriched with diamonds. His voice was shrill, but very clear and articulate, and I could distinctly hear it when I stood up. The ladies and courtiers were all most magnificently clad, so that the spot they stood upon seemed to resemble a petticoat spread on the ground, embroidered with figures of gold and silver. His Imperial Majesty spoke often to me, and I returned answers, but neither of us could understand a syllable. There were several of his priests and lawyers present (as I conjectured by their habits) who were commanded to address themselves to me, and I spoke to them in as many languages as I had the least smattering of, which were High and Low Dutch, Latin, French, Spanish, Italian, and Lingua Franca; but all to no purpose. After about two hours the court retired, and I was left with a strong guard, to prevent the impertinence, and probably the malice of the rabble, who were very impatient to crowd about me as near as they durst, and some of them had the impudence to shoot their arrows at me as I sat on the ground by the door of my house, whereof one very narrowly missed my left eye. But the colonel ordered six of the ringleaders to be seized, and thought no punishment so proper as to deliver them bound into my hands, which some of his soldiers accordingly did, pushing them forward with the butt-ends of their pikes into my reach; I took them all in my right hand, put five of them into my coat-pocket, and as to the sixth, I made a countenance as if I would eat him alive. The poor man squalled terribly, and the colonel and his officers were in much pain, especially when they saw me take out my pen-knife: but I soon put them out of fear: for, looking mildly, and immediately cutting the strings he was bound with, I set him gently on the ground, and away he ran. I treated the rest in the same manner, taking them one by one out of my pocket, and I observed both the soldiers and people were highly obliged at this mark of my clemency, which was represented very much to my advantage at court.

Toward night I got with some difficulty into my house, where I lay on the ground, and continued to do so about a fortnight; during which time the Emperor gave orders to have a bed prepared for me. Six hundred beds of the common measure were brought in carriages, and worked up in my house; a hundred and fifty of their beds sewn together made up the breadth and length, and these were four double, which however kept me but very indifferently from the hardness of the floor, that was of smooth stone. By the same computation they provided me with sheets, blankets, and coverlets, tolerable enough for one who had been so long inured to hardships as I.

As the news of my arrival spread through the kingdom, it brought prodigious numbers of rich, idle, and curious people to see me; so that the villages were almost emptied, and great neglect of tillage and household affairs must have ensued, if his Imperial Majesty had not provided, by several proclamations and orders of state, against this inconveniency. He directed that those who had already beheld me should return home, and not presume to come within fifty yards of my house without license from court; whereby the secretaries of state got considerable fees.

In the meantime, the Emperor held frequent councils to debate what course should be taken with me; and I was afterwards assured by a particular friend, a person of great quality, who was looked upon to be as much in the secret as any, that the court was under many difficulties concerning me. They apprehended my breaking loose, that my diet would be very expensive, and might cause a famine. Sometimes they determined to starve me, or at least to shoot me in the face and hands with poisoned arrows, which would soon dispatch me; but again they considered that the stench of so large a carcass might produce a plague in the metropolis, and probably spread through the whole kingdom. In the midst of these consultations, several officers of the army went to the door of the great council-chamber; and two of them being admitted, gave an account of my behavior to the six criminals above-mentioned, which made so favorable an impression in the breast of his Majesty and the whole board, in my behalf, that an Imperial Commission was issued out, obliging all the villages nine hundred yards round the city, to deliver in every morning six beeves, forty sheep, and other victuals for my sustenance; together with a proportionable quantity of bread, and wine, and other liquors; for the due payment of which his Majesty gave assignments upon his treasury. For this prince lives chiefly upon his own demesnes, seldom, except upon great occasions, raising any subsidies upon his subjects, who are bound to attend him in his wars at their own expense.

An establishment was also made of six hundred persons to be my domestics, who had board-wages allowed for their maintenance, and tents built for them very conveniently on each side of my door. It was likewise ordered, that three hundred tailors should make me a suit of clothes after the fashion of the country: that six of his Majesty's greatest scholars should be employed to instruct me in their language: and, lastly, that the Emperor's horses, and those of the nobility, and troops of guards, should be frequently exercised in my sight, to accustom themselves to me.

All these orders were duly put in execution, and in about three weeks I made a great progress in learning their language; during which time, the Emperor frequently honored me with his visits, and was pleased to assist my masters in teaching me. We began already to converse together in some sort; and the first words I learned were to express my desire that he would please give me my liberty, which I every day repeated on my knees. His answer, as I could comprehend it, was that this must be a work of time, not to be thought on without the advice of his council, and that first I must *Lumos kelmin pesso desmar lon Emposo;* that is, swear a peace with him and his kingdom. However, that I should be used with all kindness; and he advised me to acquire, by my patience and discreet behavior, the good opinion of himself and his subjects. He desired I would not take it ill, if he gave orders to certain proper officers to search me; for probably I might carry about me several weapons, which must needs be dangerous things, if they answered the bulk of so prodigious a person. I said, his Majesty should be satisfied, for I was ready to strip myself, and turn up my pockets before him. This I delivered part in words, and part in signs. He replied, that by the laws of the kingdom I must be searched by two of his officers; that he knew this could not be done without my consent and assistance; and he had so good an opinion of my generosity and justice, as to trust their persons in my hands: that whatever they took from me should be returned when I left the country, or paid for at the rate which I would set upon them. I took up the two officers in my hands, put them first into my coat-pockets, and then into every other pocket about me, except my two fobs, and another secret pocket which I had no mind should be searched, wherein I had some little necessaries that were of no consequence to any but myself. In one of my fobs there was a silver watch, and in the other a small quantity of gold in a purse. These gentlemen, having pen, ink, and paper about them, made an exact inventory of everything they saw; and when they had done, desired I would set them down, that they might deliver it to the Emperor. This inventory I afterwards translated into English, and is word for word as follows:

Imprimis, In the right coat-pocket of the Great Man-Mountain (for so I interpret the words *Quinbus Flestrin*) after the strictest search, we found only one great piece of coarse cloth, large enough to be a foot-cloth for your Majesty's chief room of state. In the left pocket we saw a huge silver chest, with a cover of the same metal, which we, the searchers, were not able to lift. We desired it should be opened, and one of us stepping into it, found himself up to the mid leg in a sort of dust, some part whereof flying up to our faces, set us both a-sneezing for several times together. In his right waistcoat-pocket we found a prodigious bundle of white thin substances, folded one over another, about the bigness of three men, tied with a strong cable, and marked with black figures; which we humbly conceive to be writings, every letter almost half as large as the palm of our hands. In the left there was a sort of engine, from the back of which were extended twenty long poles, resembling the pallisados before your Majesty's court: wherewith we conjecture the Man-Mountain combs his head; for we did not always trouble him with questions, because we found it a great difficulty to make him understand us. In the large pocket on the right side of his middle cover (so I translate the word *ranfu-lo,* by which they meant my breeches) we saw a hollow pillar of iron, about the length of a man, fastened to a strong piece of timber, larger than the pillar; and upon one side of the pillar were huge pieces of iron sticking out, cut into strange figures, which we know not what to make of. In the left pocket another engine of the same kind. In the smaller pocket on the right side, were several round flat pieces of white and red metal, of different bulk; some of the white, which seemed to be silver, were so large and heavy, that my comrade and I could hardly lift them. In the left pocket were two black pillars irregularly shaped: we could not, without difficulty, reach the top of them as we stood at the bottom of his pocket. One of them was covered, and seemed all of a piece: but at the upper end of the other, there appeared a white round substance, about twice the bigness of our heads. Within each of these was enclosed a prodigious plate of steel; which, by our orders, we obliged him to show us, because we apprehended they might be dangerous engines. He took them out of their cases, and told us, that in his own country his practice was to shave his beard with one of these, and cut his meat with the other. There were two pockets which we could not enter: these he called his fobs; they were two large slits cut into the top of his middle cover, but squeezed close by the pressure of his belly. Out of the right fob hung a great silver chain, with a wonderful kind of engine at the bottom. We directed him to draw out whatever was fastened to that chain; which appeared to be a globe, half silver, and half of some transparent metal; for, on the transparent side, we saw certain strange figures circularly drawn, and thought we could touch them, till we found our fingers stopped by that lucid substance. He put this engine to our ears, which made an incessant noise like that of a water-mill. And we conjecture it is either some unknown animal, or the god that he worships; but we are more inclined to the latter opinion, because he assured us (if we understood him right, for he expressed himself very imperfectly) that he seldom did anything without consulting it. He called it his oracle, and said it pointed out the time for every action of his life. From the left fob he took out a net almost large enough for a fisherman, but contrived to open and shut like a purse, and served him for the same use: we found therein several massy pieces of yellow metal, which, if they be real gold, must be of immense value.

Having thus, in obedience to your Majesty's commands, diligently searched all his pockets, we observed a girdle about his waist made of the hide of some prodigious animal; from which, on the left side, hung a sword of the length of five men; and on the right, a bag or pouch divided into two cells, each cell capable of holding three of your Majesty's subjects. In one of these cells were several globes or balls of a most ponderous metal, about the bigness of our heads, and requiring a strong hand to lift them: the other cell contained a heap of certain black grains, but of no great bulk or weight, for we could hold about fifty of them in the palms of our hands.

This is an exact inventory of what we found about the body of the Man-Mountain, who used us with great civility, and due respect to your Majesty's Commission. Signed and sealed on the fourth day of the eighty-ninth moon of your Majesty's auspicious reign.

CLEFRIN FRELOCK, MARSI FRELOCK.

When this inventory was read over to the Emperor, he directed me, although in very gentle terms, to deliver up the several particulars. He first called for my scimitar, which I took out, scabbard and all. In the meantime he ordered three thousand of his choicest troops (who then attended him) to surround me at a distance, with their bows and arrows just ready to discharge: but I did not observe it, for my eyes were wholly fixed upon his Majesty. He then desired me to draw my scimitar, which, although it had got some rust by the sea-water, was in most parts exceeding bright. I did so, and immediately all the troops gave a shout between terror and surprise; for the sun shone clear, and the reflection dazzled their eyes, as I waved the scimitar to and fro in my hand. His Majesty, who is a most mag-nanimous prince, was less daunted than I could expect; he ordered me to return it into the scabbard, and cast it on the ground as gently as I could, about six foot from the end of my chain. The next thing he demanded, was one of the hollow iron pillars, by which he meant my pocket-pistols. I drew it out, and at his desire, as well as I could, expressed to him the use of it; and charging it only with powder, which, by the closeness of my pouch, happened to escape wetting in the sea (an inconvenience against which all prudent mariners take special care to provide), I first cautioned the Emperor not to be afraid, and then I let it off in the air. The astonishment here was much greater than at the sight of my scimitar. Hundreds fell down as if they had been struck dead; and even the Emperor, although he stood his ground, could not recover himself in some time. I delivered up both my pistols in the same manner, as I had done my scimitar, and then my pouch of powder and bullets; begging him that the former might be kept from fire, for it would kindle with the smallest spark, and blow up his imperial palace into the air. I likewise delivered up my watch, which the Emperor was very curious to see, and commanded two of his tallest yeomen of the guards to bear it on a pole upon their shoulders, as draymen in England do a barrel of ale. He was amazed at the continual noise it made, and the motion of the minute-hand, which he could easily discern; for their sight is much more acute than ours: and asked the opinions of his learned men about him, which were various and remote, as the reader may well imagine without my repeating; although indeed I could not very perfectly understand them. I then gave up my silver and copper money, my purse, with nine large pieces of gold, and some smaller ones; my knife and razor, my comb and silver snuff-box, my handkerchief and journal-book. My scimitar, pistols, and pouch, were conveyed in carriages to his Majesty's stores; but the rest of my goods were returned to me.

I had, as I before observed, one private pocket which escaped their search, wherein there was a pair of spectacles, (which I sometimes use for the weakness of my eyes) a pocket perspective, and several other little conveniences; which being of no consequence to the Emperor, I did not think myself bound in honor to discover, and I apprehended they might be lost or spoiled if I ventured them out of my possession.

III: *The Author diverts the Emperor, and his nobility of both sexes, in a very uncommon manner—The diversions of the court of* Lilliput *described —The Author has his liberty granted him upon certain conditions.*

My gentleness and good behavior had gained so far on the Emperor and his court, and indeed upon the army and people in general, that I began to conceive hopes of getting my liberty in a short time. I took all possible methods to cultivate this favorable disposition. The natives came by degrees to be less apprehensive of any danger from me. I would sometimes lie down, and let five or six of them dance on my hand. And at last the boys and girls would venture to come and play at hide and seek in my hair. I had now made a good progress in understanding and speaking their language. The Emperor had a mind one day to entertain me with several of the country shows, wherein they exceed all nations I have known, both for dexterity and magnificence. I was diverted with none so much as that of the rope-dancers, performed upon a slender white thread, extended about two foot, and twelve inches from the ground. Upon which I shall desire liberty, with the reader's patience, to enlarge a little.

This diversion is only practised by those persons who are candidates for great employments, and high favor, at court. They are trained in this art from their youth, and are not always of noble birth, or liberal education. When a great office is vacant, either by death or disgrace, (which often happens) five or six of those candidates petition the Emperor to entertain his Majesty and the court with a dance on the rope, and whoever jumps the highest without falling, succeeds in the office. Very often the chief ministers themselves are commanded to show their skill, and to convince the Emperor that they have not lost their faculty. Flimnap, the Treasurer, is allowed to cut a caper on the straight rope, at least an inch higher than any other lord in the whole empire. I have seen him do the summerset several times together upon a trencher fixed on the rope, which is no thicker than a common pack-thread in England. My friend Reldresal, principal Secretary for Private Affairs, is, in my opinion, if I am not partial, the second after the Treasurer; the rest of the great officers are much upon a par.

These diversions are often attended with fatal accidents, whereof great numbers are on record. I myself have seen two or three candidates break a limb. But the danger is much greater when the ministers themselves are commanded to show their dexterity; for, by contending to excel themselves and their fellows, they strain so far, that there is hardly one of them who hath not received a fall, and some of them two or three. I was assured that a year or two before my arrival, Flimnap would have infallibly broke his neck, if one of the King's cushions, that accidentally lay on the ground, had not weakened the force of his fall.

There is likewise another diversion, which is only shown before the Emperor and Empress, and first minister, upon particular occasions. The Emperor lays on the table three fine silken threads of six inches long. One is blue, the other red, and the third green.[1] These threads are proposed as prizes for those persons whom the Emperor hath a mind to distinguish by a peculiar mark of his favor. The ceremony is performed in his Majesty's great chamber of state, where the candidates are to undergo a trial of dexterity very different from the former, and such as I have not observed the least resemblance of in any other country of the old or the new world. The Emperor holds a stick in his hands, both ends parallel to the horizon, while the candidates advancing one by one, sometimes leap over the stick, sometimes creep under it backward and forward several times, according as the stick is advanced or depressed. Sometimes the Emperor holds one end of the stick, and his first minister the other; sometimes the minister has it entirely to himself. Whoever performs his part with most agility, and holds out the longest in leaping and creeping, is rewarded with the blue-colored silk; the red is given to the next, and the green to the third, which they all wear girt twice round about the middle; and you see few great persons about this court, who are not adorned with one of these girdles.

The horses of the army, and those of the royal stables, having been daily led before me, were no longer shy, but would come up to my very feet without starting. The riders would leap them over my hand as I held it on the ground, and one of the Emperor's huntsmen, upon a large courser, took my foot, shoe and all; which was indeed a prodigious leap. I had the good fortune to divert the Emperor one day after a very extraordinary manner. I desired he would order several sticks of two foot high, and the thickness of an ordinary cane, to be brought me; whereupon his Majesty commanded the master of his woods to give directions accordingly; and the next morning

---

[1] Climbing, creeping, and rope-dancing are ways of winning court-favors: in England blue, red, and green ribbons represent the great orders of the Garter, the Bath, and the Thistle.

six woodmen arrived with as many carriages, drawn by eight horses to each. I took nine of these sticks, fixing them firmly in the ground in a quadrangular figure, two foot and a half square. I took four other sticks, and tied them parallel at each corner, about two foot from the ground; then I fastened my handkerchief to the nine sticks that stood erect, and extended it on all sides, till it was tight as the top of a drum; and the four parallel sticks rising about five inches higher than the handkerchief, served as ledges on each side. When I had finished my work, I desired the Emperor to let a troop of his best horse, twenty-four in number, come and exercise upon this plain. His Majesty approved of the proposal, and I took them up, one by one, in my hands, ready mounted and armed, with the proper officers to exercise them. As soon as they got into order, they divided into two parties, performed mock skirmishes, discharged blunt arrows, drew their swords, fled and pursued, attacked and retired, and in short discovered the best military discipline I ever beheld. The parallel sticks secured them and their horses from falling over the stage; and the Emperor was so much delighted, that he ordered this entertainment to be repeated several days, and once was pleased to be lifted up and give the word of command; and, with great difficulty, persuaded even the Empress herself to let me hold her in her close chair within two yards of the stage, from whence she was able to take a full view of the whole performance. It was my good fortune that no ill accident happened in these entertainments, only once a fiery horse, that belonged to one of the captains, pawing with his hoof, struck a hole in my handkerchief, and his foot slipping, he overthrew his rider and himself; but I immediately relieved them both, and covering the hole with one hand, I set down the troop with the other, in the same manner as I took them up. The horse that fell was strained in the left shoulder, but the rider got no hurt, and I repaired my handkerchief as well as I could; however, I would not trust to the strength of it any more in such dangerous enterprises.

About two or three days before I was set at liberty, as I was entertaining the court with this kind of feats, there arrived an express to inform his Majesty, that some of his subjects riding near the place where I was first taken up, had seen a great black substance lying on the ground, very oddly shaped, extending its edges round as wide as his Majesty's bedchamber, and rising up in the middle as high as a man; that it was no living creature, as they at first apprehended, for it lay on the grass without motion, and some of them had walked round it several times: that by mounting upon each other's shoulders, they had got to the top, which was flat and even, and stamping upon it they found it was hollow within; that they humbly conceived it might be something belonging to the Man-Mountain; and if his Majesty pleased, they would undertake to bring it with only five horses. I presently knew what they meant, and was glad at heart to receive this intelligence. It seems upon my first reaching the shore after our shipwreck, I was in such confusion, that before I came to the place where I went to sleep, my hat, which I had fastened with a string to my head while I was rowing, and had stuck on all the time I was swimming, fell off after I came to land; the string, as I conjecture, breaking by some accident which I never observed, but thought my hat had been lost at sea. I intreated his Imperial Majesty to give orders it might be brought to me as soon as possible, describing to him the use and the nature of it: and the next day the wagoners arrived with it, but not in a very good condition; they had bored two holes in the brim, within an inch and half of the edge, and fastened two hooks in the holes; these hooks were tied by a long cord to the harness, and thus my hat was dragged along for above half an English mile; but the ground in that country being extremely smooth and level, it received less damage than I expected.

Two days after this adventure, the Emperor, having ordered that part of his army which quarters in and about his metropolis to be in readiness, took a fancy of diverting himself in a very singular manner. He desired I would stand like a Colossus, with my legs as far asunder as I conveniently could. He then commanded his General (who was an old experienced leader, and a great patron of mine) to draw up the troops in close order, and march them under me: the foot by twenty-four in a breast, and the horse by sixteen, with drums beating, colors flying, and pikes advanced. This body consisted of three thousand foot, and a thousand horse.

I had sent so many memorials and petitions for my liberty, that his Majesty at length mentioned the matter, first in the cabinet, and then in a full council; where it was opposed by none, except Skyresh Bolgolam, who was pleased, without any provocation, to be my mortal enemy. But it was carried against him by the whole board, and confirmed by the Emperor. That minister was *Galbet,* or Admiral of the Realm, very much in his master's confidence, and a person well versed in affairs, but of a morose and sour complexion. However, he was at length persuaded to comply; but prevailed that the articles and conditions upon which I should be set free, and to which I must swear, should be drawn up by himself. These articles were brought to me by Skyresh Bolgolam in person, attended by two under-secretaries, and several persons of distinction. After they were read, I was demanded to swear to the performance of them; first in the manner of my own country, and afterwards in the method prescribed by their laws; which was to hold my right foot in my left hand, to place the middle finger of my right hand on the crown of my head, and my thumb on the tip of my right ear. But because the reader may be curious to have some idea of the style and manner of expression peculiar to that people, as well as to know the articles upon which I recovered my liberty, I have made a translation of the whole instrument word for word, as near as I was able, which I here offer to the public.

GOLBASTO MOMAREM EVLAME GURDILO SHEFIN MULLY ULLY GUE, most mighty Emperor of Lilliput, delight and terror of the universe, whose dominions extend five thousand *blustrugs* (about twelve miles in circumference) to the extremities of the globe; monarch of all monarchs, taller than the sons of men; whose feet press down to the center, and whose head strikes against the sun; at whose nod the princes of the earth shake their knees; pleasant as the spring, comfortable as the summer, fruitful as autumn, dreadful as winter. His most sublime Majesty proposeth to the Man-Mountain, lately arrived to our celestial dominions, the following articles, which by a solemn oath he shall be obliged to perform.

First, The Man-Mountain shall not depart from our dominions, without our license under our great seal.

2d, He shall not presume to come into our metropolis, without our express order; at which time, the inhabitants shall have two hours warning to keep within their doors.

3d, The said Man-Mountain shall confine his walks to our principal high roads, and not offer to walk or lie down in a meadow or field of corn.

4th, As he walks the said roads, he shall take the utmost

care not to trample upon the bodies of any of our loving subjects, their horses, or carriages, nor take any of our subjects into his hands, without their own consent.

5th, If an express requires extraordinary dispatch, the Man-Mountain shall be obliged to carry in his pocket the messenger and horse a six days journey once in every moon, and return the said messenger back (if so required) safe to our Imperial Presence.

6th, He shall be our ally against our enemies in the Island of Blefuscu, and do his utmost to destroy their fleet, which is now preparing to invade us.

7th, That the said Man-Mountain shall, at his times of leisure, be aiding and assisting to our workmen, in helping to raise certain great stones, toward covering the wall of the principal park, and other of our royal buildings.

8th, That the said Man-Mountain shall, in two moons' time, deliver in an exact survey of the circumference of our dominions by a computation of his own paces round the coast.

Lastly, That upon his solemn oath to observe all the above articles, the said Man-Mountain shall have a daily allowance of meat and drink sufficient for the support of 1728 of our subjects, with free access to our Royal Person, and other marks of our favor. Given at our Palace at Belfaborac the twelfth day of the ninety-first moon of our reign.

I swore and subscribed to these articles with great cheerfulness and content, although some of them were not so honorable as I could have wished; which proceeded wholly from the malice of Skyresh Bolgolam, the High-Admiral: whereupon my chains were immediately unlocked, and I was at full liberty; the Emperor himself in person did me the honor to be by at the whole ceremony. I made my acknowledgments by prostrating myself at his Majesty's feet: but he commanded me to rise; and after many gracious expressions, which, to avoid the censure of vanity, I shall not repeat, he added, that he hoped I should prove a useful servant, and well deserve all the favors he had already conferred upon me, or might do for the future.

The reader may please to observe, that in the last article for the recovery of my liberty, the Emperor stipulates to allow me a quantity of meat and drink sufficient for the support of 1728 Lilliputians. Sometime after, asking a friend at court how they came to fix on that determinate number; he told me that his Majesty's mathematicians, having taken the height of my body by the help of a quadrant, and finding it to exceed theirs in the proportion of twelve to one, they concluded from the similarity of their bodies, that mine must contain at least 1728 of theirs, and consequently would require as much food as was necessary to support that number of Lilliputians. By which, the reader may conceive an idea of the ingenuity of that people, as well as the prudent and exact economy of so great a prince.

IV: Mildendo, *the metropolis of* Lilliput, *described, together with the Emperor's palace—A conversation between the Author and a principal Secretary, concerning the affairs of that empire—The Author's offers to serve the Emperor in his wars.*

The first request I made after I had obtained my liberty, was, that I might have license to see Mildendo, the metropolis; which the Emperor easily granted me, but with a special charge to do no hurt either to the inhabitants or their houses. The people had notice by proclamation of my design to visit the town. The wall which encompassed it, is two foot and a half high, and at least eleven inches broad, so that a coach and horses may be driven very safely round it; and it is flanked with strong towers at ten foot distance. I stepped over the great Western Gate, and passed very gently, and sidelong through the two principal streets, only in my short waistcoat, for fear of damaging the roofs and eaves of the houses with the skirts of my coat. I walked with the utmost circumspection, to avoid treading on any stragglers, that might remain in the streets, although the orders were very strict, that all people should keep in their houses, at their own peril. The garret windows and tops of houses were so crowded with spectators, that I thought in all my travels I had not seen a more populous place. The city is an exact square, each side of the wall being five hundred foot long. The two great streets, which run across and divide it into four quarters, are five foot wide. The lanes and alleys, which I would not enter, but only viewed them as I passed, are from twelve to eighteen inches. The town is capable of holding five hundred thousand souls. The houses are from three to five stories. The shops and markets well provided.

The Emperor's palace is in the center of the city, where the two great streets meet. It is inclosed by a wall of two foot high, and twenty foot distant from the buildings. I had his Majesty's permission to step over this wall; and the space being so wide between that and the palace, I would easily view it on every side. The outward court is a square of forty foot, and includes two other courts: in the inmost are the royal apartments, which I was very desirous to see, but found it extremely difficult; for the great gates, from one square into another, were but eighteen inches high, and seven inches wide. Now the buildings of the outer court were at least five foot high, and it was impossible for me to stride over them without infinite damage to the pile, though the walls were strongly built of hewn stone, and four inches thick. At the same time the Emperor had a great desire that I should see the magnificence of his palace; but this I was not able to do till three days after, which I spent in cutting down with my knife some of the largest trees in the royal park, about a hundred yards distant from the city. Of these trees I made two stools, each about three foot high, and strong enough to bear my weight. The people having received notice a second time, I went again through the city to the palace, with my two stools in my hands. When I came to the side of the outer court, I stood upon one stool, and took the other in my hand: this I lifted over the roof, and gently set it down on the space between the first and second court, which was eight foot wide. I then stepped over the buildings very conveniently from one stool to the other, and drew up the first after me with a hooked stick. By this contrivance I got into the inmost court; and lying down upon my side, I applied my face to the windows of the middle stories, which were left open on purpose, and discovered the most splendid apartments that can be imagined. There I saw the Empress and the young Princes, in their several lodgings, with their chief attendants about them. Her Imperial Majesty was pleased to smile very graciously upon me, and gave me out of the window her hand to kiss.

But I shall not anticipate the reader with farther descriptions of this kind, because I reserve them for a greater work which is now almost ready for the press, containing a general description of this empire, from its first erection, through a long series of princes, with a particular account of their wars and politics, laws, learning, and religion: their plants and animals, their peculiar manners and customs, with other matters very curious and useful; my chief design at present being only to relate such events and transactions as happened to the public, or to myself, during a residence of about nine months in that empire.

One morning, about a fortnight after I had obtained my liberty, Reldresal, principal Secretary (as they style him) of Private Affairs, came to my house attended only by one servant. He ordered his coach to wait at a distance, and desired I would give him an hour's audience; which I readily consented to, on account of his quality and personal merits, as well as the many good offices he had done me during my solicitations at court. I offered to lie down, that he might the more conveniently reach my ear; but he chose rather to let me hold him in my hand during our conversation. He began with compliments on my liberty; said he might pretend to some merit in it: but, however, added, that if it had not been for the present situation of things at court, perhaps I might not have obtained it so soon. For, said he, as flourishing a condition as we may appear to be in to foreigners, we labor under two mighty evils; a violent faction at home, and the danger of an invasion by a most potent enemy from abroad. As to the first, you are to understand, that for about seventy moons past there have been two struggling parties in this empire, under the names of *Tramecksan* and *Slamecksan,* from the high and low heels on their shoes, by which they distinguish themselves.[1] It is alleged indeed, that the high heels are most agreeable to our ancient constitution: but however this be, his Majesty hath determined to make use of only low heels in the administration of the government, and all offices in the gift of the Crown, as you cannot but observe; and particularly, that his Majesty's Imperial heels are lower at least by a drurr than any of his court; (*drurr* is a measure about the fourteenth part of an inch). The animosities between these two parties run so high, that they will neither eat nor drink, nor talk with each other. We compute the *Tramecksan,* or High-Heels, to exceed us in number; but the power is wholly on our side. We apprehend his Imperial Highness, the Heir to the Crown, to have some tendency toward the High-Heels; at least we can plainly discover one of his heels higher than the other, which gives him a hobble in his gait. Now, in the midst of these intestine disquiets, we are threatened with an invasion from the Island of Blefuscu,[2] which is the other great empire of the universe, almost as large and powerful as this of his Majesty. For as to what we have heard you affirm, that there are other kingdoms and states in the world inhabited by human crea-

[1] High Heels and Low Heels: in England there were the High Church and the Low Church Parties between which there were bitter feuds.
[2] The Island of Blefuscu stood in relation to Lilliput as France to England.

tures as large as yourself, our philosophers are in much doubt, and would rather conjecture that you dropped from the moon, or one of the stars; because it is certain, that a hundred mortals of your bulk would, in a short time, destroy all the fruits and cattle of his Majesty's dominions. Besides, our histories of six thousand moons make no mention of any other regions, than the two great empires of Lilliput and Blefuscu. Which two mighty powers have, as I was going to tell you, been engaged in a most obstinate war for six and thirty moons past. It began upon the following occasion. It is allowed on all hands, that the primitive way of breaking eggs before we ate them, was upon the larger end: but his present Majesty's grandfather, while he was a boy, going to eat an egg, and breaking it according to the ancient practice, happened to cut one of his fingers. Whereupon the Emperor his father published an edict, commanding all his subjects, upon great penalties, to break the smaller end of their eggs.[1] The people so highly resented this law, that our histories tell us there have been six rebellions raised on that account; wherein one Emperor lost his life; and another his crown. These civil commotions were constantly fomented by the monarchs of Blefuscu; and when they were quelled, the exiles always fled for refuge to that empire. It is computed, that eleven thousand persons have, at several times, suffered death, rather than submit to break their eggs at the smaller end. Many hundred large volumes have been published upon this controversy: but the books of the Big-Endians have been long forbidden, and the whole party rendered incapable by law of holding employments. During the course of these troubles, the Emperors of Blefuscu did frequently expostulate by their ambassadors, accusing us of making a schism in religion, by offending against a funda-

[1] The Big-Endians and the Little-Endians disputed in Lilliput as the Catholics and Protestants disputed in England in Gulliver's time.

mental doctrine of our great prophet Lustrog, in the fifty-fourth chapter of the Blundecral (which is their Alcoran). This, however, is thought to be a mere strain upon the text: for the words are these; *That all true believers break their eggs at the convenient end:* and which is the convenient end, seems, in my humble opinion, to be left to every man's conscience, or at least in the power of the chief magistrate to determine. Now the Big-Endian exiles have found so much credit in the Emperor of Blefuscu's court, and so much private assistance and encouragement from their party here at home, that a bloody war has been carried on between the two empires for six and thirty moons with various success; during which time we have lost forty capital ships, and a much greater number of smaller vessels, together with thirty thousand of our best seamen and soldiers; and the damage received by the enemy is reckoned to be somewhat greater than ours. However, they have now equipped a numerous fleet, and are just preparing to make a descent upon us; and his Imperial Majesty, placing great confidence in your valor and strength, has commanded me to lay this account of his affairs before you.

I desired the Secretary to present my humble duty to the Emperor, and to let him know, that I thought it would not become me, who was a foreigner, to interfere with parties; but I was ready, with the hazard of my life, to defend his person and state against all invaders.

V: *The Author, by an extraordinary stratagem, prevents an invasion— A high title of honor is conferred upon him—Ambassadors arrive from the Emperor of* Blefuscu, *and sue for peace.*

The Empire of Blefuscu is an island situated to the north north-east side of Lilliput, from whence it is parted only by a channel of eight hundred yards wide. I had not yet seen it, and upon this notice of an intended invasion, I avoided appearing on that side of the coast, for fear of being discovered by some of the enemy's ships, who had received no intelligence of me, all intercourse between the two empires having been strictly forbidden during the war, upon pain of death, and an embargo laid by our Emperor upon all vessels whatsoever. I communicated to his Majesty a project I had formed of seizing the enemy's whole fleet: which, as our scouts assured us, lay at anchor in the harbor ready to sail with the first fair wind. I consulted the most experienced seamen, upon the depth of the channel, which they had often plumbed, who told me, that in the middle at high-water it was seventy *glumgluffs* deep, which is about six foot of European measure; and the rest of it fifty *glumgluffs* at most. I walked toward the northeast coast over against Blefuscu;

and lying down behind a hillock, took out my small pocket perspective-glass, and viewed the enemy's fleet at anchor, consisting of about fifty men of war, and a great number of transports; I then came back to my house, and gave order (for which I had a warrant) for a great quantity of the strongest cable and bars of iron. The cable was about as thick as packthread, and the bars of the length and size of a knitting-needle. I trebled the cable to make it stronger, and for the same reason I twisted three of the iron bars together, binding the extremities into a hook. Having thus fixed fifty hooks to as many cables, I went back to the northeast coast, and putting off my coat, shoes, and stockings, walked into the sea in my leathern jerkin, about half an hour before high water. I waded with what haste I could, and swam in the middle about thirty yards till I felt ground; I arrived at the fleet in less than half an hour. The enemy was so frightened when they saw me, that they leaped out of their ships, and swam to shore, where there could not be fewer than thirty thousand souls. I then took my tackling, and fastening a hook to the hole at the prow of each, I tied all the cords together at the end. While I was thus employed, the enemy discharged several thousand arrows, many of which stuck in my hands and face; and besides the excessive smart, gave me much disturbance in my work. My greatest apprehension was for my eyes, which I should have infallibly lost, if I had not suddenly thought of an expedient. I kept among other little necessaries a pair of spectacles in a private pocket, which, as I observed before, had escaped the Emperor's searchers. These I took out and fastened as strongly as I could upon my nose, and thus armed went on boldly with my work in spite of the enemy's arrows, many of which struck against the glasses of my spectacles, but without any other effect, further than a little to discompose them. I had now fastened all the hooks, and taking the knot in my hand, began to pull; but not a ship would stir, for they were all too fast held by their anchors, so that the boldest part of my enterprise remained. I therefore let go the cord, and leaving the hooks fixed to the ships, I resolutely cut with my knife the cables that fastened the anchors, receiving about two hundred shots in my face and hands; then I took up the knotted end of the cables, to which my hooks were tied, and with great ease drew fifty of the enemy's largest men of war after me.[1]

The Blefuscudians, who had not the least imagination of what I intended, were at first confounded with astonishment. They had seen me cut the cables, and thought my design was only to let the ships run adrift, or fall foul on each other: but when they perceived the whole fleet moving in order, and saw me pulling at the end, they set up such a scream of grief and despair, that it is almost impossible to describe or conceive. When I had got out of danger, I stopped awhile to pick out the arrows that stuck in my hands and face; and rubbed on some of the same ointment that was given me at my first arrival, as I have formerly mentioned. I then took off my spectacles, and waiting about an hour, till the tide was a little fallen, I waded through the middle with my cargo, and arrived safe at the royal port of Lilliput.

The Emperor and his whole court stood on the shore, expecting the issue of this great adventure. They saw the ships move forward in a large half-moon, but could not discern me, who was up to my breast in water. When I advanced to the middle of the channel, they were yet in more pain, because I was under water to my neck. The Emperor concluded me to be drowned, and that the enemy's fleet was approaching in a hostile manner: but he was soon eased of

[1] Mathematicians doubt if Gulliver could have done this. It would be the same as dragging a boat that would hold seventeen or eighteen men. Could a man up to his neck in water do this, they ask?

his fears, for the channel growing shallower every step I made, I came in a short time within hearing, and holding up the end of the cable by which the fleet was fastened, I cried in a loud voice, *Long live the most puissant Emperor of Lilliput!* This great prince received me at my landing with all possible encomiums, and created me a *Nardac* upon the spot, which is the highest title of honor among them.

His Majesty desired I would take some other opportunity of bringing all the rest of his enemy's ships into his ports. And so unmeasurable is the ambition of princes, that he seemed to think of nothing less than reducing the whole empire of Blefuscu into a province, and governing it by a viceroy; of destroying the Big-Endian exiles, and compelling that people to break the smaller end of their eggs, by which he would remain the sole monarch of the whole world. But I endeavored to divert him from this design, by many arguments drawn from the topics of policy as well as justice; and I plainly protested, that I would never be an instrument of bringing a free and brave people into slavery. And when the matter was debated in council, the wisest part of the ministry were of my opinion.

This open bold declaration of mine was so opposite to the schemes and politics of his Imperial Majesty, that he could never forgive it; he mentioned it in a very artful manner at council, where I was told that some of the wisest appeared, at least by their silence, to be of my opinion; but others, who were my secret enemies, could not forbear some expressions, which by a side-wind reflected on me. And from this time began an intrigue between his Majesty and a junto of ministers maliciously bent against me, which broke out in less than two months, and had like to have ended in my utter destruction. Of so little weight are the greatest services to princes, when put into the balance with a refusal to gratify their passions.

About three weeks after this exploit, there arrived a solemn embassy from Blefuscu, with humble offers of a peace; which was soon concluded upon conditions very advantageous to our Emperor, wherewith I shall not trouble the reader. There were six ambassadors, with a train of about five hundred persons, and their entry was very magnificent, suitable to the grandeur of their master, and the importance of their business. When their treaty was finished, wherein I did them several good offices by the credit I now had, or at least appeared to have at court, their Excellencies, who were privately told how much I had been their friend, made me a visit in form. They began with many compliments upon my valor and generosity, invited me to that kingdom in the Emperor their master's name, and desired me to show them some proofs of my prodigious strength, of which they had heard so many wonders; wherein I readily obliged them, but shall not trouble the reader with the particulars.

When I had for some time entertained their Excellencies, to their infinite satisfaction and surprise, I desired they would do me the honor to present my most humble respects to the Emperor their master, the renown of whose virtues had so justly filled the whole world with admiration, and whose royal person I resolved to attend before I returned to my own country: accordingly, the next time I had the honor to see our Emperor, I desired his general license to wait on the Blefuscudian monarch, which he was pleased to grant me, as I could perceive, in a very cold manner; but could not guess the reason, till I had a whisper from a certain person, that Flimnap and Bolgolam had represented my intercourse with those ambassadors as a mark of disaffection, from which I am sure my heart was wholly free. And this was the first time I began to conceive some imperfect idea of courts and ministers.

It is to be observed, that these ambassadors spoke to me by an interpreter, the languages of both empires differing as much from each other as any two in Europe, and each nation priding itself upon the antiquity, beauty, and energy of their own tongues, with an avowed contempt for that of their neighbor; yet our Emperor, standing upon the advantage he had got by the seizure of their fleet, obliged them to deliver their credentials, and make their speech in the Lilliputian tongue. And it must be confessed, that from the great intercourse of trade and commerce between both realms, from the continual reception of exiles, which is mutual among them, and from the custom in each empire to send their young nobility and richer gentry to the other, in order to polish themselves by seeing the world, and understanding men and manners; there are few persons of distinction, or merchants, or seamen, who dwell in the maritime parts, but what can hold conversation in both tongues; as I found some weeks after, when I went to pay my respects to the Emperor of Blefuscu, which in the midst of great misfortunes, through the malice of my enemies, proved a very happy adventure to me, as I shall relate in its proper place.

VI: *Of the inhabitants of* Lilliput; *their learning, laws, and customs, the manner of educating their children—The Author's way of living in that country—His vindication of a great lady.*

Although I intend to leave the description of this empire to a particular treatise, yet in the meantime I am content to gratify the curious reader with some general ideas. As the common size of the natives is somewhat under six inches high, so there is an exact proportion in all other animals, as well as plants and trees: for instance, the tallest horses and oxen are between four and five inches in height, the sheep an inch and a half, more or less: their geese about the bigness of a sparrow, and so the several gradations downward till you come to the smallest, which, to my sight, were almost invisible; but nature hath adapted the eyes of the Lilliputians to all objects proper for their view: they see with great exactness, but at no great distance. And to show the sharpness of their sight toward objects that are near, I have been much pleased with observing a cook pulling a lark, which was not so large as a common fly; and a young girl threading an invisible needle with invisible silk. Their tallest trees are about seven foot high: I mean some of those in the great royal park, the tops whereof I could but just reach with my fist clinched. The other vegetables are in the same proportion; but this I leave to the reader's imagination.

I shall say but little at present of their learning, which for many ages hath flourished in all its branches among them: but their manner of writing is very peculiar, being neither from the left to the right, like the Europeans; nor from the right to the left, like the Arabians; nor from up to down, like the Chinese; nor from down to up, like the Cascagians; but aslant from one corner of the paper to the other, like ladies in England.

They bury their dead with their heads directly downward, because they hold an opinion, that in eleven thousand moons they are all to rise again, in which period the earth (which they conceive to be flat) will turn upside down, and by this means they shall, at their resurrection, be found ready standing on their feet. The learned among them confess the absurdity of this doctrine, but the practice still continues, in compliance to the vulgar.

There are some laws and customs in this empire very peculiar; and if they were not so directly contrary to those of my own dear country, I should be tempted to say a little in their justification. It is only to be wished, that they were as well executed. The first I shall mention, relates to informers. All crimes against the state are punished here with the utmost severity; but if the person accused maketh his innocence plainly to appear upon his trial, the accuser is immediately put to an ignominious death; and out of his goods or lands, the innocent person is quadruply recompensed for the loss of his time, for the danger he underwent, for the hardship of his imprisonment, and for all the charges he hath been at in making his defense. Or, if that fund be deficient, it is largely supplied by the

Crown. The Emperor does also confer on him some public mark of his favor, and proclamation is made of his innocence through the whole city.

They look upon fraud as a greater crime than theft, and therefore seldom fail to punish it with death; for they allege, that care and vigilance, with a very common understanding, may preserve a man's goods from thieves, but honesty has no fence against superior cunning; and since it is necessary that there should be a perpetual intercourse of buying and selling, and dealing upon credit, where fraud is permitted and connived at, or hath no law to punish it, the honest dealer is always undone, and the knave gets the advantage. I remember when I was once interceding with the Emperor for a criminal who had wronged his master of a great sum of money, which he had received by order, and ran away with; and happening to tell his Majesty, by way of extenuation, that it was only a breach of trust; the Emperor thought it monstrous in me to offer, as a defense, the greatest aggravation of the crime: and truly I had little to say in return, farther than the common answer, that different nations had different customs; for, I confess, I was heartily ashamed.

Although we usually call reward and punishment the two hinges upon which all government turns, yet I could never observe this maxim to be put in practice by any nation except that of Lilliput. Whoever can there bring sufficient proof that he hath strictly observed the laws of his country for seventy-three moons, hath a claim to certain privileges, according to his quality and condition of life, with a proportionable sum of money out of a fund appropriated for that use: he likewise acquires the title of *Snilpall,* or Legal, which is added to his name, but does not descend to his posterity. And these people thought it a prodigious defect of policy among us, when I told them that our laws were enforced only by penalties, without any mention of reward. It is upon this account that the image of Justice, in their courts of judicature, is formed with six eyes, two before, as many behind, and on each side one, to signify circumspection; with a bag of gold open in her right hand, and a sword sheathed in her left, to show she is more disposed to reward than to punish.

It may perhaps divert the curious reader, to give some account of my domestic, and my manner of living in this country, during a residence of nine months and thirteen days. Having a head mechanically turned, and being likewise forced by necessity, I had made for myself a table and chair convenient enough, out of the largest trees in the royal park. Two hundred sempstresses were employed to make me shirts, and linen for my bed and table, all of the strongest and coarsest kind they could get; which, however, they were forced to quilt together in several folds, for the thickest was some degrees finer than lawn. Their linen is usualy three inches wide, and three foot make a piece. The sempstresses took my measure as I lay on the ground, one standing at my neck, and another at my mid-leg, with a strong cord extended, that each held by the end, while the third measured the length of the cord with a rule of an inch long. Then they measured my right thumb, and desired no more; for by a mathematical computation, that twice round the thumb is once round the wrist, and so on to the neck and the waist, and by the help of my old shirt, which I displayed on the ground before them for a pattern, they fitted me exactly. Three hundred tailors were employed in the same manner to make me clothes; but they had another contrivance for taking my measure. I kneeled down, and they raised a ladder from the ground to my neck; upon this ladder one of them mounted, and let fall a plumb-line from my collar to the floor, which just answered the length of my coat: but my waist

and arms I measured myself. When my clothes were finished, which
was done in my house, (for the largest of theirs would not have been
able to hold them) they looked like the patch-work made by the
ladies in England, only that mine were all of a color.

I had three hundred cooks to dress my victuals, in little convenient huts built about my house, where they and their families
lived, and prepared me two dishes apiece. I took up twenty waiters
in my hand, and placed them on the table: a hundred more
attended below on the ground, some with dishes of meat, and some
with barrels of wine, and other liquors, slung on their shoulders;
all which the waiters above drew up as I wanted, in a very ingenious
manner, by certain cords, as we draw the bucket up a well in
Europe. A dish of their meat was a good mouthful, and a barrel of
their liquor a reasonable draught. Their mutton yields to ours, but
their beef is excellent. I have had a sirloin so large, that I have been
forced to make three bits of it; but this is rare. My servants were
astonished to see me eat it bones and all, as in our country we do
the leg of a lark. Their geese and turkeys I usually ate at a mouthful,
and I must confess they far exceed ours. Of their smaller fowl I
could take up twenty or thirty at the end of my knife.

One day his Imperial Majesty, being informed of my way of
living, desired that himself and his Royal Consort, with the young
Princes of the blood of both sexes, might have the happiness (as he
was pleased to call it) of dining with me. They came accordingly,
and I placed them in chairs of state on my table, just over against
me, with their guards about them. Flimnap, the Lord High Treasurer, attended there likewise with his white staff; and I observed he
often looked on me with a sour countenance, which I would not
seem to regard, but ate more than usual, in honor to my dear country,
as well as to fill the court with admiration. I have some private

reasons to believe, that this visit from his Majesty gave Flimnap an opportunity of doing me ill offices to his master. That minister had always been my secret enemy, though he outwardly caressed me more than was usual to the moroseness of his nature. He represented to the Emperor the low condition of his treasury; that he was forced to take up money at great discount; that exchequer bills would not circulate under nine per cent below par; that in short I had cost his Majesty above a million and a half of *sprugs* (their greatest gold coin, about the bigness of a spangle); and upon the whole, that it would be advisable in the Emperor to take the first fair occasion of dismissing me.

I am here obliged to vindicate the reputation of an excellent lady, who was an innocent sufferer upon my account. The Treasurer took a fancy to be jealous of his wife, from the malice of some evil tongues, who informed him that her Grace had taken a violent affection for my person; and the court-scandal ran for some time, that she once came privately to my lodging. This I solemnly declare to be a most infamous falsehood, without any grounds, farther than that her Grace was pleased to treat me with all innocent marks of freedom and friendship. I own she came often to my house, but always publicly, nor even without three more in the coach, who were usually her sister and young daughter, and some particular acquaintance; but this was common to many other ladies of the court. And I still appeal to my servants round, whether they at any time saw a coach at my door without knowing what persons were in it. On those occasions, when a servant had given me notice, my custom was to go immediately to the door; and, after paying my respects, to take up the coach and two horses very carefully in my hands (for, if there were six horses, the postilion always unharnessed four) and place them on a table, where I had fixed a movable rim quite round, of five inches high, to prevent accidents. And I have often had four coaches and horses at once on my table full of company, while I sat in my chair leaning my face toward them; and when I was engaged with one set, the coachmen would gently drive the others round my table. I have passed many an afternoon very agreeably in these conversations. But I defy the Treasurer, or his two informers (I will name them, and let them make their best of it) Clustril and Drunlo, to prove that any person ever came to me *incognito,* except the secretary Reldresal, who was sent by express command of his Imperial Majesty, as I have before related. I should not have dwelt so long upon this particular, if it had not been a point wherein the reputation of a great lady is so nearly concerned, to say nothing of my own; though I then had the honor to be a *Nardac,* which the Treasurer himself is not; for all the world knows he is only a *Glumglum,* a title inferior by one degree, as that of a Marquis is to a Duke in England, although I allow he preceded me in right of his post. These false informations, which I afterwards came to the knowledge of, by an accident not proper to mention, made Flimnap, the Treasurer, show his lady for some time an ill countenance, and me a worse; and although he were at last undeceived and reconciled to her, yet I lost all credit with him, and found my interest decline very fast with the Emperor himself, who was indeed too much governed by that favorite.

VII: *The Author, being informed of a design to accuse him of high treason, makes his escape to* Blefuscu—*His reception there.*

Before I proceed to give an account of my leaving this kingdom, it may be proper to inform the reader of a private intrigue which had been for two months forming against me.

I had been hitherto all my life a stranger to courts, for which I was unqualified by the meanness of my condition. I had indeed heard and read enough of the dispositions of great princes and ministers; but never expected to have found such terrible effects of them in so remote a country, governed, as I thought, by very different maxims from those in Europe.

When I was just preparing to pay my attendance on the Emperor of Blefuscu, a considerable person at court (to whom I had been very serviceable at a time when he lay under the highest displeasure of his Imperial Majesty) came to my house very privately at night in a close chair, and without sending his name, desired admittance. The chairmen were dismissed; I put the chair, with his Lordship in it, into my coat-pocket: and giving orders to a trusty servant to say

I was indisposed and gone to sleep, I fastened the door of my house, placed the chair on the table, according to my usual custom, and sat down by it. After the common salutations were over, observing his Lordship's countenance full of concern, and inquiring into the reason, he desired I would hear him with patience in a matter that highly concerned my honor and my life. His speech was to the following effect, for I took notes of it as soon as he left me.

"You are to know," said he, "that several Committees of Council have been lately called in the most private manner on your account; and it is but two days since his Majesty came to a full resolution.

"You are very sensible that Skyresh Bolgolam (*Galbet,* or High Admiral) hath been your mortal enemy almost ever since your arrival. His original reasons I know not; but his hatred is much increased since your great success against Blefuscu, by which his glory, as Admiral, is obscured. This Lord, in conjunction with Flimnap the High Treasurer, whose enmity against you is notorious on account of his lady, Limtoc the General, Lalcon the Chamberlain, and Balmuff the Grand Justiciary, have prepared articles of impeachment against you, for treason, and other capital crimes."

This preface made me so impatient, being conscious of my own merits and innocence, that I was going to interrupt; when he entreated me to be silent, and thus proceeded.

"Out of gratitude for the favors you have done me, I procured information of the whole proceedings, and a copy of the articles, wherein I venture my head for your service."

319

Articles of Impeachment against Quinbus Flestrin
(*the* Man-Mountain).

That the said Quinbus Flestrin having brought the imperial fleet of Blefuscu into the royal port, and being afterwards commanded by his Imperial Majesty to seize all the other ships of the said empire of Blefuscu, and reduce that empire to a province, to be governed by a viceroy from hence, and to destroy and put to death not only all the Big-Endian exiles, but likewise all the people of that empire, who would not immediately forsake the Big-Endian heresy: He, the said Flestrin, like a false traitor against his most Auspicious, Serene, Imperial Majesty, did petition to be excused from the said service, upon pretense of unwillingness to force the consciences, or destroy the liberties and lives of an innocent people.

. . .

That, whereas certain ambassadors arrived from the court of Blefuscu, to sue for peace in his Majesty's court: He, the said Flestrin, did, like a false traitor, aid, abet, comfort, and divert the said ambassadors, although he knew them to be servants to a Prince who was lately an open enemy to his Imperial Majesty, and in open war against his said Majesty.

. . .

That the said Quinbus Flestrin, contrary to the duty of a faithful subject, is now preparing to make a voyage to the court and empire of Blefuscu, for which he hath received only verbal license from his Imperial Majesty; and under color of the said license, doth falsely and traitorously intend

to take the said voyage, and thereby to aid, comfort, and abet
the Emperor of Blefuscu, so late an enemy, and in open war
with his Imperial Majesty aforesaid.

.   .   .

"There are some other articles, but these are the most important,
of which I have read you an abstract.

"In the several debates upon this impeachment, it must be confessed that his Majesty gave many marks of his great lenity, often
urging the services you had done him, and endeavoring to extenuate
your crimes. The Treasurer and Admiral insisted that you should
be put to the most painful and ignominious death, by setting fire
on your house at night, and the General was to attend with twenty
thousand men armed with poisoned arrows to shoot you on the face
and hands. Some of your servants were to have private orders to
strew a poisonous juice on your shirts, which would soon make you
tear your own flesh, and die in the utmost torture. The General
came into the same opinion; so that for a long time there was a
majority against you. But his Majesty resolving, if possible, to spare
your life, at last brought off the Chamberlain.

"Upon this incident, Reldresal, principal Secretary for Private
Affairs, who always approved himself your true friend, was commanded by the Emperor to deliver his opinion, which he accordingly
did; and therein justified the good thoughts you have of him. He
allowed your crimes to be great, but that still there was room for
mercy, the most commendable virtue in a prince, and for which his
Majesty was so justly celebrated. He said, the friendship between you
and him was so well known to the world, that perhaps the most
honorable board might think him partial: however, in obedience to
the command he had received, he would freely offer his sentiments.
That if his Majesty, in consideration of your services, and pursuant

to his own merciful disposition, would please to spare your life, and only gave orders to put out both your eyes, he humbly conceived, that by this expedient, justice might in some measure be satisfied, and all the world would applaud the lenity of the Emperor, as well as the fair and generous proceedings of those who have the honor to be his counselors. That the loss of your eyes would be no impediment to your bodily strength, by which you might still be useful to his Majesty. That blindness is an addition to courage, by concealing dangers from us; that the fear you had for your eyes, was the greatest difficulty in bringing over the enemy's fleet, and it would be sufficient for you to see by the eyes of the ministers, since the greatest princes do no more.

"This proposal was received with the utmost disapprobation by the whole board. Bolgolam, the Admiral, could not preserve his temper; but rising up in fury, said, he wondered how the Secretary durst presume to give his opinion for preserving the life of a traitor: that the services you had performed, were, by all true reasons of state, the great aggravation of your crimes; that the same strength which enabled you to bring over the enemy's fleet, might serve, upon the first discontent, to carry it back: that he had good reasons to think you were a Big-Endian in your heart; and as treason begins in the heart, before it appears in overt acts, so he accused you as a traitor on that account, and therefore insisted you should be put to death.

"The Treasurer was of the same opinion; he showed to what straits his Majesty's revenue was reduced by the charge of maintaining you, which would soon grow insupportable: that the Secretary's expedient of putting out your eyes was so far from being a remedy against this evil, that it would probably increase it, as it is manifest from the common practise of blinding some kind of fowl, after which they fed the faster, and grew sooner fat: that his sacred

Majesty and the Council, who are your judges, were in their own consciences fully convinced of your guilt, which was a sufficient argument to condemn you to death, without the formal proofs required by the strict letter of the law.

"But his Imperial Majesty, fully determined against capital punishment, was graciously pleased to say, that since the Council thought the loss of your eyes too easy a censure, some other may be inflicted hereafter. And your friend the Secretary humbly desiring to be heard again, in answer to what the Treasurer had objected concerning the great charge his Majesty was at in maintaining you, said, that his Excellency, who had the sole disposal of the Emperor's revenue, might easily provide against that evil, by gradually lessening your establishment; by which, for want of sufficient food, you would grow weak and faint, and lose your appetite, and consequently decay and consume in a few months; and immediately upon your death, five or six thousand of his Majesty's subjects might, in two or three days, cut your flesh from your bones, take it away by cart-loads, and bury it in distant parts to prevent infection, leaving the skeleton as a monument of admiration to posterity.

"Thus by the great friendship of the Secretary, the whole affair was compromised. It was strictly enjoined, that the project of starving you by degrees should be kept a secret, but the sentence of putting out your eyes was entered on the books; none dissenting except Bolgolam the Admiral.

"In three days your friend the Secretary will be directed to come to your house, and read before you the articles of impeachment; and then to signify the great lenity and favor of his Majesty and Council, whereby you are only condemned to the loss of your eyes, which his Majesty doth not question you will gratefully and humbly submit to; and twenty of his Majesty's surgeons will attend, in order to see the operation well performed, by discharging very sharp-pointed arrows into the balls of your eyes, as you lie on the ground.

"I leave to your prudence what measures you will take; and to avoid suspicion, I must immediately return in as private a manner as I came."

His Lordship did so, and I remained alone, under many doubts and perplexities of mind.

It was a custom introduced by this prince and his ministry (very different, as I have been assured, from the practices of former times,) that after the court had decreed any cruel execution, either to gratify the monarch's resentment, or the malice of a favorite, the Emperor always made a speech to his whole Council, expressing his great lenity and tenderness, as qualities known and confessed by all the world. This speech was immediately published through the kingdom; nor did anything terrify the people so much as those encomiums on his Majesty's mercy; because it was observed, that the more these praises were enlarged and insisted on, the more inhuman was the punishment, and the sufferer more innocent. And as to myself, I must confess, having never been designed for a courtier either by my birth or education, I was so ill a judge of things, that I could not discover the lenity and favor of this sentence, but conceived it (perhaps erroneously) rather to be rigorous than gentle. I sometimes thought of standing my trial, for although I could not deny the facts alleged in the several articles, yet I hoped they would admit of some extenuations. But having in my life perused many state trials, which I ever observed to terminate as the judges thought fit to direct, I durst not rely on so dangerous a decision, in so critical a juncture, and against such powerful enemies. Once I was strongly bent upon resistance, for while I had liberty, the whole strength of that empire could hardly subdue me, and I might easily with stones pelt the metropolis to pieces; but I soon rejected that project with horror, by remembering the oath I had made to the Emperor, the favors I received from him, and the high title of *Nardac* he conferred upon me. Neither had I so soon learned the gratitude of courtiers, to persuade myself that his Majesty's present severities acquitted me of all past obligations.

At last I fixed upon a resolution, for which it is probable I may incur some censure, and not unjustly; for I confess I owe the preserving my eyes, and consequently my liberty, to my own great rashness and want of experience: because if I had then known the nature of princes and ministers, which I have since observed in many other courts, and their methods of treating criminals less obnoxious than myself, I should with great alacrity and readiness have submitted to so easy a punishment. But hurried on by the precipitancy of youth, and having his Imperial Majesty's license to pay my attendance upon the Emperor of Blefuscu, I took this opportunity, before the three days were elapsed, to send a letter to my friend the Secretary, signifying my resolution of setting out that morning for Blefuscu pursuant to the leave I had got; and without waiting for an answer, I went to that side of the island where our fleet lay. I seized a large man of war, tied a cable to the prow, and, lifting up the anchors, I stripped myself, put my clothes (together with my coverlet, which I brought under my arm) into the vessel, and drawing it after me between wading and swimming, arrived at the royal port of Blefuscu, where the people had long expected me: they lent me two guides to direct me to the capital city, which is of the same name. I held them in my hands till I came within two hundred yards of a gate, and desired them to signify my arrival to one of the secretaries, and let him know, I there waited his Majesty's command. I had an answer in about an hour, that his Majesty, attended by the Royal Family, and great officers of the court, was coming out to receive me. I advanced a hundred yards. The Emperor and his train alighted from their horses, the Empress and ladies from their coaches, and I did not perceive they were in any fright or concern. I lay on the ground to kiss his Majesty's and the Empress's hands. I told his Majesty, that I was come according to my promise, and with the license of the Emperor my master, to have the honor of seeing so mighty a monarch, and to offer him any service in my power, consistent with my duty to my own prince; not mentioning a word of my disgrace, because I had hitherto no regular information of it, and might suppose myself wholly ignorant of any such design; neither could I reasonably conceive that the Emperor would discover the secret while I was out of his power: wherein, however, it soon appeared I was deceived.

I shall not trouble the reader with the particular account of my reception at this court, which was suitable to the generosity of so great a prince; nor of the difficulties I was in for want of a house and bed, being forced to lie on the ground, wrapped up in my coverlet.

VIII: *The Author, by a lucky accident, finds means to leave* Blefuscu; *and, after some difficulties, returns safe to his native country.*

Three days after my arrival, walking out of curiosity to the northeast coast of the island, I observed, about half a league off, in the sea, somewhat that looked like a boat overturned. I pulled off my shoes and stockings, and wading two or three hundred yards, I found the object to approach nearer by force of the tide; and then plainly saw it to be a real boat, which I supposed might, by some tempest, have been driven from a ship; whereupon I returned immediately toward the city, and desired his Imperial Majesty to lend me twenty of the tallest vessels he had left after the loss of his fleet, and three thousand seamen under the command of his Vice-Admiral. This fleet sailed round, while I went back the shortest way to the coast where I first discovered the boat; I found the tide had driven it still nearer. The seamen were all provided with cordage, which I had beforehand twisted to a sufficient strength. When the ships came up, I stripped myself, and waded till I came within an hundred yards of the boat, after which I was forced to swim till I got up to it. The seamen threw me the end of the cord, which I fastened to a hole in the fore-part of the boat, and the other end to a man of war; but I found all my labor to little purpose; for being out of my depth, I was not able to work. In this necessity, I was forced to swim behind, and push the boat forward as often as I could, with one of my hands; and the tide favoring me, I advanced so far, that I could just hold up my chin and feel the ground. I rested two or three minutes, and then gave the boat another shove, and so on till the sea was no higher than my armpits; and now the most laborious part being over, I took out my other cables, which were stowed in one of the ships, and fastening them first to the boat, and then to nine of the vessels which attended me, the wind being favorable, the seamen towed, and I shoved till we arrived within forty yards of the shore; and waiting till the tide was out, I got dry to the boat, and by the assistance of two thousand men, with ropes and engines, I made a shift to turn it on its bottom, and found it was but little damaged.

I shall not trouble the reader with the difficulties I was under by the help of certain paddles, which cost me ten days making, to get my boat to the royal port of Blefuscu, where a mighty concourse of people appeared upon my arrival, full of wonder at the sight of so prodigious a vessel. I told the Emperor that my good fortune had thrown this boat in my way, to carry me to some place from whence I might return into my native country, and begged his Majesty's orders for getting materials to fit it up, together with his license to depart, which, after some kind expostulations, he was pleased to grant.

I did very much wonder, in all this time, not to have heard of any express relating to me from our Emperor to the court of Blefuscu. But I was afterwards given privately to understand, that his Imperial Majesty, never imagining I had the least notice of his designs, believed I was only gone to Blefuscu in performance of my promise, according to the license he had given me, which was well known at our court, and would return in a few days when that ceremony was ended. But he was at last in pain at my long absence; and after consulting with the Treasurer, and the rest of that cabal, a person of quality was dispatched with the copy of the articles against me. This envoy had instructions to represent to the monarch of Blefuscu, the great lenity of his master, who was content to punish me no farther than with the loss of my eyes; that I had fled from justice, and if I did not return in two hours, I should be deprived of my title of *Nardac,* and declared a traitor. The envoy further added, that in order to maintain the peace and amity between both empires, his master expected, that his brother of Blefuscu would give orders to have me sent back to Lilliput, bound hand and foot, to be punished as a traitor.

The Emperor of Blefuscu having taken three days to consult, returned an answer consisting of many civilities and excuses. He said, that as for sending me bound, his brother knew it was impossible; that although I had deprived him of his fleet, yet he owed great obligations to me for many good offices I had done him in making the peace. That, however, both their Majesties would soon be made easy; for I had found a prodigious vessel on the shore, able to carry me on the sea, which he had given order to fit up with my own assistance and direction; and he hoped in a few weeks both empires would be freed from so insupportable an incumbrance.

With this answer the envoy returned to Lilliput, and the monarch of Blefuscu related to me all that had passed; offering me at the same time (but under the strictest confidence) his gracious protection, if I would continue in his service; wherein although I believed him sincere, yet I resolved never more to put any confidence in princes or ministers, where I could possibly avoid it; and therefore, with all due acknowledgments for his favorable intentions, I humbly begged to be excused. I told him, that since fortune, whether good or evil, had thrown a vessel in my way, I was resolved to venture myself in the ocean, rather than be an occasion of difference between two such mighty monarchs. Neither did I find the Emperor at all displeased; and I discovered by a certain accident, that he was very glad of my resolution, and so were most of his ministers.

These considerations moved me to hasten my departure somewhat sooner than I intended; to which the court, impatient to have me gone, very readily contributed. Five hundred workmen were employed to make two sails to my boat, according to my directions, by quilting thirteen fold of their strongest linen together. I was at the pains of making ropes and cables, by twisting ten, twenty or thirty of the thickest and strongest of theirs. A great stone that I happened to find, after a long search, by the seashore, served me for an anchor. I had the tallow of three hundred cows for greasing my boat, and other uses. I was at incredible pains in cutting down some of the largest timber-trees for oars and masts, wherein I was, however, much assisted by his Majesty's ship carpenters, who helped me in smoothing them, after I had done the rough work.

In about a month, when all was prepared, I sent to receive his Majesty's commands, and to take my leave. The Emperor and Royal Family came out of the palace; I lay down on my face to kiss his hand, which he very graciously gave me: so did the Empress and young Princes of the blood. His Majesty presented me with fifty purses of two hundred *sprugs* apiece, together with his picture at full length, which I put immediately into one of my gloves, to keep it from being hurt. The ceremonies at my departure were too many to trouble the reader with at this time.

I stored the boat with the carcasses of an hundred oxen, and three hundred sheep, with bread and drink proportionable, and as much meat ready dressed as four hundred cooks could provide. I took with me six cows and two bulls alive, with as many ewes and rams, intending to carry them into my own country, and propagate the breed. And to feed them on board, I had a good bundle of hay, and a bag of corn. I would gladly have taken a dozen of the natives, but this was a thing the Emperor would by no means permit; and besides a diligent search into my pockets, his Majesty engaged my honor not to carry away any of his subjects, although with their own consent and desire.

Having thus prepared all things as well as I was able, I set sail on the twenty-fourth day of September, 1701, at six in the morning; and when I had gone about four leagues to the northward, the wind being at southeast, at six in the evening I descried a small island about half a league to the northwest. I advanced forward, and cast anchor on the lee-side of the island, which seemed to be uninhabited. I then took some refreshment, and went to my rest. I slept well, and as I conjecture at least six hours, for I found the day broke in two hours after I awaked. It was a clear night. I ate my breakfast before the sun was up; and heaving anchor, the wind being favorable, I steered the same course that I had done the day before, wherein I was directed by my pocket-compass. My intention was to reach, if possible, one of those islands, which I had reason to believe lay to the northeast of Van Diemen's Land. I discovered nothing all that day; but upon the next, about three in the afternoon, when I had by my computation made twenty-four leagues from Blefuscu, I descried a sail steering to the southeast; my course was due east. I hailed her, but could get no answer; yet I found I gained upon her, for the wind slackened. I made all the sail I could, and in half an hour she spied me, then hung out her ancient, and discharged a gun. It is not easy to express the joy I was in upon the unexpected hope of once more seeing my beloved country, and the dear pledges I had left in it. The ship slackened her sails, and I came up with her between five and six in the evening, September 26; but my heart leaped within me to see her English colors. I put my cows and sheep into my coat-pockets, and got on board with all my little cargo of provisions. The vessel was an English merchant-man, returning from Japan by the North and South Seas; the Captain, Mr. John Biddel of Deptford, a very civil man, and an excellent sailor. We were now in the latitude of 30 degrees south; there were about fifty men in the ship; and here I met an old comrade of mine, one Peter Williams, who gave me a good character to the Captain. This gentleman treated me with kindness, and desired I would let him know what place I came from last, and whither I was bound; which I did in a few words, but he thought I was raving, and that the dangers I underwent had disturbed my head; whereupon I took my black cattle and sheep out of my pocket, which, after great astonishment, clearly convinced him of my veracity. I then showed him the gold given me by the Emperor of Blefuscu, together with his Majesty's picture at full length, and some other rarities of that country. I gave him two purses of two hundred *sprugs* each, and promised, when we arrived in England, to make him a present of a cow and a sheep.

I shall not trouble the reader with a particular account of this voyage, which was very prosperous for the most part. We arrived in the Downs on the 13th of April, 1702. I had only one misfortune, that the rats on board carried away one of my sheep; I found her bones in a hole, picked clean from the flesh. The rest of my cattle I got safe on shore, and set them a-grazing in a bowling-green at Greenwich, where the fineness of the grass made them feed very heartily, though I had always feared the contrary: neither could I possibly have preserved them in so long a voyage, if the Captain had not allowed me some of his best biscuit, which, rubbed to powder, and mingled with water, was their constant food. The short time I continued in England, I made a considerable profit by showing my cattle to many persons of quality, and others: and before I began my second voyage, I sold them for six hundred pounds. Since my last return, I find the breed is considerably increased, especially the sheep; which I hope will prove much to the advantage of the woolen manufacture, by the fineness of the fleeces.

I stayed but two months with my wife and family; for my insatiable desire of seeing foreign countries would suffer me to continue no longer. I left fifteen hundred pounds with my wife, and fixed her in a good house at Redriff. My remaining stock I carried with me, part in money, and part in goods, in hopes to improve my fortunes. My eldest uncle John had left me an estate in land, near Epping, of about thirty pounds a year; and I had a long lease of the Black Bull in Fetter-Lane, which yielded me as much more; so that I was not in any danger of leaving my family upon the parish. My son Johnny, named so after his uncle, was at the Grammar School, and a towardly child. My daughter Betty (who is now well married, and has children) was then at her needle-work. I took leave of my wife, and boy and girl, with tears on both sides, and went on board the *Adventure,* a merchant-ship of three hundred tons, bound for Surat, Captain John Nicholas, of Liverpool, Commander. But my account of this voyage must be referred to the second part of my Travels.

DON QUIXOTE

OF   *MIGUEL DE CERVANTES*

Retold by
JUDGE PARRY

Illustrations by GUSTAVE DORÉ

I

AN INTRODUCTION TO DON QUIXOTE

THIS is the story that Miguel de Cervantes, Spaniard, published in 1605, which the world has been reading again and again ever since.

Once upon a time there lived in a certain village in a province of Spain called the Mancha, a gentleman named Quixada or Quesada—for indeed historians differ about this—whose house was full of old lances, halberds, and such other armors and weapons. He was, besides, the owner of an ancient target or shield, a raw-boned steed, and a swift greyhound. His pot consisted daily of common meats, some lentils on Fridays, and perhaps a roast pigeon for Sunday's dinner. His dress was a black suit with velvet breeches, and slippers of the same color, which he kept for holidays, and a suit of homespun which he wore on week-days.

On the purchase of these few things he spent the small rents that came to him every year. He had in his house a woman-servant of about some forty years old, a Niece not yet twenty, and a lad that served him both in field and at home, and could saddle his horse or manage a pruning-hook.

The master himself was about fifty years old, a strong, hard-featured man with a withered face. He was an early riser, and had once been very fond of hunting. But now for a great portion of the year he applied himself wholly to reading the old books of Knighthood, and this with such keen delight that he forgot all about the pleasures of the chase, and neglected all household matters. His mania and folly grew to such a pitch that he sold many acres of his lands to buy books of the exploits and adventures of the Knights of old. These he took for true and correct histories, and when his friends the Curate of the village, or Mr. Nicholas, the worthy Barber of the town, came to see him, he would dispute with them as to which of the Knights of romance had done the greatest deeds.

So eagerly did he plunge into the reading of these books that he many times spent whole days and nights poring over them; and in the end, through little sleep and much reading, his brain became tired, and he fairly lost his wits. His fancy was filled with those things that he read, of enchantments, quarrels, battles, challenges, wounds, wooings, loves, tempests, and other impossible follies, and those romantic tales so firmly took hold of him that he believed no history to be so certain and sincere as they were.

Finally, his wit being extinguished, he was seized with one of the strangest whims that ever madman stumbled on in this world, for it seemed to him right and necessary that he himself should become a Knight Errant, and ride through the world in arms to seek adventures and practise in person all that he had read about the Knights of old. Therefore he resolved that he would make a name for himself by revenging the injuries of others, and courting all manner of dangers and difficulties, until in the end he should be rewarded for his valor in arms by the crown of some mighty Empire. And first of all he caused certain old rusty arms that belonged to his great-grandfather, and had lain for many years neglected and forgotten in a by-corner of his house, to be brought out and well scoured. He trimmed them and dressed them as well as he could, and then saw that they had something wanting; for instead of a proper helmet they had only a morion or headpiece, like a steel bonnet without any visor. This his industry supplied, for he made a visor for his helmet by patching and pasting certain papers together, and this pasteboard fitted to the morion gave it all the appearance of a real helmet. Then, to make sure that it was strong enough, he out with his sword and gave it a blow or two, and with the very first did quite undo that which had cost him a week to make. He did not at all approve the ease with which it was destroyed, and to make things better he placed certain iron bars within it, in such a manner that made him feel sure it was now sound and strong, without putting it to a second trial.

He next visited his horse, who though he had more corners than a Spanish *real* or shilling, which in those days was anything but round, and had nothing on him but skin and bone, yet he seemed

*His fancy was filled with the things he read, of enchantments,
quarrels, battles, wounds and loves.*

to him a better steed than Bucephalus, the noble animal that carried Alexander the Great when he went to battle. He spent four days inventing a name for his horse, saying to himself that it was not fit that so famous a Knight's horse, and so good a beast, should want a known name. Therefore he tried to find a name that should both give people some notion of what he had been before he was the steed of a Knight Errant, and also what he now was; for, seeing that his lord and master was going to change his calling, it was only right that his horse should have a new name, famous and high-sounding, and worthy of his new position in life. And after having chosen, made up, put aside, and thrown over any number of names as not coming up to his idea, he finally hit upon Rozinante, a name in his opinion sublime and well-sounding, expressing in a word what he had been when he was a simple carriage horse, and what was expected of him in his new dignity.

The name being thus given to his horse, he made up his mind to give himself a name also, and in that thought labored another eight days. Finally he determined to call himself Don Quixote, which has made people think that his name was Quixada, or Quesada as others have said; and remembering that the great Knights of olden time were not satisfied with a mere dry name, but added to it the name of their kingdom or country, so he like a good Knight added to his own that also of his province, and called himself Don Quixote of the Mancha, whereby he declared his birthplace and did honor to his country by taking it for his surname.

His armor being scoured, his morion transformed into a helmet, his horse named, and himself furnished with a new name, he considered that now he wanted nothing but a lady on whom he might bestow his service and affection. "For," he said to himself, remembering what he had read in the books of knightly adventures, "if I should by good hap encounter with some Giant, as Knights Errant ordinarily do, and if I should overthrow him with one blow to the ground, or cut him with a stroke in two halves, or finally overcome and make him yield to me, it would be only right and proper that I should have some lady to whom I might present him. Then would he, entering my sweet lady's presence, say unto her with a humble and submissive voice: 'Madam, I am the Giant Caraculiambro, Lord of the Island called Malindrania, whom the never-too-much-praised Knight Don Quixote of the Mancha hath overcome in single combat. He hath commanded me to present myself to your greatness, that it may please your Highness to dispose of me according to your liking.' "

You may believe that the heart of the Knight danced for joy when he made that grand speech, and he was even more pleased when he had found out one whom he might call his lady. For, they say, there lived in the next village to his own a hale, buxom country wench with whom he was sometime in love, though for the matter of that she had never known of it or taken any notice of him whatever. She was called Aldonca Lorenso, and her he thought fittest to honor as the lady of his fancy. Then he began to search about in his mind for a name that should not vary too much from her own, but should at the same time show people that she was a Princess or lady of quality. Thus it was that he called her Dulcinea of Toboso, a name sufficiently strange, romantic, and musical for the lady of so brave a Knight. And now, having taken to himself both armor, horse, and lady fair, he was ready to go forth and seek adventures.

II

DON QUIXOTE'S FIRST SALLY

All his preparations being made, he could no longer resist the desire of carrying out his plans, his head being full of the wrongs he intended to put right, the errors he wished to amend, and the evil deeds he felt himself called upon to punish. And, therefore, without telling any living creature, and unseen of anybody, somewhat before daybreak—it being one of the warmest days in July—he armed himself from head to foot, mounted on Rozinante, laced on his strange helmet, gathered up his target, seized his lance, and through the back door of his yard sallied forth into the fields, marvelously cheerful and content to see how easily he had started on his new career. But scarcely was he clear of the village when he was struck by a terrible thought, and one which did well-nigh overthrow all his plans. For he recollected that he had never been knighted, and therefore, according to the laws of Knighthood, neither could he nor ought he to combat with any Knight. And even if he were a Knight, he remembered to have read that as a new Knight he ought to wear white armor without any device upon his shield until he should win it by force of arms.

These thoughts made him waver a little in his plan; but more for the reason that his head was full of his folly than for any other, he determined to cause himself to be knighted by the first he met, as others had done of whom he had read in the books which had so turned his brain. As to the white armor, he resolved at the first opportunity to scour his own until it should be whiter than ermine; and, having satisfied himself with these intentions, he pursued his way without following any other road than that which his horse was pleased to choose, believing that to be the most correct way of meeting with knightly adventures. And as he rode along he exclaimed to the empty air as if he had been actually in love: "O Princess Dulcinea, Lady of this captive heart, much wrong hast thou done me by dismissing me and reproaching me with thy cruel commandment not to appear before thy beauty! I pray thee, sweet Lady, to remember this thy faithful slave, who for thy love suffers so many tortures."

A thousand other ravings, after the style and manner that his books had taught him, did he add to this as he traveled along, meeting with no adventure worthy to be set down, whilst the sun mounted so swiftly and with so great heat that it would have been sufficient to have melted his brains if he had had any left.

He journeyed all that day long, and at night both he and his horse were tired and marvelously pressed by hunger, and looking about him on every side to see whether he could discover any Castle to which he might retire for the night, he saw an Inn near unto the highway on which he traveled, which was as welcome a sight to him as if he had seen a guiding star. Then spurring his horse he rode toward it as fast as he might, and arrived there much about nightfall.

There stood by chance at the Inn door two jolly peasant women who were traveling toward Seville with some carriers, who happened to take up their lodging in that Inn the same evening. And as our Knight Errant believed all that he saw or heard to take place in the same manner as he had read in his books, he no sooner saw the Inn than he fancied it to be a Castle with four turrets and pinnacles of shining silver, with a drawbridge, a deep moat, and all such things as belong to grand Castles. Drawing slowly toward it, he checked Rozinante with the bridle when he was close to the Inn, and rested awhile to see if any dwarf would mount on the battlements to give warning with the sound of a trumpet how some

Knight did approach the Castle; but seeing they stayed so long, and Rozinante was eager to get up to his stable, he went to the Inn door, and there beheld the two wenches that stood at it, whom he supposed to be two beautiful damsels or lovely ladies that did solace themselves before the Castle gates. At that moment it happened that a certain swineherd, as he gathered together his hogs, blew the horn which was wont to bring them together, and at once Don Quixote imagined it was some dwarf who gave notice of his arrival; and he rode up to the Inn door with marvelous delight. The ladies, when they beheld one armed in that manner with lance and target, made haste to run into the Inn; but Don Quixote, seeing their fear by their flight, lifted up his pasteboard visor, showed his withered and dusky face, and spoke to them thus: "Let not your ladyships fly nor fear any harm, for it does not belong to the order of Knighthood which I profess to wrong anybody, much less such high-born damsels as your appearance shows you to be."

The wenches looked at him very earnestly, and sought with their eyes for his face, which the ill-fashioned helmet concealed; but when they heard themselves called high-born damsels, they could not contain their laughter, which was so loud that Don Quixote was quite ashamed of them and rebuked them, saying: "Modesty is a comely ornament of the beautiful, and too much laughter springing from trifles is great folly; but I do not tell you this to make you the more ashamed, for my desire is none other than to do you all the honor and service I may."

This speech merely increased their laughter, and with it his anger, which would have passed all bounds if the Innkeeper had not come out at this instant. Now this Innkeeper was a man of exceeding fatness, and therefore, as some think, of a very peaceful disposition; and when he saw that strange figure, armed in such fantastic armor, he was very nearly keeping the two women company in their merriment and laughter. But being afraid of the owner of such a lance and target, he resolved to behave civilly for fear of what might happen, and thus addressed him: "Sir Knight! if your Worship do seek for lodging, we have no bed at liberty, but you shall find all other things in abundance."

To which Don Quixote, noting the humility of the Constable of the Castle—for such he took him to be—replied: "Anything, Sir Constable, may serve me, for my arms are my dress, and the battlefield is my bed."

While he was speaking, the Innkeeper laid hand on Don Quixote's stirrup and helped him to alight. This he did with great difficulty and pain, for he had not eaten a crumb all that day. He then bade the Innkeeper have special care of his horse, saying he was one of the best animals that ever ate bread.

The Innkeeper looked at Rozinante again and again, but he did not seem to him half so good as Don Quixote valued him. However, he led him civilly to the stable, and returned to find his guest in the hands of the high-born damsels, who were helping him off with his armor. They had taken off his back and breast plates, but they could in no way get his head and neck out of the strange, ill-fashioned helmet which he had fastened on with green ribands.

Now these knots were so impossible to untie that the wenches would have cut them, but this Don Quixote would not agree to. Therefore he remained all the night with his helmet on, and looked the drollest and strangest figure you could imagine. And he was now so pleased with the women, whom he still took to be ladies and dames of the Castle, that he said to them: "Never was Knight so well attended on and served by ladies as was Don Quixote. When he departed from his village, damsels attended on him and princesses on his horse. O ladies! Rozinante is the name of my steed, and I am called Don Quixote, and the time shall come when your ladyships may command me and I obey, and then the valor of mine arm shall discover the desire I have to do you service."

The women could make nothing of his talk, but asked him if he would eat, and Don Quixote replying that such was his desire, there was straightway laid a table at the Inn door. The Host brought out a portion of badly boiled haddocks, and a black, greasy loaf, which was all the Inn could supply. But the manner of Don Quixote's eating was the best sport in the world, for with his helmet on he could put nothing into his mouth himself if others did not help him to find his way and therefore one of the wenches served her turn at that, and helped to feed him. But they could not give him drink after that manner, and he would have remained dry forever if the Innkeeper had not bored a cane, and putting one end in his mouth, poured the wine down the other. And all this he suffered rather than cut the ribands of his helmet.

And as he sat at supper the swineherd again sounded his horn, and Don Quixote was still firm in the belief that he was in some famous Castle where he was served with music, and that the stale haddock was fresh trout, the bread of the finest flour, the two wenches high-born damsels, and the Innkeeper the Constable of the Castle. Thus he thought his career of Knight Errant was well begun, but he was still greatly troubled by the thought that he was not yet dubbed Knight, and could not therefore rightly follow his adventures until he received the honor of Knighthood.

III

THE KNIGHTING OF DON QUIXOTE

When he had finished his sorry supper, he took his Host with him to the stable, and shutting the door threw himself down upon his knees before him, saying: "I will never rise from this place where I am, Sir Constable, until your courtesy shall grant unto me a boon that I mean to demand of you, something which will add to your renown and to the profit of all the human race."

The Innkeeper, seeing his guest at his feet, and hearing him speak these words, stood confounded at the sight, not knowing what he would say or do next, and tried to make him arise. But all was in vain until he had promised him that he would grant him any gift that he sought at his hands.

"Signor," said Don Quixote, rising from his knees, "I did never expect less from your great magnificence, and now I will tell you that the boon which I demand of you, and which you have so generously granted, is that tomorrow in the morning you will dub me Knight. This night I will watch mine armor in the Chapel of your Castle, and in the morning, as I have said, the rest of my desires shall be fulfilled, that I may set out in a proper manner throughout the four parts of the world to seek adventures to the benefit of the poor and needy, as is the duty of Knighthood and of Knights Errant."

The Innkeeper, who was a bit of a jester, and had before thought that the wits of his guest were none of the best, was sure that his suspicions were true when he heard him speak in this manner. And in order to enjoy a joke at his expense, he resolved to fall in with his humor, and told him that there was great reason in what he desired,

345

which was only natural and proper in a Knight of such worth as he seemed to be. He added further that there was no Chapel in his Castle where he might watch his arms, for he had broken it down to build it up anew. But, nevertheless, he knew well that in a case of necessity they might be watched in any other place, and therefore he might watch them that night in the lower court of the Castle, where in the morning he, the Innkeeper, would perform all the proper ceremonies, so that he should be made not only a dubbed Knight, but such a one as should not have a fellow in the whole universe.

The Innkeeper now gave orders that Don Quixote should watch his armor in a great yard that lay near unto one side of the Inn, wherefore he gathered together all his arms, laid them on a cistern near to a well, and buckling on his target he laid hold of his lance and walked up and down before the cistern very demurely, until night came down upon the scene.

In the meantime the roguish Innkeeper told all the rest that lodged in the Inn of the folly of his guest, the watching of his arms, and the Knighthood which he expected to receive. They all wondered very much at so strange a kind of folly, and going out to behold him from a distance, they saw that sometimes he marched to and fro with a quiet gesture, other times leaning upon his lance he looked upon his armor for a good space of time without beholding any other thing save his arms.

Although it was now night, yet was the moon so clear that everything which the Knight did was easily seen by all beholders. And now one of the carriers that lodged in the Inn resolved to give his mules some water, and for that purpose it was necessary to move Don Quixote's armor that lay on the cistern.

Seeing the carrier approach, Don Quixote called to him in a loud voice: "O thou, whosoever thou art, bold Knight, who dares to touch the armor of the bravest adventurer that ever girded sword, look well what thou doest, and touch them not if thou meanest not to leave thy life in payment for thy meddling!"

The carrier took no notice of these words, though it were better for him if he had, but laying hold of the armor threw it piece by piece into the middle of the yard.

When Don Quixote saw this, he lifted up his eyes toward heaven, and addressing his thoughts, as it seemed, to his Lady Dulcinea, he said: "Assist me, dear Lady, in this insult offered to thy vassal, and let not thy favor and protection fail me in this my first adventure!"

Uttering these and other such words, he let slip his target or shield, and lifting up his lance with both hands he gave the carrier so round a knock on his pate that it overthrew him on to the ground, and if he had caught him a second he would not have needed any surgeon to cure him. This done, he gathered up his armor again, and laying the pieces where they had been before, he began walking up and down near them with as much quietness as he did at first.

But very soon afterwards another carrier, without knowing what had happened, for his companion yet lay on the ground, came also to give his mules water, and coming to take away the armor to get at the cistern, Don Quixote let slip again his target, and lifting his lance brought it down on the carrier's head, which he broke in several places.

All the people in the Inn, and amongst them the Innkeeper, came running out when they heard the noise, and Don Quixote seeing them seized his target, and, drawing his sword, cried aloud: "O Lady of all beauty, now, if ever, is the time for thee to turn the eyes of thy greatness on thy Captive Knight who is on the eve of so marvelous great an adventure."

Saying this seemed to fill him with so great a courage, that if he had been assaulted by all the carriers in the universe he would not have retreated one step.

The companions of the wounded men, seeing their fellows in so evil a plight, began to rain stones on Don Quixote from a distance, who defended himself as well as he might with his target, and durst not leave the cistern lest he should appear to abandon his arms.

The Innkeeper cried to them to let him alone, for he had already told them that he was mad. But all the time Don Quixote cried out louder than the Innkeeper, calling them all disloyal men and traitors, and that the Lord of the Castle was a treacherous and bad Knight to allow them to use a Knight Errant so basely; and if he had only received the order of Knighthood he would have punished him soundly for his treason. Then calling to the carriers he said: "As for you base and rascally ruffians, you are beneath my notice. Throw at me, approach, draw near and do me all the hurt you may, for you shall ere long receive the reward of your insolence."

These words, which he spoke with great spirit and boldness, struck a terrible fear into all those who assaulted him, and, partly moved by his threats and partly persuaded by the Innkeeper, they left off throwing stones at him, and he allowed them to carry away the wounded men, while he returned to his watch with great quietness and gravity.

The Innkeeper did not very much like Don Quixote's pranks, and therefore determined to shorten the ceremony and give him the order of Knighthood at once before anyone else was injured. Approaching him, therefore, he made apologies for the insolence of the base fellows who had thrown stones at him, and explained that

Don Quixote watching his armor at night.

349

it was not with his consent, and that he thought them well punished for their impudence. He added that it was not necessary for Don Quixote to watch his armor any more, because the chief point of being knighted was to receive the stroke of the sword on the neck and shoulder, and that ceremony he was ready to perform at once.

All this Don Quixote readily believed, and answered that he was most eager to obey him, and requested him to finish everything as speedily as possible. For, he said, as soon as he was knighted, if he was assaulted again, he intended not to leave one person alive in all the Castle, except those which the Constable should command, whom he would spare for his sake.

The Innkeeper, alarmed at what he said, and fearing lest he should carry out his threat, set about the ceremony without delay. He brought out his day-book, in which he wrote down the accounts of the hay and straw which he sold to carriers who came to the Inn, and attended by a small boy holding the end of a candle and walking before him, and followed by the two women who were staying at the Inn, he approached Don Quixote. He solemnly commanded him to kneel upon his knees, while he mumbled something which he pretended to read out of the book that he held in his hand. Then he gave him a good blow on the neck, and after that another sound thwack over the shoulders with his own sword, always as he did so continuing to mumble and murmur as though he were reading something out of his book. This being done, he commanded one of the damsels to gird on his sword, which she did with much grace and cleverness. And it was with difficulty that they all kept from laughing during this absurd ceremony, but what they had already seen of Don Quixote's fury made them careful not to annoy him even by a smile.

When she had girded on his sword, the damsel said: "May you

be a fortunate Knight, and meet with good success in all your adventures."

Don Quixote asked her how she was called, that he might know to whom he was obliged for the favors he had received. She answered with great humility that she was named Tolosa, and was a butcher's daughter of Toledo. Don Quixote replied requesting her to call herself from henceforth the Lady Tolosa, which she promised to perform. The other damsel buckled on his spurs, and when Don Quixote asked her name she told him it was Molinera, and that she was daughter of an honest miller of Antequera. Don Quixote entreated her also to call herself Lady Molinera, and offered her new services and favors.

These strange and never-before-seen ceremonies being ended, Don Quixote could not rest until he was mounted on horseback that he might go to seek adventures. He therefore caused Rozinante to be instantly saddled, leaped on his back, and embracing the Innkeeper, thanked him in a thousand wild and ridiculous ways for the great favor he had done him in dubbing him Knight. The Innkeeper, who was only eager to be rid of him without delay, answered him in the same fashion, and let him march off without demanding from him a single farthing for his food or lodging.

IV

WHAT BEFELL ON LEAVING THE INN

It was dawn when Don Quixote went out from the Inn, so full of pleasure to behold himself knighted that his very horse-girths were ready to burst for joy. But calling to memory some advice that the

Innkeeper had given him, about the necessity of carrying with him money and clean shirts when he went on his adventures, he determined to return to his house and obtain these things, and also find for himself a Squire. For this office he fixed in his own mind upon a plowman, a neighbor of his, a poor man who had many children, but yet a man who was very fit as he thought to be his Squire.

With this view he turned Rozinante toward his own village, who, knowing that he was on his way home, began to trot along with so good a will that he seemed not to touch the ground.

He had not traveled far when he heard from a thicket hard by the shrill cries of some weak and delicate mortal in grievous distress.

No sooner did he hear them than he exclaimed: "I am indeed thankful for the favor done to me by giving me so soon an opportunity of performing what is due to my profession, and gathering the fruits of my desires. These cries doubtless come from some distressed man or woman who has need of my protection and aid."

Then turning the reins, he guided Rozinante toward the place whence the voice seemed to proceed. And within a few paces after he had entered into the thicket he saw a mare tied up to one oak, and to another was tied a youth, all naked from the middle upward, of about fifteen years of age. Now it was he that cried so pitifully, and not without cause. For a sturdy fellow of a farmer was beating him soundly with a girdle, accompanying each stroke with a reproof and piece of advice, saying: "The tongue must peace and the eyes be wary." And the boy, whose name was Andrew, answered: "I will never do it again, good master, I will never do it again. I promise to have more care of your things from henceforth."

Seeing what passed, Don Quixote cried out with an angry voice: "Ill it beseems you, discourteous Knight, to deal thus with one that cannot defend himself. Mount, therefore, on horseback and take thy lance (for the Farmer had a lance leaning against the very same tree to which his mare was tied), for I will make thee know that it is the act of a coward to do that which thou dost."

The Farmer, beholding this strange figure buckled in armor, and brandishing a lance over his head, gave himself up for a dead man, and answered him with mild and submissive words, saying: "Sir Knight, the youth whom I am beating is mine own servant, and keepeth for me a flock of sheep; but he is grown so negligent that he loseth one of them every other day, and because I correct him for his carelessness and knavery, he says I do it through covetousness and miserliness so as not to pay him his due wages, but on my conscience I assure you he lies."

"What? The lie, in my presence, rascally clown!" cried Don Quixote. "By the sun that shines above us, I will run thee through and through with my lance, base Carle! Pay him instantly, without another word, or I will finish and destroy thee in a moment. Loose him forthwith!"

The Farmer, hanging down his head, made no reply, but released poor Andrew, of whom Don Quixote demanded how much his master owed him. The boy answered that it was nine months' wages at seven *reals* a month. Casting it up, Don Quixote found that it amounted to sixty-three *reals,* and commanded the Farmer to pay the money at once, unless he had a mind to die for it.

This the Farmer, who was in a terrible fright, promised to do, but said he: "The worst of it is, Sir Knight, that I have no money here. Let Andrew come with me to my house, and I will pay him his wages to the last *real.*"

"I go with him?" said the boy. "Evil befall me if I do. No, Sir. I don't intend to do that, for as soon as ever we were alone, he would flay me alive."

"He will not dare to do it," said Don Quixote, "for my command is sufficient to make him respect me. And on condition that he will swear to me to carry out his promise, by the order of Knighthood which he hath received, I will set him free and assure thee of the payment."

"Good your worship," said the youth; "mark well what you say, for this man my master is no Knight, nor did he ever receive any order of Knighthood. He is John Haldudo the rich, and lives at Quintanar."

"That is no matter," said Don Quixote, "for there may be Knights of the Haldudos."

"The good Knight speaks well, friend Andrew," said his master. "Do me but the pleasure to come with me, and I swear by all the orders of Knighthood that are in the world to pay thee, as I have said, to the last *real*."

"With this," said Don Quixote, "I will rest satisfied; and see that thou fulfillest it as thou hast sworn. If not, I swear again to thee by the same oath to return and seek thee out once more and chastise thee. And I will find thee out, though thou didst hide thyself closer than a lizard. And if thou desirest to know who it is that commands thee thus, know that I am the valiant Don Quixote of the Mancha, the righter of wrongs and the scourge of injustice."

Saying this, the Knight clapt spurs to his Rozinante, and was quickly gone from him.

The farmer followed him with his eyes, and seeing that he was beyond the wood and quite out of sight, he returned to Andrew and said: "Come to me, child, for I will pay thee what I owe thee, as that righter of wrongs hath commanded."

"Upon my word," said Andrew, "you do well to fulfill the good Knight's commandments. And I pray that he may live a thousand

*"By the sun that shines above us, I will run thee through
and through with my lance, base Carle!"*

years, for he is so brave and so just a judge that, if you pay me not, he will come back and do all he promised."

"I also do believe the same," said the Farmer; "but for the much love I bear thee, I will increase the debt that I may add to the payment." And seizing him by the arm, he tied him again to the oak, where he gave him so many blows as to leave him for dead.

"Call now, Master Andrew," said he, "for thy righter of wrongs; and thou shalt see that he cannot undo this, though I think I have not finished the doing of it, for I have yet a desire to flay thee alive as thou didst fear."

But he untied him at last, and gave him leave to go and seek out his Judge, to the end that he might execute the sentence he had pronounced. Andrew departed somewhat discontented, swearing to search for the valiant Don Quixote of the Mancha, and relate to him point for point all that had passed, that the Farmer might be repaid sevenfold. Nevertheless he wept as he went along, and his master remained behind laughing, and thus did the valiant Don Quixote right this wrong.

As for the Knight, it appeared to him that he had made a very happy and noble beginning to his feats of arms. And as he rode towards his village, he recited to himself in a low voice these words: "Well mayest thou call thyself happy above all other women of the earth, O! above all beauties, beautiful Dulcinea of Toboso; since it has fallen to thy lot to hold submissive to thy will a Knight so renowned and valorous as is and ever shall be, Don Quixote of the Mancha, who, as all the world knows, but yesterday received the order of Knighthood, and today hath destroyed the greatest outrage and wrong that injustice and cruelty could commit. Today hath he wrested the scourge from the hand of the pitiless foe who so cruelly beat the delicate infant."

Soon afterwards he came to a spot where the road branched into four, and there came into his fancy the crossways he had read of, where the Knights Errant used to ponder which of the roads they should take. And that he might imitate them, he let slip the reins on Rozinante's neck, submitting his will to that of his steed, who followed his first intention, which was to return home to his own stable. And having traveled some two miles, Don Quixote discovered a great troop of people, who, as it was afterwards known, were certain merchants of Toledo, that rode toward Murcia to buy silks. They were six in number, and came with their parasols or sun umbrellas, and four serving-men a-horseback, and three lackeys.

Scarce had Don Quixote perceived them when he straight imagined them to be a new adventure. And so that he might imitate as far as possible the passages which he had read in his books, he settled himself with a gallant air and resolute bearing firmly in his stirrups, grasped his lance, brought his target over his breast, and stood, waiting, posted in the middle of the road, for those whom he took to be Knights Errant like himself.

And when they were so near that they might hear and see him, he lifted up his voice and said: "Let all the world stand and pass no farther, if all the world will not confess that there is not in all the world a more beautiful damsel than the Empress of the Mancha, the peerless Dulcinea of Toboso."

The merchants stopped at the sound of these words to behold the marvelous and ridiculous shape of him that spake them, and at once suspected the madness of the speaker.

Curious to know the meaning of the confession he demanded from them, one of the merchants, who was a bit of a wag and very sharp-witted, said to Don Quixote: "Sir Knight, we know not who that good lady may be you speak of. Show her therefore to us, and if she be as beautiful as you report, we will with right good will, and without further trouble, confess the truth of what you demand."

"If I did show her to you," replied Don Quixote, "what merit would there be in confessing a truth which is clear to all beholders? The importance of my demand is that without seeing her you must believe it, which if you refuse to do I challenge you all to battle, ye proud preposterous crew. And now come on! One by one as the order of Knighthood requires, or all at once as is the custom and base usage of those of your breed. Here I await you, confiding in the right I have on my side."

"Sir Knight," replied the Merchant, "I request you in the name of all the Princes here present, that in order that we may not burden our conscience by confessing a thing which we have never beheld nor heard, you will be pleased to show us some portrait of the lady, although it be no bigger than a grain of wheat. For I do believe that we are already so much on your side, that though her portrait showed her to us a-squint of one eye, and wearing a hump on her back, we should say all that you wish in her favor."

"Infamous rabble," replied Don Quixote, mightily enraged; "she is neither crook-eyed nor humpbacked, but is straighter than a spindle of Guadamara. Dearly shall you pay for the foul words you have uttered against so immense a beauty as my Lady." So saying, he lowered his lance against him who had spoken, with such wrath and fury, that if Rozinante had not tripped and fallen in the midst of his career, it would have fared ill with the rash Merchant.

But, alas! Rozinante fell; his master went rolling some distance across the field, and though he struggled to arise yet was he never able, so encumbered was he by his lance, target, spurs, helmet, and the weight of his old-fashioned armor. And while he strove to rise he shouted: "Fly not, cowardly brood! Tarry a little, base caitiffs!

for not by any fault of mine, but of my horse, am I thus discomfited!"

One of the lackeys with the company, hearing these saucy speeches of the poor overthrown Knight, could not forbear returning him an answer on his ribs, and coming up to him he seized his lance, and having broken it into pieces, began with one of them to belabor him, so that, in spite of his armor, he pounded him like wheat in a mill. His masters called out to him to let the gentleman be, but the lackey was angry and would not give up the game. And running for the other pieces of the broken lance, he shivered them all over the poor fallen Knight, who never closed his mouth, but cried out against them for brigands and murderers, for such he took them to be.

At last the lackey was tired out, and the merchants followed on their way talking about the poor belabored Knight, who when he saw himself alone, again made trial to arise; but if he could not do so when sound and well, how could he after being pounded and almost beaten to a jelly? And yet he still considered himself fortunate, for he persuaded himself that this disgrace was one of those things that must of occasion happen to a Knight Errant. And though he could not rise on account of being mauled and bruised from head to foot, he put it all down to the carelessness of his steed Rozinante.

V

HOW DON QUIXOTE RETURNED HOME

Finding that he was unable to stir, the Knight pleased himself whilst lying on the ground by remembering and repeating aloud passages from his favorite books.

He was reciting the ballad of the Marquess of Mantua, in which a noble Knight has an adventure similar to his own, when there chanced to pass by a laboring man, a neighbor of Don Quixote's, who was going to take a load of wheat to the mill.

He, seeing a man stretched on the ground, came over to him and asked who he was and what mishap had befallen him.

Don Quixote at once believed that the laborer was no other than the Marquess of Mantua himself, and went on with his ballad which gave an account of his disgrace.

The laborer was astonished at all these follies, and taking off the Knight's visor, which was all broken to pieces with the beating, he wiped his face, which was covered with dust; and when he had wiped it he recognized him and cried: "Senor Quixada (for so was he named before he became a Knight Errant), who has brought your Worship to this plight?"

But the Knight only went on with his ballad, and made no answer.

Seeing this, the good man took off as well as he could his breastplate and corselet to see if he had any wound, but he found no blood nor sign of any. He tried to raise him from the ground, which he did at last with much ado. Then he mounted him upon his ass, which seemed a safer carriage than the Knight's steed. Gathering up his arms, even to the fragments of the lance, he fastened them upon Rozinante, whose bridle he took hold of, as well as of the ass's halter; and so they journeyed toward the village, Don Quixote continuing to mutter his nonsensical stories.

In this manner they arrived at last at their village about sunset, but the laborer waited until it grew somewhat dusk, so that folk should not see the Knight so simply mounted.

When he entered the village and went to Don Quixote's house, he found all in uproar there. For the Curate and the Barber—Don Quixote's great friends—were there, and his Housekeeper was crying to them at the top of her voice: "What think ye has befallen my Master? For two days both he and his horse, together with the target, lance and armor, have been missing. Woe is me! I am certain those horrid books of Knighthood have turned his brain, for I have often heard him say that he would become a Knight Errant and go and seek adventures throughout the world."

And Don Quixote's Niece, who was there also, said to Master Nicholas, the Barber: "And indeed I have known my dear Uncle continue reading these unhappy books of 'disadventures' two days and two nights together. At the end of which, throwing down the book, he would lay hand on his sword and would fall a-slashing of the walls. And when he was wearied he would say that he had slain four Giants as great as four towers. And I take great blame to myself that I did not tell you all this before, that you might have burned those wretched books which have caused all the mischief."

"So I say, too," said the Curate; "and tomorrow they shall feed the flames, so that they may do no further harm."

By this time the laborer and Don Quixote had come to the house, and all the household, hearing them arrive, ran to embrace him. And Don Quixote—who had not yet dismounted from the ass, for he was not able—said: "Stand still and touch me not, for I return very sore wounded and hurt through the fault of my steed. Carry me to bed, and summon, if it be possible, the wise Urganda, that she may examine and cure my wounds."

"Come, my dear Master," said his Housekeeper, "and welcome, for, without sending for that Urganda, we shall know how to cure thee well enough. Accursed, say I once again, and a hundred times accursed, may those books of Knighthood be which have brought you to such a pass."

With that they bore him up to his bed, and, searching for his wounds, could not find any. Then he said he was all one bruise, through having a grievous fall with his horse Rozinante, in a fight with ten Giants, the most enormous and the boldest that could be found on earth.

"So ho!" said the Curate, "there are Giants about, are there? By mine honesty, I will burn them all before tomorrow night."

The next day, while the Knight was asleep, the Curate asked the Niece for the keys of the library, which she gave him with a very good will. Then they all went in, the Housekeeper with them, and found more than a hundred very large volumes well bound, besides other smaller ones. The Curate asked the Barber to hand him down the books from their shelves one by one, that he might see whether any deserved to escape the fire.

"No, no!" cried the Niece. "You ought not to pardon any of them, seeing they have all been offenders. Better fling them all out of the window into the yard and make a heap of them, and then make a bonfire of them where the smoke will offend nobody."

With that the Housekeeper caught hold of some of the largest and flung them out of the window. But the Curate took down several from the shelves and began to examine them carefully, whilst the women cried out for their destruction.

Whilst they were thus busied, Don Quixote began to cry aloud, saying: "This way, this way, valorous Knights! Show the force of your valiant arms lest we lose the tournament."

Called away by this noise and clamor, they left the books and ran to Don Quixote, who had risen from his bed and was repeating his outcries and ravings, cutting about with his sword all over the room with slashes and back strokes, as wide awake as if he had never been asleep. Wherefore, taking him up in their arms, they returned him by main force into his bed.

With some difficulty they persuaded him to rest where he was, and after he had eaten his breakfast he fell asleep once again.

That same night the Housekeeper set fire to and burned all the books in the yard, and some went to the flames that had no harm in

The housekeeper burned all the books in the yard.

them; and thus was fulfilled the old proverb, "The Saint sometimes pays for the Sinner."

Now one of the remedies which the Curate and the Barber suggested for their friend's malady was to wall up and close his library, so that when he rose he should not find the books, and they might tell him the Enchanters had carried them off, room and all.

This was done, and when two days afterwards Don Quixote rose from his bed, the first thing he did was to go and visit his books. Not finding the library where he had left it, he went from one corner of the house to the other, looking for it. Sometimes he came to the place where the door had been, and felt it with his hands, then would turn his eyes up and down, here and there, to seek it, without speaking a word.

But at last he asked the Housekeeper where his library was. She being well schooled what she should answer, replied: "What library? There is neither library nor books in this house now, for an Enchanter has carried them all away."

"Yes, dear Uncle," said his Niece, "while you were away, an Enchanter came upon a cloud, and, alighting from a serpent on which he was riding, entered the library, and what he did therein I know not. But within a while after, he fled out at the roof of the house, and left all the place full of smoke, and when we went to see what he had done we found neither room nor books."

"This must be the work of the learned Enchanter Freston," replied Don Quixote seriously; "a great enemy of mine who has a grudge against me, for he knows through his arts and his learning that I am in course of time to fight and vanquish in single combat a Knight whom he favors. But I tell him it is useless to oppose what is decreed."

"Who doubts that, dear Uncle?" said his Niece. "But why mix yourself up in these quarrels? Better stay at home peacefully, for remember the proverb says, 'Many who go for wool come back shorn.'"

"O Niece of mine," said Don Quixote, "how little dost thou understand the matter! Before I am shorn I will pluck the beards of all who think to touch but a hair of me."

To these words the women made no reply because they saw his anger increase.

For fifteen days after this he remained quietly at home, without showing any signs of repeating his follies, and during this time he had many arguments with his friends the Curate and the Barber about his favorite Knights Errant. At the same time he was persuading a certain laborer, his neighbor, an honest man, but one of very shallow wit, to go away with him and serve him as Squire. In the end he gave him so many fair words and promises that the poor fellow determined to go with him. Don Quixote, among other things, told him that he ought to be very pleased to depart with him, for at some time or other an adventure might befall which should in the twinkling of an eye win him an Island and leave him Governor thereof. On the faith of these and other like promises, Sancho Panza (for so he was called) forsook his wife and children and took service as Squire to his neighbor.

Don Quixote then set about to provide himself with money. This he did by selling one thing, pawning another, and making bad bargains all round. At last he got a pretty sum, and having patched up his broken helmet as best he could, he told Sancho Panza the day and hour on which he meant to start. He also charged him to provide himself with a wallet, which Sancho promised to do, and said that he also meant to take a very good Ass named Dapple along which he had of his own, because he was not used to travel afoot.

In the matter of the Ass, Don Quixote hesitated a little, calling to mind whether ever he had read that any Knight Errant was ever attended by a Squire mounted on ass-back, but no such case occurred to his memory. Nevertheless, he decided that the Ass should be taken, with the intention of providing his Squire with a more dignified mount, when he had a chance, by unhorsing the first discourteous Knight he met with.

All this being arranged, Sancho Panza, without bidding his wife and children farewell, and Don Quixote, without saying good-bye to his Housekeeper and Niece, sallied forth from the village one night, unknown to any person living. They traveled so far that night that at daybreak they were safe against discovery, even if they were pursued. And Sancho Panza rode along on his beast like a patriarch with his wallet and bottle, full of a huge desire to see himself Governor of the Island which his Master had promised him.

VI

THE ADVENTURE OF THE WINDMILLS

Whilst they were journeying along, Sancho Panza said to his Master: "I pray you have good care, Sir Knight, that you forget not that government of the Island which you have promised me, for I shall be able to govern it be it never so great."

And Don Quixote replied: "Thou must understand, friend Sancho, that it was a custom very much used by ancient Knights Errant, to make their Squires Governors of the Islands and Kingdoms they conquered, and I am resolved that so good a custom shall be kept up by me. And if thou livest and I live, it may well be that I might conquer a Kingdom in six days, and crown thee King of it."

"By the same token," said Sancho Panza, "if I were a King, then should Joan my wife become a Queen and my children Princes?"

"Who doubts of that?" said Don Quixote.

"That do I," replied Sancho Panza, "for I am fully persuaded that, though it rained Kingdoms down upon the earth, none of them would sit well on my wife Joan. She is not worth a farthing for a Queen. She might scrape through as a Countess, but I have my doubts of that."

As they were talking, they caught sight of some thirty or forty windmills on a plain. As soon as Don Quixote saw them he said to his Squire. "Fortune is guiding our affairs better than we could desire. For behold, friend Sancho, how there appear thirty or forty monstrous Giants with whom I mean to do battle, and take all their lives. With their spoils we will begin to be rich, for this is fair war, and it is doing great service to clear away these evil fellows from off the face of the earth."

"What Giants?" said Sancho amazed.

"Those thou seest there," replied his Master, "with the long arms."

"Take care, Sir," cried Sancho, "for those we see yonder are not Giants but windmills, and those things which seem to be arms are their sails, which being whirled round by the wind make the mill go."

"It is clear," answered Don Quixote, "that thou are not yet experienced in the matter of adventures. They are Giants, and if thou art afraid, get thee away home, whilst I enter into cruel and unequal battle with them."

So saying, he clapped his spurs to Rozinante, without heeding the cries by which Sancho Panza warned him that he was going to encounter not Giants but windmills. For he would neither listen to Sancho's outcries, nor mark what he said, but shouted to the windmills in a loud voice: "Fly not, cowards and vile creatures, for it is only one Knight that assaults you!"

A slight breeze having sprung up at this moment, the great sail-arms began to move, on seeing which Don Quixote shouted out again: "Although you should wield more arms than had the Giant Briareus, I shall make you pay for your insolence!"

Saying this, and commending himself most devoutly to his Lady Dulcinea, whom he desired to aid him in this peril, covering himself with his buckler, and setting his lance in rest, he charged at Rozinante's best gallop, and attacked the first mill before him. Thrusting his lance through the sail, the wind turned it with such violence that it broke his weapon into shivers, carrying him and his horse after it, and having whirled them round, finally tumbled the Knight a good way off, and rolled him over the plain sorely damaged.

Sancho Panza hastened to help him as fast as his Ass could go, and when he came up he found the Knight unable to stir, such a shock had Rozinante given him in the fall.

"Bless me," said Sancho, "did I not tell you that you should look well what you did, for they were none other than windmills, nor could any think otherwise unless he had windmills in his brains?"

"Peace, friend Sancho," said Don Quixote, "for the things of war are constantly changing, and I think this must be the work of the same sage Freston who robbed me of my library and books, and he hath changed these Giants into windmills to take from me the glory of the victory. But in the end his evil arts shall avail but little against the goodness of my sword."

"May it prove so," said Sancho, as he helped his Master to rise and remount Rozinante, who, poor steed, was himself much bruised.

The next day they journeyed along toward the Pass of Lapice, a romantic spot, at which they arrived about three in the afternoon.

"Here," said Don Quixote to his Squire, "we may hope to dip our hands up to the elbows in what are called adventures. But take note of this, that although thou seest me in the greatest dangers of the world, thou are not to set hand to thy sword in my defense, unless those who assault me be base or vulgar people. If they be Knights thou mayest not help me."

"I do assure you, Sir," said Sancho, "that herein you shall be most punctually obeyed, because I am by nature a quiet and peaceful man, and have a strong dislike to thrusting myself into quarrels."

Whilst they spoke thus, two Friars of the order of St. Benedict,

The wind turned it with such violence that it broke his weapon
into shivers, carrying him and his horse after it.

369

mounted on large mules—big enough to be dromedaries—appeared coming along the road. They wore traveling masks to keep the dust out of their eyes and carried large sun umbrellas. After them came a coach with four or five a-horseback traveling with it, and two lackeys ran hard by it. In the coach was a Biscayan Lady who was going to Seville. The Friars were not of her company, though all were going the same way.

Scarcely had Don Quixote espied them than he explained to his Squire: "Either I much mistake, or this should be the most famous adventure that hath ever been seen; for those dark forms that loom yonder are doubtless Enchanters who are carrying off in that coach some Princess they have stolen. Therefore I must with all my power undo this wrong."

"This will be worse than the adventure of the windmills," said Sancho. "Do you not see that they are Benedictine Friars, and the coach will belong to some people traveling?"

"I have told thee already, Sancho," answered Don Quixote, "that thou art very ignorant in the matter of adventures. What I say is true, as thou shalt see."

So saying he spurred on his horse, and posted himself in the middle of the road along which the Friars were coming, and when they were near enough to hear him he exclaimed in a loud voice: "Monstrous and horrible crew! Surrender this instant those exalted Princesses, whom you are carrying away in that coach, or prepare to receive instant death as a just punishment of your wicked deeds."

The Friars drew rein, and stood amazed at the figure and words of Don Quixote, to whom they replied: "Sir Knight, we are neither monstrous nor wicked, but two religious men, Benedictines, traveling about our business, and we know nothing about this coach or about any Princesses."

"No soft words for me," cried Don Quixote, "for I know you well, treacherous knaves."

And without waiting for their reply he set spurs to Rozinante; and laying his lance on his thigh, charged at the first Friar with such fury and rage, that if he had not leaped from his mule he would have been slain, or at least badly wounded.

The second Friar, seeing the way his companion was treated, made no words but fled across country swifter than the wind itself.

Sancho Panza, on seeing the Friar overthrown, dismounted very speedily off his Ass and ran over to him, and would have stripped him of his clothes. But two of the Friars' servants came up and asked him why he was thus despoiling their master. Sancho replied that it was his due by the law of arms, as lawful spoils gained in the battle by his Lord and Master, Don Quixote.

The lackeys, who knew nothing of battles or spoils, seeing that Don Quixote was now out of the way, speaking with those that were in the coach, set both at once upon Sancho and threw him down, plucked every hair out of his beard and kicked and mauled him without mercy, leaving him at last stretched on the ground senseless.

As for the Friar, he mounted again, trembling and terror-stricken, all the color having fled from his face, and spurring his mule, he joined his companion, who was waiting for him hard by.

While this was happening, Don Quixote was talking to the Lady in the coach, to whom he said: "Dear Lady, you may now dispose of yourself as you best please. For the pride of your robbers is laid in the dust by this my invincible arm. And that you may not pine to learn the name of your deliverer, know that I am called Don Quixote of the Mancha, Knight Errant, adventurer, and captive of the peerless and beauteous Lady Dulcinea of Toboso. And in reward of the benefits you have received at my hands, I demand nothing else but that you return to Toboso, there to present yourself in my name before my Lady, and tell her what I have done to obtain your liberty."

All this was listened to by a Biscayan Squire who accompanied the coach. He, hearing that the coach was not to pass on but was to return to Toboso, went up to Don Quixote, and, laying hold of his lance, said to him: "Get away with thee, Sir Knight, for if thou leave not the coach I will kill thee as sure as I am a Biscayan."

"If," replied Don Quixote haughtily, "thou wert a gentleman, as thou art not, I would ere this have punished thy folly and insolence, caitiff creature."

"I no gentleman?" cried the enraged Biscayan. "Throw down thy lance and draw thy sword, and thou shalt soon see that thou liest."

"That shall be seen presently," replied Don Quixote; and, flinging his lance to the ground, he drew his sword, grasped his buckler tight, and rushed at the Biscayan.

The Biscayan, seeing him come on in this manner, had nothing else to do but to draw his sword. Luckily for him he was near the coach, when he snatched a cushion to serve him as a shield, and then they fell on each other as if they had been mortal enemies.

Those that were present tried to stop them, but the Biscayan shouted out that if he were hindered from ending the battle he would put his Lady and all who touched him to the sword.

The Lady, amazed and terrified, made the coachman draw aside a little, and sat watching the deadly combat from afar.

The Biscayan, to begin with, dealt Don Quixote a mighty blow over the target, which, if it had not been for his armor, would have cleft him to the waist. Don Quixote, feeling the weight of this tremendous blow which had destroyed his visor and carried away part of his ear, cried out aloud: "O Dulcinea, Lady of my soul, flower of all beauty, help thy Knight, who finds himself in this great danger!" To say this, to raise his sword, to cover himself with his buckler, and to rush upon the Biscayan was the work of a moment. With his head full of rage he now raised himself in his stirrups, and, gripping his sword more firmly in his two hands, struck at the Biscayan with such violence that he caught him a terrible blow on the cushion, knocking this shield against his head with tremendous violence. It was as though

He drew his sword, grasped his buckler tight, and
rushed at the Biscayan.

a mountain had fallen on the Biscayan and crushed him, and the blood spouted from his nose and mouth and ears. He would have fallen straightway from his mule if he had not clasped her round the neck; but he lost his stirrups, then let go his arms, and the mule, frightened at the blow, began to gallop across the fields, so that after two or three plunges it threw him to the ground.

Don Quixote leaped off his horse, ran towards him, and setting the point of his sword between his eyes, bade him yield, or he would cut off his head.

The Lady of the coach now came forward in great grief and begged the favor of her Squire's life.

Don Quixote replied with great stateliness: "Truly, fair Lady, I will grant thy request, but it must be on one condition, that this Squire shall go to Toboso and present himself in my name to the peerless Lady Dulcinea, that she may deal with him as she thinks well."

The Lady, who was in great distress, without considering what Don Quixote required, or asking who Dulcinea might be, promised that he should certainly perform this command.

"Then," said Don Quixote, "on the faith of that pledge I will do him no more harm."

Seeing the contest was now over, and his Master about to remount Rozinante, Sancho ran to hold his stirrups, and before he mounted, taking him by his hand, he kissed it and said: "I desire that it will please you, good my Lord Don Quixote, to bestow on me the government of that Island which in this terrible battle you have won."

To which Don Quixote replied: "Brother Sancho, these are not the adventures of Islands, but of crossroads, wherein nothing is gained but a broken pate or the loss of an ear. Have patience awhile, for the adventures will come whereby I can make thee not only a Governor, but something higher."

Sancho thanked him heartily, and kissed his hand again and the hem of his mailed shirt. Then he helped him to get on Rozinante, and leaped upon his ass to follow him.

And Don Quixote, without another word to the people of the coach, rode away at a swift pace and turned into a wood that was hard by, leaving Sancho to follow him as fast as his beast could trot.

RIP VAN WINKLE

By *WASHINGTON IRVING*

Illustrations by VICTOR PERARD

WHOEVER has made a voyage up the Hudson must remember the Catskill mountains. They are a dismembered branch of the great Appalachian family, and are seen away to the west of the river, swelling up to a noble height, and lording it over the surrounding country. Every change of season, every change of weather, indeed, every hour of the day, produces some change in the magical hues and shapes of these mountains, and they are regarded by all the good wives, far and near, as perfect barometers. When the weather is fair and settled, they are clothed in blue and purple, and print their bold outlines on the clear evening sky; but, sometimes, when the rest of the landscape is cloudless, they will gather a hood of gray vapors about their summits, which, in the last rays of the setting sun, will glow and light up like a crown of glory.

At the foot of these fairy mountains, the voyager may have descried the light smoke curling up from a village, whose shingle-roofs gleam among the trees, just where the blue tints of the upland melt away into the fresh green of the nearer landscape. It is a little village of great antiquity, having been founded by some of the Dutch colonists, in the early times of the province, just about the beginning of the government of the good Peter Stuyvesant (may he rest in peace!), and there were some of the houses of the original settlers standing within a few years, built of small yellow bricks brought from Holland, having latticed windows and gable fronts, surmounted with weather-cocks.

In that same village, and in one of these very houses (which, to tell the precise truth, was sadly time-worn and weather-beaten), there lived many years since, while the country was yet a province of Great Britain, a simple good-natured fellow of the name of Rip Van Winkle. He was a descendant of the Van Winkles who figured so gallantly in the chivalrous days of Peter Stuyvesant, and accompanied him to the siege of Fort Christina. He inherited, however, but little of the martial character of his ancestors. I have observed that he was a simple, good-natured man; he was, moreover, a kind neighbor, and an obedient, hen-pecked husband. Indeed, to the latter circumstance might be owing that meekness of spirit which gained him such universal popularity; for those men are most apt to be obsequious and conciliating abroad, who are under the discipline of shrews at home. Their tempers, doubtless, are rendered pliant and malleable in the fiery furnace of domestic tribulation; and a curtain lecture is worth all the sermons in the world for teaching the virtues of patience and long-suffering. A termagant wife may, therefore, in some respects, be considered a tolerable blessing; and if so, Rip Van Winkle was thrice blessed.

Certain it is, that he was a great favorite among all the good wives of the village, who, as usual, with the amiable sex, took his part in all family squabbles; and never failed, whenever they talked those matters over in their evening gossipings, to lay all the blame on Dame Van Winkle. The children of the village, too, would shout with joy whenever he approached. He assisted at their sports, made their playthings, taught them to fly kites and shoot marbles, and told them long stories of ghosts, witches, and Indians. Whenever he went dodging about the village, he was surrounded by a troop of them, hanging on his skirts, clambering on his back, and playing a thousand tricks on him with impunity; and not a dog would bark at him throughout the neighborhood.

The great error in Rip's composition was an insuperable aversion to all kinds of profitable labor. It could not be from want of assiduity or perseverance; for he would sit on a wet rock, with a rod as long and heavy as a Tartar's lance, and fish all day without a murmur, even though he should not be encouraged by a single nibble. He would carry a fowling-piece on his shoulder for hours together, trudging through woods and swamps, and up hill and down dale, to shoot a few squirrels or wild pigeons. He would never refuse to assist a neighbor even in the roughest toil, and was a foremost man at all country frolics for husking Indian corn, or building stone fences; the women of the village, too, used to employ him to run their errands, and to do such little odd jobs as their less obliging husbands would not do for them. In a word Rip was ready to attend to anybody's business but his own; but as to doing family duty, and keeping his farm in order, he found it impossible.

In fact, he declared it was of no use to work on his farm; it was the most pestilent little piece of ground in the whole country; everything about it went wrong, and would go wrong, in spite of him. His fences were continually falling to pieces; his cow would either go astray, or get among the cabbages; weeds were sure to grow quicker in his fields than anywhere else; the rain always made a point of setting in just as he had some outdoor work to do; so that though his patrimonial estate had dwindled away under his management, acre by acre, until there was little more left than a mere patch of Indian corn and potatoes, yet it was the worst conditioned farm in the neighborhood.

His children, too, were as ragged and wild as if they belonged to nobody. His son Rip, an urchin begotten in his own likeness, promised to inherit the habits, with the old clothes of his father. He was generally seen trooping like a colt at his mother's heels, equipped in a pair of his father's cast-off galligaskins, which he had much ado to hold up with one hand, as a fine lady does her train in bad weather.

Rip Van Winkle, however, was one of those happy mortals, of foolish, well-oiled dispositions, who take the world easy, eat white bread or brown, whichever can be got with least thought or trouble, and would rather starve on a penny than work for a pound. If left to himself, he would have whistled life away in perfect contentment; but his wife kept continually dinning in his ears about his idleness, his carelessness, and the ruin he was bringing on his family. Morning, noon, and night, her tongue was incessantly going, and everything he said or did was sure to produce a torrent of household eloquence. Rip had but one way of replying to all lectures of the kind, and that, by frequent use, had grown into a habit. He shrugged his shoulders, shook his head, cast up his eyes, but said nothing. This, however, always provoked a fresh volley from his wife; so that he

From even this stronghold the unlucky Rip was
routed by his termagant wife.

was fain to draw off his forces, and take to the outside of the house—
the only side which, in truth, belongs to a hen-pecked husband.

Rip's sole domestic adherent was his dog Wolf, who was as much
hen-pecked as his master; for Dame Van Winkle regarded them as
companions in idleness, and even looked upon Wolf with an evil
eye, as the cause of his master's going so often astray. True it is, in
all points of spirit befitting an honorable dog, he was as courageous
an animal as ever scoured the woods—but what courage can with-
stand the ever-during and all-besetting terrors of a woman's tongue?
The moment Wolf entered the house his crest fell, his tail drooped
to the ground, or curled between his legs, he sneaked about with a
gallows air, casting many a sidelong glance at Dame Van Winkle,
and at the least flourish of a broomstick or ladle, he would fly to the
door with yelping precipitation.

Times grew worse and worse with Rip Van Winkle as years of

matrimony rolled on; a tart temper never mellows with age, and a sharp tongue is the only edged tool that grows keener with constant use. For a long while he used to console himself, when driven from home, by frequenting a kind of perpetual club of the sages, philosophers, and other idle personages of the village, which held its sessions on a bench before a small inn, designated by a rubicund portrait of his Majesty George the Third. Here they used to sit in the shade through a long lazy summer's day, talking listlessly over village gossip, or telling endless sleepy stories about nothing. But it would have been worth any statesman's money to have heard the profound discussions that sometimes took place, when by chance an old newspaper fell into their hands from some passing traveler. How solemnly they would listen to the contents, as drawled out by Derrick Van Bummel, the schoolmaster, a dapper, learned little man, who was not to be daunted by the most gigantic word in the dictionary; and how sagely they would deliberate upon the public events some months after they had taken place.

The opinions of this junto were completely controlled by Nicholas Vedder, a patriarch of the village, and landlord of the inn, at the door of which he took his seat from morning till night, just moving sufficiently to avoid the sun and keep in the shade of a large tree; so that the neighbors could tell the hour by his movements as accurately as by a sun-dial. It is true he was rarely heard to speak, but smoked his pipe incessantly. His adherents, however (for every great man has his adherents), perfectly understood him, and knew how to gather his opinions. When anything that was read or related displeased him, he was observed to smoke his pipe vehemently, and to send forth short, frequent and angry puffs; but when pleased, he would inhale the smoke slowly and tranquilly, and emit it in light and placid clouds; and sometimes, taking the pipe from his mouth, and letting the fragrant vapor curl about his nose, would gravely nod his head in token of perfect approbation.

From even this stronghold the unlucky Rip was at length routed by his termagant wife, who would suddenly break in upon the tranquillity of the assemblage and call the members all to naught; nor was that august personage, Nicholas Vedder himself, sacred from the daring tongue of this terrible virago, who charged him outright with encouraging her husband in habits of idleness.

Poor Rip was at last reduced almost to despair; and his only alternative, to escape from the labor of the farm and clamor of his wife, was to take gun in hand and stroll away into the woods. Here he would sometimes seat himself at the foot of a tree, and share the contents of his wallet with Wolf, with whom he sympathized as a fellow-sufferer in persecution. "Poor Wolf," he would say, "thy mistress leads thee a dog's life of it; but never mind, my lad, whilst I live thou shalt never want a friend to stand by thee!" Wolf would wag his tail, look wistfully in his master's face, and if dogs can feel pity I verily believe he reciprocated the sentiment with all his heart.

In a long ramble of the kind on a fine autumnal day, Rip had unconsciously scrambled to one of the highest parts of the Catskill mountains. He was after his favorite sport of squirrel shooting, and the still solitudes had echoed and re-echoed with the reports of his gun. Panting and fatigued he threw himself, late in the afternoon, on a green knoll, covered with mountain herbage, that crowned the brow of a precipice. From an opening between the trees he could overlook all the lower country for many a mile of rich woodland. He saw at a distance the lordly Hudson, far, far below him, moving on its silent but majestic course, with the reflection of a purple cloud, or the sail of a lagging bark, here and there sleeping on its glassy bosom, and at last losing itself in the blue highlands.

On the other side he looked down into a deep mountain glen, wild, lonely, and shagged, the bottom filled with fragments from the impending cliffs, and scarcely lighted by the reflected rays of the setting sun. For some time Rip lay musing on this scene; evening was gradually advancing; the mountains began to throw their long blue shadows over the valleys; he saw that it would be dark long before he could reach the village, and he heaved a heavy sigh when he thought of encountering the terrors of Dame Van Winkle.

As he was about to descend, he heard a voice from a distance, hallooing, "Rip Van Winkle! Rip Van Winkle!" He looked round, but could see nothing but a crow winging its solitary flight across the mountain. He thought his fancy must have deceived him, and turned again to descend, when he heard the same cry ring through the still evening air: "Rip Van Winkle! Rip Van Winkle!"—at the same time Wolf bristled up his back, and giving a low growl, skulked to his master's side, looking fearfully down into the glen. Rip now felt a vague apprehension stealing over him; he looked anxiously in the same direction, and perceived a strange figure slowly toiling up the rocks, and bending under the weight of something he carried on his back. He was surprised to see any human being in this lonely and unfrequented place, but supposing it to be some one of the neighborhood in need of his assistance, he hastened down to yield it.

On nearer approach he was still more surprised at the singularity of the stranger's appearance. He was a short, square-built old fellow, with thick bushy hair, and a grizzled beard. His dress was of the antique Dutch fashion—a cloth jerkin strapped round the waist— several pair of breeches, the outer one of ample volume, decorated with rows of buttons down the sides, and bunches at the knees. He bore on his shoulder a stout keg, that seemed full of liquor, and made signs for Rip to approach and assist him with the load. Though

A company of odd-looking personages were playing at ninepins.

383

rather shy and distrustful of this new acquaintance, Rip complied with his usual alacrity; and mutually relieving one another, they clambered up a narrow gully, apparently the dry bed of a mountain torrent. As they ascended, Rip every now and then heard long rolling peals, like distant thunder, that seemed to issue out of a deep ravine, or rather cleft, between lofty rocks, toward which their rugged path conducted. He paused for an instant, but supposing it to be the muttering of one of those transient thunder-showers which often take place in mountain heights, he proceeded. Passing through the ravine, they came to a hollow, like a small amphitheater, surrounded by perpendicular precipices, over the brinks of which impending trees shot their branches, so that you only caught glimpses of the azure sky and the bright evening cloud. During the whole time Rip and his companion had labored on in silence; for though the former marveled greatly what could be the object of carrying a keg of liquor up this wild mountain, yet there was something strange and incomprehensible about the unknown, that inspired awe and checked familiarity.

On entering the amphitheater, new objects of wonder presented themselves. On a level spot in the center was a company of odd-looking personages playing at ninepins. They were dressed in a quaint outlandish fashion; some wore short doublets, others jerkins, with long knives in their belts, and most of them had enormous breeches, of similar style with that of the guide's. Their visages, too, were peculiar: one had a large beard, broad face, and small piggish eyes; the face of another seemed to consist entirely of nose, and was surmounted by a white sugar-loaf hat set off with a little red cock's tail. They all had beards, of various shapes and colors. There was one who seemed to be the commander. He was a stout old gentleman, with a weather-beaten countenance; he wore a laced doublet, broad belt and hanger, high-crowned hat and feather, red stockings, and high-heeled shoes, with roses in them. The whole group reminded Rip of the figures in an old Flemish painting, in the parlor of Dominie Van Shaick, the village parson, and which had been brought over from Holland at the time of the settlement.

What seemed particularly odd to Rip was, that though these folks were evidently amusing themselves, yet they maintained the gravest faces, the most mysterious silence, and were, withal, the most melancholy party of pleasure he had ever witnessed. Nothing interrupted the stillness of the scene but the noise of the balls, which, whenever they were rolled, echoed along the mountains like rumbling peals of thunder.

As Rip and his companion approached them, they suddenly desisted from their play, and stared at him with such fixed statue-like gaze, and such strange, uncouth, lack-luster countenances, that his heart turned within him, and his knees smote together. His companion now emptied the contents of the keg into large flagons, and made signs to him to wait upon the company. He obeyed with fear and trembling; they quaffed the liquor in profound silence, and then returned to their game.

By degrees Rip's awe and apprehension subsided. He even ventured, when no eye was fixed upon him, to taste the beverage, which he found had much of the flavor of excellent Hollands. He was naturally a thirsty soul, and was soon tempted to repeat the draught. One taste provoked another; and he reiterated his visits to the flagon so often that at length his senses were overpowered, his eyes swam in his head, his head gradually declined, and he fell into a deep sleep.

On waking, he found himself on the green knoll whence he had first seen the old man of the glen. He rubbed his eyes—it was a bright sunny morning. The birds were hopping and twittering among the bushes, and the eagle was wheeling aloft, and breasting the pure mountain breeze. "Surely," thought Rip, "I have not slept here all night." He recalled the occurrences before he fell asleep. The strange man with a keg of liquor—the mountain ravine—the wild retreat among the rocks—the woe-begone party at ninepins—the flagon— "Oh! that flagon! that wicked flagon!" thought Rip—"what excuse shall I make to Dame Van Winkle!"

He looked round for his gun, but in place of the clean well-oiled fowling-piece, he found an old firelock lying by him, the barrel incrusted with rust, the lock falling off, and the stock worm-eaten. He now suspected that the grave roisters of the mountain had put a trick upon him, and, having dosed him with liquor, had robbed him of his gun. Wolf, too, had disappeared, but he might have strayed away after a squirrel or partridge. He whistled after him and shouted his name, but all in vain; the echoes repeated his whistle and shout, but no dog was to be seen.

He determined to revisit the scene of the last evening's gambol, and if he met with any of the party, to demand his dog and gun. As he rose to walk, he found himself stiff in the joints, and wanting in his usual activity. "These mountain beds do not agree with me," thought Rip, "and if this frolic should lay me up with a fit of rheumatism, I shall have a blessed time with Dame Van Winkle." With some difficulty he got down into the glen; he found the gully up which he and his companion had ascended the preceding evening; but to his astonishment a mountain stream was now foaming down it, leaping from rock to rock, and filling the glen with babbling murmurs. He, however, made shift to scramble up its sides, working his toilsome way through thickets of birch, sassafras, and witch-hazel, and sometimes tripped up or entangled by the wild grapevines that

On waking, he found himself on the green knoll.

twisted their coils or tendrils from tree to tree, and spread a kind of network in his path.

At length he reached to where the ravine had opened through the cliffs to the amphitheater; but no traces of such opening remained. The rocks presented a high impenetrable wall, over which the torrent came tumbling in a sheet of feathery foam, and fell into a broad deep basin, black from the shadows of the surrounding forest. Here, then, poor Rip was brought to a stand. He again called and whistled after his dog; he was only answered by the cawing of a flock of idle crows, sporting high in air about a dry tree that overhung a sunny precipice; and who, secure in their elevation, seemed to look down and scoff at the poor man's perplexities. What was to be done? The morning was passing away, and Rip felt famished for want of his breakfast. He grieved to give up his dog and gun; he dreaded to meet his wife; but it would not do to starve among the mountains. He shook his head, shouldered the rusty firelock, and, with a heart full of trouble and anxiety, turned his steps homeward.

As he approached the village he met a number of people, but none whom he knew, which somewhat surprised him, for he had thought himself acquainted with every one in the country round. Their dress, too, was of a different fashion from that to which he was accustomed. They all stared at him with equal marks of surprise, and whenever they cast their eyes upon him, invariably stroked their chins. The constant recurrence of this gesture induced Rip, involuntarily, to do the same, when, to his astonishment, he found his beard had grown a foot long!

He had now entered the skirts of the village. A troop of strange children ran at his heels, hooting after him, and pointing at his gray beard. The dogs, too, not one of which he recognized for an old acquaintance, barked at him as he passed. The very village was altered; it was larger and more populous. There were rows of houses which he had never seen before, and those which had been his familiar haunts had disappeared. Strange names were over the doors—strange faces at the windows—everything was strange. His mind now misgave him; he began to doubt whether both he and the world around him were not bewitched. Surely this was his native village, which he had left but the day before. There stood the Catskill mountains—there ran the silver Hudson at a distance—there was every hill and dale precisely as it had always been. Rip was sorely perplexed—"That flagon last night," thought he, "has addled my poor head sadly!"

It was with some difficulty that he found the way to his own house, which he approached with silent awe, expecting every moment to hear the shrill voice of Dame Van Winkle. He found the house gone to decay—the roof fallen in, the windows shattered, and the doors off the hinges. A half-starved dog that looked like Wolf was skulking about it. Rip called him by name, but the cur snarled, showed his teeth, and passed on. This was an unkind cut indeed—"My very dog," sighed poor Rip, "has forgotten me!"

He entered the house, which, to tell the truth, Dame Van Winkle had always kept in neat order. It was empty, forlorn, and apparently abandoned. This desolateness overcame all his connubial fears—he called loudly for his wife and children—the lonely chambers rang for a moment with his voice, and then all again was silence.

He now hurried forth, and hastened to his old resort, the village inn—but it too was gone. A large, rickety, wooden building stood in its place, with great gaping windows, some of them broken and mended with old hats and petticoats, and over the door was painted, "The Union Hotel, by Jonathan Doolittle." Instead of the great tree that used to shelter the quiet little Dutch inn of yore, here now was reared a tall naked pole, with something on the top that looked like a red nightcap, and from it was fluttering a flag, on which was a singular assemblage of stars and stripes—all this was strange and incomprehensible. He recognized on the sign, however, the ruby face of King George, under which he had smoked so many a peaceful pipe; but even this was singularly metamorphosed. The red coat was changed for one of blue and buff, a sword was held in the hand instead of a scepter, the head was decorated with a cocked hat, and underneath was painted in large characters, GENERAL WASHINGTON.

There was, as usual, a crowd of folk about the door, but none that Rip recollected. The very character of the people seemed changed. There was a busy, bustling, disputatious tone about it, instead of the accustomed phlegm and drowsy tranquillity. He looked in vain for the sage Nicholas Vedder, with his broad face, double chin, and fair long pipe, uttering clouds of tobacco-smoke instead of idle speeches; or Van Bummel, the schoolmaster, doling forth the contents of an ancient newspaper. In place of these, a lean, bilious-looking fellow, with his pockets full of handbills, was haranguing vehemently about rights of citizens—elections—members of Congress—liberty—Bunker's Hill—heroes of seventy-six—and other words, which were a perfect Babylonish jargon to the bewildered Van Winkle.

The appearance of Rip, with his long, grizzled beard, his rusty fowling-piece, his uncouth dress, and an army of women and children at his heels, soon attracted the attention of the tavern politicians. They crowded round him, eyeing him from head to foot with great curiosity. The orator bustled up to him, and drawing him partly aside, inquired "on which side he voted?" Rip stared in vacant stupidity. Another short but busy little fellow pulled him by the arm, and, rising on tiptoe, inquired in his ear, "whether he was Federal or Democrat?" Rip was equally at a loss to comprehend the question; when a knowing, self-important old gentleman, in a sharp cocked hat, made his way through the crowd, putting them to the right and left with his elbows as he passed, and planting himself before Van Winkle, with one arm akimbo, the other resting on his cane, his keen eyes and sharp hat penetrating, as it were, into his very soul, demanded in an austere tone, "what brought him to the election with a gun on his shoulder, and a mob at his heels, and whether he meant to breed a riot in the village?"—"Alas! gentlemen," cried Rip, somewhat dismayed, "I am a poor quiet man, a native of the place, and a loyal subject of the king, God bless him!"

Here a general shout burst from the bystanders: "A tory! a tory! a spy! a refugee! hustle him! away with him!" It was with great difficulty that the self-important man in the cocked hat restored order; and, having assumed a tenfold austerity of brow, demanded again of the unknown culprit, what he came there for, and whom he was seeking? The poor man humbly assured him that he meant no harm, but merely came there in search of some of his neighbors, who used to keep about the tavern.

"Well—who are they?—name them."

Rip bethought himself a moment, and inquired, "Where's Nicholas Vedder?"

There was a silence for a little while, when an old man replied in a thin piping voice, "Nicholas Vedder! why, he is dead and gone these eighteen years! There was a wooden tombstone in the churchyard that used to tell all about him, but that's rotten and gone, too."

"Where's Brom Dutcher?"

"Oh, he went off to the army in the beginning of the war; some say he was killed at the storming of Stony Point—others say he was drowned in a squall at the foot of Anthony's Nose. I don't know—he never came back again."

"Where's Van Bummel, the schoolmaster?"

"He went off to the wars, too, was a great militia general, and is now in Congress."

Rip's heart died away at hearing of these sad changes in his home and friends, and finding himself thus alone in the world. Every answer puzzled him, too, by treating of such enormous lapses of time, and of matters which he could not understand: war—congress—Stony Point—he had no courage to ask after any more friends, but cried out in despair, "Does nobody here know Rip Van Winkle?"

"Oh, Rip Van Winkle!" exclaimed two or three. "Oh, to be sure! that's Rip Van Winkle yonder, leaning against the tree."

Rip looked, and beheld a precise counterpart of himself, as he went up the mountain: apparently as lazy, and certainly as ragged. The poor fellow was now completely confounded. He doubted his own identity, and whether he was himself or another man. In the midst of his bewilderment, the man in the cocked hat demanded who he was, and what was his name?

"God knows," exclaimed he, at his wits' end; "I'm not myself—I'm somebody else—that's me yonder—no—that's somebody else got into my shoes—I was myself last night, but I fell asleep on the mountain, and they've changed my gun, and everything's changed, and I'm changed and I can't tell my name, or who I am!"

The bystanders began now to look at each other, nod, wink significantly, and tap their fingers against their foreheads. There was a whisper, also, about securing the gun, and keeping the old fellow from doing mischief, at the very suggestion of which the self-important man in the cocked hat retired with some precipitation. At this critical moment a fresh, comely woman pressed through the throng to get a peep at the gray-bearded man. She had a chubby child in her arms, which, frightened at his looks, began to cry. "Hush, Rip," cried she, "hush, you little fool; the old man won't hurt you." The name of the child, the air of the mother, the tone of her voice, all awakened a train of recollections in his mind. "What's your name, my good woman?" asked he.

"Judith Gardenier."

"And your father's name?"

"Ah, poor man, Rip Van Winkle was his name, but it's twenty years since he went away from home with his gun—and never has been heard of since—his dog came home without him; but whether he shot himself, or was carried away by the Indians, nobody can tell. I was then but a little girl."

Rip had but one question more to ask; but he put it with a faltering voice:

"Where's your mother?"

"Oh, she, too, had died but a short time since; she broke a blood-vessel in a fit of passion at a New England peddler."

There was a drop of comfort, at least, in this intelligence. The honest man could contain himself no longer. He caught his daughter and her child in his arms. "I am your father!" cried he—"Young Rip Van Winkle once—old Rip Van Winkle now!—Does nobody know poor Rip Van Winkle?"

All stood amazed, until an old woman, tottering out from among the crowd, put her hand to her brow, and peering under it in his face for a moment, exclaimed, "Sure enough; it is Rip Van Winkle—it is himself! Welcome home again, old neighbor—Why, where have you been these twenty long years?"

Rip's story was soon told, for the whole twenty years had been to him but as one night. The neighbors stared when they heard it; some were seen to wink at each other, and put their tongues in their cheeks; and the self-important man in the cocked hat, who, when the alarm was over, had returned to the field, screwed down the corners of his mouth, and shook his head—upon which there was a general shaking of the head throughout the assemblage.

It was determined, however, to take the opinion of old Peter Vanderdonk, who was seen slowly advancing up the road. He was a descendant of the historian of that name, who wrote one of the earliest accounts of the province. Peter was the most ancient inhabitant of the village, and well versed in all the wonderful events and traditions of the neighborhood. He recollected Rip at once and corroborated his story in the most satisfactory manner. He assured the company that it was a fact, handed down from his ancestor the historian, that the Catskill mountains had always been haunted by strange beings. That it was affirmed that the great Hendrick Hudson, the first discoverer of the river and country, kept a kind of vigil there every twenty years, with his crew of the *Half-Moon;* being permitted in this way to revisit the scenes of his enterprise, and keep a guardian eye upon the river, and the great city called by his name. That his father had once seen them in their old Dutch dresses playing at ninepins in a hollow of the mountain; and that he himself had heard, one summer afternoon, the sound of their balls like distant peals of thunder.

To make a long story short, the company broke up, and returned to the more important concerns of the election. Rip's daughter took him home to live with her; she had a snug, well-furnished house, and a stout cheery farmer for a husband, whom Rip recollected for one of the urchins that used to climb upon his back. As to Rip's son and heir, who was the ditto of himself, seen leaning against the tree, he was employed to work on the farm; but evinced an hereditary disposition to attend to anything else but his business.

Rip now resumed his old walks and habits; he soon found many of his former cronies, though all rather the worse for the wear and tear of time, and preferred making friends among the rising generation, with whom he soon grew into great favor.

Having nothing to do at home, and being arrived at that happy age when a man can be idle with impunity, he took his place once more on the bench at the inn door, and was reverenced as one of the patriarchs of the village, and a chronicle of the old times "before the war." It was some time before he could get into the regular track of gossip, or could be made to comprehend the strange events that had taken place during his torpor. How that there had been a revolutionary war—that the country had thrown off the yoke of old England—and that, instead of being a subject of his Majesty George the Third, he was now a free citizen of the United States. Rip, in fact, was no politician; the changes of states and empires made but little impression on him; but there was one species of despotism under which he had long groaned, and that was—petticoat government. Happily that was at an end; he had got his neck out of the yoke of matrimony, and could go in and out whenever he pleased, without dreading the tyranny of Dame Van Winkle. Whenever her name was mentioned, however, he shook his head, shrugged his shoulders, and cast up his eyes; which might pass either for an expression of resignation to his fate, or joy at his deliverance.

He used to tell his story to every stranger that arrived at Mr. Doolittle's hotel. He was observed, at first, to vary on some points every time he told it, which was, doubtless, owing to his having so recently awakened. It at last settled down precisely to the tale I have related, and not a man, woman or child in the neighborhood but knew it by heart. Some always pretended to doubt the reality of it, and insisted that Rip had been out of his head, and that this was one point on which he always remained flighty. The old Dutch inhabitants, however, almost universally gave it full credit. Even to this day they never hear a thunderstorm of a summer afternoon about the Catskill, but they say Hendrick Hudson and his crew are at their game of ninepins; and it is a common wish of all hen-pecked husbands in the neighborhood, when life hangs heavy on their hands, that they might have a quieting draught out of Rip Van Winkle's flagon.

A CHRISTMAS CAROL

By CHARLES DICKENS

Illustrations by JOHN LEECH
Decorations by WARREN CHAPPELL

STAVE ONE:

MARLEY'S GHOST

MARLEY was dead: to begin with. There is no doubt what-ever about that. The register of his burial was signed by the clergyman, the clerk, the undertaker, and the chief mourner. Scrooge signed it: and Scrooge's name was good upon 'Change, for anything he chose to put his hands to. Old Marley was as dead as a door-nail.

Mind! I don't mean to say that I know, of my own knowledge, what there is particularly dead about a door-nail. I might have been inclined, myself, to regard a coffin-nail as the deadest piece of iron-mongery in the trade. But the wisdom of our ancestors is in the simile; and my unhallowed hands shall not disturb it, or the Country's done for. You will therefore permit me to repeat, emphatically, that Marley was as dead as a door-nail.

Scrooge knew he was dead? Of course he did. How could it be otherwise? Scrooge and he were partners for I don't know how many

397

years. Scrooge was his sole executor, his sole administrator, his sole assign, his sole residuary legatee, his sole friend and sole mourner. And even Scrooge was not so dreadfully cut up by the sad event, but that he was an excellent man of business on the very day of the funeral, and solemnized it with an undoubted bargain.

The mention of Marley's funeral brings me back to the point I started from. There is no doubt that Mr. Marley was dead. This must be distinctly understood, or nothing wonderful can come of the story I am going to relate. If we were not perfectly convinced that Hamlet's Father died before the play began, there would be nothing more remarkable in his taking a stroll at night, in an easterly wind, upon his own ramparts, than there would be in any other middle-aged gentleman rashly turning out after dark in a breezy spot—say Saint Paul's Churchyard for instance—literally to astonish his son's weak mind.

Scrooge never painted out Old Marley's name. There it stood, years afterwards, above the warehouse door: Scrooge and Marley. The firm was known as Scrooge and Marley. Sometimes people new to the business called Scrooge Scrooge, and sometimes Marley, but he answered to both names: it was all the same to him.

Oh! But he was a tight-fisted hand at the grindstone, Scrooge! a squeezing, wrenching, grasping, scraping, clutching, covetous, old sinner. Hard and sharp as flint, from which no steel had ever struck out generous fire; secret, and self-contained, and solitary as an oyster. The cold within him froze his old features, nipped his pointed nose, shriveled his cheek, stiffened his gait; made his eyes red, his thin lips blue; and spoke out shrewdly in his grating voice. A frosty rime was on his head, and on his eyebrows, and his wiry chin. He carried his own low temperature always about with him; he iced his office in the dog-days; and didn't thaw it one degree at Christmas.

External heat and cold had little influence on Scrooge. No warmth could warm, nor wintry weather chill him. No wind that blew was bitterer than he, no falling snow was more intent upon its purpose, no pelting rain less open to entreaty. Foul weather didn't know where to have him. The heaviest rain, and snow, and hail, and sleet, could boast of the advantage over him in only one respect. They often "came down" handsomely, and Scrooge never did.

Nobody ever stopped him in the street to say, with gladsome looks, "My dear Scrooge, how are you? When will you come to see me?" No beggar implored him to bestow a trifle, no children asked him what it was o'clock, no man or woman ever once in all his life inquired the way to such and such a place, of Scrooge. Even the blind men's dogs appeared to know him; and when they saw him coming on, would tug their owners into doorways and up courts; and then would wag their tails as though they said, "No eye at all is better than an evil eye, dark master!"

But what did Scrooge care? It was the very thing he liked. To edge his way along the crowded paths of life, warning all human sympathy to keep its distance, was what the knowing ones call "nuts" to Scrooge.

Once upon a time—of all the good days in the year, on Christmas Eve—old Scrooge sat busy in his counting-house. It was cold, bleak, biting weather: foggy withal: and he could hear the people in the court outside go wheezing up and down, beating their hands upon their breasts, and stamping their feet upon the pavement-stones to warm them. The City clocks had only just gone three, but it was quite dark already: it had not been light all day: and candles were flaring in the windows of the neighboring offices, like ruddy smears upon the palpable brown air. The fog came pouring in at every chink and keyhole, and was so dense without, that although the court was of the narrowest, the houses opposite were mere phantoms. To see the dingy cloud come drooping down, obscuring everything, one might have thought that Nature lived hard by, and was brewing on a large scale.

The door of Scrooge's counting-house was open that he might keep his eye upon his clerk, who in a dismal little cell beyond, a sort of tank, was copying letters. Scrooge had a very small fire, but the clerk's fire was so very much smaller that it looked like one coal. But he couldn't replenish it, for Scrooge kept the coal-box in his own room; and so surely as the clerk came in with the shovel, the master predicted that it would be necessary for them to part. Wherefore the clerk put on his white comforter, and tried to warm himself at the candle; in which effort, not being a man of a strong imagination, he failed.

"A Merry Christmas, uncle! God save you!" cried a cheerful voice. It was the voice of Scrooge's nephew, who came upon him so quickly that this was the first intimation he had of his approach.

"Bah!" said Scrooge, "Humbug!"

He had so heated himself with rapid walking in the fog and frost, this nephew of Scrooge's, that he was all in a glow; his face was ruddy and handsome; his eyes sparkled, and his breath smoked again.

"Christmas a humbug, uncle!" said Scrooge's nephew. "You don't mean that, I am sure."

"I do," said Scrooge. "Merry Christmas! What right have you to be merry? What reason have you to be merry? You're poor enough."

"Come, then," returned the nephew gayly. "What right have you to be dismal? What reason have you to be morose? You're rich enough."

Scrooge having no better answer ready on the spur of the moment, said, "Bah!" again; and followed it up with "Humbug."

"Don't be cross, uncle," said the nephew.

"What else can I be," returned the uncle, "when I live in such a world of fools as this? Merry Christmas! Out upon merry Christmas! What's Christmas time to you but a time for paying bills without money; a time for finding yourself a year older, but not an hour richer; a time for balancing your books and having every item in 'em through a round dozen of months presented dead against you? If I could work my will," said Scrooge, indignantly, "every idiot who goes about with 'Merry Christmas,' on his lips, should be boiled with his own pudding, and buried with a stake of holly through his heart. He should!"

"Uncle!" pleaded the nephew.

"Nephew!" returned the uncle, sternly, "keep Christmas in your own way, and let me keep it in mine."

"Keep it!" repeated Scrooge's nephew. "But you don't keep it."

"Let me leave it alone, then," said Scrooge. "Much good may it do you! Much good it has ever done you!"

"There are many things from which I might have derived good, by which I have not profited, I dare say," returned the nephew: "Christmas among the rest. But I am sure I have always thought of Christmas time, when it has come round—apart from the veneration due to its sacred name and origin, if anything belonging to it can be apart from that—as a good time: a kind, forgiving, charitable, pleasant time: the only time I know of, in the long calendar of the year, when men and women seem by one consent to open their shut-up hearts freely, and to think of people below them as if they really were fellow-passengers to the grave, and not another race of creatures bound on other journeys. And therefore, uncle, though it has never put a scrap of gold or silver in my pocket, I believe that it *has* done me good, and *will* do me good; and I say, God bless it!"

The clerk in the Tank involuntarily applauded: becoming immediately sensible of the impropriety, he poked the fire, and extinguished the last frail spark forever.

"Let me hear another sound from *you*," said Scrooge, "and you'll keep your Christmas by losing your situation. You're quite a powerful speaker, Sir," he added, turning to his nephew. "I wonder you don't go into Parliament."

"Don't be angry, uncle. Come! Dine with us tomorrow."

Scrooge said that he would see him—yes, indeed he did. He went the whole length of the expression, and said that he would see him in that extremity first.

"But why?" cried Scrooge's nephew. "Why?"

"Why did you get married?" said Scrooge.

"Because I fell in love."

"Because you fell in love!" growled Scrooge, as if that were the only one thing in the world more ridiculous than a merry Christmas. "Good afternoon!"

"Nay, uncle, but you never came to see me before that happened. Why give it as a reason for not coming now?"

"Good afternoon," said Scrooge.

"I want nothing from you; I ask nothing of you; why cannot we be friends?"

"Good afternoon," said Scrooge.

"I am sorry, with all my heart, to find you so resolute. We have never had any quarrel, to which I have been a party. But I have made the trial in homage to Christmas, and I'll keep my Christmas humor to the last. So A Merry Christmas, uncle!"

"Good afternoon!" said Scrooge.

"And A Happy New Year!"

"Good afternoon!" said Scrooge.

His nephew left the room without an angry word, notwithstanding. He stopped at the outer door to bestow the greetings of the season on the clerk, who, cold as he was, was warmer than Scrooge; for he returned them cordially.

"There's another fellow," muttered Scrooge; who overheard him: "my clerk, with fifteen shillings a week, and a wife and family, talking about a merry Christmas. I'll retire to Bedlam."

This lunatic, in letting Scrooge's nephew out, had let two other people in. They were portly gentlemen, pleasant to behold, and now stood, with their hats off, in Scrooge's office. They had books and papers in their hands, and bowed to him.

"Scrooge and Marley's, I believe," said one of the gentlemen, referring to his list. "Have I the pleasure of addressing Mr. Scrooge, or Mr. Marley?"

"Mr. Marley has been dead these seven years," Scrooge replied. "He died seven years ago, this very night."

"We have no doubt his liberality is well represented by his surviving partner," said the gentleman, presenting his credentials.

It certainly was; for they had been two kindred spirits. At the ominous word "liberality," Scrooge frowned, and shook his head, and handed the credentials back.

"At this festive season of the year, Mr. Scrooge," said the gentleman, taking up a pen, "it is more than usually desirable that we should make some slight provision for the poor and destitute, who suffer greatly at the present time. Many thousands are in want of common necessaries; hundreds of thousands are in want of common comforts, Sir."

"Are there no prisons?" asked Scrooge.

"Plenty of prisons," said the gentleman, laying down the pen again.

"And the Union workhouses?" demanded Scrooge. "Are they still in operation?"

"They are. Still," returned the gentleman, "I wish I could say they were not."

"The Treadmill and the Poor Law are in full vigor, then?" said Scrooge.

"Both very busy, Sir."

"Oh! I was afraid, from what you said at first, that something had occurred to stop them in their useful course," said Scrooge. "I'm very glad to hear it."

"Under the impression that they scarcely furnish Christian cheer of mind or body to the multitude," returned the gentleman, "a few of us are endeavoring to raise a fund to buy the Poor some meat and drink, and means of warmth. We choose this time, because it is a time, of all others, when Want is keenly felt, and Abundance rejoices. What shall I put you down for?"

"Nothing!" Scrooge replied.

"You wish to be anonymous?"

"I wish to be left alone," said Scrooge. "Since you ask me what I wish, gentlemen, that is my answer. I don't make merry myself at Christmas, and I can't afford to make idle people merry. I help to support the establishments I have mentioned: they cost enough: and those who are badly off must go there."

"Many can't go there; and many would rather die."

"If they would rather die," said Scrooge, "they had better do it, and decrease the surplus population. Besides—excuse me—I don't know that."

"But you might know it," observed the gentleman.

"It's not my business," Scrooge returned. "It's enough for a man to understand his own business, and not to interfere with other people's. Mine occupies me constantly. Good afternoon, gentlemen!"

Seeing clearly that it would be useless to pursue their point, the gentlemen withdrew. Scrooge resumed his labors with an improved opinion of himself, and in a more facetious temper than was usual with him.

Meanwhile the fog and darkness thickened so, that people ran about with flaring links, proffering their services to go before horses in carriages, and conduct them on their way. The ancient tower of a church, whose gruff old bell was always peeping slyly down at Scrooge out of a gothic window in the wall, became invisible, and struck the hours and quarters in the clouds, with tremulous vibrations afterwards as if its teeth were chattering in its frozen head up there. The cold became intense. In the main street at the corner of the court, some laborers were repairing the gas-pipes, and had lighted a great fire in a brazier, round which a party of ragged men and boys were gathered: warming their hands and winking their eyes before the blaze in rapture. The water-plug being left in solitude, its over-flowings sullenly congealed, and turned to misanthropic ice. The brightness of the shops where holly sprigs and berries crackled in the lamp heat of the windows, made pale faces ruddy as they passed. Poulterers' and grocers' trades became a splendid joke: a glorious pageant, with which it was next to impossible to believe that such dull principles as bargain and sale had anything to do. The Lord Mayor, in the stronghold of the mighty Mansion House, gave orders to his fifty cooks and butlers to keep Christmas as a Lord Mayor's household should; and even the little tailor, whom he had fined five shillings on the previous Monday for being drunk and bloodthirsty in the streets, stirred up tomorrow's pudding in his garret, while his lean wife and the baby sallied out to buy the beef.

Foggier yet, and colder! Piercing, searching, biting cold. If the good Saint Dunstan had but nipped the Evil Spirit's nose with a touch of such weather as that, instead of using his familiar weapons, then indeed he would have roared to lusty purpose. The owner of one scant young nose, gnawed and mumbled by the hungry cold as bones are gnawed by dogs, stooped down at Scrooge's keyhole to regale him with a Christmas carol: but at the first sound of

> "God bless you, merry gentleman!
> May nothing you dismay!"

Scrooge seized the ruler with such energy of action, that the singer fled in terror, leaving the keyhole to the fog and even more congenial frost.

At length the hour of shutting up the counting-house arrived. With an ill-will Scrooge dismounted from his stool, and tacitly admitted the fact to the expectant clerk in the Tank, who instantly snuffed his candle out, and put on his hat.

"You'll want all day tomorrow, I suppose?" said Scrooge.

"If quite convenient, Sir."

"It's not convenient," said Scrooge, "and it's not fair. If I was to stop half-a-crown for it, you'd think yourself ill-used, I'll be bound!"

The clerk smiled faintly.

"And yet," said Scrooge, "you don't think *me* ill-used, when I pay a day's wages for no work."

The clerk observed that it was only once a year.

"A poor excuse for picking a man's pocket every twenty-fifth of

December!" said Scrooge, buttoning his great-coat to the chin. "But I suppose you must have the whole day. Be here all the earlier next morning."

The clerk promised that he would; and Scrooge walked out with a growl. The office was closed in a twinkling, and the clerk, with the long ends of his white comforter dangling below his waist (for he boasted no great-coat), went down a slide on Cornhill, at the end of a lane of boys, twenty times, in honor of its being Christmas Eve, and then ran home to Camden Town as hard as he could pelt to play at blindman's-buff.

Scrooge took his melancholy dinner in his usual melancholy tavern; and having read all the newspapers, and beguiled the rest of the evening with his banker's-book, went home to bed. He lived in chambers which had once belonged to his deceased partner. They were a gloomy suite of rooms, in a lowering pile of building up a yard, where it had so little business to be, that one could scarcely help fancying it must have run there when it was a young house, playing at hide-and seek with other houses, and have forgotten the way out again. It was old enough now, and dreary enough, for nobody lived in it but Scrooge, the other rooms being all let out as offices. The yard was so dark that even Scrooge, who knew its every stone, was fain to grope with his hands. The fog and frost so hung about the black old gateway of the house, that it seemed as if the Genius of the Weather sat in mournful meditation on the threshold.

Now, it is a fact, that there was nothing at all particular about the knocker on the door, except that it was very large. It is also a fact, that Scrooge had seen it, night and morning, during his whole residence in that place; also that Scrooge had as little of what is called fancy about him as any man in the City of London, even including— which is a bold word—the corporation, aldermen, and livery. Let it also be borne in mind that Scrooge had not bestowed one thought on Marley since his last mention of his seven-years' dead partner that afternoon. And then let any man explain to me, if he can, how it happened that Scrooge, having his key in the lock of the door, saw in the knocker, without its undergoing any intermediate process of change: not a knocker, but Marley's face.

Marley's face. It was not in impenetrable shadows as the other objects in the yard were, but had a dismal light about it like a bad lobster in a dark cellar. It was not angry or ferocious, but looked at Scrooge as Marley used to look: with ghostly spectacles turned up on its ghostly forehead. The hair was curiously stirred, as if by breath or hot air; and though the eyes were wide open, they were perfectly motionless. That, and its livid color, made it horrible; but its horror seemed to be in spite of the face and beyond its control, rather than a part of its own expression.

As Scrooge looked fixedly at this phenomenon, it was a knocker again.

To say that he was not startled, or that his blood was not conscious of a terrible sensation to which it had been a stranger from infancy, would be untrue. But he put his hand upon the key he had relinquished, turned it sturdily, walked in, and lighted his candle.

He *did* pause, with a moment's irresolution, before he shut the door; and he *did* look cautiously behind it first, as if he half-expected to be terrified with the sight of Marley's pigtail sticking out into the hall. But there was nothing on the back of the door, except the screws and nuts that held the knocker on; so he said "Pooh, pooh!" and closed it with a bang.

The sound resounded through the house like thunder. Every room above, and every cask in the wine-merchant's cellars below, appeared to have a separate peal of echoes of its own. Scrooge was not a man to be frightened by echoes. He fastened the door, and walked across the hall, and up the stairs: slowly too: trimming his candle as he went.

You may talk vaguely about driving a coach-and-six up a good old flight of stairs, or through a bad young Act of Parliament; but I mean to say you might have got a hearse up that staircase, and taken it broadwise, with the splinter-bar towards the wall, and the door towards the balustrades: and done it easy. There was plenty of width for that, and room to spare; which is perhaps the reason why Scrooge thought he saw a locomotive hearse going on before him in the gloom. Half-a-dozen gas-lamps out of the street wouldn't have lighted the entry too well, so you may suppose that it was pretty dark with Scrooge's dip. Up Scrooge went, not caring a button for that: darkness is cheap, and Scrooge liked it. But before he shut his heavy door, he walked through his rooms to see that all was right. He had just enough recollection of the face to desire to do that.

Sitting room, bedroom, lumber room. All as they should be. Nobody under the table, nobody under the sofa; a small fire in the grate; spoon and basin ready; and the little saucepan of gruel (Scrooge had a cold in his head) upon the hob. Nobody under the bed; nobody in the closet; nobody in his dressing-gown, which was hanging up in a suspicious attitude against the wall. Lumber room as usual. Old fire-guard, old shoes, two fish-baskets, washing-stand on three legs, and a poker.

Quite satisfied, he closed his door, and locked himself in; double-locked himself in, which was not his custom. Thus secured against surprise, he took off his cravat; put on his dressing-gown and slippers, and his nightcap; and sat down before the fire to take his gruel.

It was a very low fire indeed; nothing on such a bitter night. He was obliged to sit close to it, and brood over it, before he could extract the least sensation of warmth from such a handful of fuel. The fireplace was an old one, built by some Dutch merchant long ago, and paved all round with quaint Dutch tiles, designed to illustrate the Scriptures. There were Cains and Abels, Pharaohs' daughters, Queens of Sheba, Angelic messengers descending through the air on clouds like feather-beds, Abrahams, Belshazzars, Apostles putting off to sea in butter-boats, hundreds of figures, to attract his thoughts; and yet that face of Marley, seven years dead, came like the ancient Prophet's rod, and swallowed up the whole. If each smooth tile had been a blank at first, with power to shape some picture on its surface from the disjointed fragments of his thoughts, there would have been a copy of old Marley's head on every one.

"Humbug!" said Scrooge; and walked across the room.

After several turns, he sat down again. As he threw his head back in the chair, his glance happened to rest upon a bell, a disused bell, that hung in the room, and communicated for some purpose now forgotten with a chamber in the highest story of the building. It was with great astonishment, and with a strange, inexplicable dread, that as he looked, he saw this bell begin to swing. It swung so softly in the outset that it scarcely made a sound; but soon it rang out loudly, and so did every bell in the house.

This might have lasted half a minute, or a minute, but it seemed an hour. The bells ceased as they had begun, together. They were succeeded by a clanking noise, deep down below; as if some person were dragging a heavy chain over the casks in the wine-merchant's cellar. Scrooge then remembered to have heard that ghosts in haunted houses were described as dragging chains.

The cellar-door flew open with a booming sound, and then he heard the noise much louder, on the floor below; then coming up the stairs; then coming straight towards his door.

"It's humbug still!" said Scrooge. "I won't believe it."

His color changed though, when, without a pause, it came on through the heavy door, and passed into the room before his eyes.

Marley's ghost.

Upon its coming in, the dying flame leaped up, as though it cried "I know him! Marley's Ghost!" and fell again.

The same face: the very same. Marley in his pigtail, usual waistcoat, tights and boots; the tassels on the latter bristling, like his pigtail, and his coat-skirts, and the hair upon his head. The chain he drew was clasped about his middle. It was long, and wound about him like a tail; and it was made (for Scrooge observed it

411

closely) of cash-boxes, keys, padlocks, ledgers, deeds, and heavy purses wrought in steel. His body was transparent; so that Scrooge, observing him, and looking through his waistcoat, could see the two buttons on his coat behind. Scrooge had often heard it said that Marley had no bowels, but he had never believed it until now.

No, nor did he believe it even now. Though he looked the phantom through and through, and saw it standing before him; though he felt the chilling influence of its death-cold eyes; and marked the very texture of the folded kerchief bound about its head and chin, which wrapper he had not observed before: he was still incredulous, and fought against his senses.

"How now!" said Scrooge, caustic and cold as ever. "What do you want with me?"

"Much!"—Marley's voice, no doubt about it.

"Who are you?"

"Ask me who I *was*."

"Who *were* you then?" said Scrooge, raising his voice. "You're particular—for a shade." He was going to say *"to* a shade," but substituted this, as more appropriate.

"In life I was your partner, Jacob Marley."

"Can you—can you sit down?" asked Scrooge, looking doubtfully at him.

"I can."

"Do it then."

Scrooge asked the question, because he didn't know whether a ghost so transparent might find himself in a condition to take a chair; and felt that in the event of its being impossible, it might involve the necessity of an embarrassing explanation. But the Ghost sat down on the opposite side of the fireplace, as if he were quite used to it. "You don't believe in me," observed the Ghost.

"I don't," said Scrooge.

"What evidence would you have of my reality beyond that of your senses?"

"I don't know," said Scrooge.

"Why do you doubt your senses?"

"Because," said Scrooge, "a little thing affects them. A slight disorder of the stomach makes them cheats. You may be an undigested bit of beef, a blot of mustard, a crumb of cheese, a fragment of an underdone potato. There's more of gravy than of grave about you, whatever you are!"

Scrooge was not much in the habit of cracking jokes, nor did he feel, in his heart, by any means waggish then. The truth is, that he tried to be smart, as a means of distracting his own attention, and keeping down his terror; for the specter's voice disturbed the very marrow in his bones.

To sit, staring at those fixed, glazed eyes, in silence for a moment, would play, Scrooge felt, the very deuce with him. There was something very awful, too, in the specter's being provided with an infernal atmosphere of its own. Scrooge could not feel it himself, but this was clearly the case; for though the Ghost sat perfectly motionless, its hair, and skirts, and tassels, were still agitated as by the hot vapor from an oven.

"You see this toothpick?" said Scrooge, returning quickly to the charge, for the reason just assigned; and wishing, though it were only for a second, to divert the vision's stony gaze from himself.

"I do," replied the Ghost.

"You are not looking at it," said Scrooge.

"But I see it," said the Ghost, "notwithstanding."

"Well!" returned Scrooge. "I have but to swallow this, and be for the rest of my days persecuted by a legion of goblins, all of my own creation. Humbug, I tell you—humbug!"

At this the spirit raised a frightful cry, and shook its chain with such a dismal and appalling noise, that Scrooge held on tight to his chair, to save himself from falling in a swoon. But how much greater was his horror, when the phantom taking off the bandage round its head, as if it were too warm to wear indoors, its lower jaw dropped down upon its breast!

Scrooge fell upon his knees, and clasped his hands before his face.

"Mercy!" he said. "Dreadful apparition, why do you trouble me?"

"Man of the worldly mind," replied the Ghost, "do you believe in me or not?"

"I do," said Scrooge. "I must. But why do spirits walk the earth, and why do they come to me?"

"It is required of every man," the Ghost returned, "that the spirit within him should walk abroad among his fellow-men, and travel far and wide; and if that spirit goes not forth in life, it is condemned to do so after death. It is doomed to wander through the world—oh, woe is me!—and witness what it cannot share, but might have shared on earth, and turned to happiness!"

Again the specter raised a cry, and shook its chain, and wrung its shadowy hands.

"You are fettered," said Scrooge, trembling. "Tell me why?"

"I wear the chain I forged in life," replied the Ghost. "I made it link by link, and yard by yard; I girded it on of my own free will, and of my own free will I wore it. Is its pattern strange to *you?*"

Scrooge trembled more and more.

"Or would you know," pursued the Ghost, "the weight and length of the strong coil you bear yourself? It was full as heavy and as long as this, seven Christmas Eves ago. You have labored on it, since. It is a ponderous chain!"

Scrooge glanced about him on the floor, in the expectation of finding himself surrounded by some fifty or sixty fathoms of iron cable: but he could see nothing.

"Jacob," he said imploringly. "Old Jacob Marley, tell me more. Speak comfort to me, Jacob."

"I have none to give," the Ghost replied. "It comes from other regions, Ebenezer Scrooge, and is conveyed by other ministers, to other kinds of men. Nor can I tell you what I would. A very little more, is all permitted to me. I cannot rest, I cannot stay, I cannot linger anywhere. My spirit never walked beyond our counting-house— mark me!—in life my spirit never roved beyond the narrow limits of our money-changing hole; and weary journeys lie before me!"

It was a habit with Scrooge, whenever he became thoughtful, to put his hands in his breeches pockets. Pondering on what the Ghost had said, he did so now, but without lifting up his eyes, or getting off his knees.

"You must have been very slow about it, Jacob," Scrooge observed, in a business-like manner, though with humility and deference.

"Slow!" the Ghost repeated.

"Seven years dead," mused Scrooge. "And traveling all the time!"

"The whole time," said the Ghost. "No rest, no peace. Incessant torture of remorse."

"You travel fast?" said Scrooge.

"On the wings of the wind," replied the Ghost.

"You might have got over a great quantity of ground in seven years," said Scrooge.

The Ghost, on hearing this, set up another cry, and clanked its chain so hideously in the dead silence of the night, that the Ward would have been justified in indicting it for a nuisance.

"Oh! captive, bound, and doubled-ironed," cried the phantom, "not to know, that ages of incessant labor, by immortal creatures, for this earth must pass into eternity before the good of which it is susceptible is all developed. Not to know that any Christian spirit working kindly in its little sphere, whatever it may be, will find its mortal life too short for its vast means of usefulness. Not to know that no space of regret can make amends for one life's opportunity misused! Yet such was I! Oh! such was I!"

"But you were always a good man of business, Jacob," faltered Scrooge, who now began to apply this to himself.

"Business!" cried the Ghost, wringing its hands again. "Mankind was my business. The common welfare was my business; charity, mercy, forbearance, and benevolence, were, all, my business. The dealings of my trade were but a drop of water in the comprehensive ocean of my business!"

It held up its chain at arm's length, as if that were the cause of all its unavailing grief, and flung it heavily upon the ground again.

"At this time of the rolling year," the specter said, "I suffer most. Why did I walk through crowds of fellow-beings with my eyes turned down, and never raise them to that blessed Star which led the Wise Men to a poor abode! Were there no poor homes to which its light would have conducted *me!*"

Scrooge was very much dismayed to hear the specter going on at this rate, and began to quake exceedingly.

"Hear me!" cried the Ghost. "My time is nearly gone."

"I will," said Scrooge. "But don't be hard upon me! Don't be flowery, Jacob! Pray!"

"How it is that I appear before you in a shape that you can see, I may not tell. I have sat invisible beside you many and many a day."

It was not an agreeable idea. Scrooge shivered, and wiped the perspiration from his brow.

"That is no light part of my penance," pursued the Ghost. "I am here tonight to warn you, that you have yet a chance and hope of escaping my fate. A chance and hope of my procuring, Ebenezer."

"You were always a good friend to me," said Scrooge. "Thank'ee!"

"You will be haunted," resumed the Ghost, "by Three Spirits."

Scrooge's countenance fell almost as low as the Ghost's had done.

"Is that the chance and hope you mentioned, Jacob?" he demanded, in a faltering voice.

"It is."

"I—I think I'd rather not," said Scrooge.

"Without their visits," said the Ghost, "you cannot hope to shun the path I tread. Expect the first tomorrow, when the bell tolls one."

"Couldn't I take 'em all at once, and have it over, Jacob?" hinted Scrooge.

"Expect the second on the next night at the same hour. The third upon the next night when the last stroke of twelve has ceased to vibrate. Look to see me no more; and look that, for your own sake, you remember what has passed between us!"

When it had said these words, the specter took its wrapper from the table, and bound it round its head, as before. Scrooge knew this, by the smart sound its teeth made, when the jaws were brought together by the bandage. He ventured to raise his eyes again, and found his supernatural visitor confronting him in an erect attitude, with its chain wound over and about its arm.

The apparition walked backward from him; and at every step it took, the window raised itself a little, so that when the specter reached it, it was wide open. It beckoned Scrooge to approach, which he did. When they were within two paces of each other, Marley's Ghost held up its hand, warning him to come no nearer. Scrooge stopped.

Not so much in obedience, as in surprise and fear: for on the raising of the hand, he became sensible of confused noises in the air; incoherent sounds of lamentation and regret; wailings inexpressibly sorrowful and self-accusatory. The specter, after listening for a moment, joined in the mournful dirge; and floated out upon the bleak, dark night.

Scrooge followed to the window: desperate in his curiosity. He looked out.

The air was filled with phantoms, wandering hither and thither in restless haste, and moaning as they went. Every one of them wore chains like Marley's Ghost; some few (they might be guilty governments) were linked together; none were free. Many had been personally known to Scrooge in their lives. He had been quite familiar with one old ghost, in a white waistcoat, with a monstrous iron safe attached to its ankle, who cried piteously at being unable to assist a wretched woman with an infant, whom it saw below, upon a doorstep. The misery with them all was, clearly, that they sought to interfere, for good, in human matters, and had lost the power forever.

Whether these creatures faded into mist, or mist enshrouded them, he could not tell. But they and their spirit voices faded together; and the night became as it had been when he walked home.

Scrooge closed the window, and examined the door by which the Ghost had entered. It was double-locked, as he had locked it with his own hands, and the bolts were undisturbed. He tried to say "Humbug!" but stopped at the first syllable. And being, from the emotion he had undergone, or the fatigues of the day, or his glimpse of the Invisible World, or the dull conversation of the Ghost, or the lateness of the hour, much in need of repose, went straight to bed, without undressing, and fell asleep upon the instant.

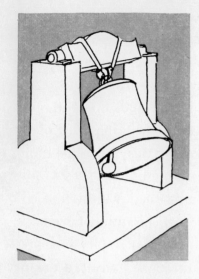

STAVE TWO:

THE FIRST OF

THE THREE SPIRITS

When Scrooge awoke, it was so dark, that looking out of bed, he could scarcely distinguish the transparent window from the opaque walls of his chamber. He was endeavoring to pierce the darkness with his ferret eyes, when the chimes of a neighboring church struck the four quarters. So he listened for the hour.

To his great astonishment the heavy bell went on from six to seven, and from seven to eight, and regularly up to twelve; then stopped. Twelve! It was past two when he went to bed. The clock was wrong. An icicle must have got into the works. Twelve!

He touched the spring of his repeater, to correct this most preposterous clock. Its rapid little pulse beat twelve; and stopped.

"Why, it isn't possible," said Scrooge, "that I can have slept through a whole day and far into another night. It isn't possible that anything has happened to the sun, and this is twelve at noon!"

The idea being an alarming one, he scrambled out of bed, and groped his way to the window. He was obliged to rub the frost off with the sleeve of his dressing-gown before he could see anything; and could see very little then. All he could make out was, that it was still very foggy and extremely cold, and that there was no noise of people running to and fro, and making a great stir, as there unquestionably would have been if night had beaten off bright day, and taken possession of the world. This was a great relief, because "three days after sight of this First of Exchange pay to Mr. Ebenezer Scrooge or his order," and so forth, would have become a mere United States security if there were no days to count by.

Scrooge went to bed again, and thought, and thought, and thought it over and over and over, and could make nothing of it. The more he thought, the more perplexed he was; and the more he endeavored not to think, the more he thought. Marley's Ghost bothered him exceedingly. Every time he resolved within himself, after mature inquiry, that it was all a dream, his mind flew back again, like a strong spring released, to its first position, and presented the same problem to be worked all through, "Was it a dream or not?"

Scrooge lay in this state until the chimes had gone three quarters more, when he remembered, on a sudden, that the Ghost had warned him of a visitation when the bell tolled one. He resolved to lie awake until the hour was passed; and, considering that he could no more go to sleep than go to Heaven, this was perhaps the wisest resolution in his power.

The quarter was so long, that he was more than once convinced he must have sunk into a doze unconsciously, and missed the clock. At length it broke upon his listening ear.

"Ding, dong!"

"A quarter past," said Scrooge, counting.

"Ding, dong!"

"Half-past!" said Scrooge.

"Ding, dong!"

"A quarter to it," said Scrooge.

"Ding, dong!"

"The hour itself," said Scrooge, triumphantly, "and nothing else!"

He spoke before the hour bell sounded, which it now did with a deep, dull, hollow, melancholy ONE. Light flashed up in the room upon the instant, and the curtains of his bed were drawn.

The curtains of his bed were drawn aside, I tell you, by a hand. Not the curtains at his feet, nor the curtains at his back, but those to which his face was addressed. The curtains of his bed were drawn aside; and Scrooge, starting up into a half-recumbent attitude, found himself face to face with the unearthly visitor who drew them: as close to it as I am now to you, and I am standing in the spirit at your elbow.

It was a strange figure—like a child: yet not so like a child as like an old man, viewed through some supernatural medium, which gave him the appearance of having receded from the view, and being diminished to a child's proportions. Its hair, which hung about its neck and down its back, was white as if with age; and yet the face had not a wrinkle in it, and the tenderest bloom was on the skin. The arms were very long and muscular; the hands the same, as if its hold were of uncommon strength. Its legs and feet, most delicately formed, were, like those upper members, bare. It wore a tunic of the purest white; and round its waist was bound a lustrous belt, the sheen of which was beautiful. It held a branch of fresh green holly in its hand; and, in singular contradiction of that wintry emblem, had its dress trimmed with summer flowers. But the strangest thing about it was, that from the crown of its head there sprang a bright clear jet of light, by which all this was visible; and which was doubtless the occasion of its using, in its duller moments, a great extinguisher for a cap, which it now held under its arm.

Even this, though, when Scrooge looked at it with increasing steadiness, was *not* its strangest quality. For as its belt sparkled and glittered now in one part and now in another, and what was light one instant, at another time was dark, so the figure itself fluctuated in its distinctness: being now a thing with one arm, now with one leg, now with twenty legs, now a pair of legs without a head, now a head without a body: of which dissolving parts, no outline would be visible in the dense gloom wherein they melted away. And in the very wonder of this, it would be itself again; distinct and clear as ever.

"Are you the Spirit, Sir, whose coming was foretold to me?" asked Scrooge.

"I am!"

The voice was soft and gentle. Singularly low, as if instead of being so close beside him, it were at a distance.

"Who, and what are you?" Scrooge demanded.

"I am the Ghost of Christmas Past."

"Long past?" inquired Scrooge: observant of its dwarfish stature.

"No. Your past."

Perhaps, Scrooge could not have told anybody why, if anybody could have asked him: but he had a special desire to see the Spirit in his cap; and begged him to be covered.

"What!" exclaimed the Ghost, "would you so soon put out, with worldly hands, the light I give? Is it not enough that you are one of those whose passions made this cap, and force me through whole trains of years to wear it low upon my brow!"

Scrooge reverently disclaimed all intention to offend, or any knowledge of having wilfully "bonneted" the Spirit at any period of his life. He then made bold to inquire what business brought him there.

"Your welfare!" said the Ghost.

Scrooge expressed himself much obliged, but could not help thinking that a night of unbroken rest would have been more conducive to that end. The Spirit must have heard him thinking, for it said immediately:

"Your reclamation, then. Take heed!"

It put out its strong hand as it spoke, and clasped him gently by the arm.

"Rise! and walk with me!"

It would have been in vain for Scrooge to plead that the weather and the hour were not adapted to pedestrian purposes; that bed was warm, and the thermometer a long way below freezing; that he was clad but lightly in his slippers, dressing-gown, and nightcap; and that he had a cold upon him at that time. The grasp, though gentle as a woman's hand, was not to be resisted. He rose: but finding that the Spirit made toward the window, clasped its robe in supplication.

"I am a mortal," Scrooge remonstrated, "and liable to fall."

"Bear but a touch of my hand *there*," said the Spirit, laying it upon his heart, "and you shall be upheld in more than this!"

As the words were spoken, they passed through the wall, and stood upon an open country road, with fields on either hand. The city had entirely vanished. Not a vestige of it was to be seen. The darkness and the mist had vanished with it, for it was a clear, cold, winter day, with snow upon the ground.

"Good Heaven!" said Scrooge, clasping his hands together, as he looked about him. "I was bred in this place. I was a boy here!"

The Spirit gazed upon him mildly. Its gentle touch, though it had been light and instantaneous, appeared still present to the old man's sense of feeling. He was conscious of a thousand odors floating in the air, each one connected with a thousand thoughts, and hopes, and joys, and cares long, long forgotten!

"Your lip is trembling," said the Ghost. "And what is that upon your cheek?"

Scrooge muttered, with an unusual catching in his voice, that it was a pimple; and begged the Ghost to lead him where he would.

"You recollect the way?" inquired the Spirit.

"Remember it!" cried Scrooge with fervor—"I could walk it blindfold."

"Strange to have forgotten it for so many years!" observed the Ghost. "Let us go on."

They walked along the road; Scrooge recognizing every gate, and post, and tree; until a little market-town appeared in the distance, with its bridge, its church, and winding river. Some shaggy ponies now were seen trotting toward them with boys upon their

backs, who called to other boys in country gigs and carts driven by farmers. All these boys were in great spirits, and shouted to each other, until the broad fields were so full of merry music, that the crisp air laughed to hear it.

"These are but shadows of the things that have been," said the Ghost. "They have no consciousness of us."

The jocund travelers came on; and as they came, Scrooge knew and named them every one. Why was he rejoiced beyond all bounds to see them! Why did his cold eye glisten, and his heart leap up as they went past! Why was he filled with gladness when he heard them give each other Merry Christmas, as they parted at crossroads and byways, for their several homes! What was merry Christmas to Scrooge? Out upon merry Christmas! What good had it ever done to him?

"The school is not quite deserted," said the Ghost. "A solitary child, neglected by his friends, is left there still."

Scrooge said he knew it. And he sobbed.

They left the highroad, by a well-remembered lane, and soon approached a mansion of dull red brick, with a little weathercock-surmounted cupola, on the roof, and a bell hanging in it. It was a large house, but one of broken fortunes; for the spacious offices were little used, their walls were damp and mossy, their windows broken, and their gates decayed. Fowls clucked and strutted in the stables; and the coach houses and sheds were overrun with grass. Nor was it more retentive of its ancient state, within; for entering the dreary hall, and glancing through the open doors of many rooms, they found them poorly furnished, cold and vast. There was an earthy savor in the air, a chilly bareness in the place, associated somehow with too much getting up by candlelight, and not too much to eat.

They went, the Ghost and Scrooge, across the hall, to a door at the back of the house. It opened before them, and disclosed a long, bare, melancholy room, made barer still by lines of plain deal forms and desks. At one of these a lonely boy was reading near a feeble fire; and Scrooge sat down upon a form, and wept to see his poor forgotten self as he had used to be.

Not a latent echo in the house, not a squeak and scuffle from the mice behind the paneling, not a drip from the half-thawed waterspout in the dull yard behind, not a sigh among the leafless boughs of one despondent poplar, not the idle swinging of an empty storehouse door, no, not a clicking in the fire, but fell upon the heart of Scrooge with softening influence, and gave a freer passage to his tears.

The Spirit touched him on the arm, and pointed to his younger self, intent upon his reading. Suddenly a man, in foreign garments: wonderfully real and distinct to look at: stood outside the window, with an ax stuck in his belt, and leading an ass laden with wood by the bridle.

"Why, it's Ali Baba!" Scrooge exclaimed in ecstasy. "It's dear old honest Ali Baba! Yes, yes, I know! One Christmas time, when yonder solitary child was left here all alone, he *did* come, for the first time, just like that. Poor boy! And Valentine," said Scrooge, "and his wild brother, Orson; there they go! And what's his name, who was put down in his drawers, asleep, at the Gate of Damascus; don't you see him! And the Sultan's Groom turned upside down by the Genii; there he is upon his head! Serve him right. I'm glad of it. What business had *he* to be married to the Princess!"

To hear Scrooge expending all the earnestness of his nature on such subjects, in a most extraordinary voice between laughing and crying; and to see his heightened and excited face; would have been a surprise to his business friends in the City, indeed.

"There's the Parrot!" cried Scrooge. "Green body and yellow tail, with a thing like a lettuce growing out of the top of his head; there he is! Poor Robin Crusoe, he called him, when he came home again after sailing round the island. 'Poor Robin Crusoe, where have you been, Robin Crusoe?' The man thought he was dreaming, but he wasn't. It was the Parrot, you know. There goes Friday, running for his life to the little creek! Halloa! Hoop! Halloo!"

Then, with a rapidity of transition very foreign to his usual character, he said, in pity for his former self, "Poor boy!" and cried again.

"I wish," Scrooge muttered, putting his hand in his pocket, and looking about him, after drying his eyes with his cuff: "but it's too late now."

"What is the matter?" asked the Spirit.

"Nothing," said Scrooge. "Nothing. There was a boy singing a Christmas Carol at my door last night. I should like to have given him something: that's all."

The Ghost smiled thoughtfully, and waved his hand: saying as it did so, "Let us see another Christmas!"

Scrooge's former self grew larger at the words, and the room became a little darker and more dirty. The panels shrank, the windows cracked; fragments of plaster fell out of the ceiling, and the naked laths were shown instead; but how all this was brought about, Scrooge knew no more than you do. He only knew that it was quite correct; that everything had happened so; that there he was, alone again, when all the other boys had gone home for the jolly holidays.

He was not reading now, but walking up and down despairingly. Scrooge looked at the Ghost, and with a mournful shaking of his head, glanced anxiously towards the door.

It opened; and a little girl, much younger than the boy, came darting in, and putting her arms about his neck, and often kissing him, addressed him as her "Dear, dear brother."

"I have come to bring you home, dear brother!" said the child, clapping her tiny hands, and bending down to laugh. "To bring you home, home, home!"

"Home, little Fan?" returned the boy.

"Yes!" said the child, brimful of glee. "Home, for good and all. Home, forever and ever. Father is so much kinder than he used to be, that home's like Heaven! He spoke so gently to me one dear night when I was going to bed, that I was not afraid to ask him once more if you might come home; and he said Yes, you should; and sent me in a coach to bring you. And you're to be a man!" said the child, opening her eyes, "and are never to come back here; but first, we're to be together all the Christmas long, and have the merriest time in all the world."

"You are quite a woman, little Fan!" exclaimed the boy.

She clapped her hands and laughed, and tried to touch his head; but being too little, laughed again, and stood on tiptoe to embrace him. Then she began to drag him, in her childish eagerness, toward the door; and he, nothing loath to go, accompanied her.

A terrible voice in the hall cried, "Bring down Master Scrooge's box, there!" and in the hall appeared the schoolmaster himself, who glared on Master Scrooge with a ferocious condescension, and threw him into a dreadful state of mind by shaking hands with him. He then conveyed him and his sister into the veriest old well of a shivering best-parlor that ever was seen, where the maps upon the wall, and the celestial and terrestrial globes in the windows, were waxy with cold. Here he produced a decanter of curiously light wine, and a block of curiously heavy cake, and administered instalments of those dainties to the young people: at the same time, sending out a meager servant to offer a glass of "something" to the postboy, who answered that he thanked the gentleman, but if it was the same tap as he had tasted before, he had rather not. Master Scrooge's trunk being by this time tied on to the top of the chaise, the children bade the schoolmaster good-bye right willingly; and getting into it, drove gayly down the garden sweep: the quick wheels dashing the hoar frost and snow from off the dark leaves of the evergreens like spray.

"Always a delicate creature, whom a breath might have withered," said the Ghost. "But she had a large heart!"

"So she had," cried Scrooge. "You're right. I'll not gainsay it, Spirit. God forbid!"

"She died a woman," said the Ghost, "and had, I think, children."

"One child," Scrooge returned.

"True," said the Ghost. "Your nephew!"

Scrooge seemed uneasy in his mind; and answered briefly, "Yes."

Although they had but that moment left the school behind them, they were now in the busy thoroughfares of a city, where shadowy passengers passed and repassed; where shadowy carts and coaches battled for the way, and all the strife and tumult of a real city were. It was made plain enough, by the dressing of the shops, that here too it was Christmas time again; but it was evening, and the streets were lighted up.

The Ghost stopped at a certain warehouse door, and asked Scrooge if he knew it.

"Know it!" said Scrooge. "Was I apprenticed here!"

They went in. At sight of an old gentleman in a Welsh wig, sitting behind such a high desk, that if he had been two inches taller he must have knocked his head against the ceiling, Scrooge cried in great excitement:

"Why, it's old Fezziwig! Bless his heart; it's Fezziwig alive again!"

Old Fezziwig laid down his pen, and looked up at the clock, which pointed to the hour of seven. He rubbed his hands; adjusted his capacious waistcoat; laughed all over himself, from his shoes to his organ of benevolence; and called out in a comfortable, oily, rich, fat, jovial voice:

"Yo ho, there! Ebenezer! Dick!"

Scrooge's former self, now grown a young man, came briskly in, accompanied by his fellow 'prentice.

"Dick Wilkins, to be sure!" said Scrooge to the Ghost. "Bless me, yes. There he is. He was very much attached to me, was Dick. Poor Dick! Dear, dear!"

"Yo ho, my boys!" said Fezziwig. "No more work tonight. Christmas Eve, Dick. Christmas, Ebenezer! Let's have the shutters up," cried old Fezziwig, with a sharp clap of his hands, "before a man can say Jack Robinson!"

You wouldn't believe how those two fellows went at it! They charged into the street with the shutters—one, two, three—had 'em up in their places—four, five, six—barred 'em and pinned 'em— seven, eight, nine—and came back before you could have got to twelve, panting like racehorses.

"Hilli-ho!" cried old Fezziwig, skipping down from the high desk, with wonderful agility. "Clear away, my lads, and let's have lots of room here! Hilli-ho, Dick! Chirrup, Ebenezer!"

Clear away! There was nothing they wouldn't have cleared away, or couldn't have cleared away, with old Fezziwig looking on. It was done in a minute. Every movable was packed off, as if it were dismissed from public life forevermore; the floor was swept and watered, the lamps were trimmed, fuel was heaped upon the fire and the warehouse was as snug, and warm, and dry, and bright a ball room, as you would desire to see upon a winter's night.

In came a fiddler with a music book, and went up to the lofty desk, and made an orchestra of it, and tuned like fifty stomach aches. In came Mrs. Fezziwig, one vast substantial smile. In came the three Miss Fezziwigs, beaming and lovable. In came the six young fol- lowers whose hearts they broke. In came all the young men and women employed in the business. In came the housemaid, with her cousin, the baker. In came the cook, with her brother's particular friend, the milkman. In came the boy from over the way, who was suspected of not having board enough from his master; trying to hide himself behind the girl from next door but one, who was proved to have had her ears pulled by her mistress. In they all came, one after another; some shyly, some boldly, some gracefully, some

Mr. Fezziwig's Ball.

awkwardly, some pushing, some pulling; in they all came, anyhow and everyhow. Away they all went, twenty couple at once, hands half round and back again the other way; down the middle and up again; round and round in various stages of affectionate grouping; old top couple always turning up in the wrong place; new top couple starting off again, as soon as they got there; all top couples at last, and not a bottom one to help them. When this result was brought about, old Fezziwig, clapping his hands to stop the dance, cried out, "Well done!" and the fiddler plunged his hot face into a pot of porter, especially provided for that purpose. But

scorning rest upon his reappearance, he instantly began again, though there were no dancers yet, as if the other fiddler had been carried home, exhausted, on a shutter; and he were a bran-new man resolved to beat him out of sight, or perish.

There were more dances, and there were forfeits, and more dances, and there was cake, and there was negus, and there was a great piece of Cold Roast, and there was a great piece of Cold Boiled, and there were mince pies, and plenty of beer. But the great effect of the evening came after the Roast and Boiled, when the fiddler (an artful dog, mind! The sort of man who knew his business better than you or I could have told him!) struck up "Sir Roger de Coverley." Then old Fezziwig stood out to dance with Mrs. Fezziwig. Top couple, too; with a good stiff piece of work cut out for them; three or four and twenty pair of partners; people who were not to be trifled with; people who *would* dance, and had no notion of walking.

But if they had been twice as many: ah, four times: old Fezziwig would have been a match for them, and so would Mrs. Fezziwig. As to *her,* she was worthy to be his partner in every sense of the term. If that's not high praise, tell me higher, and I'll use it. A positive light appeared to issue from Fezziwig's calves. They shone in every part of the dance like moons. You could n't have predicted, at any given time, what would become of 'em next. And when old Fezziwig and Mrs. Fezziwig had gone all through the dance; advance and retire, hold hands with your partner; bow and courtesy; corkscrew; thread-the-needle, and back again to your place; Fezziwig "cut"— cut so deftly, that he appeared to wink with his legs, and came upon his feet again without a stagger.

When the clock struck eleven, this domestic ball broke up. Mr. and Mrs. Fezziwig took their stations, one on either side the door, and shaking hands with every person individually as he or she went out, wished him or her a Merry Christmas. When everybody had retired but the two 'prentices, they did the same to them; and thus the cheerful voices died away, and the lads were left to their beds; which were under a counter in the back-shop.

During the whole of this time, Scrooge had acted like a man out of his wits. His heart and soul were in the scene, and with his former self. He corroborated everything, remembered everything, enjoyed everything, and underwent the strangest agitation. It was not until now, when the bright faces of his former self and Dick were turned from them, that he remembered the Ghost, and became conscious that it was looking full upon him, while the light upon its head burnt very clear.

"A small matter," said the Ghost, "to make these silly folks so full of gratitude."

"Small!" echoed Scrooge.

The Spirit signed to him to listen to the two apprentices, who were pouring out their hearts in praise of Fezziwig: and when he had done so, said: "Why! Is it not? He has spent but a few pounds of your mortal money: three or four, perhaps. Is that so much that he deserves this praise?"

"It isn't that," said Scrooge, heated by the remark, and speaking unconsciously like his former, not his latter self. "It isn't that, Spirit. He has the power to render us happy or unhappy; to make our service light or burdensome; a pleasure or a toil. Say that his power lies in words and looks; in things so slight and insignificant that it is impossible to add and count 'em up: what then? The happiness he gives, is quite as great as if it cost a fortune."

He felt the Spirit's glance, and stopped.

"What's the matter?" asked the Ghost.

"Nothing particular," said Scrooge.

"Something, I think?" the Ghost insisted.

"No," said Scrooge, "No. I should like to be able to say a word or two to my clerk just now! That's all."

His former self turned down the lamps as he gave utterance to the wish; and Scrooge and the Ghost again stood side by side in the open air.

"My time grows short," observed the Spirit. "Quick!"

This was not addressed to Scrooge, or to any one whom he could see, but it produced an immediate effect. For again Scrooge saw himself. He was older now; a man in the prime of life. His face had not the harsh and rigid lines of later years; but it had begun to wear the signs of care and avarice. There was an eager, greedy, restless motion in the eye, which showed the passion that had taken root, and where the shadow of the growing tree would fall.

He was not alone, but sat by the side of a fair young girl in a mourning dress: in whose eyes there were tears, which sparkled in the light that shone out of the Ghost of Christmas Past.

"It matters little," she said, softly. "To you, very little. Another idol has displaced me; and if it can cheer and comfort you in time to come, as I would have tried to do, I have no just cause to grieve."

"What idol has displaced you?" he rejoined.

"A golden one."

"This is the even-handed dealing of the world!" he said. "There is nothing on which it is so hard as poverty; and there is nothing it professes to condemn with such severity as the pursuit of wealth!"

"You fear the world too much," she answered, gently. "All your other hopes have merged into the hope of being beyond the chance of its sordid reproach. I have seen your nobler aspirations fall off one by one, until the master-passion, Gain, engrosses you. Have I not?"

"What then?" he retorted. "Even if I have grown so much wiser, what then? I am not changed toward you."

She shook her head.

"Am I?"

"Our contract is an old one. It was made when we were both poor and content to be so, until, in good season, we could improve our worldly fortune by our patient industry. You *are* changed. When it was made, you were another man."

"I was a boy," he said impatiently.

"Your own feeling tells you that you were not what you are," she returned. "I am. That which prom-ised happiness when we were one in heart, is fraught with misery now that we are two. How often and how keenly I have thought of this, I will not say. It is enough that I *have* thought of it, and can release you."

"Have I ever sought release?"

"In words? No. Never."

"In what, then?"

"In a changed nature; in an altered spirit; in another atmosphere of life; another Hope as its great end. In everything that made my love of any worth or value in your sight. If this had never been between us," said the girl, looking mildly, but with steadiness, upon him; "tell me, would you seek me out and try to win me now? Ah, no!"

He seemed to yield to the justice of this supposition, in spite of himself. But he said with a struggle, "You think not."

"I would gladly think otherwise if I could," she answered, "Heaven knows! When *I* have learned a Truth like this, I know how strong and irresistible it must be. But if you were free today, tomorrow, yesterday, can even I believe that you would choose a dowerless girl—you who, in your very confidence with her, weigh everything by Gain: or, choosing her, if for a moment, you were false enough to your one guiding principle to do so, do I not know that your repentance and regret would surely follow? I do; and I release you. With a full heart, for the love of him you once were."

He was about to speak; but with her head turned from him, she resumed.

"You may—the memory of what is past half makes me hope you will—have pain in this. A very, very brief time, and you will dismiss the recollection of it, gladly, as an unprofitable dream, from which it happened well that you awoke. May you be happy in the life you have chosen!"

She left him, and they parted.

"Spirit!" said Scrooge, "show me no more! Conduct me home. Why do you delight to torture me?"

"One shadow more!" exclaimed the Ghost.

"No more!" cried Scrooge. "No more. I don't wish to see it. Show me no more!"

But the relentless Ghost pinioned him in both his arms, and forced him to observe what happened next.

They were in another scene and place; a room, not very large or handsome, but full of comfort. Near to the winter fire sat a beautiful young girl, so like the last that Scrooge believed it was the same, until he saw *her,* now a comely matron, sitting opposite her daughter. The noise in this room was perfectly tumultuous, for there were more children there, than Scrooge in his agitated state of mind could count; and, unlike the celebrated herd in the poem, they were not forty children conducting themselves like one, but every child was conducting itself like forty. The consequences were uproarious beyond belief; but no one seemed to care; on the contrary, the mother and daughter laughed heartily, and enjoyed it very much; and the latter, soon beginning to mingle in the sports, got pillaged by the young brigands most ruthlessly. What would I not have given to be one of them! Though I never could have been so rude, no, no! I would n't for the wealth of all the world have crushed that braided hair, and torn it down; and as for the precious little shoe, I would n't have plucked it off, God bless my soul! to save my life. As to measuring her waist in sport, as they did, bold young brood, I could n't have done it; I should have expected my arm to have grown round it for a punishment, and never come straight again. And yet I should have dearly liked, I own, to have touched her lips; to have questioned her, that she might have opened them; to have looked upon the lashes of her downcast eyes, and never raised a blush; to have let loose waves of hair, an inch of which would be a keepsake beyond price: in short, I should have liked, I do confess, to have had the lightest license of a child, and yet been man enough to know its value.

But now a knocking at the door was heard, and such a rush immediately ensued that she with laughing face and plundered dress was borne toward it, the center of a flushed and boisterous group, just in time to greet the father, who came home attended by a man laden with Christmas toys and presents. Then the shouting and the struggling, and the onslaught that was made on the defenseless porter! The scaling him with chairs for ladders to dive into his pockets, despoil him of brown-paper parcels, hold on tight by his cravat, hug him round the neck, pummel his back, and kick his legs in irrepressible affection. The shouts of wonder and delight with which the development of every package was received! The terrible announcement that the baby had been taken in the act of putting a doll's frying pan into his mouth, and was more than suspected of having swallowed a fictitious turkey, glued on a wooden platter! The immense relief of finding this a false alarm! The joy, and gratitude, and ecstasy! They are all indescribable alike. It is enough that by degrees the children and their emotions got out of the parlor and by one stair at a time, up to the top of the house; where they went to bed, and so subsided.

And now Scrooge looked on more attentively than ever, when the master of the house, having his daughter leaning fondly on him, sat down with her and her mother at his own fireside; and when he thought that such another creature, quite as graceful and as full of promise, might have called him father, and been a spring-time in the haggard winter of his life, his sight grew very dim indeed.

"Belle," said the husband, turning to his wife with a smile, "I saw an old friend of yours this afternoon."

"Who was it?"

"Guess!"

"How can I? Tut, don't I know?" she added in the same breath, laughing as he laughed. "Mr. Scrooge."

"Mr. Scrooge it was. I passed his office window; and as it was not shut up, and he had a candle inside, I could scarcely help seeing him. His partner lies upon the point of death, I hear; and there he sat alone. Quite alone in the world, I do believe."

"Spirit!" said Scrooge in a broken voice, "remove me from this place."

"I told you these were shadows of the things that have been," said the Ghost. "That they are what they are, do not blame me!"

"Remove me!" Scrooge exclaimed, "I cannot bear it!"

He turned upon the Ghost, and seeing that it looked upon him with a face, in which in some strange way there were fragments of all the faces it had shown him, wrestled with it.

"Leave me! Take me back. Haunt me no longer!"

In the struggle, if that can be called a struggle in which the Ghost with no visible resistance on its own part was undisturbed by any effort of its adversary, Scrooge observed that its light was burning high and bright; and dimly connecting that with its influence over him, he seized the extinguisher-cap, and by a sudden action pressed it down upon his head.

The Spirit dropped beneath it, so that the extinguisher covered its whole form; but though Scrooge pressed it down with all his force, he could not hide the light, which streamed from under it, in an unbroken flood upon the ground.

He was conscious of being exhausted, and overcome by an irresistible drowsiness; and, further, of being in his own bedroom. He gave the cap a parting squeeze, in which his hand relaxed; and had barely time to reel to bed, before he sank into a heavy slumber.

STAVE THREE:

THE SECOND OF

THE THREE SPIRITS

Awaking in the middle of a prodigiously tough snore, and sitting up in bed to get his thoughts together, Scrooge had no occasion to be told that the bell was again upon the stroke of One. He felt that he was restored to consciousness in the right nick of time, for the especial purpose of holding a conference with the second messenger despatched to him through Jacob Marley's intervention. But, finding that he turned uncomfortably cold when he began to wonder which of his curtains this new specter would draw back, he put them every one aside with his own hands, and lying down again, established a sharp lookout all round the bed. For he wished to challenge the Spirit on the moment of its appearance, and did not wish to be taken by surprise and made nervous.

Gentlemen of the free-and-easy sort, who plume themselves on being acquainted with a move or two, and being usually equal to the time-of-day, express the wide range of their capacity for adventure by observing that they are good for anything from pitch-and-toss to manslaughter; between which opposite extremes, no doubt, there lies a tolerably wide and comprehensive range of subjects. Without venturing for Scrooge quite as hardily as this, I don't mind calling on you to believe that he was ready for a good broad field of strange appearances, and that nothing between a baby and a rhinoceros would have astonished him very much.

Now, being prepared for almost anything, he was not by any means prepared for nothing; and, consequently, when the Bell struck One, and no shape appeared, he was taken with a violent fit of trembling. Five minutes, ten minutes, a quarter of an hour went by, yet nothing came. All this time, he lay upon his bed, the very core and center of a blaze of ruddy light, which streamed upon it when the clock proclaimed the hour; and which, being only light, was more alarming than a dozen ghosts, as he was powerless to make out what it meant, or would be at; and was sometimes apprehensive that he might be at that very moment an interesting case of spontaneous combustion, without having the consolation of knowing it. At last, however, he began to think—as you or I would have thought at first; for it is always the person not in the predicament who knows what ought to have been done in it, and would unquestionably have done it too— at last, I say, he began to think that the source and secret of this ghostly light might be in the adjoining room, from whence, on further tracing it, it seemed to shine. This idea taking full possession of his mind, he got up softly and shuffled his slippers to the door.

The moment Scrooge's hand was on the lock, a strange voice called him by his name, and bade him enter. He obeyed.

It was his own room. There was no doubt about that. But it had undergone a surprising transformation. The walls and ceiling were so hung with living green, that it looked like a perfect grove, from every part of which, bright gleaming berries glistened. The crisp leaves of holly, mistletoe, and ivy reflected back the light, as if so many little mirrors had been scattered there; and such a mighty blaze went roaring up the chimney, as that dull petrifaction of a hearth had never known in Scrooge's time, or Marley's, or for many and many a winter season gone. Heaped up on the floor, to form a kind of throne, were turkeys, geese, game, poultry, brawn, great joints of meat, sucking-pigs, long wreaths of sausages, mince pies, plum puddings, barrels of oysters, red-hot chestnuts, cherry-cheeked apples, juicy oranges, luscious pears, immense twelfth-cakes, and seething bowls of punch, that made the chamber dim with their delicious steam. In easy state upon this couch, there sat a jolly Giant, glorious to see; who bore a glowing torch, in shape not unlike Plenty's horn, and held it up, high up, to shed its light on Scrooge, as he came peeping round the door.

"Come in!" exclaimed the Ghost. "Come in! and know me better, man!"

Scrooge entered timidly, and hung his head before this Spirit. He was not the dogged Scrooge he had been; and though the Spirit's eyes were clear and kind, he did not like to meet them.

"I am the Ghost of Christmas Present," said the Spirit. "Look upon me!"

Scrooge reverently did so. It was clothed in one simple deep green robe, or mantle, bordered with white fur. This garment hung so loosely on the figure, that its capacious breast was bare, as if disdaining to be warded or concealed by any artifice. Its feet, observable beneath the ample folds of the garment, were also bare; and on its head it wore no other covering than a holly wreath set here and there with shining icicles. Its dark brown curls were long and free; free as its genial face, its sparkling eyes, its open hand, its cheery voice, its unconstrained demeanor, and its joyful air. Girded round its middle was an antique scabbard; but no sword was in it, and the ancient sheath was eaten up with rust.

"You have never seen the like of me before!" exclaimed the Spirit.

"Never," Scrooge made answer to it.

"Have never walked forth with the younger members of my fam-

Scrooge's third visitor.

ily; meaning (for I am very young) my dear elder brothers born in these later years?" pursued the Phantom.

"I don't think I have," said Scrooge. "I am afraid I have not. Have you had many brothers, Spirit?"

"More than eighteen hundred," said the Ghost.

"A tremendous family to provide for!" muttered Scrooge.

The Ghost of Christmas Present rose.

"Spirit," said Scrooge, submissively, "conduct me where you will. I went forth last night on compulsion, and I learnt a lesson which is working now. Tonight, if you have aught to teach me, let me profit by it."

"Touch my robe!"

Scrooge did as he was told, and held it fast.

Holly, mistletoe, red berries, ivy, turkeys, geese, game, poultry, brawn, meat, pigs, sausages, oysters, pies, puddings, fruit, and punch, all vanished instantly. So did the room, the fire, the ruddy glow, the hour of night, and they stood in the city streets on Christmas morning, where (for the weather was severe) the people made a rough, but brisk and not unpleasant kind of music, in scraping the snow from the pavement in front of their dwellings, and from the tops of their houses; whence it was mad delight to the boys to see it come plumping down into the road below, and splitting into artificial little snowstorms.

The house fronts looked black enough, and the windows blacker, contrasting with the smooth white sheet of snow upon the roofs, and with the dirtier snow upon the ground; which last deposit had been plowed up in deep furrows by the heavy wheels of carts and wagons; furrows that crossed and recrossed each other hundreds of times where the great streets branched off, and made intricate channels, hard to trace, in the thick yellow mud and icy water. The sky was gloomy, and the shortest streets were choked up with a dingy mist, half thawed, half frozen, whose heavier particles descended in a shower of sooty atoms, as if all the chimneys in Great Britain had, by one consent, caught fire, and were blazing away to their dear hearts' content. There was nothing very cheerful in the climate or the town, and yet was there an air of cheerfulness abroad that the clearest summer air and brightest summer sun might have endeavored to diffuse in vain.

For, the people who were shoveling away on the house tops were jovial and full of glee; calling out to one another from the parapets, and now and then exchanging a facetious snowball—better-natured missile far than many a wordy jest—laughing heartily if it went right and not less heartily if it went wrong. The poulterers' shops were still half open, and the fruiterers' were radiant in their glory. There were great, round, pot-bellied baskets of chestnuts, shaped like the waistcoats of jolly old gentlemen, lolling at the doors, and tumbling out into the street in their apoplectic opulence. There were ruddy, brown-faced, broad-girthed Spanish Onions, shining in the fatness of their growth like Spanish Friars; and winking from their shelves in wanton slyness at the girls as they went by, and glanced demurely at the hung-up mistletoe. There were pears and apples, clustered high in blooming pyramids; there were bunches of grapes, made, in the shopkeepers' benevolence, to dangle from conspicuous hooks, that people's mouths might water gratis as they passed; there were piles of filberts, mossy and brown, recalling, in their fragrance, ancient walks among the woods, and pleasant shufflings ankle deep through withered leaves; there were Norfolk Biffins, squab, and swarthy, setting off the yellow of the oranges and lemons, and, in the great compactness of their juicy persons, urgently entreating and beseeching to be carried home in paper bags and eaten after dinner.

445

The very gold and silver fish, set forth among these choice fruits in a bowl, though members of a dull and stagnant-blooded race, appeared to know that there was something going on; and, to a fish, went gasping round and round their little world in slow and passionless excitement.

The Grocers'! oh, the Grocers'! nearly closed, with perhaps two shutters down, or one; but through those gaps such glimpses! It was not alone that the scales descending on the counter made a merry sound, or that the twine and roller parted company so briskly, or that the canisters were rattled up and down like juggling tricks, or even that the blended scents of tea and coffee were so grateful to the nose, or even that the raisins were so plentiful and rare, the almonds so extremely white, the sticks of cinnamon so long and straight, the other spices so delicious, the candied fruits so caked and spotted with molten sugar as to make the coldest lookers-on feel faint and subsequently bilious. Nor was it that the figs were moist and pulpy, or that the French plums blushed in modest tartness from their highly-decorated boxes, or that everything was good to eat and in its Christmas dress: but the customers were all so hurried and so eager in the hopeful promise of the day, that they tumbled up against each other at the door, clashing their wicker baskets wildly, and left their purchases upon the counter, and came running back to fetch them, and committed hundreds of the like mistakes in the best humor possible; while the Grocer and his people were so frank and fresh that the polished hearts with which they fastened their aprons behind might have been their own, worn outside for general inspection, and for Christmas daws to peck at if they chose.

But soon the steeples called good people all, to church and chapel, and away they came, flocking through the streets in their best clothes, and with their gayest faces. And at the same time there emerged from scores of by-streets, lanes, and nameless turnings, innumerable people, carrying their dinners to the bakers' shops. The sight of these poor revelers appeared to interest the Spirit very much, for he stood with Scrooge beside him in a baker's doorway, and taking off the covers as their bearers passed, sprinkled incense on their dinners from his torch. And it was a very uncommon kind of torch, for once or twice when there were angry words between some dinner carriers who had jostled with each other, he shed a few drops of water on them from it, and their good humor was restored directly. For they said, it was a shame to quarrel upon Christmas Day. And so it was! God love it, so it was!

In time the bells ceased, and the bakers were shut up; and yet there was a genial shadowing forth of all these dinners and the progress of their cooking, in the thawed blotch of wet above each baker's oven; where the pavement smoked as if its stones were cooking, too.

"Is there a peculiar flavor in what you sprinkle from your torch?" asked Scrooge.

"There is. My own."

"Would it apply to any kind of dinner on this day?" asked Scrooge.

"To any kindly given. To a poor one most."

"Why to a poor one most?" asked Scrooge.

"Because it needs it most."

"Spirit," said Scrooge, after a moment's thought, "I wonder you, of all the beings in the many worlds about us, should desire to cramp these people's opportunities of innocent enjoyment."

"I!" cried the Spirit.

"You would deprive them of their means of dining every seventh day, often the only day on which they can be said to dine at all," said Scrooge. "Would n't you?"

"I!" cried the Spirit.

"You seek to close these places on the Seventh day?" said Scrooge. "And it comes to the same thing."

"*I* seek!" exclaimed the Spirit.

"Forgive me if I am wrong. It has been done in your name, or at least in that of your family," said Scrooge.

"There are some upon this earth of yours," returned the Spirit, "who lay claim to know us, and who do their deeds of passion, pride, ill-will, hatred, envy, bigotry, and selfishness in our name, who are as strange to us and all our kith and kin, as if they had never lived. Remember that, and charge their doings on themselves, not us."

Scrooge promised that he would; and they went on, invisible, as they had been before, into the suburbs of the town. It was a remarkable quality of the Ghost (which Scrooge had observed at the baker's), that notwithstanding his gigantic size, he could accommodate himself to any place with ease; and that he stood beneath a low roof quite as gracefully and like a supernatural creature, as it was possible he could have done in any lofty hall.

And perhaps it was the pleasure the good Spirit had in showing off this power of his, or else it was his own kind, generous, hearty nature, and his sympathy with all poor men, that led him straight to Scrooge's clerk's; for there he went, and took Scrooge with him, holding to his robe; and on the threshold of the door the Spirit smiled, and stopped to bless Bob Cratchit's dwelling with the sprinklings of his torch. Think of that! Bob had but fifteen "Bob" a week himself; he pocketed on Saturdays but fifteen copies of his Christian name; and yet the Ghost of Christmas Present blessed his four-roomed house!

Then up rose Mrs. Cratchit, Cratchit's wife, dressed out but poorly in a twice-turned gown, but brave in ribbons, which are cheap and make a goodly show for sixpence; and she laid the cloth, assisted by

Belinda Cratchit, second of her daughters, also brave in ribbons; while Master Peter Cratchit plunged a fork into the saucepan of potatoes, and getting the corners of his monstrous shirt collar (Bob's private property, conferred upon his son and heir in honor of the day) into his mouth, rejoiced to find himself so gallantly attired, and yearned to show his linen in the fashionable Parks. And now two smaller Cratchits, boy and girl, came tearing in, screaming that outside the baker's they had smelt the goose, and known it for their own; and basking in luxurious thoughts of sage-and-onion, these young Cratchits danced about the table, and exalted Master Peter Cratchit to the skies, while he (not proud, although his collars nearly choked him) blew the fire, until the slow potatoes bubbling up, knocked loudly at the saucepan-lid to be let out and peeled.

"What has ever got your precious father then?" said Mrs. Cratchit. "And your brother, Tiny Tim! And Martha warn't as late last Christmas Day by half-an-hour!"

"Here's Martha, Mother!" said a girl, appearing as she spoke.

"Here's Martha, Mother!" cried the two young Cratchits. "Hurrah! There's *such* a goose, Martha!"

"Why, bless your heart alive, my dear, how late you are!" said Mrs. Cratchit, kissing her a dozen times, and taking off her shawl and bonnet for her with officious zeal.

"We'd a deal of work to finish up last night," replied the girl, "and had to clear away this morning, mother!"

"Well! Never mind so long as you are come," said Mrs. Cratchit.

"Sit ye down before the fire, my dear, and have a warm, Lord bless ye!"

"No, no! There's father coming," cried the two young Cratchits, who were everywhere at once. "Hide, Martha, hide!"

So Martha hid herself, and in came little Bob, the father, with at least three feet of comforter exclusive of the fringe, hanging down before him; and his threadbare clothes darned up and brushed, to look seasonable; and Tiny Tim upon his shoulder. Alas for Tiny Tim, he bore a little crutch, and had his limbs supported by an iron frame!

"Why, where's our Martha?" cried Bob Cratchit, looking round.

"Not coming," said Mrs. Cratchit.

"Not coming!" said Bob, with a sudden declension in his high spirits; for he had been Tim's blood horse all the way from church, and had come home rampant. "Not coming upon Christmas Day!"

Martha didn't like to see him disappointed, if it were only in joke; so she came out prematurely from behind the closet door, and ran into his arms, while the two young Cratchits hustled Tiny Tim, and bore him off into the washhouse, that he might hear the pudding singing in the copper.

"And how did little Tim behave?" asked Mrs. Cratchit, when she had rallied Bob on his credulity, and Bob had hugged his daughter to his heart's content.

"As good as gold," said Bob, "and better. Somehow he gets thoughtful, sitting by himself so much, and thinks the strangest things you ever heard. He told me, coming home, that he hoped the people saw him in the church, because he was a cripple, and it might be pleasant to them to remember upon Christmas Day, who made lame beggars walk and blind men see."

Bob's voice was tremulous when he told them this, and trembled more when he said that Tiny Tim was growing strong and hearty.

His active little crutch was heard upon the floor, and back came Tiny Tim before another word was spoken, escorted by his brother and sister to his stool before the fire; and while Bob, turning up his cuffs—as if, poor fellow, they were capable of being made more shabby—compounded some hot mixture in a jug with gin and lemons, and stirred it round and round and put it on the hob to simmer; Master Peter, and the two ubiquitous young Cratchits went to fetch the goose, with which they soon returned in high procession.

Such a bustle ensued that you might have thought a goose the rarest of all birds; a feathered phenomenon, to which a black swan was a matter of course—and in truth it was something very like it in that house. Mrs. Cratchit made the gravy (ready beforehand in a little saucepan) hissing hot; Master Peter mashed the potatoes with incredible vigor; Miss Belinda sweetened up the apple sauce; Martha dusted the hot plates; Bob took Tiny Tim beside him in a tiny corner at the table; the two young Cratchits set chairs for everybody, not forgetting themselves, and mounting guard upon their posts, crammed spoons into their mouths, lest they should shriek for goose before their turn came to be helped. At last the dishes were set on, and grace was said. It was succeeded by a breathless pause, as Mrs. Cratchit, looking slowly all along the carving-knife, prepared to plunge it in the breast; but when she did, and when the long expected gush of stuffing issued forth, one murmur of delight arose all around the board, and even Tiny Tim, excited by the two young Cratchits, beat on the table with the handle of his knife, and feebly cried Hurrah!

There never was such a goose. Bob said he didn't believe there ever was such a goose cooked. Its tenderness and flavor, size and cheapness, were the themes of universal admiration. Eked out by the apple sauce and mashed potatoes, it was a sufficient dinner for the whole family; indeed, as Mrs. Cratchit said with great delight (surveying one small atom of a bone upon the dish), they had n't ate it all at last! Yet everyone had had enough, and the youngest Cratchits in particular were steeped in sage and onion to the eyebrows! But now, the plates being changed by Miss Belinda, Mrs. Cratchit left the room alone—too nervous to bear witnesses—to take the pudding up and bring it in.

Suppose it should not be done enough! Suppose it should break in turning out! Suppose somebody should have got over the wall of the back yard, and stolen it, while they were merry with the goose —a supposition at which the two young Cratchits became livid! All sorts of horrors were supposed.

Hallo! A great deal of steam! The pudding was out of the copper. A smell like a washing day! That was the cloth. A smell like an eating house and a pastry cook's next door to each other, with a laundress next door to that! That was the pudding! In half a minute Mrs. Cratchit entered—flushed, but smiling proudly—with the pudding, like a speckled cannon ball, so hard and firm, blazing in half of half-a-quartern of ignited brandy, and bedight with Christmas holly stuck into the top.

Oh, a wonderful pudding! Bob Cratchit said, and calmly, too, that he regarded it as the greatest success achieved by Mrs. Cratchit since their marriage. Mrs. Cratchit said that now the weight was off her mind, she would confess she had had her doubts about the quantity of flour. Everybody had something to say about it, but nobody said or thought it was at all a small pudding for a large family. It would have been flat heresy to do so. Any Cratchit would have blushed to hint at such a thing.

At last the dinner was all done, the cloth was cleared, the hearth swept, and the fire made up. The compound in the jug being tasted, and considered perfect, apples and oranges were put upon the table, and a shovelful of chestnuts on the fire. Then all the Cratchit family drew around the hearth, in what Bob Cratchit called a circle, meaning half a one; and at Bob Cratchit's elbow stood the family display of glass. Two tumblers and a custard cup without a handle.

These held the hot stuff from the jug, however, as well as golden goblets would have done; and Bob served it out with beaming looks, while the chestnuts on the fire sputtered and cracked noisily. Then Bob proposed:

"A Merry Christmas to us all, my dears. God bless us!"

Which all the family re-echoed.

"God bless us every one!" said Tiny Tim, the last of all.

He sat very close to his father's side upon his little stool. Bob held his withered little hand in his, as if he loved the child, and wished to keep him by his side, and dreaded that he might be taken from him.

"Spirit," said Scrooge, with an interest he had never felt before, "tell me if Tiny Tim will live."

"I see a vacant seat," replied the Ghost, "in the poor chimney corner, and a crutch without an owner, carefully preserved. If these shadows remain unaltered by the Future, the child will die."

"No, no," said Scrooge. "Oh, no, kind Spirit! say he will be spared."

"If these shadows remain unaltered by the Future, none other of my race," returned the Ghost, "will find him here. What then? If he be like to die, he had better do it, and decrease the surplus population."

Scrooge hung his head to hear his own words quoted by the Spirit, and was overcome with penitence and grief.

"Man," said the Ghost, "if man you be in heart, not adamant, forbear that wicked cant until you have discovered What the surplus is, and Where it is. Will you decide what men shall live, what men shall die? It may be, that in the sight of Heaven, you are more worthless and less fit to live than millions like this poor man's child. O God! to hear the Insect on the leaf pronouncing on the too much life among his hungry brothers in the dust!"

Scrooge bent before the Ghost's rebuke, and trembling cast his eyes upon the ground. But he raised them speedily, on hearing his own name.

"Mr. Scrooge!" said Bob; "I'll give you Mr. Scrooge, the Founder of the Feast!"

"The Founder of the Feast indeed!" cried Mrs. Cratchit, reddening. "I wish I had him here. I'd give him a piece of my mind to feast upon, and I hope he'd have a good appetite for it."

"My dear," said Bob, "the children! Christmas Day."

"It should be Christmas Day, I am sure," said she, "on which one drinks the health of such an odious, stingy, hard, unfeeling man as Mr. Scrooge. You know he is, Robert. Nobody knows it better than you do, poor fellow!"

"My dear," was Bob's mild answer, "Christmas Day."

"I'll drink his health for your sake and the Day's," said Mrs. Cratchit, "not for his. Long life to him! A Merry Christmas and a Happy New Year! He'll be very merry and happy, I have no doubt!"

The children drank the toast after her. It was the first of their proceedings which had no heartiness in it. Tiny Tim drank it last of all, but he didn't care twopence for it. Scrooge was the Ogre of the family. The mention of his name cast a dark shadow on the party, which was not dispelled for full five minutes.

After it had passed away, they were ten times merrier than before, from the mere relief of Scrooge the Baleful being done with. Bob Cratchit told them how he had a situation in his eye for Master Peter, which would bring in, if obtained, full five-and-sixpence weekly. The two young Cratchits laughed tremendously at the idea of Peter's being a man of business; and Peter himself looked thoughtfully at the fire from between his collars, as if he were deliberating what particular investments he should favor when he came into the receipt of that bewildering income. Martha, who was a poor apprentice at a milliner's, then told them what kind of work she had to do, and how many hours she worked at a stretch, and how she meant to lie abed tomorrow morning for a good long rest; tomorrow being a holiday she passed at home. Also how she had seen a countess and a lord some days before, and how the lord "was much about as tall as Peter"; at which Peter pulled up his collars so high that you couldn't have seen his head if you had been there. All this time the chestnuts and the jug went round and round; and by-and-by they had a song, about a lost child traveling in the snow, from Tiny Tim, who had a plaintive little voice, and sang it very well indeed.

There was nothing of high mark in this. They were not a handsome family; they were not well-dressed; their shoes were far from being waterproof; their clothes were scanty; and Peter might have known, and very likely did, the inside of a pawnbroker's. But, they were happy, grateful, pleased with one another, and contented with the time; and when they faded, and looked happier yet in the bright sprinklings of the Spirit's torch at parting, Scrooge had his eye upon them, and especially on Tiny Tim, until the last.

By this time it was getting dark, and snowing pretty heavily; and as Scrooge and the Spirit went along the streets, the brightness of the roaring fires in kitchens, parlors, and all sorts of rooms, was wonderful. Here, the flickering of the blaze showed preparations for a cozy dinner, with hot plates baking through and through before the fire, and deep red curtains, ready to be drawn to shut out cold and darkness. There, all the children of the house were running out into the snow to meet their married sisters, brothers, cousins, uncles, aunts, and be the first to greet them. Here, again, were shadows on the window blind of guests assembling; and there a group of handsome girls, all hooded and furbooted, and all chattering at once, tripped lightly off to some near neighbor's house, where, woe upon the single man who saw them enter—artful witches; well they knew it—in a glow!

But if you had judged from the numbers of people on their way to friendly gatherings, you might have thought that no one was at home to give them welcome when they got there, instead of every house expecting company, and piling up its fires half-chimney high. Blessings on it, how the Ghost exulted! How it bared its breadth of breast, and opened its capacious palm, and floated on, outpouring, with a generous hand, its bright and harmless mirth on everything within its reach! The very lamplighter, who ran on before dotting the dusky street with specks of light, and who was dressed to spend the evening somewhere, laughed out loudly as the Spirit passed: though little kenned the lamplighter that he had any company but Christmas.

And now, without a word of warning from the Ghost, they stood upon a bleak and desert moor, where monstrous masses of rude stone were cast about, as though it were the burial place of giants; and water spread itself wheresoever it listed, or would have done so, but for the frost that held it prisoner; and nothing grew but moss and furze, and coarse, rank grass. Down in the west the setting sun had left a streak of fiery red, which glared upon the desolation for an instant, like a sullen eye, and frowning lower, lower, lower yet, was lost in the thick gloom of darkest night.

"What place is this?" asked Scrooge.

"A place where Miners live, who labor in the bowels of the earth," returned the Spirit. "But they know me. See!"

A light shone from the window of a hut, and swiftly they advanced toward it. Passing through the wall of mud and stone, they found a cheerful company assembled round a glowing fire. An old, old man and woman, with their children and their children's children, and another generation beyond that, all decked out gayly in their holiday attire. The old man, in a voice that seldom rose above the howling of the wind upon the barren waste, was singing them a Christmas song; it had been a very old song when he was a boy; and from time to time they all joined in the chorus. So surely as they raised their voices, the old man got quite blithe and loud; and so surely as they stopped, his vigor sank again.

The Spirit did not tarry here, but bade Scrooge hold his robe, and passing on above the moor, sped whither? Not to sea? To sea. To Scrooge's horror, looking back, he saw the last of the land, a frightful range of rocks, behind them; and his ears were deafened by the thundering of water, as it rolled, and roared, and raged among the dreadful caverns it had worn, and fiercely tried to undermine the earth.

Built upon a dismal reef of sunken rocks, some league or so from shore, on which the waters chafed and dashed, the wild year through, there stood a solitary lighthouse. Great heaps of seaweed clung to its base, and storm birds—born of the wind one might suppose, as seaweed of the water—rose and fell about it, like the waves they skimmed.

But even here, two men who watched the light had made a fire, that through the loophole in the thick stone wall shed out a ray of brightness on the awful sea. Joining their horny hands over the rough table at which they sat, they wished each other Merry Christmas in their can of grog; and one of them, the elder, too, with his face all damaged and scarred with hard weather, as the figure head of an old ship might be: struck up a sturdy song that was like a Gale in itself.

Again the Ghost sped on, above the black and heaving sea—on, on—until, being far away, as he told Scrooge, from any shore, they lighted on a ship. They stood beside the helmsman at the wheel, the lookout in the bow, the officers who had the watch; dark, ghostly figures in their several stations; but every man among them hummed a Christmas tune, or had a Christmas thought, or spoke below his breath to his companion of some bygone Christmas Day, with homeward hopes belonging to it. And every man on board, walking or sleeping, good or bad, had had a kinder word for another on that day than on any day in the year; and had shared to some extent in its festivities; and had remembered those he cared for at a distance, and had known that they delighted to remember him.

It was a great surprise to Scrooge, while listening to the moaning of the wind, and thinking what a solemn thing it was to move on through the lonely darkness over an unknown abyss, whose depths were secrets as profound as Death: it was a great surprise to Scrooge, while thus engaged, to hear a hearty laugh. It was a much greater surprise to Scrooge to recognize it as his own nephew's and to find himself in a bright, dry, gleaming room, with the Spirit standing smiling by his side, and looking at that same nephew with approving affability.

"Ha, ha!" laughed Scrooge's nephew. "Ha ha, ha!"

If you should happen, by any unlikely chance, to know a man more blest in a laugh than Scrooge's nephew, all I can say is, I should like to know him, too. Introduce him to me, and I'll cultivate his acquaintance.

It is a fair, even-handed, noble adjustment of things, that while there is infection in disease and sorrow, there is nothing in the world so irresistibly contagious as laughter and good humor. When Scrooge's nephew laughed in this way: holding his sides, rolling his head, and twisting his face into the most extravagant contortions: Scrooge's niece, by marriage, laughed as heartily as he. And their assembled friends being not a bit behindhand, roared out, lustily.

"Ha, ha! Ha, ha, ha, ha!"

"He said that Christmas was a humbug, as I live!" cried Scrooge's nephew. "He believed it, too!"

"More shame for him, Fred!" said Scrooge's niece, indignantly. Bless those women; they never do anything by halves. They are always in earnest.

She was very pretty: exceedingly pretty. With a dimpled, surprised-looking, capital face; a ripe little mouth, that seemed made to be kissed—as no doubt it was; all kinds of good little dots about her chin, that melted into one another when she laughed; and the sunniest pair of eyes you ever saw in any little creature's head. Altogether she was what you would have called provoking, you know; but satisfactory, too. Oh, perfectly satisfactory!

"He's a comical old fellow," said Scrooge's nephew, "that's the truth; and not so pleasant as he might be. However, his offenses carry their own punishment, and I have nothing to say against him."

"I'm sure he is very rich, Fred," hinted Scrooge's niece. "At least you always tell me so."

"What of that, my dear!" said Scrooge's nephew. "His wealth is of no use to him. He don't do any good with it. He don't make himself comfortable with it. He hasn't the satisfaction of thinking—ha, ha, ha!—that he is ever going to benefit Us with it."

"I have no patience with him," observed Scrooge's niece. Scrooge's niece's sisters, and all the other ladies, expressed the same opinion.

"Oh, I have!" said Scrooge's nephew. "I am sorry for him; I couldn't be angry with him if I tried. Who suffers by his ill whims? Himself, always. Here, he takes it into his head to dislike us, and he won't come and dine with us. What's the consequence? He don't lose much of a dinner."

"Indeed, I think he loses a very good dinner," interrupted Scrooge's niece. Everybody else said the same, and they must be allowed to have been competent judges, because they had just had dinner; and, with the dessert upon the table, were clustered around the fire, by lamplight.

"Well! I'm very glad to hear it," said Scrooge's nephew, "because I haven't any great faith in these young housekeepers. What do *you* say, Topper?"

Topper had clearly got his eyes upon one of Scrooge's niece's sisters, for he answered that a bachelor was a wretched outcast, who had no right to express an opinion on the subject. Whereat Scrooge's niece's sister—the plump one with the lace tucker: not the one with the roses—blushed.

"Do go on, Fred," said Scrooge's niece, clapping her hands. "He never finishes what he begins to say! He is such a ridiculous fellow!"

Scrooge's nephew reveled in another laugh, and as it was impossible to keep the infection off; though the plump sister tried hard to do it with aromatic vinegar; his example was unanimously followed.

"I was only going to say," said Scrooge's nephew, "that the consequence of his taking a dislike to us, and not making merry with us, is, as I think, that he loses some pleasant moments, which could do him no harm. I am sure he loses pleasanter companions than he can find in his own thoughts, either in his moldy old office, or his dusty chambers. I mean to give him the same chance every year, whether he likes it or not, for I pity him. He may rail at Christmas till he dies, but he can't help thinking better of it—I defy him—if he finds me going there, in good temper, year after year, and saying 'Uncle Scrooge, how are you?' If it only puts him in the vein to leave his poor clerk fifty pounds, *that's* something; and I think I shook him yesterday."

It was their turn to laugh now at the notion of his shaking Scrooge. But being thoroughly good-natured, and not much caring what they laughed at, so that they laughed at any rate, he encouraged them in their merriment, and passed the bottle joyously.

After tea, they had some music. For they were a musical family, and knew what they were about, when they sang a Glee or Catch, I can assure you: especially Topper, who could growl away in the bass like a good one, and never swell the large veins in his forehead, or get red in the face over it. Scrooge's niece played well upon the harp; and played among other tunes a simple little air (a mere nothing: you might learn to whistle it in two minutes), which had been familiar to the child who fetched Scrooge from the boarding-school, as he had been reminded by the Ghost of Christmas Past. When this strain of music sounded, all the things that Ghost had shown him, came upon his mind; he softened more and more; and thought that if he could have listened to it often, years ago, he might have cultivated the kindnesses of life for his own happiness with his own hands, without resorting to the sexton's spade that buried Jacob Marley.

But they didn't devote the whole evening to music. After a while they played at forfeits; for it is good to be children sometimes, and never better than at Christmas, when its mighty Founder was a child himself. Stop! There was first a game at blind-man's buff. Of course there was. And I no more believe Topper was really blind than I believe he had eyes in his boots. My opinion is, that it was a done thing between him and Scrooge's nephew: and that the Ghost of Christmas Present knew it. The way he went after that plump sister in the lace tucker, was an outrage on the credulity of human nature. Knocking down the fire irons, tumbling over the chairs, bumping up against the piano, smothering himself among the curtains, wherever she went, there went he. He always knew where the plump sister was. He wouldn't catch anybody else. If you had fallen up against him, as some of them did, and stood there; he would have made a feint of endeavoring to seize you, which would have been an affront to your understanding; and would instantly have sidled off in the direction of the plump sister. She often cried out that it wasn't fair and it really was not. But when at last, he caught her; when, in spite of all her silken rustlings, and her rapid flutterings past him, he got her into a corner whence there was no escape; then his conduct was the most execrable. For his pretending not to know her; his pretending that it was necessary to touch her headdress, and further to assure himself of her identity by pressing a certain ring upon her finger, and a certain chain about her neck; was vile, monstrous! No doubt she told him her opinion of it, when, another blind man being in office, they were so very confidential together, behind the curtains.

Scrooge's niece was not one of the blind-man's buff party, but was made comfortable with a large chair and a footstool, in a snug corner, where the Ghost and Scrooge were close behind her. But she joined in the forfeits, and loved her love to admiration with all the letters of the alphabet. Likewise at the game of How, When and Where, she was very great, and to the secret joy of Scrooge's nephew, beat her sisters hollow: though they were sharp girls, too, as Topper could have told you. There might have been twenty people there, young and old, but they all played, and so did Scrooge; for, wholly forgetting in the interest he had in what was going on, that his voice made no sound in their ears, he sometimes came out with his guess quite loud, and very often guessed quite right, too; for the sharpest needle, best Whitechapel, warranted not to cut in the eye, was not sharper than Scrooge: blunt as he took it in his head to be.

The Ghost was greatly pleased to find him in this mood, and looked upon him with such favor, that he begged like a boy to be allowed to stay until the guests departed. But this the Spirit said could not be done.

"Here is a new game," said Scrooge. "One half-hour, Spirit, only one!"

It is a Game called Yes and No, where Scrooge's nephew had to think of something, and the rest must find out what; he only answering to their questions yes or no, as the case was. The brisk fire of questioning to which he was exposed, elicited from him that he was thinking of an animal, a live animal, rather a disagreeable animal, a savage animal, an animal that growled and grunted sometimes, and talked sometimes, and lived in London, and walked about the streets, and wasn't made a show of, and wasn't led by anybody, and didn't live in a menagerie, and was never killed in a market, and was not a horse, or an ass, or a cow, or a bull, or a tiger, or a dog, or a pig, or a cat, or a bear. At every fresh question that was put to him, this nephew burst into a fresh roar of laughter; and was so inexpressibly tickled, that he was obliged to get up off the sofa and stamp. At last the plump sister, falling into a similar state, cried out:

"I have found it out! I know what it is, Fred! I know what it is!"

"What is it?" cried Fred.

"It's your Uncle Scro-o-o-o-oge!"

Which it certainly was. Admiration was the universal sentiment, though some objected that the reply to "Is it a bear?" ought to have been "Yes"; inasmuch as an answer in the negative was sufficient to have diverted their thoughts from Mr. Scrooge, supposing they had ever had any tendency that way.

"He has given us plenty of merriment, I am sure," said Fred, "and it would be ungrateful not to drink his health. Here is a glass of mulled wine ready to our hand at the moment; and I say, 'Uncle Scrooge!'"

"Well! Uncle Scrooge!" they cried.

"A Merry Christmas and a Happy New Year to the old man, whatever he is!" said Scrooge's nephew. "He wouldn't take it from me, but may he have it, nevertheless. Uncle Scrooge!"

Uncle Scrooge had imperceptibly become so gay and light of heart, that he would have pledged the unconscious company in return, and thanked them in an inaudible speech, if the Ghost had given him time. But the whole scene passed off in the breath of the last word spoken by his nephew; and he and the Spirit were again upon their travels.

Much they saw, and far they went, and many homes they visited, but always with a happy end. The Spirit stood beside sick beds and they were cheerful; on foreign lands, and they were close at home; by struggling men, and they were patient in their greater hope; by poverty, and it was rich. In almshouse, hospital, and jail, in misery's every refuge, where vain man in his little brief authority had not made fast the door, and barred the Spirit out, he left his blessing, and taught Scrooge his precepts.

It was a long night, if it were only a night; but Scrooge had his doubts of this, because the Christmas Holidays appeared to be condensed into the space of time they passed together. It was strange, too, that while Scrooge remained unaltered in his outward form, the Ghost grew older, clearly older. Scrooge had observed this change, but never spoke of it, until they left a children's Twelfth Night party, when, looking at the Spirit as they stood together in an open place, he noticed that its hair was gray.

"Are spirits' lives so short?" asked Scrooge.

"My life upon this globe is very brief," replied the Ghost. "It ends tonight."

"Tonight!" cried Scrooge.

"Tonight at midnight. Hark! The time is drawing near." The chimes were ringing the three quarters past eleven at that moment.

"Forgive me if I am not justified in what I ask," said Scrooge, looking intently at the Spirit's robe, "but I see something strange, and not belonging to yourself, protruding from your skirts. Is it a foot or a claw?"

"It might be a claw, for the flesh there is upon it," was the Spirit's sorrowful reply. "Look here."

From the foldings of its robe, it brought two children: wretched, abject, frightful, hideous, miserable. They knelt down at its feet, and clung upon the outside of its garment.

"Oh, Man! look here. Look, look, down here!" exclaimed the Ghost.

They were a boy and girl. Yellow, meager, ragged, scowling, wolfish; but prostrate, too, in their humility. Where graceful youth should have filled their features out, and touched them with its freshest tints, a stale and shriveled hand, like that of age, had pinched, and twisted them, and pulled them into shreds. Where angels might have sat enthroned, devils lurked, and glared out menacing. No change, no degradation, no perversion of humanity, in any grade, through all the mysteries of wonderful creations, has monsters half so horrible and dread.

Scrooge started back, appalled. Having them shown to him in this way, he tried to say they were fine children, but the words choked themselves, rather than be parties to a lie of such enormous magnitude.

"Spirits! are they yours?" Scrooge could say no more.

"They are Man's," said the Spirit, looking down upon them. "And they cling to me, appealing from their fathers. This boy is Ignorance. This girl is Want. Beware them both, and all of their degree, but most of all beware this boy, for on his brow I see that written which is Doom, unless the writing be erased. Deny it!" cried the Spirit, stretching out its hand toward the city. "Slander those who tell it ye! Admit it for your factious purposes, and make it worse! And bide the end!"

"Have they no refuge or resource?" cried Scrooge.

"Are there no prisons?" said the Spirit, turning on him for the last time with his own words. "Are there no workhouses?"

The bell struck twelve.

Scrooge looked about him for the Ghost, and saw it not. As the last stroke ceased to vibrate, he remembered the prediction of old Jacob Marley, and lifting up his eyes, beheld a solemn Phantom, draped and hooded, coming, like a mist along the ground, toward him.

STAVE FOUR:

THE LAST OF

THE SPIRITS

The Phantom slowly, gravely, silently approached. When it came near him, Scrooge bent down upon his knees; for in the very air through which this Spirit moved it seemed to scatter gloom and mystery.

It was shrouded in a deep black garment, which concealed its head, its face, its form, and left nothing of it visible save one outstretched hand. But for this it would have been difficult to detach its figure from the night, and separate it from the darkness by which it was surrounded.

He felt that it was tall and stately when it came beside him, and that its mysterious presence filled him with a solemn dread. He knew no more, for the Spirit neither spoke nor moved.

"I am in the presence of the Ghost of Christmas Yet To Come?" said Scrooge.

The Spirit answered not, but pointed downward with its hand.

"You are about to show me shadows of the things that have not happened, but will happen in the time before us," Scrooge pursued. "Is that so, Spirit?"

The upper portion of the garment was contracted for an instant in its folds, as if the Spirit had inclined its head. That was the only answer he received.

Although well used to ghostly company by this time, Scrooge

feared the silent shape so much that his legs trembled beneath him, and he found that he could hardly stand when he prepared to follow it. The Spirit paused a moment, as observing his condition, and giving him time to recover.

But Scrooge was all the worse for this. It thrilled him with a vague uncertain horror, to know that behind the dusky shroud there were ghostly eyes intently fixed upon him, while he, though he stretched his own to the utmost, could see nothing but a spectral hand and one great heap of black.

"Ghost of the Future!" he exclaimed, "I fear you more than any Specter I have seen. But, as I know your purpose is to do me good, and as I hope to live to be another man from what I was, I am prepared to bear you company, and do it with a thankful heart. Will you not speak to me?"

It gave him no reply. The hand was pointed straight before them.

"Lead on!" said Scrooge. "Lead on! The night is waning fast, and it is precious time to me, I know. Lead on, Spirit!"

The Phantom moved away as it had come toward him. Scrooge followed in the shadow of its dress, which bore him up, he thought, and carried him along.

They scarcely seemed to enter the city; for the city rather seemed to spring up about them, and encompass them of its own act. But there they were, in the heart of it; on 'Change, amongst the merchants; who hurried up and down, and chinked the money in their pockets, and conversed in groups, and looked at their watches, and trifled thoughtfully with their great gold seals; and so forth, as Scrooge had seen them often.

The Spirit stopped beside one little knot of business men. Observing that the hand was pointed to them, Scrooge advanced to listen to their talk.

"No," said a great fat man with a monstrous chin, "I don't know much about it, either way. I only know he's dead."

"When did he die?" inquired another.

"Last night, I believe."

"Why, what was the matter with him?" asked a third, taking a vast quantity of snuff out of a very large snuffbox. "I thought he'd never die."

"God knows," said the first, with a yawn.

"What has he done with his money?" asked a red-faced gentleman with a pendulous excrescence on the end of his nose, that shook like the gills of a turkey cock.

"I haven't heard," said the man with the large chin, yawning again. "Left it to his Company, perhaps. He hasn't left it to *me*. That's all I know." This pleasantry was received with a general laugh.

"It's likely to be a very cheap funeral," said the same speaker; "for upon my life I don't know of anybody to go to it. Suppose we make up a party and volunteer?"

"I don't mind going if a lunch is provided," observed the gentleman with the excrescence on his nose. "But I must be fed, if I make one." Another laugh.

"Well, I am the most disinterested among you, after all," said the first speaker, "for I never wear black gloves, and I never eat lunch. But I'll offer to go, if anybody else will. When I come to think of it, I'm not at all sure that I wasn't his most particular friend; for we used to stop and speak whenever we met. Bye, bye!"

Speakers and listeners strolled away, and mixed with other groups. Scrooge knew the men, and looked toward the Spirit for an explanation. The Phantom glided on into a street. Its finger pointed to two persons meeting. Scrooge listened again, thinking that the explanation might lie here.

He knew these men, also, perfectly. They were men of business: very wealthy, and of great importance. He had made a point always of standing well in their esteem: in a business point of view, that is; strictly in a business point of view.

"How are you?" said one.

"How are you?" returned the other.

"Well!" said the first. "Old Scratch has got his own at last, hey?"

"So I am told," returned the second. "Cold, isn't it?"

"Seasonable for Christmas time. You're not a skater, I suppose?"

"No. No. Something else to think of. Good morning!"

Not another word. That was their meeting, their conversation, and their parting.

Scrooge was at first inclined to be surprised that the Spirit should attach importance to conversations apparently so trivial; but feeling assured that they must have some hidden purpose, he set himself to consider what it was likely to be. They could scarcely be supposed to have any bearing on the death of Jacob, his old partner, for that was Past, and this Ghost's province was the Future. Nor could he think of any one immediately connected with himself, to whom he could apply them. But nothing doubting that to whomsoever they applied they had some latent moral for his own improvement, he resolved to treasure up every word he heard, and everything he saw; and especially to observe the shadow of himself when it appeared. For he had an expectation that the conduct of his future self would give him the clew he missed, and render solution of these riddles easy.

He looked about in that very place for his own image; but another man stood in his accustomed corner, and though the clock pointed to his usual time of day for being there, he saw no likeness of himself among the multitudes that poured in through the Porch. It gave him little surprise, however; for he had been revolving in his mind a change of life, and thought and hoped he saw his new-born resolutions carried out in this.

Quiet and dark, beside him stood the Phantom, with its out-stretched hand. When he roused himself from his thoughtful quest, he fancied from the turn of the hand, and its situation in reference to himself, that the Unseen Eyes were looking at him keenly. It made him shudder, and feel very cold.

They left the busy scene, and went into an obscure part of the town, where Scrooge had never penetrated before, although he recognized its situation, and its bad repute. The ways were foul and narrow; the shops and houses wretched; the people half-naked, drunken, slipshod, ugly. Alleys and archways, like so many cesspools, disgorged their offenses of smell, and dirt, and life, upon the straggling streets; the whole quarter reeked with crime, filth, misery.

Far in this den of infamous resort, there was a low-browed, beetling shop, below a pent-house roof, where iron, old rags, bottles, bones, and greasy offal, were brought. Upon the floor within, were piled up heaps of rusty keys, nails, chains, hinges, files, scales, weights, and refuse iron of all kinds. Secrets that few would like to scrutinize were bred and hidden in mountains of unseemly rags, masses of corrupt fat, and sepulchers of bones. Sitting in among the wares he dealt in, by a charcoal-stove, made of old bricks, was a gray-haired rascal, nearly seventy years of age; who had screened himself from the cold air without, by a frowzy curtaining of miscellaneous tatters, hung on a line, and smoked his pipe in the luxury of calm retirement.

Scrooge and the Phantom came into the presence of this man, just as a woman with a heavy bundle slunk into the shop. But she had scarcely entered, when another woman, similarly laden, came in too; and she was closely followed by a man in faded black, who was no less startled by the sight of them, than they had been upon the recognition of each other. After a short period of blank astonishment, in which the old man with the pipe had joined them, they all three burst into a laugh.

"Let the charwoman alone to be the first!" cried she who had entered first. "Let the laundress alone to be the second, and let the undertaker's man alone to be the third. Look here, old Joe, here's a chance! If we have n't all three met here without meaning it!"

"You could n't have met in a better place," said old Joe, removing his pipe from his mouth. "Come into the parlor. You were made free of it long ago, you know; and the other two ain't strangers. Stop till I shut the door of the shop. Ah! How it skreeks! There ain't such a rusty bit of metal in the place as its own hinges; I believe; and I'm sure there's no such old bones here, as mine. Ha, ha! We're all suitable to our calling, we're well matched. Come into the parlor. Come into the parlor."

The parlor was the space behind the screen of rags. The old man raked the fire together with an old stair rod, and having trimmed his smoky lamp (for it was night) with the stem of his pipe, put it in his mouth again. While he did this, the woman who had already spoken threw her bundle on the floor, and sat down in a flaunting manner on a stool; crossing her elbows on her knees, and looking with a bold defiance at the other two.

"What odds then! What odds, Mrs. Dilber?" said the woman. "Every person has a right to take care of themselves. *He* always did!"

"That's true, indeed!" said the laundress. "No man more so."

"Why, then, don't stand staring as if you was afraid, woman: who's the wiser? We're not going to pick holes in each other's coats, I suppose?"

"No, indeed!" said Mrs. Dibler and the man together. "We should hope not."

"Very well, then!" cried the woman. "That's enough. Who's the worse for the loss of a few things like these? Not a dead man, I suppose."

"No, indeed," said Mrs. Dibler, laughing.

"If he wanted to keep 'em after he was dead, a wicked old screw," pursued the woman, "why was n't he natural in his lifetime? If he had been, he'd have had somebody to look after him when he was struck with Death, instead of lying gasping out his last there, alone."

"It's the truest word that ever was spoke," said Mrs. Dilber. "It's a judgment on him."

"I wish it was a little heavier one," replied the woman; "and it should have been, you may depend upon it, if I could have laid my hands on anything else. Open that bundle, old Joe, and let me know the value of it. Speak out plain. I'm not afraid to be the first, nor afraid for them to see it. We knew pretty well we were helping ourselves, before we met here, I believe. It's no sin; open the bundle, Joe."

But the gallantry of her friends would not allow of this; and the man in faded black, mounting the breach first, produced *his* plunder. It was not extensive. A seal or two, a pencil case, a pair of sleeve buttons, and a brooch of no great value, were all. They were severally examined and appraised by old Joe, who chalked the sums he was disposed to give for each, upon the wall, and added them up into a total when he found there was nothing more to come.

"That's your account," said Joe, "and I would n't give another sixpence, if I was to be boiled for not doing it. Who's next?"

Mrs. Dilber was next. Sheets and towels, a little wearing apparel, two old-fashioned silver teaspoons, a pair of sugar-tongs, and a few boots. Her account was stated on the wall in the same manner.

"I always give too much to ladies. It's a weakness of mine, and that's the way I ruin myself," said old Joe. "That's your account.

If you asked me for another penny, and made it an open question, I'd repent of being so liberal and knock off half-a-crown."

"And now undo my bundle, Joe," said the first woman.

Joe went down on his knees for the greater convenience of opening it, and having unfastened a great many knots, dragged out a large and heavy roll of some dark stuff.

"What do you call this?" said Joe. "Bed curtains!"

"Ah!" returned the woman, laughing and leaning forward on her crossed arms. "Bed curtains!"

"You don't mean to say you took 'em down, rings and all, with him lying there?" said Joe.

"Yes, I do," replied the woman. "Why not?"

"You were born to make your fortune," said Joe, "and you'll certainly do it."

"I certainly shan't hold my hand, when I can get anything in it by reaching it out, for the sake of such a man as He was, I promise you, Joe," returned the woman, coolly. "Don't drop that oil upon the blankets, now."

"His blankets?" asked Joe.

"Whose else's do you think?" replied the woman. "He isn't likely to take cold without 'em, I dare say."

"I hope he didn't die of anything catching? Eh?" said old Joe, stopping in his work, and looking up.

"Don't you be afraid of that," returned the woman. "I ain't so fond of his company that I'd loiter about him for such things, if he did. Ah! you may look through that shirt till your eyes ache; but you won't find a hole in it, nor a threadbare place. It's the best he had, and a fine one, too. They'd have wasted it, if it hadn't been for me."

"What do you call wasting of it?" asked old Joe.

"Putting it on him to be buried in, to be sure," replied the woman with a laugh. "Somebody was fool enough to do it, but I took it off again. If calico ain't good enough for such a purpose, it isn't good enough for anything. It's quite as becoming to the body. He can't look uglier than he did in that one."

Scrooge listened to this dialogue in horror. As they sat grouped about their spoil, in the scanty light afforded by the old man's lamp, he viewed them with a detestation and disgust, which could hardly have been greater, though they had been obscene demons, marketing the corpse itself.

"Ha, ha!" laughed the same woman, when old Joe, producing a flannel bag with money in it, told out their several gains upon the ground. "This is the end of it, you see! He frightened everyone away from him when he was alive, to profit us when he was dead! Ha, ha, ha!"

"Spirit!" said Scrooge, shuddering from head to foot. "I see, I see. The case of this unhappy man might be my own. My life tends that way, now. Merciful Heaven, what is this!"

He recoiled in terror, for the scene had changed, and now he almost touched a bed: a bare, uncurtained bed: on which, beneath a ragged sheet, there lay a something covered up, which, though it was dumb, announced itself in awful language.

The room was very dark, too dark to be observed with any accuracy, though Scrooge glanced round it in obedience to a secret impulse, anxious to know what kind of room it was. A pale light, rising in the outer air, fell straight upon the bed; and on it, plundered and bereft, unwatched, unwept, uncared for, was the body of this man.

Scrooge glanced toward the Phantom. Its steady hand was pointed to the head. The cover was so carelessly adjusted that the slightest raising of it, the motion of a finger upon Scrooge's part, would have disclosed the face. He thought of it, felt how easy it would be to do, and longed to do it; but had no more power to withdraw the veil than to dismiss the specter at his side.

Oh, cold, cold, rigid, dreadful Death, set up thine altar here, and dress it with such terrors as thou hast at thy command: for this is thy dominion! But of the loved, revered, and honored head, thou canst not turn one hair to thy dread purposes, or make one feature odious. It is not that the hand is heavy and will fall down when released; it is not that the heart and pulse are still; but that the hand WAS open, generous, and true; the heart brave, warm, and tender; and the pulse a man's. Strike, Shadow, strike! And see his good deeds springing from the wound, to sow the world with life immortal!

No voice pronounced these words in Scrooge's ears, and yet he heard them when he looked upon the bed. He thought, if this man could be raised up now, what would be his foremost thoughts? Avarice, hard dealing, griping cares? They have brought him to a rich end, truly!

He lay, in the dark empty house, with not a man, a woman, or a child, to say that he was kind to me in this or that, and for the memory of one kind word I will be kind to him. A cat was tearing at the door, and there was a sound of gnawing rats beneath the hearthstone. What *they* wanted in the room of death, and why they were so restless and disturbed, Scrooge did not dare to think.

"Spirit!" he said, "this is a fearful place. In leaving it, I shall not leave its lesson, trust me. Let us go!"

Still the Ghost pointed with an unmoved finger to the head.

"I understand you," Scrooge returned, "and I would do it, if I could. But I have not the power, Spirit. I have not the power."

Again it seemed to look upon him.

"If there is any person in the town, who feels emotion caused by this man's death," said Scrooge quite agonized, "show that person to me, Spirit, I beseech you!"

The Phantom spread its dark robe before him for a moment, like a wing; and withdrawing it, revealed a room by daylight, where a mother and her children were.

She was expecting someone, and with anxious eagerness; for she walked up and down the room; started at every sound; looked out from the window; glanced at the clock; tried, but in vain, to work with her needle; and could hardly bear the voices of the children.

At length the long-expected knock was heard. She hurried to the door, and met her husband; a man whose face was careworn and depressed, though he was young. There was a remarkable expression in it now; a kind of serious delight of which he felt ashamed, and which he struggled to repress.

He sat down to the dinner that had been hoarding for him by the fire; and when she asked him faintly what news (which was not until after a long silence), he appeared embarrassed how to answer.

"Is it good," she said, "or bad?"—to help him.

"Bad," he answered.

"We are quite ruined?"

"No. There is hope yet, Caroline."

"If *he* relents," she said amazed, "there is! Nothing is past hope, if such a miracle has happened."

"He is past relenting," said her husband. "He is dead."

She was a mild and patient creature if her face spoke truth; but she was thankful in her soul to hear it, and she said so, with clasped hands. She prayed forgiveness the next moment, and was sorry; but the first was the emotion of the heart.

"What the half-drunken woman whom I told you of last night, said to me, when I tried to see him and obtain a week's delay; and what I thought was a mere excuse to avoid me; turns out to have been quite true. He was not only very ill, but dying, then."

"To whom will our debt be transferred?"

"I don't know. But before that time we shall be ready with the money; and even though we were not, it would be bad fortune indeed to find so merciless a creditor in his successor. We may sleep tonight with light hearts, Caroline!"

Yes. Soften it as they would, their hearts were lighter. The children's faces, hushed, and clustered round to hear what they so little understood, were brighter; and it was a happier house for this man's death! The only emotion that the Ghost could show him, caused by the event, was one of pleasure.

"Let me see some tenderness connected with a death," said Scrooge; "or that dark chamber, Spirit, which we left just now, will be forever present to me."

The Ghost conducted him through several streets familiar to his feet; and as they went along, Scrooge looked here and there to find himself, but nowhere was he to be seen. They entered poor Bob Cratchit's house; the dwelling he had visited before; and found the mother and the children seated round the fire.

Quiet. Very quiet. The noisy little Cratchits were as still as statues in one corner, and sat looking up at Peter, who had a book before him. The mother and her daughters were engaged in sewing. But surely they were very quiet!

" 'And he took a child, and set him in the midst of them.' "

Where had Scrooge heard those words? He had not dreamed them. The boy must have read them out, as he and the Spirit crossed the threshold. Why did he not go on?

The mother laid her work upon the table, and put her hand up to her face. "The color hurts my eyes," she said.

The color? Ah, poor Tiny Tim!

"They're better now again," said Cratchit's wife. "It makes them weak by candlelight; and I would n't show weak eyes to your father when he comes home, for the world. It must be near his time."

"Past it rather," Peter answered, shutting up his book. "But I think he's walked a little slower than he used, these few last evenings, mother."

They were very quiet again. At last she said, and in a steady cheerful voice, that only faltered once:

"I have known him walk with—I have known him walk with Tiny Tim upon his shoulder, very fast indeed."

"And so have I," cried Peter. "Often."

"And so have I," exclaimed another. So had all.

"But he was very light to carry," she resumed, intent upon her work, "and his father loved him so, that it was no trouble—no trouble. And there is your father at the door!"

She hurried out to meet him; and little Bob in his comforter—he had need of it, poor fellow—came in. His tea was ready for him on the hob, and they all tried who should help him to it most. Then the two young Cratchits got upon his knees and laid, each child a little cheek, against his face, as if they said, "Don't mind it, father. Don't be grieved!"

Bob was very cheerful with them, and spoke pleasantly to all the family. He looked at the work upon the table, and praised the industry and speed of Mrs. Cratchit and the girls. They would be done long before Sunday he said.

"Sunday! You went today, then, Robert?" said his wife.

"Yes, my dear," returned Bob. "I wish you could have gone. It would have done you good to see how green a place it is. But you'll see it often. I promised him that I would walk there on a Sunday. My little, little child!" cried Bob. "My little child!"

He broke down all at once. He couldn't help it. If he could have helped it, he and his child would have been farther apart perhaps than they were.

He left the room, and went upstairs into the room above, which was lighted cheerfully, and hung with Christmas. There was a chair set close beside the child, and there were signs of someone having been there, lately. Poor Bob sat down in it, and when he had thought a little and composed himself, he kissed the little face. He was reconciled to what had happened, and went down again quite happy.

They drew about the fire, and talked; the girls and mother working still. Bob told them of the extraordinary kindness of Mr. Scrooge's nephew, whom he had scarcely seen but once, and who, meeting him in the street that day, and seeing that he looked a little—"just a little down you know," said Bob—inquired what had happened to distress him. "On which," said Bob, "for he is the pleasantest-spoken gentleman you ever heard, I told him. 'I am heartily sorry for it, Mr. Cratchit,' he said, 'and heartily sorry for your good wife.' By the bye, how he ever knew *that*, I don't know."

"Knew what, my dear?"

"Why, that you were a good wife," replied Bob.

"Everybody knows that!" said Peter.

"Very well observed, my boy!" cried Bob. "I hope they do. 'Heartily sorry,' he said, 'for your good wife. If I can be of service to you in any way,' he said, giving me his card, 'that's where I live. Pray come to me.' Now, it wasn't," cried Bob, "for the sake of anything he might be able to do for us, so much as for his kind way, that this was quite delightful. It really seemed as if he had known our Tiny Tim, and felt with us."

"I'm sure he's a good soul!" said Mrs. Cratchit.

"You would be surer of it, my dear," returned Bob, "if you saw and spoke to him. I shouldn't be at all surprised, mark what I say, if he got Peter a better situation."

"Only hear that, Peter," said Mrs. Cratchit.

"And then," cried one of the girls, "Peter will be keeping company with someone, and setting up for himself."

"Get along with you!" retorted Peter, grinning.

"It's just as likely as not," said Bob, "one of these days; though there's plenty of time for that, my dear. But however and whenever we part from one another, I am sure we shall none of us forget poor Tiny Tim—shall we—or this first parting that there was among us?"

"Never, father!" cried they all.

"And I know," said Bob, "I know, my dears, that when we recollect how patient and how mild he was; although he was a little, little child; we shall not quarrel easily among ourselves, and forget poor Tiny Tim in doing it."

"No, never, father!" they all cried again.

"I am very happy," said little Bob, "I am very happy!"

Mrs. Cratchit kissed him, his daughters kissed him, the two young Cratchits kissed him, and Peter himself shook hands. Spirit of Tiny Tim, thy childish essence was from God!

"Specter," said Scrooge, "something informs me that our parting moment is at hand. I know it, but I know not how. Tell me what man that was whom we saw lying dead?"

The Ghost of Christmas Yet To Come conveyed him, as before—though at a different time, he thought: indeed, there seemed no

The last of the spirits.

order in these latter visions, save that they were in the Future—into the resorts of business men, but showed him not himself. Indeed, the Spirit did not stay for anything, but went straight on, as to the end just now desired, until besought by Scrooge to tarry for a moment.

"This court," said Scrooge, "through which we hurry now, is where my place of occupation is, and has been for a length of time. I see the house. Let me behold what I shall be, in days to come!"

The Spirit stopped; the hand was pointed elsewhere.

"The house is yonder," Scrooge exclaimed. "Why do you point away?"

The inexorable finger underwent no change.

Scrooge hastened to the window of his office, and looked in. It was an office still, but not his. The furniture was not the same, and the figure in the chair was not himself. The Phantom pointed as before.

He joined it once again, and wondering why and whither he had gone, accompanied it until they reached an iron gate. He paused to look round before entering.

A churchyard. Here, then, the wretched man whose name he had now to learn, lay underneath the ground. It was a worthy place. Walled in by houses; overrun by grass and weeds, the growth of vegetation's death, not life; choked up with too much burying; fat with repleted appetite. A worthy place!

The Spirit stood among the graves, and pointed down to One. He advanced toward it trembling. The Phantom was exactly as it had been, but he dreaded that he saw new meaning in its solemn shape.

"Before I draw nearer to that stone to which you point," said Scrooge, "answer me one question. Are these the shadows of the things that Will be, or are they shadows of things that May be, only?"

Still the Ghost pointed downward to the grave by which it stood.

"Men's courses will foreshadow certain ends, to which, if persevered in, they must lead," said Scrooge. "But if the courses be departed from, the ends will change. Say it is thus with what you show me!"

The Spirit was immovable as ever.

Scrooge crept toward it, trembling as he went; and following the finger, read upon the stone of the neglected grave his own name, Ebenezer Scrooge.

"Am *I* that man who lay upon the bed?" he cried, upon his knees.

The finger pointed from the grave to him, and back again.

"No, Spirit! Oh no, no!"

The finger still was there.

"Spirit!" he cried, tight clutching at its robe, "hear me! I am not the man I was. I will not be the man I must have been but for this intercourse. Why show me this, if I am past all hope!"

For the first time the hand appeared to shake.

"Good Spirit," he pursued, as down upon the ground he fell before it: "Your nature intercedes for me, and pities me. Assure me that I yet may change these shadows you have shown me, by an altered life!"

The kind hand trembled.

"I will honor Christmas in my heart, and try to keep it all the year. I will live in the Past, the Present, and the Future. The Spirits of all Three shall strive within me. I will not shut out the lessons that they teach. Oh, tell me I may sponge away the writing on this stone!"

In his agony, he caught the spectral hand. It sought to free itself, but he was strong in his entreaty, and detained it. The Spirit, stronger yet, repulsed him.

Holding up his hands in one last prayer to have his fate reversed, he saw an alteration in the Phantom's hood and dress. It shrank, collapsed, and dwindled down into a bedpost.

STAVE FIVE:

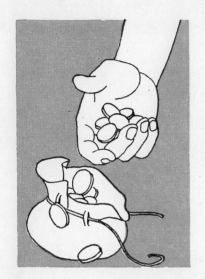

THE END OF IT

Yes! and the bedpost was his own. The bed was his own, the room was his own. Best and happiest of all, the Time before him was his own, to make amends in!

"I will live in the Past, the Present, and the Future!" Scrooge repeated, as he scrambled out of bed. "The Spirits of all Three shall strive within me. Oh, Jacob Marley! Heaven, and the Christmas Time be praised for this! I say it on my knees, old Jacob, on my knees!"

He was so fluttered and so glowing with his good intentions, that his broken voice would scarcely answer to his call. He had been sobbing violently in his conflict with the Spirit, and his face was wet with tears.

"They are not torn down," cried Scrooge, folding one of his bed curtains in his arms, "they are not torn down, rings and all. They are here: I am here: the shadows of the things that would have been, may be dispelled. They will be. I know they will!"

His hands were busy with his garments all this time: turning them inside out, putting them on upside down, tearing them, mislaying them, making them parties to every kind of extravagance.

"I don't know what to do!" cried Scrooge, laughing and crying in the same breath; and making a perfect Laocoon of himself with his stockings. "I am as light as a feather, I am as happy as an angel, I am as merry as a schoolboy. I am as giddy as a drunken man. A

Merry Christmas to everybody! A Happy New Year to all the world. Hallo here! Whoop! Hallo!"

He had frisked into the sitting room, and was now standing there: perfectly winded.

"There's the saucepan that the gruel was in!" cried Scrooge, starting off again, and frisking round the fireplace. "There's the door, by which the Ghost of Jacob Marley entered! There's the corner where the Ghost of Christmas Present sat! There's the window where I saw the wandering Spirits! It's all right, it's all true, it all happened. Ha, ha, ha!"

Really, for a man who had been out of practice for so many years, it was a splendid laugh, a most illustrious laugh. The father of a long, long line of brilliant laughs!

"I don't know what day of the month it is!" said Scrooge. "I don't know how long I've been among the Spirits. I don't know anything. I'm quite a baby. Never mind. I don't care. I'd rather be a baby. Hallo! Whoop! Hallo here!"

He was checked in his transports by the churches ringing out the lustiest peals he had ever heard. Clash, clang, hammer, ding, dong, bell. Bell, dong, ding, hammer, clang, clash! Oh, glorious, glorious!

Running to the window, he opened it, and put out his head. No fog, no mist; clear, bright, jovial, stirring, cold; cold, piping for the blood to dance to; golden sunlight; heavenly sky; sweet fresh air; merry bells. Oh, glorious! Glorious!

"What's today?" cried Scrooge, calling downward to a boy in Sunday clothes, who perhaps had loitered in to look about him.

"Eh?" returned the boy, with all his might of wonder.

"What's today, my fine fellow?" said Scrooge.

"Today!" replied the boy. "Why, CHRISTMAS DAY."

"It's Christmas Day!" said Scrooge to himself. "I haven't missed it. The Spirits have done it all in one night. They can do anything they like. Of course they can. Of course they can. Hallo, my fine fellow!"

"Hallo!" returned the boy.

"Do you know the Poulterer's, in the next street but one, at the corner?" Scrooge inquired.

"I should hope I did," replied the lad.

"An intelligent boy!" said Scrooge. "A remarkable boy! Do you know whether they've sold the prize Turkey that was hanging up there? Not the little prize Turkey: the big one?"

"What, the one as big as me?" returned the boy.

"What a delightful boy!" said Scrooge. "It's a pleasure to talk to him. Yes, my buck!"

"It's hanging there now," replied the boy.

"Is it?" said Scrooge. "Go and buy it."

"Walk-ER!" exclaimed the boy.

"No, no," said Scrooge, "I am in earnest. Go and buy it, and tell 'em to bring it here, that I may give them the direction where to take it. Come back with the man, and I'll give you a shilling. Come back with him in less than five minutes, and I'll give you half-a-crown!"

The boy was off like a shot. He must have had a steady hand at a trigger who could have got a shot off half so fast.

"I'll send it to Bob Cratchit's!" whispered Scrooge, rubbing his hands, and splitting with a laugh. "He shan't know who sends it. It's twice the size of Tiny Tim. Joe Miller never made such a joke as sending it to Bob's will be!"

The hand in which he wrote the address was not a steady one, but write it he did, somehow, and went downstairs to open the street door, ready for the coming of the poulterer's man. As he stood there, waiting his arrival, the knocker caught his eye.

"I shall love it, as long as I live!" cried Scrooge, patting it with his hand. "I scarcely ever looked at it before. What an honest expression it has in its face! It's a wonderful knocker!—Here's the Turkey. Hallo! Whoop! How are you! Merry Christmas!"

It *was* a Turkey! He could never have stood upon his legs, that bird. He would have snapped 'em short off in a minute, like sticks of sealing wax.

"Why, it's impossible to carry that to Camden Town," said Scrooge. "You must have a cab."

The chuckle with which he said this, and the chuckle with which he paid for the turkey, and the chuckle with which he paid for the cab, and the chuckle with which he recompensed the boy, were only to be exceeded by the chuckle with which he sat down breathless in his chair again, and chuckled till he cried.

Shaving was not an easy task, for his hand continued to shake very much; and shaving requires attention, even when you don't dance while you are at it. But if he had cut the end of his nose off, he would have put a piece of sticking plaster over it, and been quite satisfied.

He dressed himself "all in his best," and at last got out into the streets. The people were by this time pouring forth, as he had seen them with the Ghost of Christmas Present; and walking with his hands behind him, Scrooge regarded everyone with a delighted smile. He looked so irresistibly pleasant, in a word, that three or four good-humored fellows said, "Good morning, Sir! A Merry Christmas to you!" And Scrooge said often afterwards, that of all the blithe sounds he had ever heard, those were the blithest in his ears.

He had not gone far, when coming on toward him he beheld the portly gentleman, who had walked into his counting house the day before and said, "Scrooge and Marley's, I believe?" It sent a pang across his heart to think how this old gentleman would look upon him when they met; but he knew what path lay straight before him, and he took it.

"My dear Sir," said Scrooge, quickening his pace, and taking the old gentleman by both his hands. "How do you do? I hope you succeeded yesterday. It was very kind of you. A Merry Christmas to you, Sir!"

"Mr. Scrooge?"

"Yes," said Scrooge. "That is my name, and I fear it may not be pleasant to you. Allow me to ask your pardon. And will you have the goodness"—here Scrooge whispered in his ear.

"Lord bless me!" cried the gentleman, as if his breath were gone. "My dear Mr. Scrooge, are you serious?"

"If you please," said Scrooge. "Not a farthing less. A great many back-payments are included in it, I assure you. Will you do me that favor?"

"My dear Sir," said the other, shaking hands with him. "I don't know what to say to such munifi——"

"Don't say anything, please," retorted Scrooge. "Come and see me. Will you come and see me?"

"I will!" cried the old gentleman. And it was clear he meant to do it.

"Thank'ee," said Scrooge. "I am much obliged to you. I thank you fifty times. Bless you!"

He went to church, and walked about the streets, and watched the people hurrying to and fro, and patted children on the head, and questioned beggars, and looked down into the kitchens of houses, and up to the windows; and found that everything could yield him pleasure. He had never dreamed that any walk—that anything—could give him so much happiness. In the afternoon, he turned his steps toward his nephew's house.

He passed the door a dozen times, before he had the courage to go up and knock. But he made a dash, and did it:

"Is your master at home, my dear?" said Scrooge to the girl. Nice girl! Very.

"Yes, Sir."

"Where is he, my love?" said Scrooge.

"He's in the dining room, Sir, along with mistress. I'll show you upstairs, if you please."

"Thank'ee. He knows me," said Scrooge, with his hand already on the dining room lock. "I'll go in here, my dear."

He turned it gently, and sidled his face in, round the door. They were looking at the table (which was spread out in great array); for these young housekeepers are always nervous on such points, and like to see that everything is right.

"Fred!" said Scrooge.

Dear heart alive, how his niece by marriage started! Scrooge had forgotten, for the moment, about her sitting in the corner with the footstool, or he wouldn't have done it, on any account.

"Why, bless my soul!" cried Fred, "who's that?"

"It's I. Your uncle Scrooge. I have come to dinner. Will you let me in, Fred?"

Let him in! It is a mercy he didn't shake his arm off. He was at home in five minutes. Nothing could be heartier. His niece looked just the same. So did Topper when *he* came. So did the plump sister, when *she* came. So did everyone when *they* came. Wonderful party, wonderful games, wonderful unanimity, won-der-ful happiness!

But he was early at the office next morning. Oh, he was early there. If he could only be there first, and catch Bob Cratchit coming late! That was the thing he had set his heart upon.

And he did it; yes he did! The clock struck nine. No Bob. A quarter past. No Bob. He was full eighteen minutes and a half behind his time. Scrooge sat with his door wide open, that he might see him come into the Tank.

His hat was off, before he opened the door; his comforter, too. He was on his stool in a jiffy; driving away with his pen, as if he were trying to overtake nine o'clock.

"Hallo!" growled Scrooge, in his accustomed voice as near as he could feign it. "What do you mean by coming here at this time of day?"

"I am very sorry, Sir," said Bob. "I *am* behind my time."

"You are?" repeated Scrooge. "Yes. I think you are. Step this way, Sir, if you please."

"It's only once a year, Sir," pleaded Bob, appearing from the Tank. "It shall not be repeated. I was making rather merry yesterday, Sir."

"Now, I'll tell you what, my friend," said Scrooge, "I am not going to stand this sort of thing any longer. And therefore," he continued, leaping from his stool, and giving Bob such a dig in the waistcoat that he staggered back into the Tank again: "and therefore I am about to raise your salary!"

Bob trembled, and got a little nearer to the ruler. He had a momentary idea of knocking Scrooge down with it; holding him; and calling to the people in the court for help and a strait-waistcoat.

"A Merry Christmas, Bob!" said Scrooge, with an earnestness that could not be mistaken, as he clapped him on the back. "A merrier Christmas, Bob, my good fellow, than I have given you for many a year! I'll raise your salary, and endeavor to assist your struggling family, and we will discuss your affairs this very afternoon, over a

Christmas bowl of smoking bishop, Bob! Make up the fires, and buy another coal scuttle before you dot another i, Bob Cratchit!"

Scrooge was better than his word. He did it all, and infinitely more; and to Tiny Tim, who did NOT die, he was a second father. He became as good a friend, as good a master, and as good a man, as the good old city knew, or any other good old city, town, or borough, in the good old world. Some people laughed to see the alteration in him, but he let them laugh, and little heeded them; for he was wise enough to know that nothing ever happened on this globe, for good, at which some people did not have their fill of laughter in the outset; and knowing that such as these would be blind anyway, he thought it quite as well that they should wrinkle up their eyes in grins, as have the malady in less attractive forms. His own heart laughed: and that was quite enough for him.

He had no further intercourse with Spirits, but lived upon the Total Abstinence Principle, ever afterwards; and it was always said of him, that he knew how to keep Christmas well, if any man alive possessed the knowledge. May that be truly said of us, and all of us!

And so, as Tiny Tim observed, God Bless Us, Every One!

SOURCES OF STORIES IN VOLUME V

Alice's Adventures in Wonderland, by Lewis Carroll. The Macmillan Company.

The King of the Golden River, by John Ruskin. George Allen & Unwin, Ltd., London.

Jackanapes, from Jackanapes and Other Tales, by Juliana Horatia Ewing. Little, Brown & Company.

A Midsummer Night's Dream, from Tales from Shakespeare, by Charles and Mary Lamb. The Macmillan Company.

The Gold Bug, by Edgar Allan Poe. P. F. Collier & Son Corporation.

Tales from the Travels of Baron Munchausen, from The Children's Book, edited by Horace E. Scudder. Houghton Mifflin Company.

Gulliver's Voyage to Lilliput, from Gulliver's Travels, edited by Padraic Colum. The Macmillan Company.

Don Quixote, from The Story of Don Quixote, retold by Judge Parry. Dodd, Mead & Company, Inc.

Rip Van Winkle, from The Sketch Book, by Washington Irving. Frederick A Stokes Company.

A Christmas Carol, by Charles Dickens. Little, Brown & Company.